I0614099

Georgia Peach

by

Carissa Hyde

Georgia Peach

Contact Information: info@thewildrosepress.com

Cover Art by *Diana Carlile*

The Wild Rose Press, Inc.
PO Box 708
Adams Basin, NY 14410-0708
Visit us at www.thewildrosepress.com

Publishing History
First Edition, 2023
Trade Paperback ISBN 978-1-5092-4752-3
Digital ISBN 978-1-5092-4753-0

Published in the United States of America

"When Raegan was little," I finally said, breaking the quiet, "about four or five years old, she used to have these nightmares. On and off for an entire year, an hour after she would fall asleep, she would wake up screaming. When the nightmares first started, I would run to her bedside, panicked and asking her what was wrong, over and over again.

"Eventually, I stopped asking what was wrong and just held her. I would shush her and tell her everything was fine. That she didn't have to cry. It was just a nightmare, and she would feel better once she calmed down." I slowly turned over to face him.

"The logical part of me knows that's what this is. I know it's just a nightmare, and eventually everything will be fine. But for now, in this moment, I can't make sense of it, and I can't calm down. I'm panicking, and my brain can't stop thinking about everything that could go wrong."

Landon moved closer to me, still holding my hand in his. "Then I'll be the one to tell you it's okay and hold you until it's over. You're right, everything will be fine, eventually. This is all just a hiccup in the grand scheme of life. But until you can regain your bearings and know for certain everything will sort itself out, I'll be the one to comfort you. I will sit here with you through this nightmare."

Dedication

To my friends and family: thank you for your unyielding support. I love you all.

Acknowledgments

I am fortunate to have an entire team of people who support me as an author and who are ready to talk me off a ledge whenever necessary. Every single one of them came through for me during the creation of this book, playing their supportive roles like Oscar nomination season is 365 days a year. While there are dozens of people I want to thank, I'm limited in space. Below are just a few of the many individuals who constantly push me to reach my greatest potential, and I will be forever indebted to them.

Jeff, my wonderful, *very* understanding husband—thank you for putting up with me and encouraging me. Thank you for listening to me cry and threaten to quit writing a dozen times a week before enveloping me in your arms and telling me to keep going. I couldn't have done any of this without your love and support. My babies—you're my reason why.

Mom—thank you for being my first editor and for always giving me honest feedback. I know you don't *have* to love my stories but knowing that you do makes me believe in myself that much more. Your help and opinions are invaluable and I appreciate everything you do for me. Mitchell—thank you for reading what you refer to as "romantic books you normally wouldn't be caught dead reading." I appreciate you taking one for the team because you're my brother and you love me.

Carolyn and Verusca—thank you for *always* being my cheerleaders. You two are sunshine and make me feel like I can accomplish anything. Heather—thank you for happily and willingly reading my manuscripts and always feeling them so deeply. Laura—thank you for listening to me and being there with wine and chocolate. Forever my octopus you will be. Angela, thank you for being a magical unicorn. Your ability to see the good in all things and lift me up is just...magical. You're extraordinary. Thank you for coming into my life all those years ago and accepting and loving me for who I am. I'd be lost without you.

Rachel, AKA Pookie—you've known me since the era of pedal pushers and scrunchies, and despite truly, really knowing me for nearly three decades, you've never left my side. From *very* late-night anxiety-ridden Facetimes to flying to California and reading my latest manuscript from the confines of my closet, you've always talked me down and cheered me on. Thank you for reading and editing all of my stories, but most importantly, thank you for being one of the greatest people in my life. I love you forever.

Genalea—thank you for befriending me, a random stranger when we first interacted, on Twitter. You're the only person I have met online who I've become close with (because, you know, creepers), and I'm so grateful we took a chance on each other. You're my only true writer friend, and your knowledge and understanding of the entire writing and publishing industry is incomparable. Thank you for always listening to me rant and for giving me advice. I can't wait to see you change the world through your books.

Fitz—thank you for reading my book and providing me with amazing feedback and unrelenting support. Ken, "Remember-I-am-not-a-Georgia-lawyer" (and Maryann, who let me borrow Ken for many hours during the research process), thank you for all your legal expertise, despite the fact that you are NOT a Georgia lawyer. You pointed me in the right direction and answered my endless questions without hanging up on me (though I wouldn't blame you if you had).

And lastly, to the two people who made my wildest dream come true, Morena and Rhonda at The Wild Rose Press—thank you for giving *Georgia Peach* and me a chance. I don't think I'll ever be able to put into words just how happy you've made me. I have dreamt of being a published author since I was five years old after writing my first story, and you've made my wish a reality. For that, I will be eternally grateful.

CHAPTER ONE

I was hovering mere inches above the chair behind the nurses' station when the call light for room five flickered on. Wistfully peering into the coffee cup in front of me, I saw that the steam had long since dissipated, and after wrapping my hands around the porcelain mug, it was obvious that my hot coffee had since become a cold brew. Glancing across the hallway, I expelled a long, slow sigh. Mr. Keenan was one of my favorite patients, and normally, seeing him was the highlight of my day. But morning rounds had left me exhausted, and I really, really needed a serotonin boost in the form of caffeine.

When my five-second pity party ended, I returned my coffee to the desk and made the short walk to his room. "Whatcha need, Mr. Keenan?" I asked, pushing back the curtain and turning off the call light.

Over the years, I had watched Mr. Keenan's ebony skin sag more and more, and now in the final stages of kidney failure, the whites of his eyes were tinted yellow, signaling his limited time with us. He glanced up at me and smiled.

"Ms. Hawley, I can't seem to find the book my granddaughter brought me yesterday. Have you seen it?"

Glancing around, I didn't see it on any of the obvious surfaces, so I opened the drawer of the bedside table next to him. Sliding the book out and handing it to him, I smiled, a gesture which he returned.

"I'm sorry to bother you, Ms. Hawley. I know you're a busy woman. Thank you for finding it," Mr. Keenan breathed heavily before dissolving into a coughing fit.

Patting his arm, I shook my head. "Mr. Keenan, I told you to call me Sam, so you have to stop with the 'Ms. Hawley' nonsense, ya hear?" I grinned, and he managed to squeeze in a laugh before coughing again.

Hearing anyone refer to me as "Ms. Hawley" made me cringe, and I begged nearly everyone I met to call me by my first name. However, as much as I hated my last name, I was keeping it for the sake of my children. All of the terrible connotations it carried were just something I was going to have to get over, along with the dissolution of my nearly two-decade-long marriage.

Exiting his room, I heard the nurses' station phone ring. Head down, I started toward the desk, but as I glanced up, the call light for room eight flickered on. Seeing Linda out of the corner of my eye, I motioned for her to answer the phone while I veered toward the illuminated room number.

As she spoke into the phone, the heaviness of Linda's Southern drawl made me grin. No matter how much coffee I ingested, I could never muster enough energy to sound as Southern as the people around me. After living in Madison, Georgia for more years than I cared to admit, I assumed I would sound like I was born and raised here. But even if I had managed to acquire a native accent, the extremely tight-knit, lifelong residents in the community would never let me forget I was an outsider. My scarlet letter followed me everywhere; everyone would forever see me as the freshman college girl who got pregnant by the son of one of the wealthiest Madison families.

"She probably did it on purpose to marry into wealth."

"The audacity of that girl, moving into our city and acting like she was forced to. She should be so lucky to live here, married into the Hawley family. That is basically every unwed Madison woman's dream."

The less-than-subtle whispers that swirled throughout the city like a tornado lasted for years before simmering down, but the quiet was short-lived. The drama in my life over the last six months started tongues wagging and rumors flying all over again, and honestly, I was tired of it.

Just as my hand grazed the doorframe of room eight, Linda called out to me.

"Hey, boss? You need to take this," she said, shaking the phone. "I'll get Mrs. Sanchez."

"Who is it?" I asked, our paths crossing in front of the nurses' station.

She cast her gaze downward. "It's Raegan's school."

"Shit," I said, probably a little too loudly, and quickened my pace to the desk. Sliding into the chair closest to the phone, I counted to ten before picking up the receiver. "Hello?"

The all too familiar voice of Raegan's principal came on the other line. "Ms. Hawley, I hate to interrupt you at work, but I wouldn't call if this wasn't important." Unlike Linda, his Southern accent had lost its charm after hearing it dozens of times over the last three and a half years.

Placing my head in my hands, I suppressed a groan.

"What's up?"

"We need you to come to the school, Ms. Hawley. We found Ritalin on Raegan, and one of the teachers saw her handing some off to another child in exchange for money. Your daughter is facing major disciplinary actions."

Just what I needed. Noticing the clock on the wall, I saw that it was nine-thirty a.m. on a Tuesday—only four hours into my shift. I still had another eight hours left, but I obviously couldn't leave Raegan sitting in the principal's office for that long, though it was tempting.

"I'll be there," I said through a sigh, promptly hanging up the phone. Linda circled back to me and sat down.

"What trouble has she gotten herself into now?" she asked, peeling back a banana and taking a bite. Turning my chair to look at her, I said, "She was caught dealing Ritalin to a classmate."

She paused, mid-chew. "Ritalin? Where did she get Ritalin? And why?"

I ran my fingers over my scalp and stopped when I reached my tightly wound bun. "Only the good Lord knows, but I'm about to find out for myself. Tell Carly she's going to have a break from fetching and restocking bedpans soon—Raegan is going to be coming back with me, no doubt."

Linda chuckled. "You could just take the rest of the day off, you know. We could call in someone else."

I stood, grabbing my jacket from the back of the chair. "I can't afford to take time off. If she's going to keep getting into trouble, she's going to learn what kind of jobs she can get after she's done time in prison. Hell, collecting bedpans may be a luxurious job for her. I'm done with this kid. Lord help me over the fence."

She waved me off. "Good luck, darlin'. I'll hold down the fort while you're gone."

A blast of cold air hit my face the second I barreled through the stairwell exit, burning my cheeks and stinging my eyes. Hugging my jacket against my torso, I rushed toward the parking lot. God, I hated this city. In fact, I hated Georgia, and everything that had led me here. I missed home.

Southern Californians couldn't handle cold winters and humid summers—we were raised with less-cold months and summers overwhelmed by dry heat. To be fair, the Madison winters didn't bother me as much as the warmer months. The humidity was what annoyed me—I wasn't used to it, even after all these years of living in the South. Southern California's dry heat was upfront, direct. Georgia humidity had a way of sneaking through my hair and under my clothes, making me drip sweat before I even realized just how suffocating the air was around me. Humidity was sneaky and undermining, just like the people in this city.

When I reached my fifteen-year-old beat-up sedan, I couldn't feel my face, and I had only run less than a block. Cranking over the engine and turning up the heater, I mentally prepared myself for more drama as I backed out of the parking lot and headed to Madison High. Two minutes into the drive, my windshield started to cloud, leaving me no choice but to roll down my windows. I really needed to consider getting a newer car with a better defroster if I was going to be forced to stick around here much longer.

A block away from the school, an unmistakable voice rang out in the silence as I slowed for an approaching stop sign.

"Howdy, Samantha!" Mrs. Peters, the local bookstore owner, called as she waved to me from the front stoop of her shop. "Is everything alright, dear? You look a little troubled. Is it Harrison?"

I really, *really* needed to get a newer car with a better defroster. If my windows had been up, I could have easily avoided this situation. A pause at the stop sign and a slight wave of my hand would have been a hundred times better than actually striking up a conversation with one of the nosiest people in the community.

I gave her a tight smile. "Everything is fine, Mrs. Peters. Harrison is fine. I'm just going to the school to see about Raegan."

"Oh, bless her heart." Her face pulled into a frown. "Dear girl seems to be getting into some trouble lately. Do let me know if you need anything."

I saluted her before rolling up my windows and continuing on to the last block before the school. I would rather peer through the foggy windows than risk speaking with more neighbors. After pulling into the nearest open parking space, I took another deep breath.

I would not lose my mind in public.

I would not lose my mind in public.

Flipping down the car visor, I stared at myself in the tiny mirror. My wavy brunette hair was a static nightmare, and my face resembled how I was feeling ninety-nine percent of the time—worn out. I had permanent wrinkles between my brows from frowning far too often, and my hazel eyes seemed to darken as the years wore on. At thirty-six years old, I felt like I should look a lot younger than I actually did, but I guess this was what happened when self-care wasn't a priority.

With a dejected groan, I slung my purse over my shoulder and walked the well-known path to the principal's office while smoothing out my navy-colored scrubs under my jacket.

Although, I thought as I hiked up the steps to the school's doors, if I lost my mind in a public setting and was placed on a psych hold, I could get three meals a day and perhaps uninterrupted sleep. Grabbing one of the double door handles, the cold gave way to blazing heat inside the building.

Who was I kidding—no one would care for my son, Harrison, if I went to jail. At least, not long term.

When I knocked on Mr. Prior's door, it swung open almost immediately to reveal the principal and Raegan with a man I'd never seen before towering over the balding administrator.

"Please, come in, Ms. Hawley," Mr. Prior said, dabbing his sweaty forehead. I was convinced Mr. Prior was going to suffer a heart attack if he didn't get his anxiety under control, and surely having Raegan out of his school would drastically lessen his stress.

I glared at my daughter before sitting next to her. Her dyed jet-black hair was pulled into a ponytail, and her makeup made her seem like she could be a stand-in for a heavy metal frontrunner. Her clothes weren't much better—black skinny jeans with enough holes in them to make me wonder if we had moths in our house, a shirt that barely covered her midsection, and black combat boots. I reminded myself to chastise her later regarding her outfit choice.

Mr. Prior repositioned himself behind his desk, while the man standing next to him didn't move a muscle. And speaking of muscle—I could see that man's biceps bulging through his shirt. Good Lord. Talk about a distraction. Moving my eyes from the unfamiliar man to Mr. Prior in an attempt to keep my focus, I sat at the edge of the chair. "What exactly happened this morning?" I was almost afraid to hear him recount the details.

Mr. Prior folded his hands. "Mr. Standford, one of our math teachers, caught Raegan taking money from one of the football players and handing him these," he said, removing a small bag from his desk. Inside the bag were three pills, and after taking it from him, I saw Mr. Prior was right—it *was* Ritalin.

Still holding the bag, I turned to face Raegan once again. "Ritalin? Really, Raegan? I just—" I paused, words failing me. How did my daughter, an AP student and teacher favorite for the past three years of high school, morph into *this* her senior year? I thought my impending divorce would only improve our lives, but clearly, I was wrong.

Raegan simply stared at the wall behind Mr. Prior's head. Rage boiled inside me, but I tried to force it down. *Don't lose your mind in a public setting.* Through clenched teeth, I managed to utter, "You better tell me where this came from, Raegan. I have to get back to work. I can't sit here all day and play this game with you."

Mr. Prior cleared his throat again. "I am sorry we had to call you away from the hospital. We tried getting ahold of Mr. Hawley, but he was unavailable."

What a surprise, I thought. He was probably too busy screwing his latest secretary to be a parent. If I had to put money on it, I would wager his new concubine was a tall, skinny brunette—not unlike me—who had artificial voluptuous breasts and thought Charles was the greatest man alive—very much unlike me.

I would have been amazed if Mr. Prior *had* managed to reach him. Never once in the last six months since I forcefully evicted him from our home had he been in contact with me, Raegan, or Harrison, but that wasn't shocking. Even when we lived under the same roof, communication with him was nonexistent. The only thing that emanated from that toxic man was disdain for his family and lust toward other women.

When Raegan remained silent, I glanced back at the principal. "Bottom line it for me, Mr. Prior. What's going to happen to Raegan?"

He looked at the mystery man before speaking. "Raegan will be suspended for the rest of the week, and upon her return, with your consent of course, she will be seeing our school counselor, Dr. Ford," he gestured to the statuesque man, "for counseling twice a week. We believe talking with someone could greatly benefit her…situation." Mr. Prior said the last word slowly.

"But, if Raegan is caught doing anything illegal or something that goes against school policy again, she will be expelled. Raegan is on strike three. Actually, she's probably on strike five, but given the circumstances and her relation to, well, you know…" he trailed off.

Of course. Raegan got special treatment because her daddy was the mayor of Madison and the Hawleys were longtime residents and huge benefactors of the city. It was my turn to roll my eyes, and when they finally stilled, my gaze landed yet again on the wordless man next to Mr. Prior.

Dr. Ford's beard was neatly trimmed and, along with his side-swept medium brown hair, had dashes of gray throughout. Studying him further, his peppered hair confused me, as he didn't appear to be old enough to exhibit the classic sign of aging. It honestly seemed like he had just stepped away from his college graduation and driven straight here. His commanding blue eyes were stern, yet small wrinkles in the upper corners of his face made it apparent Dr. Ford smiled a lot. I found myself wondering what it looked like.

Moving my eyes downward, I could feel a trickle of sweat begin its descent in the recess between my shoulder blades. Judging by how his button-down dress shirt hugged his arms, Dr. Ford frequently hit the gym, and I could only imagine what his legs were like under his fitted dress pants.

Why? Why did I go there? He looked to be in his mid-twenties, tops. And even though I needed a rebound relationship after my marriage crumbled years ago (but not legally, as of yet), I vowed right then and there it wouldn't be with a man tied to my daughter's school.

"Ms. Hawley?" Mr. Prior asked, snapping me out of my derailed thoughts.

I looked from Dr. Ford to the principal, my jaw dropping open in the process. "This is the school psychologist?" I asked, my question directed at Mr. Prior.

Raegan's principal nodded. "Dr. Ford joined us this year from a high school in New England, where he counseled students for nearly eight years." Before he finished his sentence, I could have sworn Mr. Prior was going to say, "…where he graduated from."

"How old are you?" I heard myself ask, this time addressing Dr. Ford.

"Mom." Raegan scowled at me, but I ignored her.

Dr. Ford stared directly at me and finally spoke. "I'm thirty-eight. I know, I know, I look younger, but I promise you, I'm not only gray because of my profession." He smiled, and my stomach clenched. There it was, that smile, and it was better than I imagined.

This man was two years older than me, *and* he looked like that? Goodness gracious. The trickle of sweat was turning into a downpour. I realized I was still staring at Dr. Ford with my mouth slightly agape. Quickly shutting it, I stood up. This was clearly not the time to be ogling a man. "Yes, I consent to counseling for Raegan, and hopefully, she won't get expelled five months before graduation." I turned to Raegan, who quickly averted her gaze.

Mr. Prior and Dr. Ford walked around the desk. "It was nice to meet you, Mrs. Hawley," Dr. Ford said, reaching out for a professional handshake. I wanted to correct the "Mrs." but decided against it.

Casually regarding the hand that was still at his side, I noticed his ring finger was bare. "Nice to meet you, Dr. Ford." I briefly shook his outstretched hand. "I apologize in advance for the gray hairs that appear in the future because of my child and her glaringly apparent desire to finish high school from a juvenile facility."

Dr. Ford smiled and shook his head slightly. "It's my job. If I wanted easy, I wouldn't do this."

With that, I turned around and nearly dragged Raegan out of the principal's office. "Well, I hope you had a fun week of bedpan collection and restocking in mind, because that's what your ass will be doing every day until you go back to school," I grumbled, marching slightly ahead of her down the hallway with my car keys in hand.

Raegan let out a dramatic sigh. "You don't even work all of those days," she whined.

I spun on my heels and stalked back in her direction. When I was half a foot away from her face, I responded. "I don't care. You will be collecting bedpans starting today, all the way until Sunday. You keep messing up, Raegan, and fetching used bedpans is going to be your equivalent to working as one of Hollywood's best makeup artists."

For the last few years, Raegan's ultimate goal was to own a hair and makeup business. Looking at her now, though, I was concerned that might no longer be her ideal career choice. Normally, Raegan's facial appearance was on point. On fleek? I had no idea what the kids said these days. But today, her makeup was questionable at best.

"And what the hell are you wearing, might I add? You look like you got dressed in the dark. Was there a power outage? It's winter, for crying out loud. Where did you even get those clothes?"

Raegan marched past me and through the high school doors. "Hannah gave them to me."

"Well, cross yet another friend off the list, because you aren't hanging out with her anymore." Following her down the steps and across the parking lot, I sunk into the driver's seat seconds after Raegan collapsed into the passenger seat.

Recalling a meditative exercise a past therapist had taught me, I took several long breaths—in for five, out for five—before I felt mentally prepared to have a serious discussion.

"Okay, Rae. Talk to me. You've only been back in school for," I glanced at my watch, "a week and a half since winter break ended. What's going on?" I turned slightly in my seat to stare at the side of her head.

Raegan's secured black locks fell down around one shoulder as she began to pick at her cuticles (a habit we'd both tried to break her of dozens of times). "A friend asked me to give the bag to someone I was having my next class with," she answered quietly, still looking down at her nails.

"Is this friend a *friend*, or an acquaintance?" I asked.

Finally, Raegan's eyes met mine. "He's not even that. He's a guy I barely know. But he's friends with a guy I like, so I figured…" She shrugged.

"Rae, honey," I said. "This is the third time you've been caught doing this. First, we know for sure you are *not* a discreet drug dealer, which, if I'm being honest, I am super thrilled about. Second, if this guy liked you, he wouldn't make you do stuff like this for him. And finally, let's not date boys who are associated with drugs, yeah?"

Raegan sighed. "I know. I know all those things. I'm just…I'm struggling. This whole thing with you and Dad, and graduation coming up, and I still don't know what universities I got accepted to. I'm stressed, and anxious, and I don't know. Maybe slightly depressed?"

The overwhelming feeling that Rae was perhaps partially depressed because of my life choices made me want to scream into the void. Instead, I leaned over and ruffled her ponytail. "Oh, baby. I know things have been difficult and stressful lately, and I'm so sorry. Are you open to discussing things with Dr. Ford? Or do you want me to find you a different therapist outside of school?"

Raegan raised an eyebrow at me. "I'm not as open as you probably are to discussing things with Dr. Ford."

I felt redness dash across my cheeks. "Stop it. I'm

serious."

She shrugged. "So am I. I saw how you were looking at him. But yeah, I'm open to it."

I moved my hand to her cheek. "I love you, Rae of Sunshine. I'm sorry things are tough right now. But you know you can always talk to me, right?"

Snorting, she asked, "In between you working and taking care of Harrison? Can I pencil in a time?"

Like tiny little knives hitting me all at once, her words caused me to drop my hand from her face.

"I'm sorry," she rushed, her eyes widening as she stared at me. "That was below the belt."

I shook my head. "You aren't wrong. I haven't been there for you in all the ways you've needed me to be, and I hate it," I admitted. As selfish as it sounded, I needed work to maintain what little sanity I had left. The combination of Charles and his philandering ways and everyday life left me feeling like I was drowning most days. I needed an escape every once in a while, and my job gave me just that. True, I had to cater to grumpy people laid up in a hospital, but they weren't *my* grumpy people. Plus, I didn't want to rely on Charles for money. Or anything else, for that matter.

"Do I really have to collect and restock bedpans for the next five days?" Raegan asked softly.

I turned the key in the ignition. "I loved our talk, but don't think for a second that got you out of bedpan duty, missy. A lesson is a lesson. Besides, I know how much you love hearing stories from my geriatric patients about their glory days. That, and receiving *so* much unsolicited advice. It'll be like a little personalized Raegan vacation."

"UGH," Raegan groaned, crossing her arms. "It'll

be my personalized hell. Life sucks."

I smirked as we pulled out of the school parking lot. She didn't know the half of it.

CHAPTER TWO

"Ritalin, huh?" my best friend Andrea, an emergency room nurse at Morgan Medical Center, asked quietly, as Raegan traipsed by with a bag full of dirty bedpans for the third time in four hours. This was one of those moments I was thrilled my floor was filled with only bed-ridden elderly people.

Sitting behind the desk at the nurses' station, I took a bite of my apple as I watched Raegan disappear into another room. As pieces of the fruit became smaller, I raised my hand to my mouth and responded. "Ritalin, Drea. RITALIN. And you know why? Because the guy she likes is friends with the guy who asked her to hand off the drugs. It's for a boy. She is going to get kicked out of school months before graduation for a BOY."

Drea raised an eyebrow at me while I continued to chomp away at the apple. Her tall frame leaned against the counter, one of her ebony arms resting on the ledge, the rest of her body facing away to survey the area. Her thick, black hair was up in a ponytail, but multiple strands had sprung free from the hair tie and were sticking out at all angles.

"Gee, I wonder where she got that from? Doing stupid crap for a man? Could...could it be you?" she asked, and before she could shield herself, the core of my apple went flying at her face. Drea shrieked before dissolving into hysterics.

16

I rolled my eyes and threw my feet up onto the desk. Leaning back in the chair, I gathered my staticky, wavy mess of hair into a high ponytail. "I never said I didn't know where she got it from. I'm just astounded she's making poor choices in men after seeing how my life turned out when I've made nothing but terrible decisions relating to the opposite sex. Or really, just one man in particular."

Drea shrugged. "She's seventeen. It's all about making bad choices when you're that age. Plus, you're her mom. You don't count."

After securing my hair with a scrunchie, I withdrew my legs from the shared workspace. The sound of my shoes hitting the floor, along with my slow, long sigh, echoed throughout the halls. "I'm taking five outside." Grabbing my puffer jacket, I stood and stretched before sticking my arms into the sleeves.

She stared at me. "You better not be smoking, Peach."

Peach had been Drea's nickname for me since I started working at the hospital, and the irony wasn't lost on anyone. I had gone off on a patient during my very first shift, and unbeknownst to me, everyone at the nurses' station heard me lose my cool. Drea's eyes had widened upon seeing me exit the patient's room, her mouth gaping open. "Well, you're a real peach, aren't you?" She had smirked. The nickname, along with my reputation of having an attitude when goaded, had stuck with me ever since.

I shot Drea a glance before making my way to the double doors that led to the hospital's main hallway. "You can't tell me what to do. I'm a grown-ass woman."

"A grown-ass woman who continues to use poor

judgement, apparently," she called, and I flipped her off as the doors closed behind me.

For the most part, I had quit smoking six years ago. But every so often, a type of stress arose that was only minimized by a quick inhale of a cigarette. I kept a pack in my locker, and every shift, I would stick one cigarette in my scrubs pocket with a lighter, in case the desperate need to smoke ever struck me. I hated myself for it, but taking a drag of nicotine occasionally was better than me having a full-fledged mental breakdown. I didn't have time for that.

Leaning against the brick façade of the hospital wall, I reached into my pocket to grab the lighter. No sooner had I placed the cigarette in my mouth when a shadow darkened the cement in front of me. With the lighter in one hand and the other shielding my eyes from the glaring sun, I saw Dr. Ford looming over me. At five feet, eight inches tall, I wasn't exactly short, but Dr. Ford had at least half a foot on me.

"Crap," I muttered, quickly removing the cigarette.

Dr. Ford gave a sly smile and waved his hand at the ground. "Don't stop on my account. I just saw you leaving the hospital and thought I'd say hi."

I was really, really looking forward to a moment of peace with my faithful friend nicotine. But alas, the handsome doctor stood in front of me, so I tucked my lighter and cigarette back into my shirt pocket. Unlike when I saw him at the high school, Dr. Ford was wearing fitted jeans, gray slip-ons, and a more casual button-down shirt with the sleeves rolled to just below his elbows. Apparently, the man was immune to the cold. "What are you doing here?"

Dr. Ford looked around, and after a lone person

wandered into the hospital, he spoke, his tone hushed. "I was visiting someone."

His wife? Girlfriend? Fiancée? "Whoever it is, I hope they will be okay," I offered lamely. As a nurse, someone might think I would have something better to say to a person upon learning they had a loved one in the hospital. Nothing had come to me as of yet, though, and I had been an RN for years.

Dr. Ford nodded. "They will be. They're going to be transferred to a teen recovery center in Athens. I've had a few patients really excel there, so I'm hoping this one will, too."

I refrained from smacking my head. He was visiting *a student.* Why did I feel relieved knowing this? "Do you visit all your patients if they end up in the hospital?" I asked as I folded my arms across my chest, curiosity getting the better of me.

"Always. Whenever a student is admitted, they are inundated with unfamiliar medical professionals, social workers, etc. I try to show up as soon as possible to help them and their parents navigate everything. It's overwhelming for everyone when a teen thinks they are better off dead."

A lump rose in my throat. I hoped Raegan truly understood that I was always there for her, even if she didn't want to, or couldn't, talk to me most days. The thought of losing either of my children made me nauseous.

Dr. Ford looked at me, his head cocked. "I know you're worried about Raegan, ma'am, but she seems like a good kid. If I ever suspect anything, I won't keep you in the dark."

God, how easy was I to read? Swallowing my

anxiety, I gave him a slight smile. "I appreciate that. I never want Raegan to feel like suicide is the only option. That would kill me, no pun intended. Also, please don't call me ma'am. I know it's a Southern thing, but it makes me feel so old."

Dr. Ford laughed, and his eyes crinkled the second his smile reached them. I couldn't decide if he really was incredibly good-looking, or if I was just desperate to move on from my train wreck of a marriage. Besides, he was a shrink. My *daughter's* shrink, at that. Were psychologists allowed to be that attractive? Hell, I would consider taking up therapy again if I could land someone like Dr. Ford. Although talking would probably not be the first thing I'd want to accomplish behind closed doors with that man.

"The things kids have to deal with nowadays," he said, running his left hand through his hair. *Again, no wedding ring.* "It's exhausting just listening to it. I'm amazed that only a few of my students a year end up in a recovery center."

I stared at him through squinted eyes. "I can only imagine. I'm sure your job is very difficult, but I'm glad you're there for the kids at Raegan's school. Teenagers often need someone to listen, offer them advice. Mine is no different, since she clearly can't discuss things with me."

Dr. Ford straightened his head and rubbed his hands together before shoving them into his front pockets. His body emitted a small shiver, which I would have missed if I hadn't been watching him so closely. In a panic to move my gaze away from him, I stared at a tree across from the hospital entrance. Its branches were stripped bare, its trunk bent with age. The poor thing looked how

I felt—drained and downtrodden. I shuddered to think of myself in twenty years, considering how I looked and felt now.

"You know kids rarely talk to their parents voluntarily," he said. "Raegan isn't an exception. I know I didn't talk to my parents when I was that age. I would have rather talked to a wall."

My eyes met his again. He had a point. While I loved my mom and dad, I didn't exactly think of us as close when I was a teenager.

"I obviously haven't spoken with her yet, but I really do have a good feeling about Raegan. I've seen her exceptional grades—up until this year, of course—and all of the wonderful things former teachers said about her. It's clear she's been going through something these last few months, and I'm fairly certain we can get to the bottom of it. Sometimes an outsider's perspective can do wonders."

I glanced down at my feet, using the sole of one of my shoes to create tiny scuff marks on the cement. "I really hope you can help in the areas where I've failed. Having been raised alongside a sibling with special needs and lacking a father figure the majority of her life, Raegan hasn't had the easiest of times. She deserves to have someone listen to her and give her advice she will actually heed."

Dr. Ford nodded. "I think you've done all that you know how to do with Raegan, Mrs. Hawley. Don't be too hard on yourself."

"It's Ms. Hawley," I finally corrected him. "Ms. Or Sam. You can call me Sam. Sam is great. But not Mrs. Definitely not Mrs. I'm in the process of getting divorced. And I'm rambling." This time I brought my hand to my forehead. "I'm sorry. You do not need to know my marital history." *What in the hell was wrong with me?*

Dr. Ford grinned. "What can I say? I'm a psychologist. I exude trust. Complete strangers have told me a lot more about themselves with less context. At least I kind of know you."

Biting the inside of my cheek, I shook my head. "If you knew even a little bit about me, Dr. Ford, you would have run in the opposite direction the second you saw me."

He rocked back on his heels. "It's Landon, and I doubt that. I get the feeling that anyone who runs away from you is an idiot. I'm sure I'll see you around, Ms. Sam." He winked, and I was grateful for the bitter chill in the air and my already-red cheeks, as they masked just how fiercely I blushed. Before I could fully register his remarks—or the wink—he turned and walked away.

Landon Ford, I thought to myself, watching him disappear. I considered taking the cigarette out of my pocket again, but then realized I wasn't as stressed as I was when I'd headed out here.

Landon Ford.

As my feet carried me back to my unit, my mind was still replaying the image of him fading into the parking lot. He was clearly not from around here, or he would know to stay far away from me. My life was messy, to put it mildly, and any single man in Madison knew not to get involved in my business in any way, shape, or form. But, if Landon was an outsider, he might not be fully aware of my chaotic life, which could either work for or against me.

His not being a Madison native also meant *I* knew

nothing about *him*. While he wasn't wearing a wedding ring the two times I'd seen him, it might not mean he was available. I had a hard time believing a guy like that wasn't married, but then again, some psychologists had a tendency to be weird.

Just as I picked up a file to enter a patient's vitals into my computer, Mr. Keenan's room light flickered on.

Groaning, I shimmied out of my jacket and started down the hallway. I was about to enter Mr. Keenan's room when Raegan shuffled by me, this time with a bag full of soiled hospital gowns in hand. Raising my eyebrows at her, she gave a sickeningly sweet fake smile, complete with a head tilt.

Drea was right—Raegan was just like me.

****

"Hey, McKenna," I called, tossing my purse on the kitchen table before grabbing myself a glass of water from the tap. My temples had been throbbing since noon, and while subconsciously I knew my headache was far too severe to be eliminated with water, I was sure as hell going to try anyway.

A head covered in gorgeous brunette waves popped up from below the back of the couch in the next room over. McKenna was at the far end where the seat stopped, Harrison's wheelchair sitting next to her on the other side of the armrest.

"Hey, Sam." Her eyes moved to Harrison before she stood and joined me in the kitchen. They were watching *Fight Club*, again, and occasionally I would hear Harrison happily grunt from the living room.

"How did today go?" I asked as she stood opposite me, the kitchen island separating us.

She chewed on her lip. "He refused the smoothie I

offered at lunch, so we just stuck to the G-tube. And when I suggested going for a roll around the neighborhood in the afternoon, he started yelling, so here we've sat. He did finally humor me with a bit of yogurt at dinner, though. I'm not sure if something is going on, or what. Him pushing back on food is one thing, but he almost always wants to get out of the house."

McKenna came to us fresh out of high school five years ago and planned on staying until she finished her Master's Degree in Special Education. At only five feet, three inches tall, I almost didn't hire her, since a large part of caring for Harrison is picking him up and moving him from one place to another. I soon found out, though, that she had been a gymnast for fifteen years, and she could probably bench press a two-seater car without breaking a sweat. She carried him just as easily on her first day when he was only nine years old as she did now, and at fourteen years old, my son wasn't light.

I dreaded the day McKenna would leave us—she had made my life easier and Harrison's life better in so many ways. She single-handedly restored my faith in humanity moments after meeting her. The day of her interview, she greeted me with a brisk, firm handshake, waltzed into my living room, and nodded at Harrison. "Is that him?" she asked, and before I could confirm, she marched up and hunched over to make eye contact with him.

"Hey, Harrison, I'm McKenna. I hear you're in the market for a new friend. I, too, am looking for a new buddy, and I think you just might fit the bill. You want to go roll around the neighborhood for a little bit? Test out my theory?"

After giving her a quizzical stare, Harrison offered

her one of the biggest smiles I had ever seen, and he and McKenna rolled out of the house like they had been friends for years. She immediately treated him like a person, and both Harrison and I instantly loved her for that. The other caregivers I had interviewed before her were so delicate with Harrison—almost as if they were afraid of him. But McKenna breezed in, treated him how he and I longed for him to be treated by outsiders, and that was it.

"I'll talk to him. It *is* odd he didn't want to leave the house." I stared at the back of his wheelchair before addressing McKenna again. "Regardless, thank you for everything, Kenny. I appreciate you so much," I said before downing the glass of water. Sure enough, my headache was still there.

"You tell me that every day, Sam." Her brown eyes glinted with amusement.

"That's because I mean it every day. You want to stay for dinner?"

She shook her head. "I told Kevin I would meet him for a date if you got home in time. I think if I ever want a shot at a lasting relationship, I should spend time with the person I like once in a while. But obviously not *too* much time. That's when things tend to go south."

My chin jutted out as I nodded. "Good call. I'll see you Monday. Tell Kevin I said hi and that I'm sorry for hijacking his girlfriend for days on end."

As McKenna left, I walked over and collapsed onto the couch next to Harrison. His eyes moved from the television to me for a split second before returning his intense gaze to Brad Pitt.

"Hey, Harry. I heard it was a difficult day."

Harrison gave me his signature lazy smile, and it

was in that moment I realized he had played McKenna. Tsking, I patted his knee. "You know, you still may be able to trick McKenna, but you can't fool me, pal. That smile gave you away."

He side-eyed me, his face expressionless.

"McKenna only has your best interest in mind. Don't give her hell about leaving the house just because you're obsessed with this movie and want to watch it over and over again until your eyeballs fall out of your skull. You need to get out once in a while. Smell some fresh air, see some trees. It's good for you. This crap," I gestured to the television, "is not."

Harrison grunted.

Rubbing the sides of my head, I stared blankly at the TV, not processing any of it. Instead, I found myself wondering how my life turned into what it was. Not that it was bad, but if someone had told me twenty years ago that I would be a divorcee with two kids—one with a severe disability and the other with a severe attitude problem—I would have laughed. Or maybe gulped down a bottle of wine in one swig.

My future wasn't something I worried about when I was younger. I thrived on living in the moment, handling everything as it came. The small stuff didn't matter, and I never planned anything more than a few hours in advance. Looking back now, my lack of forethought explained almost all of my questionable teenage choices. Meeting and sleeping with my kids' father the first month of my freshman year of college and becoming pregnant with Raegan halfway through the first semester was one of those instances.

As if she could read my mind, Raegan, who I'd given the day off from bedpan collection duty, appeared from her black hole of a bedroom and flopped down next to me on the couch. When she hadn't been at the hospital this week, she had locked herself in her bedroom, completely withdrawn and barely speaking to me. Her silence and lack of presence throughout the house was noticeable, as our home was fairly small. It was the house Charles' parents had gifted us when we relocated to Madison after Charles graduated college.

Because it was a single-story ranch-style home, we never considered moving after having Harrison. As time wore on, I had equipped it with everything we needed for him, and while a larger one-story house would be nice, it would be a costly endeavor to start over and alter a space with everything required for a special needs child. Moving was never an issue of affordability, because Charles obviously had more than enough money to buy us a mansion and have it completely remodeled to fit Harrison's needs. It was just simply never a topic of discussion in the past, and now, it didn't matter.

Ever since I kicked him out six months ago, I had two goals: divorce his sorry ass and get me and my children out of this suffocating city as quickly as possible. I just had to somehow convince Charles to agree to the divorce and sign over the kids in order for that to happen.

"Pizza?" Raegan asked. "It's Friday."

Friday had become pizza night the first week after Charles left, and we decided to make it a weekly thing. Partly because pizza was delicious and it made us happy, and partly because I was too tired to cook ninety percent of the time.

"Call it in?" I asked her, and she nodded, taking her phone out of her pocket. Leaning back against the cushions, I closed my eyes and inhaled slowly.

I didn't realize having a carefree, happy attitude early in life meant everything stressful and maddening would catch up to me as I got older. Never did I think I would become depressed, much less suffer a depression so dark and deep it felt like I was trapped in a cement box buried in quicksand. While I did manage to pull myself out of it with the aid of therapy and medication, it was still a daily struggle not to fall back into my old habits and ways of thinking. Every morning, I had to fight the inner voices that told me I wasn't strong enough or good enough. I had to be louder than them every time I faced a challenging situation so I wouldn't break. If I collapsed, Harrison and Raegan wouldn't have anyone else to rely on. It was me; it had always been just me. If I fell apart, everything else around me would too, including my kids.

Now seeing those same signs of depression in Raegan, I was determined to swim beneath her and force her head above water until she was strong enough to tread solo again. The three of us had been dealt some difficult cards, but what didn't kill us would make us stronger. That's how the saying went, right? Or was it, what didn't kill us would give us a warped sense of humor and borderline depression?

Either way, I'm sure we would be fine. We had to be.

CHAPTER THREE

Creeping into Harrison's room, I gently climbed onto his partially-reclined bed and snuggled up against him, breathing in the scent of fresh laundry and teenage boy. He stirred and let out a soft groan as I wrapped my arm around him.

"Hey, Handsome Harry. It's my day off. I'm thinking we should do something fun—get out of Madison for a bit. Maybe visit your favorite museum? If we get there when it opens, we can check out the exhibits, come back here for some lunch, and then chill until Raegan gets home. How does that sound?"

I propped myself up so I could see his face. When his blue eyes met mine, he grinned, and my heart melted into a giant puddle of emotion. Seeing this kid happy made my entire day.

Making my way to the other side of the bed, I looked at him. "Change, then breakfast?" He smiled again, and I lowered his bed so he was laying mostly flat. After removing his pajamas and changing his undergarments, I grabbed a long sleeve shirt and pants out of the nearby dresser and carefully pulled the clothes over his rigid limbs. Dressing Harrison was a challenge because his muscles randomly and rapidly contracted and released. I could be halfway through putting his pants on when his knees would jerk upward toward his chest, startling both of us.

Once he was changed, I raised the mattress again and gently placed Harrison into a sitting position. "You ready for some breakfast?" I asked, holding him upright.

He grunted. Sliding one hand under his legs and keeping one hand behind his back, I lifted him into the wheelchair that waited beside his bed. After buckling him in, I directed his wheelchair out of the bedroom and down the hall to the kitchen. Leaving him sitting by the kitchen table, I turned his favorite playlist up on my phone and began making breakfast. As I was blending his favorite smoothie, I turned to see he was staring at me. Offering him a smile, he returned the gesture before looking down at the table.

Moving my focus to the frozen fruit, vegetables, and oat milk whirring and blending beneath my hand, I watched as the colors spun around, disappearing into the thickening beverage. His doctor had suggested I make Harrison smoothies from the time he was a toddler because he was incredibly limited when it came to types of food he could actually eat.

Stealing another glance at my son, my heart constricted. The moment I saw Harrison after giving birth, I knew something was different. Doctors soon began muttering "cerebral palsy" to one another as they put Harrison through a plethora of scans and tests during his first few months of life, but they remained hopeful and refused to diagnose him when he was an infant. They wanted to see if things improved as he got older, but my intuition told me time wasn't going to solve anything. As the months wore on, Harrison failed to meet growth and development milestones, and doctors eventually diagnosed him with spastic quadriplegia cerebral palsy—an incredibly daunting and heartbreaking disability.

He was wheelchair-bound from the time he woke up until the time he went to bed and required around-the-clock supervision. Like many others who had severe forms of cerebral palsy, Harrison had a gastrostomy tube, or G-tube, but we occasionally orally fed him specific liquids if he was in the mood to humor us. Though Harrison wasn't paralyzed, he could not control his limbs, and he suffered from seizures, which were unfortunately common in individuals who had spastic quadriplegia.

Harrison's low groan pulled me from my thoughts, and I glanced down to realize the blender had stopped. Sitting next to him, I slowly spooned the cool beverage into his mouth.

"Is this one a keeper?" I asked, studying his face. He looked like his father when Charles was younger, but far more handsome. Harrison's facial features drooped slightly, but even lack of muscle tone could not conceal his striking features. His sandy brown hair and pale blue eyes made him seem like he belonged on a beach instead of in the middle of the country, surrounded by barely any water at all.

He grunted and pulled his lips into a smile.

"Well, joke's on you, kid. I managed to sneak spinach into this one, and you just admitted you liked it." I let out an evil laugh, causing Harrison's smile to stretch and his eyes to twinkle. "Victory is mine!" As I raised the smoothie above my head, he laughed, small, short bursts of air and sound emanating from his hunched frame.

Within the hour, we were on the road, heading to one of Harrison's favorite natural history museums, in the city of Atlanta. It had been a while since our last visit, but today seemed like as good a day as any to temporarily escape Madison. Getting Harrison out of the house always improved his mood, and Lord knows I needed some fresh air.

As we made our way around the museum, my gaze constantly shifted between Harrison and the people around us. Whispers were inevitable. Almost everyone who noticed him stared; their brows furrowed as they tried to figure out exactly what was "wrong" or different about him. Then, after a few seconds, they realized they were staring too long and quickly averted their eyes.

When we reached the seventy-five acre outdoor portion of the museum, I directed Harrison along one of the handicap accessible pathways and took in the beautiful scenery. The sound of his wheelchair bumping along the wooden pathway and a breeze whispering through the trees filled the otherwise quiet air. No one else seemed to want to brave the winter chill, but this area was Harrison's favorite part of the entire museum. His eyes constantly darted upward, his face illuminated by rays of sunlight that managed to break through the thick tree cover above and around us.

After nearly an hour of exploring, Harrison and I made the joint decision to head back inside. On the way, we passed a woman and a young boy, who stopped in his tracks and stared as Harrison rolled by. Seconds later, the boy broke away from the woman to catch up with us. "Hey!" he shouted, shielding his eyes from the sun while gazing at Harrison. "How come you get to roll everywhere instead of walk?"

Taking my hand off of the joystick that controlled Harrison's wheelchair, we stopped along the boardwalk.

Harrison grinned as I knelt down next to him so I could be on the same level as the boy. "He can't talk," I explained.

The child looked Harrison over. "Why? He can't walk, either?"

As fast as her legs could carry her, the woman came up behind the boy and placed her hands on his shoulders. "I am so sorry, ma'am." Her cheeks flushed with embarrassment.

Staring up at her, I shook my head. "Don't apologize. It's great that he is asking questions instead of assuming things about my son." I turned back to the boy. "He can't walk or talk because he has something called cerebral palsy. It affects the way he moves, talks, eats, things like that."

I could see the gears shifting in the little boy's brain. "Do you like movies?" I asked him, and he nodded enthusiastically.

"Yeah! I love action movies. They're my favorite."

Grinning, I nodded at Harrison. "This guy loves action movies, too. He can spend hours watching them if I let him. What about being outside? You like playing outdoors?"

The boy nodded again. "Totally. My mom only lets me watch one movie a day, so the rest of the time when I'm not in school, I play in my treehouse."

"Harrison loves being outside, too! You both have some things in common."

As kids usually did, the boy forgot about why Harrison was in a wheelchair, and instead, started talking to him about movies. "I saw this one movie yesterday, where there was this bad guy, and he had bright green hair, and—"

Standing up, I looked at the woman, who had noticeably relaxed. "Thank you for letting him talk with us. I always prefer when people speak to my son, instead of pretending he's not there. Or worse, acknowledging that he's there and then ignoring him. You're raising a good kid."

The little boy continued talking to Harrison until we reached the doors that led to the inside of the museum. After noticing where we were, he reluctantly waved goodbye before skipping off down the wooden outdoor pathway, his mom trailing behind him. I watched them disappear before I turned and steered Harrison to the next exhibit. More people stared as we went past them, and I found myself wishing everyone could be more like that kid. I longed for the outside world to see Harrison the way I saw him.

In my eyes, he was a teenager who loved going for long rides in the car so he could see colors and shapes whiz by. He hated trying new foods, but eventually came around to liking almost all of them. He loved action movies; the more explosions and fight scenes, the better. His laugh was infectious, and his joyous personality was apparent when someone got to know him. Harrison was a blessing, though many people couldn't understand that. A majority of the population simply saw a young man in a wheelchair, but I saw my entire world.

After taking a few laps around the museum and staring at the dinosaurs for what felt like hours, Harrison and I called it a day. When we arrived home forty-five minutes later, I glanced at him in the rearview mirror. He was sitting behind me, his wheelchair secured to the van's floorboards with tiedowns. "Was today nice, Harry?"

His torso was slanted forward, unintentionally testing the durability of his shoulder harnesses. The hunch of his spine was more severe when he was tired, and I could tell by his glassy stare that today had worn him out.

Once I moved him inside the house, I quickly prepared his lunch and inserted it into his gastrostomy tube. When the food was gone, I gently lifted Harrison out of his wheelchair and carried him into his bedroom. Changing his clothes and undergarments once more, I settled him into bed and grabbed a book from the nearby bookcase. Three pages in, I felt his body relax against mine and I quietly closed the story.

Instead of getting up and tending to various neglected chores, I remained on top of the duvet, listening to my son's breathing. While trying to take in the moment, I was suddenly overcome with memories of him and me sitting together in his room over the years.

The room had changed a lot—from baby blue hues to a neutral light gray—but the most significant change happened right after he was born. Because Harrison's official diagnosis didn't come until months after his birth, we planned a run-of-the-mill nursery. A wooden crib, a mobile of stars, a navy-blue glider. After I returned home from the hospital four months ahead of Harrison, I almost gutted his room. Gone was the crib to make way for a special bed. Certain sounds, as we discovered in the hospital, drove Harrison to cry for hours on end, so I tossed the mobile in the trash out of fear it would upset him. The only thing that remained the same was the glider. It was still in the corner of his room, and on rare occasions, I would still hold Harrison like I did when he was little, gently rocking us back and forth.

It felt sorely out of place now, though, as the room clearly looked like it belonged to a teenager. Framed movie posters adorned Harrison's wall, along with the random tranquil nature photographs I hung to counter the violence depicted on said posters. Whenever he showed an interest in another action movie, a poster from the film would appear on his wall within a week. Seeing his smile when he noticed the new addition was worth putting dozens of holes in the walls.

Charles had thought differently. That man had ignored nearly everything that happened in our home, but whenever he'd heard me hammering, he was out of his office faster than green grass through a goose. He thought décor and knickknacks were tacky and a waste of money. But he didn't have a say in what we did under this roof anymore.

I liked to think that if I had finished college after getting pregnant with Raegan, I may have gotten a job and left Charles much sooner; thereby preventing some of the terrible memories my children rightfully associated with Charles. Hell, had I gone down that path, I may not have married him at all. If I had held fast to my beliefs and vision for my future, my life would have looked different. But the moment the plus sign appeared on that home pregnancy test, fear clouded my dreams and I folded under the Hawleys' pressure. Charles and his family took over everything and shamed me for wanting to finish college.

"Mothers put their children first. If you had wanted to finish college, you wouldn't have coerced Charles into having sex with you. Now your job is to be a good mother to the next Hawley heir and live with your decisions."

And that was what I did. The first few years of being

a stay-at-home mother were a struggle, but ultimately, it was what was best for my children. Charles' inability and unwillingness to care for Raegan and Harrison would have made finishing college or having any sort of career challenging for everyone. And after Harrison was born, I was habitually exhausted. Between the myriad of hospital visits during his first few years of life and Raegan still being a young child, obtaining my nursing degree was the last thing on my mind.

But once things started to settle, I began feeling trapped. Between barely leaving the house and constantly being at the mercy of young children and a demanding husband, something inside me shifted.

When I felt the time was right, I returned to college online and earned my registered nurse license when Raegan was nearing the end of elementary school. During the day, I would care for Harrison: get him out of the house and take him places that could expand his mind and illuminate more of the world around him. When Raegan returned home from school, we would do homework, I would cook dinner, and the kids would be in bed by eight. Once the house was clean, the laundry was folded and put away, and I was mentally and physically exhausted, it was then time for me to start my *own* schooling for the evening.

I spent years following that schedule, taking only one or two online classes at a time so my education wouldn't impede my children's own schooling and lives. In fact, I never required additional care for Harrison until clinicals started, and even then, Harrison was only out of my sight for a few hours at a time. I managed to schedule them while Raegan was at school to ensure minimal disruption of the kids' routines.

I'm fairly certain Charles never even suspected I'd returned to college until I got a job locally and the neighbors did what they did best—gossip. My textbooks were always hidden away and the money I pulled from our joint account to pay for my courses was always gradually deducted. When I applied for and landed a part-time job in the emergency room after I passed my licensing exam, however, it was the kiss of death for my secret. The moment I stepped out in public wearing scrubs and a name tag, the good ol' residents of Madison couldn't help but talk.

"Look at you, picking up a hobby," I remembered a few ladies saying, giggling when they passed me on the street. As if going to school every night for years on end and studying my ass off for a licensing exam was a "hobby." Other people referred to my career as "cute," "a good distraction," and "ambitious, but a waste of time, seeing as how your children need you."

No one really took me or my job seriously until McKenna arrived in our lives and I switched to full-time work at the medical center. The caretaker I had for Harrison before McKenna was nice and could do the bare minimum, but I never felt comfortable being away from him for long. With McKenna, though, I knew immediately she was more than capable of caring for my son, and I moved from part-time to full-time with ease.

Life had almost seemed calm for a bit, with Raegan, Harrison, and I adjusting to the routine where I was a full-time mother *and* nurse. But staying true to the nature of our lives, my kicking Charles out of our house disturbed the peace. Rumors began spreading like wildfire, and the most audacious neighbors began approaching me in public to barrage me with questions.

How could I possibly parent two children while working full time with Charles gone?

Who would raise my kids now that both of their parents were away from the home?

What possessed me to bring harm upon my family by divorcing such a beloved, thoughtful man?

It was nearly impossible to keep secrets in a small city, but I made damn sure everyone knew as little as possible about my family's business. With Charles being in local politics, I'd put on an act every time I appeared in public with him. Giant smiles, my arm wrapped around his waist, me staring adoringly into his eyes every time he spoke. But the moment the front door to our house closed and we were all safely inside, the smiles disappeared. Charles and I never touched each other. Staring at any part of him made me feel ill.

What the good people of Madison didn't know was that their beloved mayor never paid any attention to his family. Never once did he help in any aspect related to his children, hence my need for McKenna. She and I took care of everything, so when Charles left our home and marriage, nothing was different in my world of parenting. I was just as alone as I had been when we were together.

Harrison stirred, and I instinctively moved closer to him, ready to wrap my arms around his frame to minimize any muscle spasms that might occur and wake him from his slumber. We remained like this for a few minutes; my arms hovering over him, my breathing measured and light to ensure I wouldn't wake him, and him asleep, completely unaware of my presence. After I finally convinced myself that he was fine, I relaxed against the pillows again.

Because I struggled with my own issues while raising Harrison and Raegan, I was under no illusion that I was the world's greatest mother during my children's formative years. I wanted to give Raegan and Harrison equal attention so no one would feel left out, but it was impossible. I was only one person, and I couldn't pull the weight of being a mother *and* father. I was drowning, and the only thing that saved me, and subsequently my children, was returning to school and eventually getting a job.

Becoming a nurse, in the end, was a game-changer for both Harrison and me. He became exposed to more people than just our family. I got out of the house a few times a week and could focus on other people and their problems instead of wallowing in my own.

Somewhere in my brain, I registered the front door unlocking, and I inched off Harrison's bed to greet Raegan. She was already sitting on the couch, staring at her phone.

"Hey, Rae of Sunshine," I said quietly. She briefly blinked in my direction before returning to her phone. "How was school?"

She shrugged. "Passable. Thanks for letting me use the car."

On the days I didn't work, I let Raegan take my car to school, because I could only use the handicap-equipped van to transport Harrison. When I was at the hospital, McKenna either hauled both kids in the van to drop Raegan off at school, or Raegan would catch a ride with a friend. The school wasn't *that* far from the house, but the Madison winters were chilly, and the spring and summer months were disgustingly humid. Driving beat walking any day of the year.

Sitting next to her, I watched her fingers rapidly move across the screen as she responded to friends' text messages. Absent-mindedly, she raised a hand to her lips and began biting her cuticles, her focus still lasered in on the small screen in front of her. Seeing her like this—a near-adult just months away from graduating high school—made it difficult for me to remember Raegan ever being a little kid. So much of her childhood was overshadowed by the challenges of her brother's medical diagnosis, and while it obviously impacted us differently, she ended up coping in ways I didn't expect.

When she was young, she was the stereotypical sibling of a special needs child—loud, rebellious, chaotic. I used to know what was on her mind at all times; I could hear her rage and disappointment when plans were cancelled because of something that came up with Harrison. She was starving for attention, any attention, and rarely was she rewarded with it.

Realizing her former coping mechanisms got her nowhere, Raegan transformed into an entirely different person once she hit puberty. I no longer knew what she was feeling or thinking via tantrums and vocalizations. She began suffering silently—everything she once expressed outwardly turned inward. These days, I could only feel anger radiating from her small frame like ripples from a skipping stone in a lake as she quickly brushed past me in the hall. I saw the red in and around her eyes and the stains on her cheeks from the tears that had fallen minutes before, as she left the house. She barely talked to me anymore, leading me to decide that it was far scarier having a silent teenager than a screaming toddler.

I wished I had the opportunity to go back and do

things differently when Raegan and Harrison were younger. I was so overwhelmed with what-ifs, mom guilt, soul-sucking depression, and crippling anxiety that my own mental and physical health took a dive. I couldn't prioritize what needed to be done and who needed attention because I was exhausted. Had I known there would be a light at the end of the tunnel and we would mostly be okay a few years down the road, I think I would have been a better mom. I would have made an effort to repair my mental health faster and spend more quality time with my kids. Instead, the darkness that originated in my mind slowly seeped throughout my body for years, rendering me all but useless.

As I stared at her, I couldn't help but wonder if Dr. Ford could truly advise Raegan on how to deal with the consequences of her less-than-ideal childhood. Could therapy fix all those years of damage and neglect that I had caused? Leaning back against the couch, I massaged my temples. What would happen if it couldn't?

CHAPTER FOUR

Sitting at a table next to one of the dozen windows in the hospital cafeteria, I stared out into the distance, my mind threatening to shut down for the day if it didn't receive some type of stimulation soon. Taking in the dormant brown grass, the dreary weather, and the flat terrain surrounding the medical center, I realized looking outside wasn't the answer. What I needed was sunshine and green landscapes, but I would be hard-pressed to find either of those things around here during the winter months. For the millionth time this year, I chastised myself for still living in this godforsaken city, and it was only January.

I didn't hear Drea join me at the table until she plopped her lunch tray down in front of mine, revealing a salad, a bottled water, and a fruit cup. Peering down at what had been my lunch ten minutes earlier, I saw the remnants of spaghetti, a burnt edge of the garlic bread, and two empty cans of Coke sitting in the corner of the tray. I was waiting for the caffeine to kick in before returning to work, but for some reason, my body was refusing to get out of first gear.

Drea eyed my food. "I don't know how you stay so damn skinny and eat like that. Then there's me, who eats salads and exercises four times a week and is still the 'before' model in a weight loss advertisement."

I rolled my eyes. "First off, you're smoking hot.

Second, it's the stress. You just need more stress. Tell Marcus to go screw his secretary, completely neglect your children so one of them starts dealing drugs at the local high school, and then come back to me. I'm convinced stress, carbs, and caffeine hit differently when you're always seconds away from a mental breakdown."

Drea shook her head. "Marc is too afraid of me to screw his secretary." She paused. "Not that Charles wasn't afraid of you. He's just—" she stopped herself.

Grinning, I held up my hand. "Let me take the shovel away from you before you dig yourself into a deeper hole. Charles *wasn't* afraid of me when we first met. I was an unsure eighteen-year-old college freshman who was out on her own for the first time. But after getting pregnant and being subjected to his controlling family for years, there is now a rage burning inside of my soul fueled entirely by my disdain for that man. Does he know this? Probably not." I swirled a lone spaghetti around my fork. "But he will surely find out if he decides to contest our divorce."

She stared at me. "Ever since I've known you, you've always been the opinionated, sassy woman I see before me, so it's hard to imagine you as a quiet woman who *didn't* give everyone a piece of her mind. In the same vein, though," she cocked her head, "You're also one of the sweetest, most caring people I've ever met. Really, I guess, your nickname should be Spikey Peach. Prickly on the outside, soft on the inside."

My laughter rang out across the cafeteria. "Spikey Peach doesn't have quite the same ring as Peach."

Her lips pursed as she nodded. "You're right. Peach you will forever be." She gulped down a bite of salad before waving her fork in the air. "Circling back to the rest of what you said—you do *not* neglect your children. You work full time to pay for your kids' needs because your piece of crap ex doesn't pay anything. You also work to maintain what little sanity you have left, because of your piece of crap ex *and* your children. When you aren't at work, you put one hundred and ten percent into parenting your babies. Rae is just struggling right now because of everything that's been going on. She will level out. You're a good mom, Peach. I promise."

I held Drea's gaze for a minute before abruptly exhaling. "Sometimes I don't feel like it."

She shrugged. "All moms feel like failures at least three times a day. And if they don't, they either have other people raising their children for them or are on a secret drug that eliminates mom guilt."

A small chuckle escaped me. "Thanks, Drea."

She reached over and rubbed my arm. "You got this, okay?"

"I sure hope so. I shudder to imagine what would happen if I don't got this."

Raising another forkful of salad to her mouth, she wiggled her eyebrows at me. "Can we talk about something else? That man I saw outside the other day talking with you? He looks familiar, but I can't place him. What's his deal? He is *fine* as *hell*." She gave a low whistle before ingesting the leafy green vegetables.

I could feel heat rushing to my cheeks. "Creeper. That's Rae's school psychologist."

Clearly forgetting she had food in her mouth, Drea's jaw dropped, revealing her half-masticated salad. "If he didn't have graying hair, I would have thought he just graduated from college."

Nodding, I tried not to picture Landon, because my

focus was already shot for the day. "I said the exact same thing when I met him, which he found humorous. But he claims he's thirty-eight. I'm not sure I believe it."

Drea bobbed her head back and forth. "Mhmm, mhm, mhmmmm. I know you're not actively searching for a man right now, girl, but damn. He's like, right here. Right in your lap."

"I've had worse things in my lap," I smirked.

She snorted. "That's right, you have. Things can only really go up from here. You going to pursue it?"

Glancing at my watch, I realized my lunch was over ten minutes ago. As I stood up and grabbed my tray from the cafeteria table, I stared down at her. "No. Besides, no sane man would want to be with me. And I can't handle anymore narcissistic assholes."

She tutted. "He's into you. I could tell by the way he was looking at you."

"Then he's a narcissistic asshole, and I'm not interested." Tossing my trash into the bin and placing the tray on top of it, I turned to give Drea a quick hug. "I'll see you later, okay? Thanks for the pep talk, as always."

She kissed my cheek. "Someone has to do it to ensure you keep going, babe. Kick ass and get that therapist's number."

****

The rest of my shift dragged on with no eventful happenings. As a geriatric nurse, a boring workday was great for my patients, because it meant everyone pulled through to see another sunrise. However, the mundanity of rounds and changing bedpans and garments made completing my twelve-hour shift incredibly difficult. It was days like these that I missed the adrenaline rush I felt working in the emergency room.

As I trudged to the parking structure after clocking out, I felt my phone vibrate in my pocket. Panic washed over me when I saw the school's number appear on the screen. Raegan couldn't have messed up again, right? Or had she? Was this it, the last straw? Would I be scrambling to find my daughter a new school only a few months before graduation?

When I heard Landon's voice in place of Mr. Prior's, a different type of fear flooded my brain.

"Ms.—" Landon stopped himself. "Sam. It's Dr.— Landon. It's Landon."

"Hey. Is everything okay?" Checking my watch, I saw it was seven p.m. Why would anyone from the school be calling this late unless it was serious?

"Everything is fine. I just wanted to take a quick break from paperwork to fill you in on something. Mr. Prior has been on me for a few months to hire someone to help with my caseload, and I finally conceded his point. Yesterday we hired a female therapist, Dr. Miranda Ridley."

Why was he telling me this?

"I'm informing you of this staff addition because Raegan opted to switch to Miranda. You mentioned that Raegan doesn't speak with you on a regular basis, so I felt like I should mention the change, in the event Raegan doesn't say anything. I vetted Miranda and trust her implicitly, and I think she can help Raegan more than I can in various ways." There was a pause before I heard Landon quickly inhale. "Besides, as much as I wanted to help Raegan, her choosing Miranda over me is better for personal and ethical reasons, as well."

Throwing open my rusting car door and blindly chucking my purse inside, I fell into the seat behind the wheel and shut myself in the vehicle. A long sigh escaped me as my head hit the headrest and my eyes slowly closed. While I was staring at the inside of my eyelids, I fully processed the last part of his explanation. "Wait, what personal and ethical reasons?"

He ignored my question. "Did I catch you at a bad time?"

"Not really. I just got off work. When I saw the school number on my phone, I was worried Raegan finally blew it. Between that moment of panic and a horrendously boring shift, I'm ready for today to be done," I admitted. "But it's definitely not the worst time for you to call."

"I'm really sorry," he said, his voice dropping an octave. The polite phone voice gave way to his normal, casual voice. "I didn't mean to panic you. I didn't even realize the time until right now. I should have held off calling until tomorrow."

Pressing the speaker button, I placed the phone on my thigh and slowly massaged my scalp. "It's totally fine. If you're anything like me, you have to do things while you're thinking about them, otherwise they will never get done."

He laughed, the rich tones of his voice seeping through the phone. "I feel like everyone over the age of thirty has that problem. Throw in kids, work, life—it's amazing adults remember anything at all."

"Ain't that the truth. Do you always work this late? Because not sleeping also impairs one's memory. I've both experienced and read studies about this," I quipped.

"Hey, now." He chuckled. "Just because school ends at three p.m. doesn't mean my work ends at three p.m. Sometimes paperwork gets the best of me, and I opt to stay after hours to finish it. If I don't stay on campus and do it, I'll take it home, and I've tried to avoid doing that once the pandemic ended. You know, boundaries and all that."

I could feel myself grinning. "Look at you, practicing what you preach." Landon laughed again, and I found myself slowly falling in love with the sound.

"I had to. Rarely leaving my house for all those months made me a little stir crazy. When I returned to seeing patients face-to-face, I vowed to make my home a work-free place again."

I flipped open the mirror on the sun visor as he spoke. The dark circles under my eyes made me resemble a raccoon, and my mascara had almost completely flaked off after a day's worth of wear. Relieved Landon was on the phone instead of in person, I rolled my eyes at myself. Twelve-hour-shift Sam was not my best look.

Shutting the visor, I refocused on our conversation. "I commend you for sticking to working at work and relaxing at home. I can't imagine what it was like during the pandemic, working from home and then signing off for the day, only to still be at home. One nice thing about having a job outside of the house is that it makes you more appreciative of your own personal space."

Landon hummed in agreement. "I shouldn't complain, though. I know you probably struggled more than most people during the pandemic."

I shrugged. "I wouldn't say more than most, but yeah, it was definitely a challenge. Although, living in this city feels just as suffocating as sheltering at home does, I'm assuming. Kudos to you for moving here after a global pandemic."

"I'm actually from Madison," he admitted slowly. "So really, I just moved back."

I froze. "Seriously?"

"Yes, ma'am. Born and raised. I left the second I graduated high school. After being around the same people for nearly two decades, I needed to get the hell out of dodge. Granted, I didn't attend a university on the other side of the country like I originally wanted to, but I did get out, *and* stayed out, for a while."

"Why in the Sam Hill did you come back?"

"My parents. They were old and I'm an only child. I felt guilty for leaving them alone for years, but it was too hard to come back to Madison after college. There is too much history, too many bad memories for me in this place. I would visit during the holidays, but I never stayed for more than a week at a time. When their health started declining, I forced myself to suck it up and accepted the offer at the high school so I could move back to care for them. Too little, too late, though." His words hung heavy with regret.

"They passed away." It was more of a statement from me than a question, as his tone left little to suspect.

"Both of them died within a few months of me being back."

"I'm so sorry, Landon. If it's any consolation, I'm sure the time you *did* spend with them was precious and meant more to them than you'll ever know. And I realize it's not the same, but my parents live in Southern California, and I haven't seen them since Raegan was two months old. They don't travel well. My mom is one of those grips-the-airplane-armrests-and-screams-during-turbulence kind of flyers."

"Is that where you're from? Southern California?"

he asked.

I guffawed. "How do you know I'm not from Georgia?"

Landon tried to suppress another laugh but failed. "Sam, I'm not going to tell you your accent is terrible, but as a Georgia native, it's passable, at best."

I put my hand over my heart, feigning offense. "No way. I have the accent down pat, sir. How dare you accuse me of not being Southern enough," I said in my heaviest, sweetest drawl. "Bless your heart, heavens to Betsy, you've gone cattywampus." I rattled off a few more stereotypical Southern phrases as Landon snickered in the background.

"Okay, okay. I'll placate you. Let's call your accent believable then, but your demeanor alone proves you're a transplant. You know how Southern women are. Sweet to your face, utterly charming, you can almost see honey oozing out of every pore. But it's usually a front— they're really just being ugly. You know it, they know it, everyone knows it. The second you turn around, most women are talking about you to every person with a pulse. Many of them are conniving and bored. And while we've only spoken less than a handful of times, I can almost guarantee you aren't like that."

He was right on the money. Madison was the stereotypical small Southern city that drove me absolutely mental with its cliques and gossiping women. "Well, I won't argue with you on that. Though I have talked about you behind your back."

The joy in Landon's voice instantly disappeared. "All good things, I hope?"

Before I could think, I heard myself say, "Of course, all good things. I mean, have you met you? Have you seen you? There's nothing bad to report, as of yet." My hand flew over my mouth and heat crept across my cheeks the second I finished speaking. Oh my gosh. I really *was* tired. My filter was gone.

Silence followed my confession, and as time ticked on, I could feel myself sinking further into my seat.

"I—" I began, but he cut me off.

"Why, Sam," he said, his voice even lower, "do you think I'm attractive?"

With my hand still over my mouth, I clenched my fingers into a fist and actually thought about how I was going to reply. "I didn't not say you were attractive." It wasn't my best work, and the fact that I wasn't good at flirting was becoming glaringly and rapidly apparent.

He chuckled, softer this time. "Well, then it's my turn to admit the final reason I know you aren't from around here, passable Southern accent and demeanor aside. Unless you want to guess it?"

I shook my head and shrugged as if he could see me. "I've got nothing."

"You, Samantha Hawley, aren't from around here because without a doubt in my mind, I would have remembered seeing someone as beautiful as you around these parts growing up. Had you been here when I was, I would have thought twice about leaving this city."

My cheeks flushed again, and I was fairly certain my heart did a cartwheel. "I doubt that."

"Eh, maybe you're right. I wouldn't have stayed, but I would have taken you with me."

This entire conversation had taken a turn I couldn't have seen coming with a map and a magnifying glass. I had no idea what to say next. Years away from the dating game left me completely useless when it came to romantic banter. Why couldn't I think of something witty?

"And this circles back to my comment about how I'm grateful Raegan is no longer under my care. Ethically, I cannot flirt with a patient's mother, and personally, I would feel gross about it. But now…Miranda is a hero for multiple reasons in my book."

My body had sunk so far down into the driver's seat of my car that my knees were nearly touching the space above the pedals.

"On that note," Landon said cheerfully, "I'm going to go. Thank you for giving me a reprieve from notes. I have a feeling Miranda and Raegan will hit it off."

Thank God. Operation Panic-About-Flirting ended before it really began.

I bit my lip. "I hope they do." Just as I was about to hit the end call button, I took the phone off speaker and brought it to my ear. "Hey, Landon?"

"Yes?"

"I'm glad Raegan isn't your patient anymore, too." And with that, I hung up and headed home. Strolling into the kitchen a few minutes later, I threw a microwave dinner in and got changed into pajamas while it cooked. Raegan was locked in her room, and Harrison was in his chair next to the couch, watching an action flick with McKenna.

As I sat down next to McKenna a few minutes later, she gave me a once-over. "Long day?"

I nodded, shoveling pieces of warmed-over chicken breast into my mouth. "Slow day. All of my patients remained on this side of the dirt, which is great. But man, I miss the ER."

Her face softened. "I bet. I know one day, though, you'll have the opportunity to go back."

Glancing down the hall, I crossed my legs and put my dinner on my lap. "Do you think Raegan is going to be okay?" I nearly whispered. Raegan most likely had her headphones in and was blasting music at an ungodly volume, but I didn't want to risk it.

McKenna cocked her head. "I think so."

"I wish she would let me help her."

She patted my arm gently. "I think she knows you'll always be there for her, but it's hard for teenagers to talk to their moms. I didn't talk to mine until I was basically in college. I know you know; being a teenager is a struggle. And then what happened with you and Char—her dad," she stumbled, "it's just a lot."

"You can say his name." I gave her a smile. "He's not some evil movie villain. Technically, anyway."

"Yeah, he's a real-life villain. I despise that man so much, it's hard to think of him as a human with a name. In my brain, he's the poop emoji."

I snorted. "Kenny, have I told you recently that I love you?"

She laughed. "But honestly, I think she will be okay. It's good she's in therapy. I think everyone could benefit from seeing a therapist. The world would be much better off."

Picking up my dinner, I finished the rest of the chicken and the soggy, limp green beans. McKenna helped with the washing up before leaving, and after Harrison's movie finished, we started down the hallway to begin our evening routine.

An hour later, I fell into my own bed, completely spent. Rolling onto my side, I studied the empty spot next to me. Charles had technically only been out of the house for a few months, but that spot beside me had been vacant for years. As I closed my eyes, Landon popped into my head, and I recalled our conversation.

He had said Madison had too much history, too many bad memories. What did that mean? Was it stereotypical small-city stuff, or something bigger? He seemed like such a nice guy that I had a hard time thinking he was ever involved in something nefarious, but I vowed to Google him tomorrow when I had more energy.

Landon Ford.

I ignored the tingling feeling in the lower half of my body as I thought about his face, and his arms, and how his legs looked in his fitted pants. His flirtatious remarks from our call earlier left me feeling almost giddy, but I knew I couldn't let my guard down. Being in a relationship had only brought me trouble in the past, and I didn't need any more drama in my life. Protecting my heart was the safest move, even though in this moment, shying away from Landon was the last thing I wanted to do.

CHAPTER FIVE

My body reacted to the sound before my brain did. By the time I was fully awake, I was already in Harrison's room, rolling him onto his side and holding his convulsing frame against mine. The monitor beneath his bed was still sending pages to the device I had abandoned next to my bed; its shrill tone alerting everyone within a thousand-foot radius that Harrison was having a seizure.

"It's okay, Harrison. It's okay," I said, knowing good and well he couldn't process what was going on, much less what I was saying.

Staring at my watch while his body shuddered, I realized we had passed the amount of time for it to be categorized as a partial seizure. I needed to call 911. One minute later, the ambulance was on its way, and Harrison's body had finally calmed. The blueness in his lips and face started to fade, and he let out a sigh before his breathing began to regulate.

"Hey, baby. It's okay, it's over now." I rubbed his back reassuringly, letting him know he wasn't alone. His clammy face remained in my lap, and I watched as his clenched muscles slowly relaxed. My heart, on the other hand, thumped against my ribcage like a discontented prisoner as adrenaline coursed through my veins.

"That was a really bad one." Raegan's voice drifted into the room, and I moved my head to see her standing in the doorway.

"It was a grand mal seizure; I had to call 911." My voice cracked as I stared at her. She remained at the entrance of Harrison's room, her gaze cast downward, her fingertips brushing aimlessly against her lips.

Pounding on the front door echoed throughout the house, and Raegan left to user the emergency personnel inside.

"Another bad one, huh?" Tom, one of the six paramedics in Madison, asked as he came up beside me and examined Harrison.

"It went on for nearly three minutes," I said. "I can't remember the last time he had one that lasted more than a minute."

No matter how many seizures Harrison had experienced, they always scared me. There was always a tiny part of me that feared the effects of it would kill him. When Harrison had prolonged seizures, a blocked airway, heart attack, or neck injury were at the forefront of my mind until I saw him regain his standard bodily functions. This episode was no exception.

While Tom and Chris, one of the local firefighters, lifted Harrison onto the gurney, I ran to my bedroom to grab a hoodie. Throwing it over my head, I simultaneously shoved my feet into the pair of shoes that sat right inside my doorway for this very reason and shuffled to grab my purse on the way out the front door. I watched as they wheeled Harrison inside the ambulance. Normally I would ride with him, but I decided to follow in my car with the hope that I could sneak home later while Harrison was sleeping to shower and change into real clothes. I nodded to Tom. "See you at the hospital."

Turning to tell Raegan I was leaving, I saw her hovering in the shadows on the front stoop. "Do you want to come, Rae?" I called, and she paused before nodding. We drove to the hospital in silence, and when I pulled into the parking lot, I noted it was three in the morning.

"Mom?" Rae's voice was barely above a whisper. "Do you ever wish your life was normal?"

I shut off the car and faced her. "What do you mean?"

She sighed. "You know what I mean. Do you ever wish you had normal kids? Like ones that don't have health problems and obedience problems. And a soon-to-be-ex-husband who isn't a piece of crap."

I tried so hard not to talk about my issues with Raegan and Harrison's father in front of them, but despite my best efforts, Raegan was aware of her father's infidelity. I never asked or wanted her to pick sides, but she relayed to me early on that she would always stand by me. She hadn't voluntarily seen her father in months, and honestly, his lack of involvement made all our lives a lot easier.

Dropping the car keys into my purse, I shook my head. "Raegan Marie, I'm going to clarify a few things. One, I would be lying if I said I was happy Harrison has cerebral palsy. No mother wants their child to suffer from anything, ever. A child constantly in any kind of pain, be it mental, physical, etc., is a mother's worst nightmare. So of course, I wish things could be different in that sense. But wishing doesn't change anything, and I sure as hell can't waste my time on useless activities like fantasizing about a different life. I was dealt the cards I have, and I'm playing them to the best of my ability.

"Two," I continued, "My other child does not have obedience problems. You make yourself sound like a dog. You are not a dog; you are a teenager. A teenager who has grown up with a brother who requires special care and with a parental unit that became less than ideal very early on in her life. There is nothing wrong with you. At your worst, you don't know how to handle things when life gets particularly tough, and you deal with it the way you think you should. We all do that. Sometimes you don't handle things fantastically, but it is what it is. I'm hoping Dr. Ridley will arm you with some amazing coping skills so you have the ability to handle life's bullshit a bit better."

A slight smile appeared on Raegan's shadowed face.

"As for your father," I said, pulling my purse onto my shoulder and exiting the vehicle, "stuff happens. I made choices and they ultimately led me to you and your brother, so they weren't all bad. But yeah. I'm not too thrilled with how things ended up with him."

"He's an asshole," Raegan muttered, falling into sync with me as I walked toward the emergency room doors.

I shrugged. "I can't argue with you there, kid. I'm just sorry he's an asshole who isn't around for you like he should be."

The nurses huddled around the front desk nodded at Raegan and me and one leapt up to open the doors leading to the emergency room. We walked down the deserted corridor, our footsteps echoing off the walls.

"Just know," I paused, touching her arm and waiting for her eyes to meet mine before I continued. "The decisions you make at this point in your life—they can change the *rest* of your life. I met your father freshman year of college, when I wasn't much older than you, and my entire life changed because of that. Again, not necessarily a bad thing, but the choices you make now, as a senior in high school—those can either bring your life to a complete standstill or propel you forward. You have choices to make, Raegan, and you have to think about those choices before you decide what you want to do."

She sighed. "This is about the Ritalin."

I resumed walking. "Yes, but it's about other things too. Everything, really. Just think. Think before you act, so you don't end up with regrets."

After peeking through a few curtained partitions, we located Harrison and sat beside him, the sounds of the ER replacing our desires to talk. Within a few hours, he was moved into a room for observation, and I took out my phone after he had been settled in.

I eyed Raegan. "I can call you out for school today, or I can take you home and then run you to school. You may be a little late, but I'll talk with the front desk. Which do you want?"

"You would let me miss school?" she asked, raising an eyebrow.

I let my head fall forward, the exhaustion of the morning temporarily overtaking me. "It's already been a long day and it's not even eight a.m. yet, Rae. I don't want you to fall asleep in class. But I also don't want you to get behind. Just tell me what you want to do, and I'll do it."

The rhythmic beeping of Harrison's oxygen monitor filled the room while I waited for Raegan's response. "I think I'll go to school. I have a session with Dr. Ridley and I kind of don't want to miss it," she said eventually.

Snapping my head up, I tossed my phone into my purse and stood. "Great. Let's go."

"Harrison," I said softly, leaning down to him. "I'll be back, okay? I'm going to take Raegan home and then to school." No response.

Raegan walked over and gently kissed him on the forehead. "I'll see you later, kid. Keep everyone in check around here, okay?"

He opened his eyes long enough to give her a slight smile. It wasn't shocking that he acknowledged Raegan over me. He adored his sister, and she was his biggest cheerleader.

While Raegan was inside the house changing, I waited in the car, doing everything I could to keep my eyes open. I had tossed and turned the majority of the night, Landon's face randomly appearing in my head every so often, causing my heartrate to speed up and ruining my attempts at keeping my mind clear. Picking up bits of trash in the front seat, I dropped them in the cupholder and looked around. Rolling down the window, the cold air wandered in, but even it wasn't enough to jolt me out of my impending slumber.

Think of Landon. Think about what he said to you on the phone. My pulse quickened, but the exhaustion quickly brought it back to its resting rate. Eyelids closing, I could feel my head falling forward as the car door slammed. Jerking upright, I gave Raegan an unconvincing smile.

"Are you okay to drive?" she asked, her voice full of concern.

Nodding, I backed out of the driveway, keeping the window open and praying we didn't see anyone on the street.

About a block away from school, Raegan spoke up again. "I really like Dr. Ridley."

I glanced over at her, not wanting to ask too little or too much in that moment. "You do? Do you feel like she's listening to you, giving you good advice?" I decided to possibly ask too much.

She shrugged. "Yeah. She's pretty solid. I liked Dr. Ford, but you know, Dr. Ridley is a woman. She's easier to talk with."

Nodding, I signaled to turn into the school lot. "That's really great, honey. I'm proud of you for being open to meeting with her."

Following Raegan up the steps to the office, she muttered something that resembled, "Goodbye," under her breath before heading to class. After explaining the situation to the secretary, Raegan's tardiness was excused, and I headed for the exit. Just as my hand touched the door, a voice called out to me.

"Ms.—Sam."

Landon. I could hear the smile in his voice, and it made it hard not to do the same.

Gently stepping past me, he leaned against the door and held it open after walking outside. "How is Harrison?" he asked as we descended the steps.

"Wow, word really does travel fast in this place," I said, taking my time walking back to the car. He fell into step with me, matching my meandering pace.

"Yep. Faster than a knife fight in a phone booth." He slid both of his hands into his freshly pressed dress pants' pockets, just as he did the day we spoke outside of the hospital.

Noting his seemingly effortless magnetism, I was

fully aware I looked like I had stood outside during a hurricane for a better part of the night. I didn't even know what I was wearing. Did I have a bra on under my hoodie? I slowly puffed out my chest, eventually feeling the tight constraint of the underwire. Thank the Lord, I hadn't taken it off from the day before.

"I'm not sure how he's doing. They're running tests, but I'm hoping nothing has changed for the worse. I don't know if I can handle anything else right now," I said, immediately regretting putting that out in the universe. *Could* I handle anything else? I suppose. Did I *want* to deal with more chaos? Absolutely not.

When we reached the row of cars where mine was parked, Landon stepped closer to me, clearing a path for a car that was cruising up the lane. His arm briefly brushed against mine in the process, and the second I felt the heat from his body, I nearly jumped sideways. Stealing a glance at him, he appeared unaware that my pounding heart was about to claw its way out of my chest.

Once the car passed, he reached out and touched my wrist before stopping. "I wish I could say something uplifting and positive, but the only thought that comes to mind is that I truly hope he's going to be alright. My internet search of cerebral palsy and seizures left me feeling more confused than I initially was, so forgive me if I'm completely off-base; I hope Harrison's seizure was just a random occurrence, not because something is seriously wrong."

"How did you know Harrison has cerebral palsy?" I was almost certain I'd never mentioned it to him.

Circling a finger in the air, he chuckled. "The people in this community doing what they do best—gossiping—

means I involuntarily know a lot about everyone. I get stopped in the grocery store frequently by my friends' grandmas, aunts, you name it. However, I figured Harrison having cerebral palsy wasn't a story concocted by a bored old woman."

Rolling my eyes, I sighed. "I should have known." Bringing a hand up to shield my eyes from the sun, I met his gaze. "So, you *do* know stuff about me."

He cocked his head as his eyes narrowed. "What do you mean?"

"When we spoke outside of the hospital that one day, I mentioned that if you knew anything about me, you would run in the opposite direction."

His face broke into a grin. "You're right, you did say that. And I also recall saying anyone would be stupid to run away from you." He pulled his elbows away from his sides, hands still in his pockets. "I stand by that. The majority of what I hear is gossip. Until you can confirm what I've heard, I'm not believing anything, good or bad."

I bit the inside of my lip. "Oh, yeah? When and how would this confirmation happen? Would you call me into your office after hours, or…?" My eyes widened in horror as I realized that what I thought was going to be a funny question sounded like a trashy pickup line from a porno. I *really* needed to stop talking to people when I was exhausted. Especially Landon.

Watching the color drain from Landon's cheeks as his eyes squeezed shut, I could deduce he also misinterpreted my poor attempt at humor and took it as the latter. Drawing his arms tight against his torso, he exhaled slowly. "I feel like I cannot answer that question while on campus out of fear I will get fired."

I nearly doubled over with laughter. "I am so sorry; I swear I meant it as a joke. I didn't realize just how…flirtatious…?" That didn't seem like the right word. Slutty was probably more accurate. Shaking my head as I straightened, I continued. "Anyway, I didn't realize how it would come across until it was too late."

Landon pretended to wipe his brow. "If that was you *not* trying to be coy, mercy, Sam." He looked around before lowering his voice and leaning in. "Don't think less of me when I admit this, but I would love to hear your intended lewd comments one day."

My face turned crimson as he winked at me. Clearly, I could dish it but couldn't take it. "And on that note…"

He nodded. "On that note, I'm going to get back to work, and I'm assuming you're heading back to the hospital. I look forward to seeing you again. It's always a pleasure."

As I drove away, I noticed him in my rearview mirror turn and watch me until he and the school disappeared.

****

When Harrison was an infant and toddler, his seizures would land us in the hospital after every occurrence. He had what was referred to as "tonic-clonic" seizures, which was the most common and most severe type of generalized seizures. Most of them would last for a minute or less, but if they went longer, I had to bring him in to ensure brain damage didn't occur. As he grew older, his seizures lessened, but they still happened. Every few months he had less-severe ones, but about twice a year, he and I would find ourselves in the hospital because of seizures that lasted more than a minute and a half.

Hospital stays with Harrison never get easier, even though he spent more than half of his early childhood in medical facilities. Never would I get used to seeing my child lying in a hospital bed, wires spewing out of his body every which way. Hospitals were bittersweet for me as a mom—they reminded me of how lucky my son was to have access to such amazing medical professionals and tools, while also reminding me that Harrison wasn't invincible, and his last moments could be just around the corner.

I knew I should have taken the day off, but because his doctors decided to keep him overnight, I ended up changing into the backup scrubs from my locker and working the latter half of my shift. I needed to take my mind off the situation, and Harrison was under the best possible care, just a few floors away from mine.

After I clocked out for the evening, I circled back to his room with a book I had grabbed from the children's ward a few hours before on my break.

He smiled when he saw me, but his eyes were tired. Sitting next to him on the bed, I produced the book from my purse. "Some reading before some shut eye, Handsome Harry?"

He grunted, so I began, intentionally keeping my voice quiet. He was asleep before I finished, but I read until the last page all the same. I laid with him for a few minutes, listening to his breathing and the beeping of the monitors. I hated this life for my son.

Feeling my eyes start to close, I reluctantly pulled myself away from him and headed to my car. I desperately needed to shower and change before returning to the hospital so that he wouldn't be alone overnight. I knew it wasn't necessary, and that the doctors would alert me to any changes, but mom guilt always trumped logic. I could never leave him alone—not when he was an infant, and not now.

Head down, I dug through my purse for my car keys as I walked across the hospital grounds. My bag was a black hole—filled with stuff I never remembered putting in there, and yet, there the most random objects were, and there they stayed. After finally locating the keys, I looked up and nearly screamed. Landon was leaning against the hood of my car in the parking garage, still dressed in his work clothes.

I placed my palm over my racing heart. "What are you doing here?"

He put his hands up, his face apologetic. "I needed to speak with you, and when I called the hospital, they told me you had just clocked out. Not wanting to miss you, I decided that waiting here was my best option."

"Speak with me about what? The dangers of not being aware of your surroundings at night? Because if that's the case, my lesson has been learned. You gave me a freaking heart attack." For the second time today actually, but I kept that last bit to myself.

Landon lowered his hands. "I'm sorry, I really am. I didn't mean to scare you. I just…" He surveyed the area before shaking his head. "I can't get you off my mind. I wanted to make sure you were okay. And, of course, I wanted to see how Harrison is doing."

"You could have called my cell," I pointed out, sounding snarkier than I meant to.

He sighed. "I know, but you can pretend to be okay over the phone. It's harder to fake how you're feeling when someone is standing right in front of you."

Snorting, I tried to unlock my car with the fob, but

of course, it didn't work. The battery must have died. Resisting the urge to throw my keys, I jammed the correct one into the door lock and turned it. "I faked happiness so well during my nearly twenty-year-long marriage that my estranged husband claimed to have never predicted me kicking him out. I call bullshit on your theory."

He closed his mouth before opening it again. "Can I do *anything* for you?"

His offer was sweet but completely unfeasible, and instead of feeling grateful that someone cared enough to offer to help, I felt mad. Mad that no one *could* help me, even if I wanted them to. "No. There's nothing you can do, short of swapping bodies with me and taking over my life for a bit."

Shifting his weight and staring at the ground, Landon sighed. "I'm serious, Sam."

What little self-control I had disappeared with his reaction. "Landon, you don't get it." I could hear how loud my voice was, but I couldn't calm down. Every emotion from today was now coming out during this conversation. "No one can help me. No one can take care of Harrison minus me, Raegan, and his caregiver. Not even his own damn father will step in and help. He's off screwing God knows who while pretending to run this asinine city. He doesn't care about his children. Never has, never will. And to be honest, I'm used to not having help. When people volunteer to help, there's a strong possibility they will let me down in some way, and I've had enough disappointment to last a lifetime. I'm fine being on my own. I'm aware that some days I struggle to cope, but my kids are alive and I'm not in jail, and truly, that's all I can ask for."

He was still leaning against my car, but his hands were now in his pockets and his gaze remained focused on the cement. Eventually, he spoke. "I'm sorry." He raised his head, regret reflecting in his eyes. "I just…I worry about you."

It was my turn to sigh. "That's sweet, Landon, but I don't know why. I'm not your problem. Trust me, you don't want to be a part of this. I worked the last half of my shift because I'm scared to relax. If I stop moving and doing things, I start thinking, and if that happens, I will be placed on a psych hold." I gestured to myself. "Avoid this at all costs."

He shook his head. "There's something about you. I know it sounds crazy. Hell, it feels crazy. But I can't stop thinking about you, and frankly, I don't want to."

My heart stopped beating before it plummeted into my stomach. "You seem like a nice guy, Landon. Like, a *really* nice guy. But being with me is like running into a burning building. The ashes—my problems—are already affecting you, and for that, I'm sorry. But just let it be ashes. Don't let it be fire."

"Sam," Landon started, but I shook my head, stopping him.

"It's for the best. Now if you'll please excuse me, I have to go."

Head down, he moved away from my car, and for the second time in less than twelve hours, I watched him in my rearview mirror as I drove away. The tears I held in all day finally sprung free, running down my cheeks and falling onto my lap. Was I interested in Landon? Of course, but I couldn't date him. I couldn't drag anyone into my messy life and expect them to stay. Who would want to be involved with a thirty-six-year-old mother who constantly looked and felt like a dumpster fire? His revelation *did* break me a little, though.

Part of me wanted to give him a shot—offer him front row seats to my life so he could make the decision as to whether or not he could handle everything being with me entailed. But was it the right move?

Sighing, I turned up the radio in my car. My brain and heart were fighting, and I couldn't deal.

CHAPTER SIX

Head in my hands, I leaned over the kitchen island as I processed the email Raegan's English teacher had just sent me. Harrison was in his wheelchair next to the dinner table, where my neglected cup of coffee sat beside his smoothie. Hearing her footsteps come down the hall, I took a deep, slow breath, forcing myself to remain as calm as possible. Yelling wouldn't solve anything, and Harrison didn't do well with loud noises.

I straightened as she trudged past the island. "As if Monday mornings aren't fun enough, do you want to know what made mine much more exciting? Receiving an email from Mrs. Farrell."

Her hand froze on the fridge door, her body facing away from me.

"Want to know what it said?"

Raegan slowly turned. "I know what it said," she replied, staring me straight in the eye. "She's a bitch and she's freaking out about a couple assignments I forgot to turn in."

Think of Harrison.

Think of Harrison.

Yelling wouldn't fix any—did she just call her teacher a bitch?

My slight sense of calm vanished. "You will *not* refer to a teacher as a bitch, especially one who is actively trying to help you raise your grade. You're

71

missing five assignments, Raegan. FIVE. THREE OF THOSE ARE ESSAYS. Due WEEKS ago. Did you just figure you wouldn't do them and see if you could still pass English? Because guess what, buttercup? You won't. Mrs. Farrell informed me that she will accept the late assignments, but you only have until five p.m. Friday. Otherwise, she's marking those assignments as zeros, and you WILL NOT PASS YOUR SENIOR YEAR OF ENGLISH."

Raegan pressed her lips into a firm line and glared at me, which made my pulse skyrocket even more. Behind me, Harrison made a noise.

"Don't you give me that look, Raegan Marie. Talk to me. What are you thinking?"

Her face was emotionless, her eyes cold. "I don't know, Mom. Probably what I'm always thinking, which is only the wrong stuff. Ritalin, not handing in assignments...I think I want to fail English, too."

I wanted to simultaneously scream and punch a hole in the wall. Instead, I clenched my fists and tried to regulate my breathing. "RAEGAN. You set yourself up for these things. Hand in your assignments when they're due. Don't hang around with people who expect you to deal drugs for them. You aren't a victim—you make those choices. No one else makes them for you. Your phone, your iPad, TV—they're gone until you turn in those assignments. And as an added bonus, I'm going to email the rest of your teachers and ask if you're missing papers in their classes, too."

Harrison moaned from across the room. I needed to stop yelling.

Raegan continued to stare at me. "Well, when you email Mrs. Farrell back, ask her to welcome you into the club."

My anger momentarily gave way to confusion. "What are you talking about?"

Raegan turned away from me and started back up the hallway. "The 'I'm the biggest BITCH in the world' club," she yelled.

My face flushed with unadulterated rage. "RAEGAN MARIE, YOU ARE GROUNDED UNTIL GRADUATION," I screamed after her.

Harrison began to moan louder, but just as I was about to comfort him, Raegan came flying back into the room. "YOU CAN'T GROUND ME UNTIL GRADUATION," she roared, inches away from my face.

"I JUST DID," I responded, willing myself not to smack her. "YOU MAKE BAD CHOICES; YOU LIVE WITH THE RESULTS."

Harrison's groaning grew louder by the second.

"Please, Raegan." I put my hands up in an attempt to calm everyone. "We have to stop yelling. It's upsetting your brother."

"Yeah, and we wouldn't FREAKING want that," she spat.

Without further warning, Harrison let out an ear-splitting screech. Whipping our heads around to look at him, we saw tears streaming down his cheeks as he repeatedly threw himself against the back of his wheelchair. I immediately fell to my knees in front of him.

"Harrison, honey, I'm so sorry, baby. We're done now. I'm so sorry."

Raegan folded her arms and rolled her eyes. "I'm getting ready for school," she said, vanishing up the hall.

I chastised myself as I looked Harrison over. I stupidly allowed myself to fight with a teenager, and in turn, upset my son, who was only three days out of the hospital. How big of a jerk was I? Maybe I should email Mrs. Farrell and ask if the club had jackets. I could always go for a good jacket.

****

I checked my phone. It had been two hours since I'd heard from McKenna, assuring me that Harrison was fine. I still felt awful about this morning, but McKenna had confirmed numerous times that he was doing okay. Work was slow, and that didn't help, either. I needed something to do. I needed a distraction. My mind kept ping-ponging between Raegan and my conversation with Landon, and I couldn't do anything about either of those issues while on the clock.

As I was about to duck out for a smoke break, I heard someone approach the nurses' station. Glancing up with my usual half-fake smile, my face immediately froze.

Landon stared at me. "Are you alright? That's an odd face you're making."

My eyes widened before my expression returned to normal. "I was not expecting to see you here," I said, glancing at my watch. "It's school hours, Dr. Ford. Aren't you supposed to be counseling children? Plus, some may consider this stalker behavior."

He laughed and shook his head. "It's my lunch break, and you and I need to talk. Can we go outside for a minute?"

I heard someone come up behind me. "Yes, yes. Absolutely she can. I'm Drea, by the way. Peach—*Sam's* best friend," she corrected herself as she stuck out her hand.

I rolled my eyes. "You don't even work on this floor, Drea. You have no idea what my schedule looks like."

Drea spotted Linda as she exited a patient's room. "Linda, can Sam take a quick break?"

Linda surveyed Landon, then moved her attention to me. "Of course. Take all the time you need, boss." She winked, and I let out an internal groan.

"I hate you all," I whispered in Drea's ear as I stalked past her. She responded with a huge grin.

Landon and I walked in silence until we stepped out of the hospital's double front doors. "About the other day," I began, but he waved at me to continue walking until we reached the back of the hospital.

"No prying eyes and listening ears back here," he explained. If I doubted him before, this action alone made me believe he was indeed from Madison. "*I* want to apologize for ambushing you in the parking lot the other night," he said, finally turning to face me. "And now here. But the moment I saw you in Mr. Prior's office, I knew I was a goner. You've been on my mind ever since that meeting, and while I would love to stop thinking about you because I know you don't want to get involved with me, I can't." His steel-blue eyes gazed into mine.

"Landon, it's not that I don't want to get involved with you."

His eyes softened at my revelation. "It's not?"

I shook my head. "I mean, I think you're certifiable for wanting to go out with me, but you're a grown man who is completely capable of making his own choices. You just need to understand that I'm a mess. I'm barely taking care of myself and my kids. When you could have anyone else in this city, why choose me?"

He took a step toward me, the space between us decreasing. Even though it was cold enough outside to see my breath, the sun temporarily peeked out from behind a cloud, illuminating the space around us. The sudden heat from the rays of the sun and Landon's proximity was making me feel unnaturally warm on such a frigid day.

"Why not choose you?" he asked, slowly reaching out to trace my jawline.

My eyes instinctively closed at his touch, but when the sun retreated behind the clouds, the darkening skies snapped me out of my daze. "I can give you so many reasons. Plus, I know nothing about you. For all I know, you could be a serial killer."

Landon dropped his hand from my face and burst out laughing. "Come out with me, then. I'm an open book, I swear."

I bit the inside of my cheek as a thought resurfaced from weeks before. "That night, when you called to tell me Raegan was switching to Miranda. You said Madison was full of bad memories. What did you mean?"

Gazing downward and shuffling his feet, he ran a hand through his hair. "I was involved in something when I was sixteen years old. It…it nearly ruined me. I can tell you about it now, or I can tell you about it over dinner where alcohol may be involved, because I might need it to dredge up my past."

I nodded. Fair enough.

"If you don't want to go to dinner, that's fine, and I respect your decision. But if there is any chance, a small inkling, that you are curious about me and would date me at some point in the future, come out with me. I will make it worth your while." He shoved both hands into his pockets before raising his eyes to meet mine.

I knew he would make it worth my while. He would probably make it worth my while and then some. After studying him for a few seconds, I sighed. "Can you hold that thought for a few days? Raegan and I had a huge fight this morning, and I need to be in a better place with her before I can accept your dinner invitation."

His face dropped. "Absolutely, yes. I'm sorry, I didn't realize the poor timing of this." He slowly started to turn. "I'll ambush you again maybe next week, then? Two weeks? Regardless, I hope you and Raegan can patch things up, for various reasons." He gave me a small smile and a wink.

I grinned. "Thank you. And also, thank you for understanding."

Landon nodded before raising a hand. "Goodbye, Sam. Have a good rest of your shift." He started walking in the direction of the parking structure, leaving me to stare at his backside.

Snapping out of my trance when he was a few yards away from where I was still standing, I called out to him. "Hey, Landon?"

He spun around. "Yeah?"

"I'm looking forward to our future dinner date."

His grin was so wide, I was certain it could be seen from the next town over. "Me too."

****

Drea stared at me as I shoved lukewarm mac and cheese into my mouth, my teeth angrily mashing the soft noodles into swallowable pieces. Usually the cafeteria food was passable, but today, it was absolute crap, and honestly, that summed up my entire week so far.

"Two days?" There was zero context behind her question, but I knew what she was referring to. We had been friends for almost ten years; background information before starting conversations was rarely necessary.

"Two days." I angrily jabbed the soggy cheese-covered shells. "TWO," *stab*, "FREAKING," *stab*, "DAYS." After taking another bite, I decided I couldn't stomach the rest and shoved the lunch tray aside. Not realizing the force of my anger, the tray nearly went over the edge of the table. Luckily, it stopped a little more than halfway, teetering on the edge like the rest of my sanity.

Drea's expression was one of surprise and amusement. "And you're doing...*fine*?"

I exhaled forcefully. "I don't understand why she's doing stupid crap and letting her grades slip the last year of high school. Of all the freaking years, this is not the one to screw around and fail classes. And her getting mad at me isn't abnormal, but we've never not spoken for this long before. I just...I don't know what I'm doing wrong." It also didn't help that every moment we were still fighting made me feel like my date with Landon wasn't actually going to happen. I was worried he was going to give up and move on if things took much longer.

"She hasn't said a single thing to you?" Drea asked.

Shaking my head, I glanced out the nearby window. "And I don't know how to make her talk to me. When she was younger, Rae told me everything. Things I wanted to know, things I didn't want to know, then she hit puberty, and BAM. I became the enemy overnight. Now with graduation looming, I know if she passes her damn classes, she's going to get as far away from here as possible." Tears that had stayed dormant all morning suddenly threatened to fall. Blinking, I quickly wiped away the moisture from my eyes with my sleeve.

"What if she shuts me out for good? What if we can't come back from this? I don't know how to help her if she can't tell me what's wrong. I feel like I'm failing her, and it's killing me."

Drea reached across the table and grasped my hand. "I'm so sorry, Peach. I really am. You can have Auntie D talk with her. I'll get to the bottom of it."

Sniffing, I managed to give her a small smile. "Thanks for offering. Hopefully I can get through to her soon and we can move past this mess."

By the time I got home that night, Harrison was sound asleep and McKenna, bless her heart, had loaded and started the dishwasher. The light was on in Raegan's room when I walked by, but when I knocked on the door, it quickly flickered off.

I spent half the night staring at the ceiling, pondering what I could do about Raegan. Hours later, it came to me. When she threw open her bedroom door the following morning, I was waiting in the hallway, leaning against the wall opposite her room. "You aren't going to school today."

She squinted at me. "Why would I not be going to school?"

Temporarily ignoring her question, I made my way to the kitchen to start a pot of coffee. Once the ancient machine sputtered to life, I turned to her, resting my hands against the counter.

"We're going somewhere. When Kenny gets here, you and I are taking off. Unless you want to go in that outfit," I gestured to her pajama bottoms and white tank top, "I would change."

"What do I wear?"

Tilting my head, I tried to silence the dozens of sarcastic comments that sprung to mind. "It's winter, Rae. Something warm. And bring an extra jacket."

I could tell she wanted to ask more questions, but she also knew I wasn't going to answer them. Releasing an exasperated sigh, she left me alone with my coffee. McKenna walked in five minutes later, chipper as usual.

"Good morning, Sam," she said in a sing-song voice. "What is everyone up to this morning?" Before I could answer, Raegan appeared next to McKenna. "Well, hello to you too, smiley."

Raegan folded her arms, but I could see the small hint of a smile across her face. It was difficult to be mad around McKenna—she was the personification of sunshine. "Rae and I are off to an undisclosed location," I answered.

McKenna looked from me to Raegan, eyebrows raised. "Should I be worried?" She knew what was going on, and even she was surprised by Raegan's silent treatment toward me.

I laughed. "Offing one of my children will not be a part of today's trip. Last I checked, Harrison was still sleeping, but that was a few minutes ago." Throwing back my coffee, I left the mug on the counter and saluted McKenna. "We will be back in a while!"

When we hit the highway, Raegan finally spoke. "Can you tell me where we are going now?" she asked, and I shook my head. "Can you tell me why we are going where we are going?"

Turning down the radio, I glanced at her. "Because I don't like how things have been between us lately."

When we passed a road sign twenty minutes later, Raegan bolted up in her seat. "Wait, are we going to—?"

"You'll see."

Five minutes later, we pulled into the public parking area for Lake Oconee. Climbing out of the car and taking in a deep, slow breath, I let the sound of the lake meeting the shore pull me to the waterfront. Plopping down in a spot away from the few people present, I sighed. This place was heaven on earth, and it almost made me forget how much I hated Georgia.

Almost.

Raegan appeared at my side, gingerly sitting down before staring at me and then out at the lake. "You took me here when I was three," she said quietly.

"You said you didn't remember that trip when I asked you about it a few years ago," I pointed out.

"I don't. But that picture of us together, here, on the shore—it's one of my favorite pictures," she admitted.

The picture hung in our hallway, and I thought of that day often as I trekked to and from the bedrooms to the living room and kitchen. It was only a few days before I had Harrison, my stomach swollen like a balloon about to burst. I had begged for one last "family of three" outing, even though most of our outings only consisted of me and Raegan. I don't remember much about that trip other than Raegan laughing. She giggled nearly the entire day, joyous about nothing and everything at the same time.

In the wooden frame was a snapshot of me holding Raegan in my arms, her brunette hair wet and matted around her shoulders, her freckles activated by a summer of sun. Our hazel eyes matching, our elated expressions the same. It was a memory of simpler times.

"I'm almost done with my assignments for English. And I'm not missing anything else in any other class." Raegan's words were rushed as she stared at the water.

"I know, sweetheart," I whispered. "Your teachers emailed me back. But can you tell me what happened? Your English teacher said you were doing great up until a few weeks ago. What changed?"

The wind swirled around us, prompting Raegan to huddle against me for warmth. "She asked my class to write an essay about 'what this city symbolizes.' And when I sat down to write it, I realized I couldn't turn in what I want to say. I want to write that this city symbolizes broken hearts, shattered dreams, and narrow-mindedness. Being here is a constant reminder that my family's been torn apart because my stupid father couldn't stick by you and Harrison and me when things got hard. And the fact that everyone glorifies him and has no clue just how much damage he has caused our family exemplifies the community members' inability or unwillingness to see bullshit that's right in front of their faces. All because he is 'one of their own' and you aren't."

Immediately wrapping my arms around her, I pulled her close. "Rae," I whispered, burying my face into her shoulder. "Honey."

She was crying then, and I could feel my own cheeks dampen. We sat there, embracing each other and the silence between us as the waves lapped against the shore. Eventually, Raegan wiped her eyes and pulled away from me.

"Therapy has really helped me uncover a lot of feelings." She tried to laugh, but it came out as more of a sob. "But that's the only assignment I have left. I still don't know what to write."

I stared at her. "Write what you feel. I will send in a note with your essay telling the teacher how we discussed the prompt and we decided it's best for you to express your thoughts. If she wants to know what the city means to you, tell her your truth. And if she gives you anything less than a passing grade, well, then I'll agree with you. She's a bitch."

A slow grin spread across Raegan's face. "I'm sorry I didn't tell you. I just know you're hurting enough as it is."

I hugged her tighter. "I want you to tell me everything, always. It doesn't matter what I'm feeling or doing. You're my daughter, Rae. You and Harrison are my everything. You will never burden me with anything. I want to be here for you, no matter what."

Placing her head against mine, we sat there until our bodies were numb, staring out at the water and the shoreline dotted with trees as far as we could see.

"I can't feel my face anymore. Should we head home? I can start my essay." Raegan offered me a smile.

Smirking, I nodded slowly. "Yeah, coming here in winter wasn't the best idea, but it was my only idea, so I ran with it."

As the lake disappeared in the rearview mirror, Raegan spoke up. "Do you like Dr. Ford?"

My eyebrows shot up. "What?"

She began fiddling with the radio. "He seems to like you. Not that he's said anything to me, but I just get that vibe. I saw how he was looking at you in Mr. Prior's office."

I pursed my lips, uncertain if I wanted to cross a

boundary with Raegan, but since it sort of involved her, I decided to feel out the situation. "I'm not sure. I don't really know a lot about him. But if Lan—Dr. Ford and I were to date, would you be upset?"

Wiggling her eyebrows, she laughed. "Landon, huh? You guys are on a first-name basis? I don't even want to know how, but I'm impressed."

I rolled my eyes. "I'm serious, Rae. I would never want you to feel uncomfortable about a guy I date. Or possibly date. I guess I haven't agreed to anything yet with him."

"He's asked you out! What did you say?"

"I told him to ask me again when the timing was better," I admitted.

Raegan was quiet for a minute. "I guess it would be kind of weird because he works at my school, but it's not like he's my therapist anymore. I…I think you should go for it. I think it would be good for you to get out. Besides, he seems like a really nice guy. All the girls at school are in love with him. They will be so jealous of you."

I snorted. "Great. That's my goal—to make dozens of high school girls jealous of my dating life."

When we pulled into the driveway, she jumped out of the car and raced to the house. "I'll let you know when I'm done with my essay," she called, leaving me to walk the remainder of the steps leading up to the front porch alone.

I stepped inside and leaned against the door with my eyes closed. Between visiting the lake, and Raegan and I working things out, I felt so much lighter. Although now I had to deal with the next conundrum that was giving me anxiety: Landon. Was I truly ready to risk putting my heart on the line for a second time?

Don't think about the heartbreak, a voice from somewhere within my brain shouted. *Think about the six-pack abs you know are under his fitted shirts and deal with the emotions later.*

I gulped. The relief I was feeling seconds ago morphed into panic, and I wasn't sure if the thought of dating again was to blame, or if it was the possibility of seeing Landon naked. As my heart thudded in my chest, I dropped my purse on the entryway table. I guess I would find out soon enough.

CHAPTER SEVEN

The following afternoon, I purposely took my lunch later than usual and drove to the high school when I knew most of the faculty would be gone for the day. Boldly assuming Landon would be staying late on a Friday, I pulled into the parking lot and squinted.

Only a handful of cars remained in the otherwise deserted area, but I had no idea what he drove. For all I knew, my instincts were wrong, and he left when the students were dismissed an hour ago. Drumming my hands on the steering wheel, I waited a few more minutes, feeling stupider by the second. I was about to drive off when the double doors of the school's office swung open, revealing Landon. His laptop bag was dangling off his right shoulder, his peppered hair slightly disheveled. My breath caught in my throat. How was that man so gorgeous?

He grinned when he saw me get out of my car and nearly jogged to where I was standing. "Well, this is a surprise," he said, stopping a few inches from me.

"I really don't know what it is about us and parking lots." I bit the inside of my cheek, trying to conceal a smile.

"Could be worse. Could be bathrooms."

I laughed. "Touché." My pulse quickened as he stared at me. The way his eyes bore into mine left me feeling completely exposed. Crossing my arms and pulling them tightly against my chest, I cleared my throat. "Anyway."

Landon smiled. "Anyway. How are things with Raegan and Harrison?"

"Back to normal and fine, for now, thank God."

He adjusted his bag, his eyes twinkling. "So does this mean what I think it means?"

I cast my gaze downward, inspecting the worn asphalt. "If you still want to, yes."

He fist-pumped the air in front of us. "Samantha Hawley," he breathed, "will you go out with me?"

How could I not smile? His excitement was contagious. "This is your last chance to back out," I warned.

He violently shook his head. "Nope. No way."

Shrugging, I replied, "Well, then yes. Yes, I will."

His grin spread from ear to ear. "May I have your phone number?" he asked, unlocking his phone and handing it to me.

I returned his phone after creating a new contact for myself. "Not to be presumptuous, but I'm off this weekend and McKenna, Harrison's caregiver, has offered to give me a night off."

He slipped his phone into his back pocket. "I guess you'll be hearing from me soon then." Tipping an imaginary hat, he winked at me. "Have a great night, Sam. I know I will."

As I drove back to work, my phone vibrated.

Landon—*Dinner tomorrow? You pick the time, I pick the place?*—

When I walked into the living room the following evening, McKenna let out a shrill whistle. "Damn, Sam. You're as pretty as a peach. He's clearly not taking you to any restaurant 'round here. Where are y'all going?" McKenna always sounded more Southern when she was excited—a characteristic I found utterly endearing.

Releasing a pair of heels from my grip, they dropped to the floor, and I slid them on my feet. "Hell, no, we aren't going anywhere in Madison. I don't need any more rumors flying around this godforsaken city. We are going to Athens. That way, there's a smaller chance we will run into someone either of us know." Grabbing a black cardigan from the hall closet, I stared at myself in the mirror hanging on the inside of the door before shutting it. This was as good as it was going to get.

McKenna raised an eyebrow. "Athens is nearly an hour away. If he's willing to drive that far on a first date, he must really like you."

I grumbled. "He doesn't even know me. But he's very persistent and attractive so here we are."

Raegan came down the hallway and stood next to me. "You look really nice, Mom," she said softly, touching one of my long curls. "I'm glad you're finally getting out after…everything."

It had been a hot minute since I had ventured out in public for something other than a local political event. To find a decent pair of shoes, I had to dig through my closet for nearly ten minutes. The last time I wore anything formal was when Raegan and Harrison's father ran for mayor, and we campaigned around the city.

When Landon chose a "fancy" restaurant for our date, I'd panicked about what I could wear that didn't remind me of Charles. After staring at my wardrobe for forty-five minutes and making a phone call to Drea, I decided to go with a plum-colored dress that fell just above the knee. The three-quarter-length sleeves were lace and I loved the deep-V neckline, but I remembered the price tag was still attached because Charles forbade me from wearing it.

"It's too revealing. What are you trying to do, make yourself look like a whore?"

I had tucked it into the far corner of my closet after he'd admonished me, and there it hung. Until now. I never felt that it was a trashy dress, but the amount of cleavage it showed when I put it on all these years later made me feel slightly uncomfortable. To be fair, the entire idea of dating someone made me slightly uncomfortable. I either had to embrace the discomfort and move on with my life, or seriously consider adopting hordes of cats. Tonight, I was choosing the first option.

A knock came from the other side of the front door, and I shot McKenna an anxious look. "You're sure you're going to be okay? You're sure you're fine being here on your day off?" I smoothed my dress, trying to ignore the fact my hands were shaking.

McKenna gave me a long stare. "Sam, I've told you a million times, you can go out anytime and I will stay with Harrison. He's my best buddy, and you need a break once in a while. We are fine. Rae and I are going to trash-talk all the guys at her school before she leaves for the party, and Harrison will drown us out with an action flick. Leave. Now," she commanded.

Because Raegan had completed all of her assignments, I agreed to let her go to a friend's party tonight under the condition she was home by midnight and would call me for a ride if she or her friends had any alcohol. I also knew the parents would be home, which put my mind at ease.

After kissing both kids' foreheads, I boldly walked

to the front door. Throwing it open, I had a feeling my face matched Landon's when he saw me. He was wearing a black dinner jacket over a light blue button-down shirt that was tucked into a pair of fitted dress pants. Not one strand of his immaculately gelled hair was out of place, and his beard was trimmed to perfection. A slight breeze blew past us, wafting his sandalwood and citrus cologne in my direction. *Good Lord almighty, this man.* I was genuinely starting to think it was impossible for him not to look like at any given moment, he could model every article of clothing that adorned his body.

"Hey," he managed to utter, still staring at me. "You look…amazing. Absolutely amazing." He offered me his arm, and I glanced back one last time into the house. Raegan and McKenna quickly whipped their heads around to watch the TV. Rolling my eyes, I stepped out onto the porch and closed the door behind me.

Proving chivalry wasn't dead, Landon opened the passenger door for me, jokingly bowing as I slid into the car. After I was safely tucked inside, he closed the door and reappeared in the driver's seat seconds later. As we headed toward the highway, I glanced at him. "I'm sorry again for making you drive so far."

Landon smiled. "If driving an hour for dinner makes you feel more comfortable, I will make this drive anytime you wish. Plus, it will be nice to dodge the rumors we both know will fly if anyone in Madison sees us together. At least, for now."

As we drove north, my nerves gradually began to settle. "So, Landon Ford, we have some time in the car. Tell me a little more about yourself."

I could feel him tense almost immediately. "We aren't even halfway there, yet. What if I say something you don't like and you want to turn around before we make it to the restaurant?"

I shrugged. "Choose your words wisely, then."

Landon gave an unconvincing laugh. "The pressure is on, then. Okay, well, I was born and raised in Georgia. Moved to Connecticut for college and ended up staying in New England for graduate school. I saw an opening for a school psychologist a few towns over from where I was living a couple weeks before I graduated with my doctorate and applied, even though I thought I wanted to start my own practice. I interviewed for it the day I turned in my thesis, landed the position, and have yet to start my own practice."

"Why did you even want to interview for a school psychologist position if you had dreams of private practice?" I asked.

He let out a long sigh. "I just happened to come across the job posting and thought to myself, 'Hey, I could do some good while gaining enough experience to open my own practice.' But once I started working with kids…" he paused. "I couldn't abandon them. Every few semesters, I get a kid that really needs help—like, a lot of help. A teen who reminds me of myself when I was in high school. And just how my former therapist helped me, I want to be able to help them turn their lives around and do amazing things. After one set of kids graduates, I find myself thinking I'll quit and start my own practice, but then another really troubled kid comes along, and I stay. It's a vicious cycle, but I love helping them.

"And I realize I can open my own practice and solely counsel children and teens, but I enjoy the school setting. I like the fact that they have a designated time carved out to see me. They have nowhere else to be—they can't make excuses for why they can't show up. The faculty and the parents approve a time during a school day for them to receive counseling, so the kids just have to show up and talk. Even if they fight it in the beginning, they always end up talking because they need someone to listen. I get to be that person for them. It's…" he trailed off.

"Gratifying," I nodded. "I used to feel that way about being a nurse. I worked in the ER for about a year before transferring to the geriatric floor. In the ER, it's almost always life or death, and I got to battle death with medicine time and time again. Of course, we lost some, but we always tried our best, and when someone was at death's door only to be brought back to life with our assistance, it felt amazing."

"Why did you leave the ER?"

"It came down to the stress. I loved the ER and thrived on the adrenaline rush, but between Harrison and his health problems, and Rae and her everyday problems, *plus* my marriage problems, I couldn't do it. Geriatric care is the pace I need at this stage of my life," I admitted.

"That makes sense. And I'm sure you still make a difference in your patients' lives."

"I suppose," I said, staring ahead.

He briefly took his eyes off the road to glance at me. "I don't know what is required of you at your job, but I doubt you do the bare minimum. I have a feeling you're holding a patient's hand as they slip away so they aren't alone. I'm confident you bring some brightness to their final days. Don't sell yourself short." Landon's eyes lingered on the side of my face before finally returning to the highway.

It was my turn to stare at him. His eyes were focused

on the road, his mouth pulled taut in determination. "Why do you think I'm such a good person?" I asked quietly. "So far, you know my ex cheated on me, my oldest child was caught dealing drugs at school, and I'm sure by now you've figured out nearly everyone in Madison hates me. None of those things equate to me being a good person. In fact, they all really point to the opposite."

Landon cleared his throat. "I'm going to make a bold statement: I sense you carry a lot of guilt. Maybe about your son, possibly about Raegan's issues, and probably about your marriage. And because of that, I think you project the guilt you feel onto the people around you, making you believe everyone thinks you're a bad person when they might not think that at all. Besides, your husband cheating on you, Raegan dealing drugs at school, and everyone hating you has nothing to do with you. It has to do with them and their choices."

Holy wow. He just therapied me.

His eyes darted from the darkness in front of us to me, his face and shoulders instantly drooping with regret. "I'm sorry, I just shrinked you. I absolutely hate when I do that to people other than my students. Please ignore those comments. I just…I want you to know you aren't a bad person, at least, not in my eyes. Charles made terrible choices, your daughter is a normal teenager, and not everyone in Madison hates you." He glanced at the road before eyeing me again. "I wish I could make you see what other people see."

Shaking my head, I leaned back against the seat. "I promise you, you're one of the few individuals who likes me in the community. A vast majority of the city thinks I'm an unfit wife and mother."

Landon cocked his head, his nose scrunched with confusion.

"I'll elaborate. The good people of Madison only believe what they want to believe and see what they want to see, no matter how outlandish or inaccurate their views and convictions are. They believe my husband moved out of our shared home months ago because we were having 'irreconcilable differences' but that the issues were my fault. They think I'm a bad mom because I work full time instead of spending every waking hour with my children." I sighed. This was going to be one hell of a monologue.

"What they don't see is that I kicked my husband out six months ago because someone finally sent me an anonymous message with a picture of him screwing his latest secretary. I knew it had been happening for a while, but I never had proof, and frankly, I didn't care. Charles had one foot out the door the minute I told him I was pregnant with Raegan, and then after Harrison's diagnosis, he slammed that door and cemented it shut for good measure." I winced, hating that I was recalling all of this on a first date, but I kept going.

"He abandoned our family in nearly every sense of the word. He rarely spoke to us, rarely came home. On the weekends, he would schedule golf games or hide out in his office. He only came to Raegan's extracurriculars if he knew other residents would be there.

"It was always about his image. When he first ran for mayor, he forced us to go to all of his campaigns; threatened us if we didn't smile. He made Harrison come along, even though Harrison hates loud noises and crowds of people, because having a child with special needs showed the world just how compassionate Charles was. Or at least, that's what he thought. But honestly, never in his life has Charles spent more than five minutes with his son. He despises Harrison because in Charles' eyes, Harrison failed him the moment he was diagnosed with cerebral palsy.

"Never will Harrison play baseball like his father did, or attend college and become a fraternity brother. Harrison can't continue the family legacy in city politics and run for mayor, like his father and grandfather did. And unless Charles has another son with someone else, the Hawley name ends with Harrison, which is detrimental to such a conceited, self-important man like Charles. Bottom line, Harrison will never meet my husband's expectations, and because of his hatred toward our son, my loathing for Charles when we were together grew stronger by the minute. I wanted to leave him so badly, but I didn't know how.

"Finally, when someone sent me a picture of him cheating, that was it—he was gone. I spent the next two months finding an attorney with the skills and determination to go against Charles in court, and we served him with divorce papers the following month. His lawyer responded, but we haven't moved forward with the proceedings."

Landon raised his eyebrows. "Why not?"

"When I say it out loud, it sounds terrible, but Charles hasn't bothered us since he moved out. He's kept to himself; he hasn't even attempted to see the kids. I'm afraid once the divorce proceedings start, he's going to make my life a living hell. He may fight for full custody of the kids—not because he loves them, but because he's bitter and wants to hurt me. And to be honest, I'm exhausted.

"I don't have enough energy to amp myself up for a custody battle. Not yet. All those years of dealing with him left me drained. I'm so, so tired. He stripped me of nearly everything. Granted, I allowed it to happen, but nonetheless, I'm beat. What happens if I lose my children? I can't live without them." The thought of not seeing Raegan and Harrison every day instantly made me tear up, and before I could stop it, a sob escaped my lips. In an attempt to pull myself together, I ducked my head.

I could feel the car drift to the right and looked up to see Landon exiting the highway. When we reached a place to park, he shut the car off and offered me his hand. Sliding mine into his, I immediately felt calmer.

"Bottom line, I'm scared to rock the boat with Charles, but I know I'll have to soon. I can't be married to that man forever." I sniffed, wiping my fingers under my eyes in an attempt to salvage my mascara. "But of course, no one in Madison knows this. And even if they did, they would still favor Charles over me because I'm not from around here."

"Sam," he said. "I'm so sorry."

I tried to laugh. "If it is not blazingly apparent, I haven't dated in a really long time, and I'm clearly unaware of solid first-date discussion points."

Landon humored me with a quiet laugh before turning serious. "We can go home," he offered, but I shook my head.

"You want to go out. *I* want to go out. As long as we talk about something else, anything else, I'll be fine the rest of the night," I promised.

Landon squeezed my hand. "I want you to talk to me about whatever is on your mind. You've been through a lot in the past two decades. If you need to get stuff off your chest, I'm here."

I snorted. "Because you don't do that every day with your students. I'm just what you need; one more person to offload her crap onto you."

"Hey, I didn't go into this blindly. You warned me you have baggage, remember? It doesn't bother me. I like hearing about your life, even the really terrible parts."

Landon got us back onto the highway and drove the rest of the way to Athens, his hand never leaving mine until he shut off the car. I quickly checked my makeup in the visor mirror as he got out, pleased to find I didn't look as terrible as I feared I would.

Opening the passenger door, he took my hand once again as we slowly made our way to the restaurant. It took everything in me not to pull away when we walked inside, paranoid someone would see us. Instead, I stepped closer to him, our arms touching as we followed the maître d' to our table. When we separated to sit across from each other, I was strangely aware of the void his hand left in mine. Glancing around, I noticed we were in the far back corner of the restaurant, tucked away from nearly everyone else. "Did you ask for this table?"

He nodded. "You told me you didn't want to risk having anyone see you. I understood the assignment." His mouth turned upward, a smile illuminating his entire face.

Between the simple, thoughtful gesture of pulling over when I was crying and him going above and beyond to ensure I was comfortable on our date, I knew it would be easy to fall for Landon. Hell, it might already be happening.

Swallowing hard, I threw back the glass of water the

waiter had filled and stared at Landon across the table. He offered me another grin and I quickly looked down. This man had no clue he had the potential to either completely obliterate what was left of my heart or possibly be the one to piece it back together. No pressure, Landon.

Absolutely no pressure at all.

CHAPTER EIGHT

The upper half of Landon's face appeared above the menu as the waiter placed two glasses of wine in front of us. "Have you been here before?"

I shook my head, scanning the long list of appetizing options. This place was my nightmare. Too many things looked good and I was rapidly feeling overwhelmed by choices.

Placing the menu on the table, Landon shrugged off his dinner jacket. The dress shirt he was wearing clung to his biceps for dear life, making me temporarily forget about the vast selection of food. Was I the only one entranced by this man? Subtly looking around behind the safety of my menu, I noticed a few other patrons glancing at Landon. Nope, it wasn't just me.

"If too many things appeal to you, I suggest randomly picking something. You really can't go wrong with anything—it's all delicious. This used to be my parents' favorite restaurant, so I've tried just about everything." His face fell ever so slightly when he mentioned his parents. "I think my mom would have really liked you. She was a sucker for a dark sense of humor and dry wit. Guess the apple didn't fall far from the tree."

Taking his advice, I set my menu atop his as I tilted my head and smiled at him. "Well, seeing how you turned out, I'm sure I would have liked her, too."

He glanced around quickly before sliding off the chair across from me and into the seat next to mine. "Now I can hold your hand again," he said softly.

Lord help me. Feeling him this close made me want to rip my clothes off and straddle him right there. Unfortunately, it wasn't that type of dining establishment, and thankfully, the server returned to take our order.

Once the waiter disappeared, Landon started fiddling with the silverware. "I went to school with Charles," he revealed slowly. "I never really knew him, since he was older than me, but I knew of him and his family. They are…" he paused.

"There's no politically-correct way to explain Charles and his family," I told him. "They are self-absorbed assholes who use their money and power to get what they want. Charles thinks the sun comes up just to hear him crow."

He raised his eyebrows before nodding. "Yep. That pretty much sums them up. Also, one point for using a Southern phrase." He winked.

"I told you I can pass as Southern," I said, laughing. "His mother accused me of purposely getting pregnant with Raegan to derail Charles' future, but then forced us to get married in order to protect Charles' image. Political families are one thing, rich Southern families are something else, and when you combine the two of them, it's a completely different ball game. Even though they forced Charles and me to stay together to protect the family name, Charles' parents had nothing to do with the kids and me the entire time Charles and I were together. I don't think Raegan and Harrison have seen Lydia, Charles' mom, more than three times in their whole lives. And I'm fairly certain they never met Charles' father, since he passed away when Harrison was a baby."

Remembering the glasses of wine, I raised mine to my lips, inhaling slowly before taking a sip. It was delicious, and within seconds, the drink was gone. Landon flagged down the server and signaled for another round of drinks as he finished his own. "Charles was captain of the football team senior year. Treated everyone like trash, slept with every cheerleader on the squad. He was the embodiment of a rich, Southern boy. Great physique, killer charm, an ego the size of Texas. I always wondered if he would follow in his father's footsteps. Turns out, he did."

I rolled my eyes. "Like cheating asshole father, like cheating asshole son."

Charles' father was rumored to have had numerous affairs while in office, but because of his wealth and status, no one ever outed him, and Lydia, Charles' mom, stayed with him. Without his money, Lydia would have nothing, but unlike me, she was obviously too cowardly to start over on her own. She needed her husband, and I didn't; a fact I'm sure made her resent me even more.

"It's ironic, because Lydia got pregnant with Charles around the same age that I got pregnant with Raegan. And yet, she judged and hated me—still hates me—and I just find it baffling. If Raegan goes out of state for college, which I hope she does, I'm genuinely going to consider moving. The South is a gorgeous but vicious place, and we have nothing keeping us here. Well, minus a custody order, potentially."

Landon hummed in agreement. "People either love or hate the South. I'm sorry everyone here has been so horrible to you. They don't take kindly to outsiders.

Especially gorgeous ones like you who threaten the entire population of run-down beauty queens."

The second round of drinks appeared, and half of mine vanished in one sip. Putting my elbow on the table and resting my head on my fist, I stared at Landon. "I really wish I had known you eighteen years ago. This insight would have been extremely helpful."

"If you had known me then, I doubt you would have given me a second glance. I'm a completely different person now." He held my hand a little tighter, and a warmth spread from the tips of my fingers to unmentionable regions throughout my body.

"If it hadn't been for your parents, would you have come back to Madison?" I asked.

Shaking his head, Landon replied, "Absolutely not. And now that they are gone, I'm not opposed to leaving again. It's been very difficult being back." He stared at me, his eyes full of worry. "I want to tell you about my past, but I'm scared you will run screaming into the night after I reveal everything."

I couldn't help but chuckle. "You haven't run away from me, yet, and I have enough baggage to fill a double-decker passenger plane. I'm not sure what your past entails, but I'm hopeful yours is far less dramatic."

He slowly released my hand. "I killed a little girl."

I could feel the color drain from my face. "Oh my gosh." And I'd made a serial killer joke yesterday. I was the epitome of insensitive.

Raising his hands to his face, Landon stared down at the table and drew in a shaky breath. "My mom and I were driving home from a math competition in Atlanta when I was sixteen years old. I had just gotten my driver's license a few weeks before and my mom was exhausted, so I had volunteered to drive us back to Madison. As we crossed into Morgan County, my mom told me to take a backroad so we could avoid other cars.

"The speed limit was forty-five, which I was going. But a black sedan without its lights on came careening out from a side road about ten feet in front of me. I couldn't stop. I tried. I tried so hard to stop." His voice cracked. I wanted to reach out to comfort him, but I was frozen, the details of his story rendering me immobile.

"I just remember the sound of my mom screaming and the crunching of metal. It was awful. The little girl was only two years old—she never stood a chance. Her dad, who survived, was so intoxicated he hadn't put her in the car seat correctly. The mom's wails echoing throughout the hospital when she learned about her daughter will haunt me for the rest of my life." He swallowed hard, his eyes still cast downward.

"Both of my legs were broken upon impact, but when I found out what had happened to the toddler, I didn't even care how much pain I was in. I felt I deserved it—and more. I refused to return to school, I stopped letting my friends visit me. I couldn't live with myself, knowing I killed a child, accident or not. I just laid in bed, wishing I could die. I even…I tried to kill myself."

I couldn't begin to image the immense pain he felt all those years ago, because as he recalled the story now, regret and remorse nearly seeped from every crevice of his body.

"My mom had me transferred to the inpatient program here in Athens. I received in-house treatment for a month and then three months of outpatient services. Once I finished the program, my mom found me a therapist closer to home, and I saw her until I graduated high school."

My hand found his, which he gratefully accepted. "Therapy saved your life."

He nodded. "And that's why I do what I do. The teens who are lost, depressed, despondent. I want them to know suicide not only isn't a good option, but it's also not their *only* option. I want them to know life can go on after a tragedy, even when it seems like it can't." He moved his free hand toward the wine glass and wrapped his fingers around the stem. Absentmindedly, he wiped the condensation from the sides with his thumb, creating indiscernible patterns.

"The pain you must have felt then, and even now, is incomprehensible to someone who hasn't been in your situation. But it's pretty incredible that you were able to take something that could have stopped your life and transformed it into the will to do something great. Seriously, Landon. Your actions are inspiring."

He shook his head. "I feel like it's the least I can do. The little girl's mom lived on the outskirts of Madison, so I didn't run into her very much before I graduated high school, but the need to flee was overpowering. When I got into a university in Connecticut, an inexpressible weight was lifted from my shoulders. The second I crossed the Georgia-South Carolina border, I actually cried." His cheeks reddened slightly at his confession. "Driving down that road today still makes me nauseous."

"Understandable. If it were me, I wouldn't be able to drive on that road at all."

He lifted his chin, his eyes finally meeting mine. "Do you want to leave?" His palpable sorrow transformed into fear as he searched my gaze. I could feel his palm begin to sweat against mine as he prepared himself for the worst.

I gently leaned against him as I studied our intertwined hands. "No. What happened was an accident. I could never think badly about you because of that. My heart breaks for your teenage self who felt so helpless. I'm glad your mom saw you were struggling, because in turn, you've probably helped hundreds of teenagers the same way your therapist helped you." Without giving it much thought, I rubbed his arm with my free hand. "And it also means you're still here, walking amongst the living, and now, in a surprising turn of events, at dinner with me."

He grinned before turning serious again. "I'm sorry I didn't tell you sooner."

Shaking my head and abandoning his forearm, I took a sip of wine. "Don't apologize. You said you would tell me, and you did. I appreciate it."

We sat in silence for a few moments, listening to the clinking of glasses and the tinging of silverware against plates. As the waitstaff passed us to and from the kitchen, I was hyperaware of the fact that nearly all of them stared at Landon. Still holding his hand, I gave it a small squeeze. "Not to change the subject, but also to change the subject," I glanced around, "if you do decide I'm too much, I think you have a pretty good shot with any woman in this place. All eyes have been on you since the moment we walked in."

He chuckled. "How do you know they aren't staring at you? You're drop dead gorgeous—they're all probably jealous. Hell, *I'm* jealous of me right now. And even if things were different, I would never date anyone within a forty-mile radius of Madison. I know too much about every woman around here, and honestly, likewise for them about me."

"Is that why you're attracted to me? I'm an outsider?" I asked. I tried keeping my tone light to ensure he knew I was mostly kidding, but there was also a need for truth. It was still beyond me why he would seek me out, especially when our first meeting was in the principal's office due to my daughter's conspicuous drug dealing.

He tucked a strand of my hair behind my ear, leaving me nothing to hide behind. "There are a multitude of reasons why I'm attracted to you," he whispered. "Being an outsider is on the list, but it's pretty far down."

Our faces were now mere inches apart, but I knew if I kissed him then, there was a strong possibility we would miss dinner. My pulse had gone from normal to near tachycardic in milliseconds, and my lungs were starting to ache. Forcing myself to take a deep breath, I exhaled slowly. *Get a hold of yourself, Sam.*

"We can't kiss, yet," I said.

"Why?" His voice was low and husky.

More warmth spread to the unmentionable places. "Because I won't want to stop, and dinner is arriving as we speak. I got dressed up for this and debated what to order for ten minutes. We have to make it through this meal," I whispered back, plates of food appearing in my peripheral vision.

He pulled away from me and smiled at the server. "Thank you, sir." The waiter nodded at us before walking through the silver double doors leading to the kitchen.

My cheeks and chest were flushed pink from mild embarrassment and pure, unadulterated lust. A man hadn't made me feel this way in my entire life. It was amazing and discombobulating at the same time, and I was struggling to maintain what little composure I had left. The second we moved away from each other, my heart rate returned to a typical pace.

"Stereotypical first date question: if you could go anywhere in the world, where would you go?" he asked, pausing between bites.

I chewed slowly, pondering his question. "Money, time, life, logistics off the table?" I asked, and he nodded.

"It's hard to pick just one place. I have a bucket list a mile long filled with cities and countries I would love to see. I thought I was going to study abroad my junior year of college and travel the world, but that clearly didn't happen, seeing as I got pregnant freshman year. Switzerland, the United Kingdom, Peru, Japan. Egypt, New Zealand—the list goes on. Have you traveled much?"

He swallowed a bite of steak while shaking his head. "I went straight to college from high school, and then onto the graduate and doctorate programs before landing a job. I tell myself every summer I'll go somewhere epic, but then June rolls around, and I don't go. I know traveling alone can be a great experience, but I think at this point in my life, I would really like to share seeing the world with someone I love spending time with." Cocking his head, a hint of a smile formed on his lips. "What are your summer plans?"

The restaurant lighting suddenly dimmed around us, and waiters stopped at every table to light the centerpiece candles. Looking sideways, I saw that Landon was still gorgeous in the terrible lighting. I had never wanted to finish a meal and get out of a place faster in my life. I shook my head. "It's two and a half hours into our first date, and I've already cried and made us late for our reservation. You should think really hard about a second date, let alone traveling across the globe with me."

Placing his napkin on his plate to signal he had finished eating, he stared at me. "I'm thinking that this is the best date I've ever been on, and that I can't wait to do it again. That is, if you want to."

Watching shadows dance across his face in the candlelight, I suppressed another urge to slide off my chair and onto his lap. The desire to show him just how much I wanted to have dinner with him again—and more, if he was up for it—was overwhelming. I wished my practically sexless marriage was to blame for the way I was feeling, but I wasn't sure it was entirely at fault. I think it was a combination of that mixed with Landon's entire essence.

"Dessert?" the waiter interrupted us, and Landon looked at me expectingly. Wasn't Landon the dessert?

"We have a long drive home," I managed to tell the waiter. "The check would be great." If anything else delayed us from leaving this restaurant, I would scream. I just wanted to get out of there so I could finally kiss this ridiculously attractive man sitting next to me.

Landon handed the waiter his credit card, in spite of my insistence that we split it. "I promise, you can get the next dinner," he said. "If there is a next dinner?"

I knew I was leaving him hanging, but hopefully within a few minutes, my response would be obvious. Until then, I avoided eye contact.

With his dinner jacket draped over his arm, he and I exited the restaurant in silence, my mind racing too much to make conversation. Just as he started to open the passenger door, I put my hand on his arm, stopping him.

Turning to face me, I ignored the warning signals in my brain and stepped toward him. "Now that we aren't running the risk of eating a cold dinner, can we please, *please* kiss?" I asked.

Closing the short distance between us with one step, Landon tossed his jacket onto the top of the car before placing his hand behind my head and pulling my face to his. The instant we connected, my stomach dropped and my knees weakened. The feel of his lips against mine was intoxicating, and I wrapped my arms around his waist, pulling every inch of him closer. I could practically feel his abs through his thin shirt, and it did things to me I wasn't proud to admit.

He slowly turned us so that I was leaning against the car, the cold metal bringing a sense of relief to my body, which felt like it was on fire. His tongue explored my mouth, and I untucked the front part of his shirt so I could run my hand across his stomach. There was at least a six pack, possibly an eight pack, and part of me died a little. This man was sinfully attractive. When we finally parted, I nearly gasped for air. "There will definitely be a second dinner."

He grinned. "That took you a while to answer. I was getting worried."

After a few more minutes of an intense game of tonsil hockey, I managed to pull away. "I can do this all night, but I should be getting home so McKenna can leave. However, I'm not against you joining me at my house, as long as you can sneak out before Raegan notices you're there."

Landon swung open the passenger door with such force, I thought it would come unhinged. "I spent many nights in college preparing for this moment."

As I settled in, he grabbed his jacket and attempted to pull a *Dukes of Hazzard* hood slide but got stuck halfway. By the time he scooted off the car and climbed into the driver's seat, I was doubled over, tears of laughter streaming down my cheeks.

"That would have been much hotter if I had made it work," he admitted, "but you got what I meant."

"I don't think you can be a true Georgia native if you can't successfully hood slide," I snorted.

He tsked me. "To be honest, I've never even tried it before. You inspired me. And now I know I need to work on those skills." We started the journey back to Madison, our hands once again interlocked. When we were ten minutes outside of the city, my phone started to vibrate. Pulling it out of my purse, I saw that it was Drea.

"Hey, what's going on?" I answered, knowing good and well she wouldn't call unless it was an emergency, as she was aware of my date.

"It's Raegan, Sam. You have to get to the hospital. There's been an accident," Drea started.

I pulled my hand from Landon's as Drea gave me all the details she knew, which wasn't much. When she hung up, I turned to him. "We need to get to the hospital, now."

Without a second thought, he pressed down on the gas pedal, rocketing the car towards Madison. "What happened? What's wrong?"

"It's Raegan," I said, panic ripping through my body. "There's been an accident. She's been shot."

CHAPTER NINE

"I need my mom. You can't take me into surgery until I see her." The pain and fear in Raegan's voice were apparent, and I could feel my anxiety skyrocket as I rounded the corner of the ER bay. As a nurse, I knew seeing her and learning the extent of her injuries would put my mind at ease in some odd way, but as a mother, I was petrified to see my child in agony. I had no idea what I was in for, as Drea didn't know the exact details of the incident when she'd called. We only knew that Raegan was conscious and on her way to the hospital via ambulance due to a gunshot wound.

Following the sound of her voice to bed three, I pushed my way past the throng of nurses and doctors. "I'm here, Rae," I managed to call out, momentarily overcoming the terror that constricted my chest and throat.

Landon had ignored every speed limit to get me here, and he was now sitting in the waiting room, the fear of overstepping preventing him from joining me. I didn't have time to dispute his feelings, so I left him, sprinting down the corridor of the Morgan Medical Center's emergency room in high heels.

A wave of nausea hit me the moment I saw her face. Smears of blood covered her hair and cheeks, causing her light skin to appear even more ashen. "It's going to be okay." Clasping her trembling hand, I swept sticky, matted hair away from her forehead. "Where is the pain?" I instinctively asked, as if she were four years old again.

Raegan pinched her lips together and gestured to her thigh. "In my leg. The idiot shot me in the freaking thigh."

I briefly registered a police officer on my way into the ER bay, and I turned around to scan the area. Seeing her pressed up against the wall directly behind me, my eyes connected with hers. "What the hell happened?"

Drea came up beside me. "We need to take her to surgery now," she said, placing her hand on my arm. "I'll be in there with her, Peach. I'll update you when I can."

I shook my head. "She can't be in there alone. I have to go with her."

"She won't be," Drea said firmly. "I'm going in there, because you can't. Go wait in the conference room and someone will come get you when we are done."

"We have her, Sam," Dr. Jacobs, one of the ER doctors, nodded at me. "She will be okay."

Raegan's hand slipped from mine as they began wheeling her away, and I watched as panic welled in her eyes and tears streamed down her cheeks. Mouthing, "It's going to be fine," to her, she gave me a small nod before disappearing behind the double doors that led to the operating room.

When they were out of sight, I walked backwards until I hit the wall and felt my legs give out. Sinking into a heap on the floor, my emotions hit me all at once. My daughter was shot. How had letting her go to a supervised gathering led to this? Now she was lying on an operating table with a bullet hole in her thigh. I let her go to one stupid party and it could have gotten her killed.

And of course, this all happens on the one night I took for myself after years of never leaving the house for anything other than work and doctors' appointments. Guilt crashed over me, then, and I could feel bile rising in my esophagus. I shouldn't have let her go. I should have asked her to stay home, and we could have had a movie night with Harrison. But I allowed her to leave, and I went on a date with Landon. Now everything was a disaster.

The police officer gently put a hand on my shoulder. "A kid called in saying a couple of teens got into the parents' gun safe, and they took a few of the rifles out back for target practice. Raegan was walking to her friend's car to leave, completely unaware of what the other kids were doing, and she stepped into the line of fire."

As I processed her words, rage replaced my sadness. Teenagers had gotten ahold of guns. My daughter could have been shot somewhere far worse than her thigh. I could have been in the morgue right now, identifying her corpse. As if my body was radiating the flames I felt inside, the officer immediately removed her hand.

"My colleagues are bringing everyone to the station now, including the parents of the kid who shot Raegan. We have every intention of fining the registered owners of the guns," she explained.

My legs wobbling like a newborn foal, I picked myself up off the floor. "They should be tried for attempted manslaughter. Neglect. Anything and everything. They didn't lock up their guns and now my child is lying in an OR with a bullet hole in her leg. I swear to God—" I stopped as the officer put her hands up.

"It's an ongoing investigation, ma'am. I will keep you posted. And I'll be back later to take Raegan's statement." She left me alone in the now empty room. After standing in the silence for who knows how long, I found my phone in my purse and dialed the number of the man I despised.

Of course, my call went unanswered. I left a voicemail, telling him to call me immediately, and walked back out to the ER waiting area. Landon was rubbing his hands back and forth, his right leg bouncing at the speed of light at the far end of the room. I could feel his uneasiness as I approached him, heightening my anxiety even further. When he finally spotted me, he stood up.

"What happened?" he asked. "Is she okay? Is she going to be alright?"

Nodding at the handful of people around us, I said, "We are going to wait in the conference room. The last thing I need right now is people asking about Raegan AND what my business is with you."

Wordlessly, he followed me through the hospital hallways until we reached the deserted conference room. I couldn't remember the last time a conference was actually held in there, and the space smelled of neglect and musty furniture. Collapsing into the nearest chair, a cloud of dust that had coated the cushion billowed up around me. Coughing, he slowly sat next to me, careful not to disturb the layers of abandonment on his chair.

"Can you tell me what happened? Or do you need time to process?" he asked, placing a hand on my leg.

I studied how his fingers looked against my skin as I told him what the police officer told me.

Landon's face transformed before me. His eyes,

once filled with worry, clouded with fury. "The kids got into a gun safe? How in the hell did that happen? Was it not locked? Did the kids have the combination? The entire purpose of a gun safe is to keep the guns SAFE. Out of reach from CHILDREN. I'm going to find those parents and—"

The charming, Southern Landon was gone, and I had to admit, I found his wrath refreshing.

"I feel the exact same way," I said. "I will help you find them. I just have to make sure Raegan gets out of surgery safely before I land myself in the slammer."

Jail immediately made me think of how Harrison would be alone, and I realized I hadn't called McKenna. Pulling my phone from my purse once more, I dialed her number and explained everything. Through her tears, she assured me she would stay the night with Harrison and made me promise to keep her updated. When I ended the call, a new wave of nausea hit me. How was this happening?

"I'm so sorry about all of this," he said, looking over at me. "I can't believe it." His leg started bouncing again.

"Are *you* okay?" I asked him, and confusion muddled his face until his eyes followed mine. Immediately stilling his limb, he drew his hands into fists and crossed his arms as he pulled them close to his stomach. "Hospitals make me nervous."

Raising an eyebrow, I cocked my head. "Did you feel this way every time you visited me while I was working?"

He nodded, still staring down. "It's a whole mind-over-matter thing. When I ambushed you those few times, your presence managed to ease all negative associations of being near and in the hospital. Right now, though, I'm freaked out about Raegan and it's making it nearly impossible to ignore my fear of this place. There are too many memories of my accident and I'm feeling very overwhelmed."

I was both in awe and shock that he was even here. "You don't have to stay, Landon. I completely understand if you want to go. I'll be fine. Once she gets into a room, I'm going to stay with her anyway."

He shook his head. "I can't leave until I know she's okay. Plus, I want to be here for you. I just need to concentrate on refocusing all of this stuff I'm feeling for a minute. Or five."

I watched as he closed his eyes and rhythmically inhaled and exhaled, his shoulders slowly relaxing in the process. Witnessing him change before me, I found myself seriously considering returning to therapy. The last thing to relax were his fingers, which he slowly unfurled after a few minutes of timed breathing. Finally, he opened his eyes and turned to me. "I'm so, so sorry, Sam. This is not how I wanted tonight to go."

I half-heartedly guffawed. "Me neither. I'm just relieved Raegan wasn't killed. It could have been so much worse. So much freaking worse." I thought I was calmer after observing him work through his nervousness, but another round of tears overcame me, and I couldn't stop them even if I wanted to.

Pushing the chair away from the table, he reached over and gathered me in his arms, his body rocking back and forth with me in his lap while I cried. While it was for the best that we were in an abandoned room, I noted that in this moment, I didn't care who saw me with Landon, or what they would tell other people. For the first time in a very long time, with my head pressed against his chest, one of his hands on my waist, and the other arm holding me close, I felt safe.

When my tears finally slowed, my tired eyes threatened to close, but I knew I couldn't give in. I had to stay awake and alert.

"Want me to go find us some coffee?" he asked the top of my head.

He was a saint and a mind reader rolled into one stunning package. "Yes, please," I whispered, sliding off his lap. "There's a vending machine at the end of this hallway."

Settling back in the chair next to his, I checked my phone. I didn't even know when they took Raegan into surgery, but I imagined it couldn't be much longer before we heard something. The conference room door opened and shut again, and the waft of hospital coffee preceded Landon. Grimacing, he set the paper cup on the table in front of me. "I think this is the worst coffee I've ever smelled, and the machine in the teacher's lounge at work is pretty awful."

Taking a small sip, I quickly discovered he was right. "During the first hour of my first shift here, I was told just how disgusting the vending machine coffee was, so I avoided it at all costs, until now. And wow, everyone was correct. I can feel my stomach lining dissolving already."

He swirled the liquid in his cup before placing it back on the table. "I don't think I'm brave enough."

Setting my coffee next to his, we watched as steam rose from the cups and dissipated before us.

"How long were you in the hospital?" I asked, desperate to focus on something other than the impending sense of dread I was feeling.

He rubbed his beard and stared at the ceiling. "A couple of weeks, if I recall correctly. My left leg was broken in multiple places and required two different surgeries. My right one only required one surgery, but I was in a cast from the waist down for what seemed like months. I remember my dad had to carry me throughout the house. He would move me from my bed to the couch before he went to work, and from the couch to my bed when he got home each night. After the casts came off and I had completed a few rounds of physical therapy, I was able to drag myself to the bathroom. I never truly appreciated the ability to use a toilet until the accident. Bedpans were my life for a few months, and as you know from dealing with bedridden patients, they are demoralizing."

I nodded. "I wish catheters weren't so painful and problematic for people. Besides running the risk of infection, they're uncomfortable as all get out, but I think there needs to be a happy medium between bedpans and catheters. I just don't know what it would be."

"It was rough. My mom was a trooper. From changing my bedpans to sponge-bathing me, I'll forever be indebted to her. She was a real-life superhero. Kind of like you are to your patients." He smiled.

"How did your dad handle your depression following the accident? Was he as supportive as your mom?" I knew I was rapid-firing questions, but he didn't seem to mind.

"He was as supportive as he knew how to be, if that makes sense. He grew up in a household that didn't exactly discuss personal feelings. If my dad or his brothers were upset, my grandparents told them to get over it. Never once did I see my dad cry, and I honestly think it's because he didn't know how. He was probably so out of touch with his emotions after keeping them inside for so long, he had just become numb to everything.

"When I was stranded on the couch one evening after the accident, I overheard my mom telling him that she was worried about me, and he couldn't understand why. He approached me a few times, telling me how I needed to move on and get over it, as 'wallowing wouldn't solve anything'." Landon sighed, lowering his head to focus on the wall in front of us. "The night I tried to overdose on pain meds, it was following one of my dad's very one-sided discussions about how real men don't show their feelings."

My stomach churned. "I'm so sorry, Landon."

"Eventually, he came around, but I'm sure my mom was the impetus for that. He showed up at one of my family therapy sessions when I was a part of the inpatient program in Athens and apologized. I never felt any ill will toward him, but it was nice of him to make an effort."

The conference room door clicked open, startling us both. Spinning around in our chairs, we saw Dr. Jacobs standing in the doorway. "Raegan is going to be fine," he said, giving me a small smile. "It missed the femoral artery. She will be sore for a while and will require PT to ensure she doesn't baby it and the affected muscles don't atrophy, but overall, she's good. She may even get out of here within the next day or two if she plays her cards right."

Overcome by emotions, I leapt from the chair to hug him. Taken aback by my gesture, Dr. Jacobs rubbed my back awkwardly. "I'll bring you back to see her in a few minutes."

"Thank you. I appreciate everything you have done and will continue to do for my family." Returning to Landon's side after the doctor left the room, I let out a slow, measured breath. "She's okay. Thank God, she's okay."

He nodded, staring intently at me. "Can I go find the parents now?"

I couldn't conceal my smile. "I suppose it's better you than me, but I kind of like having you around. Plus, a lot of kids depend on you."

He grinned. "I think orange could be my color, though." His hand found its way back to my thigh, and as he relaxed against the chair and shut his eyes, another emotion blindsided me—love. I think I loved Landon.

I knew we were mostly joking about going to jail to ensure justice for Raegan, but I also got the impression that if push came to shove, he would do it. This man had known me for less than two months. We just had our first date hours earlier. But he was already doing what no other man in my life had done—stepped up for me and my children.

I couldn't tell him how I felt, though. It wasn't the time or place, so I shoved my idiotic adoration of him back down into my heart and locked the door. That emotional revelation would be dealt with later.

Dr. Jacobs returned, and when I stood to follow him, Landon hung back. "You can come, if you want," I said, turning to him.

He cracked his knuckles, his eyes avoiding mine. "I don't want to intrude on family time. I'm fine sitting in here. Can you let me know how she is when you have a chance, though, please?" His voice broke at the end, and he drew his arms tightly across his stomach again.

Motioning for Dr. Jacobs to wait, I knelt down in front of Landon and placed my hands on his jittery knees. "Landon." I tried to get him to look at me. Finally, he did, and I saw that his eyes were red.

"Landon," I whispered. "Please come see Raegan with me. You aren't intruding, I swear. Besides, you'll feel better once you see she's recovering, just like I know I will. And then you can stop torturing yourself and leave this place without feeling guilty."

He clenched his fists a few times before eventually nodding. This time, we both rose and followed Dr. Jacobs.

Raegan was drowsy, but the second she saw me, her face lit up. "Mommy," she whispered. A single tear trickled down her now-cleaned cheek.

"Rae of Sunshine." I moved to her side and rested my forehead on top of hers.

Her eyes darted to where Landon stood awkwardly in the doorway. "Is he crying?" she asked quietly.

I nodded. "You had us both really worried, baby. And he really, really doesn't like hospitals."

Her gaze lingered on him for a few more seconds before she peered at me through swollen eyelids. "I ruined your date night." Silent tears sprang from her eyes, and I quickly reached up with my thumb to wipe them away.

"No, baby, you didn't. You didn't ruin anything. Besides, there is nowhere else I would rather be than here with you. When Drea called me..." I paused, a sob interrupting my train of thought. I convinced myself to take a few slow breaths before beginning again. "When she called me, I was so scared. She only knew you had been shot; she didn't know any details. The drive here felt like an eternity. I was so, so scared."

Raegan started uncontrollably sobbing, so I gently crawled into the bed and held her as close as I could, barring all of the wires she was connected to. A few minutes later, she was sound asleep, and when I looked at Landon, I could see his fatigue mirrored mine.

Coming up beside me, his lips brushed against my forehead. "If you text McKenna and ask if she can pack a bag with some clothes in it for you and Raegan, I can run by and grab it on my way home. Then I'll come back here in the morning with the bag, fresh coffee, and some bagels. Does that sound alright?" he asked quietly, giving my hand a squeeze, and I nodded my reply. Slipping my phone out of my purse, I handed the bag to him, which he placed on the bedside table before silently leaving.

After I texted McKenna, I put my phone on vibrate and slipped it under my leg that was furthest from Raegan. I couldn't put it on silent in the event something happened with Harrison, but the vibrations would wake me up just as easily as my ringtone could.

Closing my eyes, I let out a long sigh. This was definitely not how I expected the night to end, but I was thankful things hadn't been worse. Sending up a silent prayer, I begged for a few weeks of peace. Between Harrison's latest hospital stint and Raegan's injury, we needed a break from the chaos. Everyone needed time to heal.

CHAPTER TEN

Years of hearing his commanding gait up and down the halls of our home made the sound of his approach as familiar as his face. When I heard the telltale footsteps coming up the hospital corridor, my eyes flew open. Scrambling to sit up, I glanced over at Raegan, who was still sound asleep. I needed to stop him before he barreled in and woke her up. The man had no regard for anyone but himself.

Trying to move my arm out from underneath her, I could hear him growing nearer, and the panic was rising rapidly from the confines of my chest. Finally, I decided to quickly yank my arm away and hope Raegan would stay asleep; and she did. I was crawling out of the hospital bed just as he rounded the corner to her room, flanked by the person I wanted to see even less than Charles—his mother, Lydia.

"Was anyone going to tell me my daughter had been shot?" he nearly yelled, his ostentatious voice echoing throughout the otherwise quiet hospital. I glared at him before gesturing to Raegan, who had only slightly stirred.

"Can we talk about this outside of our sleeping daughter's room, since you clearly don't know how to use an indoor voice?" I asked, and his mother rolled her eyes at me. It took every ounce of self-control not to throttle that woman.

Grabbing my phone from the bed, I ushered them out into the hallway and closed Raegan's door softly behind us.

"What the hell, Samantha? Were you even going to tell me? A buddy of mine on the force came to my front door this morning to give his condolences. I had no clue what he was talking about," Charles started.

Unlocking my phone, I opened my call log and showed him the screen. "Did you even check your voicemail? Don't you dare come in here and accuse me of not contacting you when you can't even check your freaking voicemail," I hissed.

"Don't talk to my son that way," Lydia stepped in front of Charles, as if to shield him from my words.

My eyes narrowed. "I'm sorry, why are you even here?" At only five feet tall, Lydia was tiny in comparison to me, and I never realized how good it felt to tower over her until now. "You haven't given a crap about your grandchildren for the last seventeen years. Why now? What sort of appearance are you trying to keep up, Lydia? Raegan can barely pick you out of a lineup of ragged former beauty queens. Go home. You are too old to be fighting your son's battles, and you sure as hell aren't welcome here."

Lydia opened her mouth but before she could utter any words, I heard someone come up behind me.

"Who the hell are you?" Charles asked.

I felt a gentle touch on the small of my back before he appeared beside me, bagels and a duffle bag of clothes in hand. *Talk about timing.*

Lydia answered Charles before Landon could. "Landon Ford. Betty and Paul's son, right?" she asked, and Landon nodded.

"Yes, ma'am."

That Southern charm flowed seamlessly from him again, and Lydia smiled.

"Well, what a surprise. I haven't seen you since you were in high school. Are you back in the city for good? And how do you know our Raegan?" she asked.

I snorted. "Our Raegan? Her father hasn't seen her in months, and you haven't seen her, well, hardly ever. Rich. Really rich."

Landon remained calm. "Raegan attends the school I work at."

I knew he was going to leave it at that to try to maintain what little peace was left, but I didn't care anymore. Something in me snapped, and my desire to tolerate the Hawleys' bullshit from here on out was gone. I was done.

"Landon and I are also seeing each other. And unlike you," I glared accusingly at Charles, "Landon actually showed up for Raegan last night."

"I'm sorry, but if you think you are going to replace me in my wife and daughter's life," Charles began, starting toward him.

I threw my arm out, ensuring a safe distance between the two men. "I'm not your wife anymore, Charles. I'm meeting with my attorney as soon as possible and we are moving forward with this divorce." It was a spur-of-the-moment decision, but I was sticking to it. "And you were never in your daughter's life enough to warrant a replacement. The father figure in Raegan's life has been vacant since the day she was born."

Lydia gave Charles an incredulous stare. "You aren't divorced yet?"

I sighed, directing my gaze to Lydia. "I'm sure your

125

son thinks he married someone exactly like you. A dutiful, clueless wife who sticks by her cheating husband no matter what. Someone who will always come running back after every fight, claiming it's out of love, but really, it's for the financial stability. And that's where Charles is wrong, because I am the polar opposite of you. It's taken me a few months to solidify things, but I'm not coming back, Charles. I was never going to come back. Our children deserve better. I deserve better. Bottom line, I'm not weak like your mother." I nearly poked Lydia in the chest with my finger, but Landon pulled me back.

"I think we should all maybe step outside. Get some fresh air," he suggested, but Charles pushed past him.

"I'm going to see my daughter."

"Why?" I challenged. "You never visit Harrison when he's in the hospital. Are you worried your buddy on the force will think less of you if he hears you didn't show up at your daughter's bedside? Wouldn't want you to be embarrassed now, would we?"

Ignoring me, he threw open the door and marched over to Raegan.

Slightly dazed from the commotion and anesthesia, Raegan slowly sat up and looked around. Finally, everything hit her.

"Mom, you called Dad?" she asked, betrayal flashing across her face. Somewhere in my stomach, I felt a stabbing pain. I walked around to the other side of her bed, as far away from Charles as possible.

"He's your father, honey. I had to."

She shook her head as she scooted closer to me. "No, you didn't. I don't want him here. He needs to leave."

As much as I hated Charles, it destroyed me that my children didn't want him around, either. I wished they loved him and that he returned the sentiment. I longed for the resentment to just be between the two of us. But he failed all of us, and now he was paying the price.

Charles stared at me his eyes ablaze with anger. "Do you see this? You've poisoned our daughter's mind with all the bullshit you feed her."

Risking looking like I was submitting to his awful behavior, I held back what I wanted to say. I hated arguing in front of the kids. The entire time Charles and I were together, I would purposely avoid fights until after they were in bed and out of earshot. Because of Raegan's presence now, I wouldn't fight Charles. It could wait.

"No," came a loud, stern voice. Everyone turned to see Landon standing in the doorway, in the exact same spot he had been twelve hours earlier.

"No," he said again firmly, taking a few steps into the room. "Samantha doesn't need to feed your daughter anything. Raegan is a smart, capable young woman who can make her own choices and decisions—no one has poisoned her mind. And she's asked you to leave. If you have any shred of decency left, you'll go."

Raegan and I gawked at each other.

"Get. Out. Of. My. Daughter's. Room," Charles seethed through clenched teeth.

Raegan sat up further. "No, Dad. *You* get out of my room. And take that horrid woman with you."

Never in my life had I been rendered speechless until this moment.

Looking from me, to Landon, to Raegan, Charles finally let out a huff and stomped out of the room, Lydia close on his heels. As she passed by Landon, she shook her head. "Your mother and father would be so disappointed in you, wasting your life with a woman like this after you've overcome so much," she gestured to me, then scurried after her son.

"Yeah, well, your precious son wasted half his life with me, but God forbid you admit your disappointment in him. Hell would freeze over before you ever talked poorly about your little boy," I said under my breath, knowing very well she couldn't hear me.

Landon's eyes widened before he shut them. "What in the actual hell is wrong with that family?" he muttered to himself, rubbing his forehead with both pointer fingers.

A strange feeling rose inside me, bubbling up until it burst out of my mouth. *Laughter.* I sat down in the nearest chair, holding my chest. Seconds later, I heard Raegan start laughing. We both doubled over in fits of hysterics, leaving Landon standing in the middle of the room completely perplexed at our reaction. When I finally regained my composure, I stood up. "Raegan, honey, you might want to close your eyes."

Walking up to him, I wrapped my arms around his waist and kissed him. "I have never seen anyone stand up to Charles like that," I said between kisses. "That was the most amazing, romantic, sexiest thing I've ever witnessed in my entire life."

Raegan faked vomiting through a grin. "That was epic, Dr. Ford. No one has put my dad in his place before, and you just handed him his ass. Watching him get served was a thing of beauty."

He still looked slightly dubious. "I can't believe the nerve of him. How dare he talk to women like that? Especially the mother of his children and his own daughter? It took everything in me not to punch him. Holy moly," he said, rocking on his heels and running his hands through his hair, causing it to stand up in odd places. "I need to go get some air and decompress. I'll be quick, I promise. Please call me if he comes back. I'm just going to take a quick lap around the building so I don't wind up in a fist fight."

Once he was gone, Raegan eyed me. "He's going to stick around, right?"

I glanced back to where he had been standing. "I hope so, kid. I really hope so."

****

McKenna called later that morning to tell me she was planning on taking Harrison to the park down the street after lunch. We agreed that she would text me when they got back, and I would head home to give her a break. Drea had driven my car to the hospital a few hours earlier and dropped the keys with me before clocking in for her shift, so I was no longer without my vehicle.

At first, McKenna insisted she didn't need me to come home, and when I offered to ask Drea to see if she could step in for the night, McKenna straight up refused. But after some cajoling, she agreed to go to her apartment, shower, and change her clothes before I headed back to the hospital.

When Landon returned from his walk, he bore all forms of chocolate from the gift shop and dropped them onto the tray table next to Raegan like they were pilfered goods. He also managed to sneak in Raegan's favorite meal from a local restaurant, much to her surprise.

"How did you know?" she asked, hungrily digging in.

He smiled. "I may or may not have asked your mom. I know hospital food is terrible, and lunch is an incredibly important meal. It should not be wasted eating cardboard..." he lifted up the now abandoned hospital food tray, "bread and rubberized turkey. Eat up. I can't promise I can do the same tonight for dinner. I think the security guard is on to me."

After she finished eating, Raegan's eyes slowly began to droop, and within a few minutes, she was asleep. Landon and I sat in the two chairs next to her bedside; my hand was in his, his thumb rubbing the grooves of my knuckles.

"Why don't you get some rest? I'm sure you didn't sleep well last night. When Raegan wakes up or if the doctor comes in, I promise I'll wake you," he whispered, pulling his hand away so he could wrap his arm around my shoulders. Leaning against him, I closed my eyes.

"Just let me sleep for a little bit, okay?"

Him gently nudging me roused me from my slumber, and I glanced down at my phone to check the time only to discover the battery had died. *Crap.* Moving my eyes from my phone to the clock just above Raegan's bed, I saw that it was nearly four p.m. McKenna had to be home with Harrison by now.

Dr. Jacobs was standing next to Raegan, examining her wound. "It's looking good, Raegan. I think you can bust out of here later, if you want." He looked from her to me. "Maybe tonight after shift change?"

Raegan nodded enthusiastically. "Yes, please. As nice as everyone is, I would love not to be woken up every hour for a blood pressure check."

"I'll circle back in a few hours, then. If you are still feeling good and the wound remains unchanged, I'll ask a nurse to start the discharge process."

I stood and stretched my limbs after Dr. Jacobs left, feeling nearly every bone in my body crack as a result of sleeping in an uncomfortable chair. I definitely wasn't as young as I used to be, and this instance drove the fact home. "Are you going to be fine while I relieve McKenna for an hour? In the event you aren't discharged tonight, I want her to have clean clothes and a shower before spending another night with Harrison," I explained. Raegan's face dropped ever so slightly. Joining me at my side, Landon cocked his head.

"I can stay with her until you get back if she doesn't want to be alone," he offered quietly. "If everyone is comfortable with me being here."

I raised my eyebrows at her. "Do you feel okay having him stay with you? You can say no. No one's feelings would be hurt." Landon shook his head for extra emphasis.

"Would you mind?" she asked him.

He tried to stifle a grin but failed. "Not at all. I bought a deck of cards from the giftshop, and I'm known to play a mean game of Go Fish."

Raegan snickered and rolled her eyes. "It's blackjack or nothing, bro."

Giving him a peck on the cheek, I whispered, "Thank you. And for the record, you will be rewarded for your valiant efforts today. Hopefully soon, if no one else winds up in the hospital."

Landon gently grabbed my arm and pulled me in for a kiss. "Don't threaten me with a good time." He flashed a devilish grin as I pulled away.

As I was crossing the parking garage, the sound of someone yelling my name made me stop dead in my tracks. It was Drea, and she was sprinting across the grassy area, coming at me like something was on fire. "Are you going home?" she asked when she reached me, doubling over and putting her hands on her knees.

"Yeah, why? What's wrong? You don't run unless something is wrong."

Drea shook her head, still panting. "I just got a call from McKenna, but I couldn't understand what she was saying. She's hysterical, Sam. You gotta get home. Something's up."

It was my turn to sprint. Jumping in my car, I peeled out of the parking garage and sped toward the house. When I paused at a red light, I plugged my phone into the car charger, and a minute later, my phone screen came to life and began pinging almost nonstop for ten seconds. Missed call. Voicemail. Missed call. Missed call. Voicemail.

Pulling onto my street, the thudding in my ears sounded like the hooves of stampeding wild horses. Yanking my phone from the charger, I tossed it into my purse and screeched to a halt in the driveway. McKenna was off to my right, hunched over on the front steps, with her face buried in her arms. Throwing open the car door, I raced to the front of the house. Fear of the unknown left me almost breathless as I collapsed onto my knees in front of her.

"Kenny, what's wrong?"

She moved her head to look at me, and I saw that her cheeks were flushed crimson and covered in tears. "I-I, he—" she started, but she couldn't catch her breath. The front door was open behind her, and I glanced into the house.

"Is it Harrison? Is he okay?"

She tried to speak again, but the only thing she could muster were short, panicked bursts of tears and air. "I—he just, he just appeared, and I—I couldn't stop him," she sobbed, entombing her face in her arms again.

Dropping my purse on the cement walkway, I nearly leapt over her small body and into the house. Harrison wasn't in the living room or the kitchen. Racing up the hallway, I checked his room. It was empty.

"McKenna," I nearly screamed, running back to the porch and crouching in front of her. "Where is he? Where is Harrison?" My eyes searched hers as she lifted her chin.

"Charles took him. He came up to us while we were at the park and told me he was going to take Harrison. I argued with him; I told him he couldn't just up and leave with him. He started yelling at me—saying Harrison is his child and that he has every right to take him. I—I tried to stop him. I really did, Sam. I swear."

Chills and nausea washed over me.

"I'm sorry. I tried calling you, but it just went to voicemail. I called you so many times." She was nearly hyperventilating. "I couldn't get through to the hospital. I didn't know what to do; I couldn't breathe. Drea eventually answered her cell, but it was too late. Harrison's been gone for nearly an hour. Charles had a van with him—I don't even know how or where he got it from. But he loaded Harrison into it and just left. The look on Harrison's face…his sounds…Oh, Sam," she cried. "I tried so hard, but—"

Harrison was gone. Charles, a man who had never once cared for his children, had taken my son away from the only people he knew. And I could have stopped it had I paid attention to my phone's battery. Instead, I had fallen asleep and left McKenna alone to deal with all of it. My phone rang from within the depths of my purse.

I ran my fingers over my scalp, ignoring it. "This isn't happening. None of this is happening right now." I tried to breathe, but my lungs were burning. How could Charles take Harrison? And why? Just to get back at me? Was he really going to jeopardize our son's wellbeing as a form of revenge?

My phone rang again, but I let it go unanswered as I tried to process everything. Charles had Harrison. My daughter was in the hospital because she was shot at a party. How had everything gone so wrong so fast?

The shrill ring once again filled my purse and my ears, causing me to finally jam my hand into my bag in search of my phone. Grabbing the back of it and flipping it over, I saw Landon's name on the screen. "I don't want you to be calling because of an emergency, but this better be an emergency," I said through gritted teeth.

"Sam, Charles came to the hospital a few minutes ago and demanded Raegan be discharged. I tried to stop him, but I had no leg to stand on. I'm so sorry."

He was still talking as I slowly pulled the phone away from my ear and ended the call. McKenna looked at me, her eyes wide. "What happened?"

Swallowing hard, I shook my head and rose to my feet. "In the event that Charles taking Harrison wasn't bad enough, that asshole discharged Raegan from the hospital and has her now, too. They're both gone, McKenna. And I'm not sure I can do anything about it."

CHAPTER ELEVEN

I stared blankly into the house, trying to figure out my next move as McKenna cried on the steps below me. *Jules.* I needed to call Jules Parker, my lawyer. She would know what I could legally do. As I was scrolling through my contacts, the sound of tires turning into my driveway made me whip my head around. A pearl-colored Cadillac Escalade rolled to a stop behind my car, kicking up a cloud of dust.

Just when I thought things couldn't get worse.

A man dressed in embarrassingly stereotypical butler attire jumped out of the driver's seat before racing around to the other side of the SUV. Opening both passenger doors simultaneously, I stared as Lydia and a woman in scrubs stepped out of the car and made their way up the driveway. Even though I was looking in their direction, I wasn't processing what any of this could mean. I was only thinking about Raegan and Harrison, and how I needed to get them out of this mess. How scared Harrison must have been. How scared he probably still was. How vulnerable and angry Raegan must feel. I had no clue where they were; if they were safe.

Lydia stopped a foot away from me and cleared her throat.

Glaring at her, I said, "If I were in the mood, I would try to guess what opening to a joke this is, but I don't have time. My children were just taken by a man who hasn't bothered to see them in months," I paused, "and I'm sure you encouraged this outlandish plan, so you need to leave. Now. You have no business being here."

"We are here for Harrison's things," she announced, her face not registering my anger.

"You're bullshitting me, right?" I glanced at McKenna, whose jaw was hanging open.

Lydia shook her head. "No, my son wanted to see his children and he knew you would keep them from him for as long as possible. He had no choice. Besides, you don't have a custody order in place, and in the eyes of the law, you're still married. He has every right to see his kids. And now that he has them, we need Harrison's things until Charles can get the proper equipment for his own place."

Glancing down at my phone and turning my back to Lydia, I pressed the number for Jules as I crossed the threshold of the house. She picked up on the second ring, despite it being after business hours. "Long story," I rushed, "but Charles just took Raegan from the hospital while I was away and all but kidnapped Harrison from the park while he was with McKenna. Please, please tell me he can't do that." I stood in the doorway, blocking Lydia and her entourage from entering my home. I needed Jules to tell me I could legally tell them to screw themselves and that I could get my kids back tonight. This couldn't be acceptable.

Jules was silent on the other line for a few seconds. "Holy crap, Sam." I then heard her muttering to herself over the shuffling of papers. "Because he and his lawyer haven't agreed to mediation or set a court hearing, we don't have any paperwork stating custody. Nothing has been agreed upon in terms of who has the kids and when. I know you didn't want to keep nudging him because you had the kids full time and not hearing from him was working. But this is why we should have pushed him. Right now, I can't help you. Charles has every right to take Harrison and Raegan. He's their father. And if they are in a safe setting and Charles is caring for them, we can't do anything about this situation tonight."

I didn't remember the phone sliding out of my hand, but one minute I was holding it, and the next it was clattering onto the floor. "No," I whispered.

Lydia's voice came from behind me. "I told you. Now please, let this nice nurse in. She can help you gather everything Harrison needs for the next few days. If you forget anything, you can bring it by my place."

I moved robotically, forbidding my mind to wander. This was what I had to do. I couldn't fight Lydia and refuse to give them what they needed for Harrison. It would only hurt him, not Charles, and I couldn't let my son pay the price for my mistakes; although, maybe he already was.

When I reached Harrison's room, I froze. I had to do this. I had to allow my son to stay with someone who was essentially a complete stranger and expect him to be okay. Swallowing a sob and walking slowly into the room, I started opening drawers. This was all my fault. I hadn't followed through on the divorce and now my children were suffering because of my shortcomings. Harrison wouldn't thrive under Charles' and some random nurse's care. He struggled with McKenna and me sometimes, and we were his sole caregivers. I've cared for him since he was inside me. Now I had to just…let him go?

Somehow, I managed to find a duffel bag and packed what Harrison needed for at least a week, including my seizure monitor. "He needs this sensor for his bed," I told the nurse. "He has seizures and the sensor alerts the caregiver via pager. You need to get one as soon as possible, because I will need mine back. It's non-negotiable. And he can't eat normal food. I give him some liquids and pureed food via mouth, but most of his nutrients come from the blended foods through his G-tube. He can't eat what you and I eat—he can choke very easily. He can only handle smoothies, protein drinks, and pureed fruits and vegetables in addition to the G-tube, but the G-tube is the priority. Everything else is secondary."

She nodded, taking out her phone and making a note. Once I zipped the bag shut, I handed it to her and set off for the kitchen. Grabbing some feeding tube bags, I slipped them into the front pouch of the duffel. "Please," I whispered to her. "Please take care of my son."

She nodded again; her eyes were full of empathy. "I'm sorry."

We made our way to the front door where McKenna and Lydia stood, and it was there I realized they hadn't asked for any of Raegan's belongings. Surely, they didn't plan on buying her all new items, but even if they tried, I knew Raegan wouldn't accept anything out of sheer stubbornness and anger. Signaling for them to give me a minute, I ran to her room and grabbed a handful of clothes, her headphones, her phone charger, and the school textbooks she had on her desk. I placed everything into the abandoned backpack next to Raegan's bed before zipping it closed and rejoining the nurse, Lydia, and McKenna in the entryway.

With both bags in hand, the nurse offered me a sympathetic smile before she descended the front steps and made her way to the Escalade. She slid into the car when the butler opened the door. The second the nurse was safely out of earshot, Lydia turned to me and smirked. "I hope you use this newfound silence to think about what you've done." Stepping off the porch, she climbed into the car. Seconds later, they were gone.

My legs began to tremble, and I reached out to the doorframe for support. I wasn't going to be able to keep it together for much longer. "Kenny, you should go home."

She shook her head. "I can't. I can't leave you alone like this. This is my fault. I let him—"

"McKenna, please. I know you wouldn't have let Harrison go unless you had no other choice. I'm not upset with you. I just need time to process all of this. Go home, see Kevin, and please know I don't blame you."

Staring at me for a moment, her shoulders finally sagged in defeat. "Please let me know what happens," she whispered.

I managed to nod. "Of course, I will, Kenny. Drive safe."

Once she drove away, I closed the door, officially shutting myself out from the rest of the world. While everyone's day continued on as normal, mine had just stopped. The deafening silence overtook me, and I heard myself utter a low, animalistic wail before my body sunk onto the stone tile in the foyer. My children were gone. Had I fought for sole legal and physical custody months ago, this never would have happened. I should have fought harder for my children.

But I hadn't, and now they were gone.

Tears came. Multiple times I found myself wondering if I could perish from crying too hard. My breathing was ragged and I could feel what little energy I had left drain out of me as my body convulsed with sobs on the freezing tile. I cried until my body was depleted: until my strength was gone, until my tears had dehydrated every ounce of me, until my willpower to do anything was nonexistent.

Then sleep came. When I woke again, more tears flooded down my cheeks and onto the floor, and the cycle repeated itself in what felt like an endless loop. At one point, the sun hit the tiles in front of me, nearly blinding me for what felt like days, but as it continued on its path, the cold darkness returned.

My children were gone.

I vaguely remember my phone ringing in the background of my haze, but I couldn't find it without moving, and that felt like an impossible task. After hearing it go off at least two dozen times, though, I finally gathered the strength to sit up and I spotted it a few feet away, facedown near the entryway table. Fumbling to pick it up, I saw ten missed calls from Raegan, two missed calls from Jules, eight missed calls from Landon, and the rest of the unanswered calls were from Drea.

I immediately dialed Raegan, who answered on the first ring.

"Harrison is fine, Mom," she said, her breathing uneven. She had been crying. "And I'm okay. I'm taking care of Harrison. I tried to get Dad to call McKenna and get rid of the stupid, clueless nurse, but he won't do it. I can't leave Harrison alone with her. Also, Lydia is constantly looking over my shoulder, so I'm not sure how much I'll be able to text you."

I curled back into the fetal position, my endless torrent of tears robbing me of my ability to speak.

"Mom?" Raegan said. "We are going to be fine until you can come get us, I'll make sure of it. But please hurry."

I couldn't breathe. My children weren't here.

"I'm so sorry, baby," I managed to utter. "You shouldn't be saddled with any of this, ever, but especially after what happened at the party. You should be healing, not juggling additional responsibilities and stress. I'm so, so sorry."

Raegan started crying again. "It's not your fault. Just get us home." She hung up, and I pulled my phone to my chest, my eyes clenched shut. Please, God, tell me this was a nightmare.

When my phone rang again, Jules' name popped up on the screen. "I'm getting paperwork together so we can file an *ex parte* application for custody orders on Wednesday morning. If all goes well, Sam, you can have your children back by Wednesday afternoon. But you will need to be there with me in court. A judge is going to ask why you need emergency custody, and you have to be prepared to tell him all the reasons Charles is an unfit parent. Once that's done, it will start the ball rolling for the divorce and custody hearing, so we need to prepare for that. Hang tight. I'll keep you in the loop."

The sun was high in the sky when a knock came from the front door behind me. Not having the energy to verbally respond, much less pull myself off the floor to answer it, I ignored it. A minute later, a knock came again, and I raised my arms above my head, blocking out the sound and wishing for whoever it was to go away.

"Sam?" My hands over my ears caused the voice to sound muffled, but I recognized the dress shoes and pants as soon as I opened my eyes. When he realized I was curled below him, he fell onto his hands and knees beside me. "Sam, what are you doing on the floor?"

"They're gone, Landon," I whispered, wrapping my arms around my body and staring straight ahead. "He took them."

He placed his hands under my armpits and managed to prop my limp body up against the front door. "I tried to reach you last night and this morning a bunch of times, but I thought maybe you were mad that I let Charles take Raegan. I was going to give you a few more hours before I came begging for forgiveness. Then Raegan called me at the school. She explained what happened; that Charles took Harrison last night, too. She told me where the spare key was because she knew you wouldn't answer your phone. My God, Sam." He finally stopped to take a breath.

My head slumped forward. I was too drained and my head was throbbing too much to interact with another person right now, even if it was Landon.

"When is the last time you've eaten?" he asked, taking me in his arms and slowly standing up.

"I don't know. Lunch, yesterday maybe," I said. "At the hospital. I had a few bites of cardboard bread and rubberized turkey."

Wordlessly, he carried me down the hall and after finding Raegan's and Harrison's rooms, he located my bedroom and pulled back the sheets with one hand. As gently as he'd picked me up, he slid me onto the bed, pulled the duvet up to my shoulders, and disappeared.

Moments later, he walked in with a bag of cheese puffs, four bottles of water, an entire bag of candy, a banana, and a bottle of ibuprofen. After setting them on the nightstand behind me, he crawled onto the bed.

"You can cry and wallow and hate yourself and get angry, but you also have to eat. Eventually, you will need your strength to fight back, and now you have options conveniently located right next to you."

I knew he was right—I would eventually need to retaliate. But I wasn't at the anger stage yet, and without fury motivating me to pull myself together, I couldn't do it. All I could do was lie there.

He settled against the pillows next to me, snaking his hand underneath the blanket to find mine. When our fingers connected, I closed my eyes. We sat in silence for a bit, me under the duvet and him on top of the covers, holding my hand.

"When Raegan was little," I finally said, breaking the quiet, "about four or five years old, she used to have these nightmares. On and off for an entire year, an hour after she would fall asleep, she would wake up screaming. When the nightmares first started, I would run to her bedside, panicked and asking her what was wrong, over and over again. She was always half-asleep, so even if she knew what was wrong, she wasn't coherent enough to make any sense of it.

"Eventually, I stopped asking what was wrong and just held her. I would shush her and tell her everything was fine. That she didn't have to cry. It was just a nightmare, and she would feel better once she calmed down." I slowly turned over to face him.

"The logical part of me knows that's what this is. I know it's just a nightmare, and eventually everything will be fine. But for now, in this moment, I can't make sense of it, and I can't calm down. I'm panicking, and my brain can't stop thinking about everything that could go wrong."

He moved closer to me. "Then I'll be the one to tell you it's okay and hold you until it's over. You're right, everything will be fine, eventually. This is all just a hiccup in the grand scheme of life. But until you can regain your bearings and know for certain everything will sort itself out, I'll be the one to comfort you. I will sit here with you through this nightmare.

"I have no idea what you're going through, so I won't say I understand. But I do want you to know that I'm going to be here for you every step of the way—whatever that looks like. You won't be alone."

Tears returned upon hearing his reassurance, but after a while, my crying turned into shallow breaths, and those gave way to sleep. When I awoke again, he was no longer next to me, but the impression his body made on the duvet and pillows was still prominent. Feeling the spot, I discovered it was still warm—he hadn't been gone long. The entire room was dark, the open window revealing a crescent moon hanging midway in the evening sky.

I pulled a water bottle close and after a few seconds of struggling, I managed to crack it open. The entire bottle was gone in three long gulps. Opening another, I fetched two pills from the ibuprofen bottle and quickly swallowed them, along with the rest of the water.

My next instinct was to open the bag of cheese puffs, but I knew I needed something relatively healthy before diving into the junk food. Reluctantly, I peeled back the banana and sat up. Just as I was taking the last bite,

Landon walked in.

"Hey," he said softly, coming and sitting next to me. "I'm glad to see you're eating." He had taken off his shoes and rolled up his shirt sleeves, revealing just enough of his forearms to distract me, but only momentarily.

"What time is it?" I asked. He unhooked my phone from the charger on my nightstand and handed it to me.

"It's eleven. Monday night. I took a half day today, and I'm planning on staying the night on the couch, just in case you need anything."

"You don't have to stay," I said. "My lawyer is trying to get paperwork together to file for an emergency, albeit temporary, custody arrangement Wednesday morning. She's hoping to get the kids back to me by that afternoon. The *ex parte* will kickstart the divorce and custody agreement battle, so I need to meet with her on Thursday or Friday to discuss our plan of attack. I'm sure you have better things to do than watch me wallow until all that happens. Thank you for offering, though."

He shook his head. "I want to be here for you as much as possible. I can't cancel on my students, but the second I finish my last session, I will be here. Every day."

"Thank you," I whispered, laying the banana peel on my nightstand and slumping back into bed.

He covered me with the duvet and stared at me, his eyes searching mine.

"I'm so, so sorry, Sam. I wish I could help somehow. I wish I could get the kids back to you faster." He placed his head in his hands, slowly rubbing his forehead. "I always knew Charles was an asshole, but this…this is just evil."

"Honestly, it tracks. I should have seen this coming. Charles doesn't give a crap about our children; he only cares about hurting me. And the only way he knows how to get revenge for me leaving him is by taking away Raegan and Harrison."

He sighed. "He is truly a trash human."

"That, he is."

Moving my pillow, I wiggled into a comfortable position, exhausted from the little effort I had exerted from eating and drinking. I was definitely weak from not taking care of myself the last twenty-four hours.

Before I could close my eyes, Landon stood up and started walking out of my bedroom.

"Wait," I said, stopping him in his tracks. "Don't sleep on the couch. I can't—in fact, I won't—guarantee a good time tonight, but I would like it if you stayed in here with me. If you want," I added.

He spun around and made his way to the opposite side of the bed. Undoing his belt and loosening his shirt by a few buttons, he pulled back the duvet and settled in next to me. "I would love that. And don't believe for a second that any time spent with you in any capacity *isn't* a good time. We clearly don't need to be naked for me to want to be around you 24/7."

Grinning, I asked, "Do you think we can hold hands again?"

I heard him smile in the dark. "Always," he whispered.

CHAPTER TWELVE

Landon was gone when I woke up the following morning. It was a little past nine a.m., and I knew I needed to get up and deal with reality. Pulling myself into a sitting position against the headboard, my pounding head and racing thoughts immediately made me want to slither back under the covers. But I had to get up. *Come on, Sam. Get up.*

The sound of a key turning in the front door lock made my heart stop. Could it be…?

"I'm here with the goods!" a voice yelled as the door slammed shut.

I sighed. It wasn't the kids. It was Drea. Coffee in both hands and two pastry bags between her teeth, she swept into the room seconds later and sat down beside me. "It's a brand new day, you beautiful human. Let's get some coffee and food in you before you make this day your b—"

"Let me guess, this is not your first cup," I interrupted her, taking a croissant and coffee cup from her outstretched hands.

"Absolutely not. Now you need to get on my level and get going. We need to move past the woe-is-me stage and get angry. You want to punch holes in the walls? Marc can come by later and drywall over those suckers. You want to scream? Come at me. But you cannot lay here any longer. You cannot give Charles any reason to

147

keep your children permanently. Because how you look right now," she eyed me, "I'm not sure I would grant you custody if I were a judge. You look a little unhinged."

I rolled my eyes. "I can always count on you to make me feel better."

She shrugged. "I'm just being honest. And the Peach I know; she doesn't let anyone push her around. Get up, Sam. Fight back."

She was right. Placing the croissant and coffee on the nightstand, I stripped myself of the clothes McKenna had packed in the bag Landon brought to the hospital and changed into an old t-shirt and sweats. Picking up the food, I marched out of my bedroom, down the hall, and into the kitchen. Spinning around to take everything in, I saw it was exactly how I had left it four days ago—before Raegan was in the hospital. Dishes were in the sink, dust bunnies were congregating on the wood floors, the counters were a disaster from Raegan making God knows what before she left for the party.

Holy crap. My life *and* my house were a mess. Fantastic. "I'm going to clean," I started.

She nodded in approval. "I support that."

"And then I'm going to shower," I added.

Her head bobbed up and down. "Yep, yep. All good things, love it."

"And tomorrow, Jules and I are going to court to file an *ex parte* application for a custody order, and by tomorrow afternoon, I should hopefully have my kids back. That's my plan. Here we go. Go, team," I said, amping myself up, and Drea cheered.

"And now that you're out of bed and motivated, I gotta go. Landon had asked if I could stop by at some point to ensure you were still breathing, but since I'm your hype girl, I wanted to come by early to make sure your day started off right."

I stared at her. "Landon called you?"

"Girl, when he rang the hospital yesterday, he told me he found you on the floor in the foyer. Now, I'm not saying there is a right and wrong way to grieve, but I sure as hell wasn't going to let you do that again today. Don't let Charles win, Peach. If you need anything, you call, you hear?" Just as fast as she came in, she was gone.

My eyes moved from the front door back to the kitchen. Throwing back my coffee, I retrieved my phone from my bedroom, picked a motivational music playlist, and slowly started getting my life back together. Sia's "Unstoppable" blasted through the kitchen while I tackled the dishes.

Five songs later, the area was pristine, and I continued to make my way through the house, cleaning everything as I went. I couldn't remember when I deep cleaned my house last, but judging by how everything looked, it had been a while.

By the time I made it to my bathroom, I could feel my rage waning and my regret attempting to make a comeback. Even with music blasting, the fact that I was alone in my house was overpowering. As I violently scrubbed the shower grout, the sponge in my grip started to crumble, pieces flaking off and floating down the drain.

I was that sponge. What little mental stability I had left before this happened was starting to disintegrate right before my eyes. The more I thought about it, the more I suspected that Charles had plotted this when he realized I wasn't going to come crawling back to him that afternoon at the hospital. When he saw that his control over me was slipping, he took away what I lived for—my children. Now *I* was the one who was slipping, grasping at thin branches of sanity as I tumbled down a mental ravine, the rushing waters of hopelessness waiting for me at the bottom.

When I glanced up a few minutes later, I saw Landon standing in the doorway, his hands in his pockets. "The house is very clean."

"Yes, well, rage cleaning does wonders."

He came up next to the shower. "Maybe you should take a break. We could go for a walk? Get some fresh air?"

For some reason, his comment inspired my rage to make a swift return, and I glared at him. "First, you're upset that I'm too depressed to get off the floor, and now you're upset that I'm being productive?" The sponge continued to dissolve as I kept scrubbing.

Jerking his head back, he raised his hands slightly. "No, that's not what I meant. I just—"

My anger was escalating, but it was misdirected, and while I knew this, I couldn't contain the rage I felt burning a hole inside of me. I turned my head slightly. "Why are you here, Landon? You don't have to be here whenever you have a spare moment. I appreciate you coming over, and even sending Drea with food this morning, but I'm fine now. You can leave." As the words left my mouth, I knew I didn't mean them, but I was angry. So, so angry.

At the wrong man.

He shifted his weight. "Sam, I want to be here. I want to help you get through this. That's what partners do, right? I know you aren't used to having someone in your corner, but now that I'm here, don't force me out of it."

Throwing the cleaning supplies onto the shower tiles, I stood up to face him. "We've been on one date. Are we in a relationship, Landon? Or did you sense that I was a wounded person the moment I walked into Mr. Prior's office a month and a half ago and thought to yourself, 'Hey! I can fix her!' Am I your partner, or am I a challenge?"

I watched as his eyes widened and his shoulders dropped, but I kept going, not caring in that moment how much I was hurting him. "I've said it before, and I'll say it again to really drive it home; I'm a mess, Landon. And I know because of your profession and your past, you are attracted to messy things. You think you can fix all the broken people you meet, and in most cases, I'm sure that's true. But it's not true for me. You can't fix this. I am what I am."

His face revealed the true sting of my words, showing they were worse than any type of physical pain I could have inflicted. Climbing back into the shower, I continued scrubbing, despite everything becoming blurry through my tears. I had to keep going.

He remained standing behind me, as if he were rooted to the spot. My frantic scrubbing and crying filled the silence between us.

Eventually, he spoke. "Please get up, Sam."

I wanted to ignore him, but something in his voice made me put down the sponge and stand again. He was now leaning against the double sink, his hands reaching out for mine.

Exhausted, I traipsed out of the shower and collapsed into him. Enveloping me in a firm embrace, he stood still as I cried.

I failed. I failed my children; I failed myself. I tried to keep my family together, and instead, it epically fell apart.

Gently sliding the ponytail holder out of my hair, Landon began massaging my scalp. Moving my attention from my overwhelming feelings to Landon's movements and his rhythmic breathing, my body further relaxed against his.

"I didn't mean to hurt you," I whispered. "You've been here for me through all of this, and I was ugly."

He hugged me tighter. "I know you didn't mean it. And I will sit here with you while you clean every inch of this house with a toothbrush if that's what you need to do. After eighteen years, Sam, you don't have to be alone anymore."

I sniffled. "I'm tired of cleaning."

Above me, I heard him smile. "Great. Do you want food? Alcohol? Ice cream?"

I eased away from him and glanced at myself in the mirror. My eyes were red and puffy, my face swollen from endless crying, and my holey old t-shirt was smeared with dust and cleaning supplies. "I want nothing more than to get the hell out of here and get drunk, but I feel like those two things can't happen because of how terrifying I look. Plus, I have court in the morning."

Landon stood behind me. "I'll tell you what. We'll go to my place, and on the way there, I'll run inside the liquor store on the corner. That way, you get a change of scenery without being in public, *and* you can enjoy an adult beverage or two before getting a good night's sleep so you're ready for court."

"Your place, huh?" I asked, leaving him in the bathroom and heading toward the front door. He didn't have to ask me twice.

He trailed me, his hands in the air. "Only if you want. Otherwise, we can go to a park or take a drive or something."

Waiting for him to walk past me, I grabbed my purse and shut the door behind us, locking it. "Trust me, the amount of alcohol I need to temporarily forget about all of this is way past the legal limit, and the last thing I need is to be arrested for public intoxication. Your place sounds amazing."

Fifteen minutes later, we were walking up the steps of a modest, ranch-style single story home. Throwing open the door, Landon ushered me in. "Welcome to my rental home."

I was surprised at what I saw. Black leather furniture with wooden accents were arranged neatly throughout a gray-toned living room off to the right, and the kitchen immediately in front of us was white and immaculately clean. "I'm impressed," I admitted. "I thought your house would either resemble a prison or a frat house. You continue to surprise me, Dr. Ford."

Landon removed a cork from one of the wine bottles he had purchased at the liquor store before handing it over with a glass. "My mother raised me to have *some* sense of style. I'm not going to apply for a job with Joanna Gaines, but I think my taste in home décor is passable."

"The fact that you know who Joanna Gaines is makes me like you even more, and I wasn't sure that was possible," I said quietly, flopping onto his couch with the wine. I placed the glass on the ottoman in front of me before taking a swig straight from the bottle. There was no point in dirtying a glass when I knew I was going to drink every last ounce of that delicious fermented grape juice. I hardly ever drank, but if one occasion called for it, this was it.

Within half an hour, a majority of the alcohol was gone. Landon was busy at the stove, cooking something that was beginning to smell delicious. Pulling myself off the couch, I walked over to the kitchen island and sat down on one of the barstools, my wine sitting next to me on the counter. As I watched him cook, I could feel the alcohol start to take effect, but the pain from the last few days was still very much present. I took a long sip, draining the rest of the bottle.

He turned around. "I would love to get some food in you so you don't throw up all that hard work." He nodded at the wine bottle. "Give me ten more minutes, and then by all means, continue."

I glanced down the hall. "Would it be possible for me to take a shower in those ten minutes?"

He stared at me for a beat before nodding. "My bathroom is through the primary room—end of the hall to the left. Clean towels are under the sink. I have to warn you, though, my soap will make you smell like a forest."

"It beats Clorox and Windex." I headed down the hallway and into his room, and I couldn't help but temporarily picture a gloriously naked Landon in the bed I passed on the way to the bathroom. Turning the shower on full blast, I stripped off my clothes and stood under the scalding water, feeling it hit every inch of my body. My tense muscles started to loosen, letting me know the wine was finally starting to do its job as I washed off four days of grime and grief.

When I pulled myself from the shower, a knock came from the bathroom door. Slowly opening it, I saw

Landon's outstretched hand, a pair of plaid pajama pants and a black t-shirt sitting in his palm.

"If you wanted clean clothes to go with your clean self," he said, respectably averting his eyes. Grinning, I took the outfit and shut the door. Because I had two kids, I refastened my bra around my chest, but ultimately decided to forgo underwear.

Mouthwatering aromas hit me the second I opened the bathroom door. Reclaiming my seat at the kitchen island, he smiled as he handed me a plate of steak, green beans, and mashed potatoes. A full bottle of wine had replaced the empty one, and he had poured himself what appeared to be a glass of whiskey. From the living room came the gentle crackle of the fireplace.

"Thank you for dinner," I said, as he sat down next to me with his own plate.

"You're welcome. Hopefully it's good. I haven't cooked for anyone in a long time. I'm my only house guest, and I don't have high standards." He laughed.

The second the steak hit my mouth, I closed my eyes, reveling in the taste. Alcohol and low expectations aside, I had never eaten something this good outside of a restaurant. "Well just to let you know, you must have higher standards than most, because this is delicious. Perfectly executed, perfectly presented," I gestured to the plate. "Ten out of ten would eat here again."

His eyes crinkled as he smiled. "I hope you will."

We ate in silence for the rest of the meal, and although I was tempted to drink the second bottle of wine, the responsible part of my brain told me it wasn't a good idea, before succumbing to the effects of the first bottle. After having a brief argument with Landon, I stood at the sink, loading the dirty utensils, plates, and pans into the dishwasher before turning it on. He remained seated, watching me the entire time. Finally, I turned to face him. "Did you have a girlfriend before moving back here?"

His focus moved to the glass in his hand as he swirled the amber liquid around. "I did. It ended a few months before I left."

"How long were you together?"

"Three years. I called it quits because she wanted something I didn't."

I raised an eyebrow. "Which was?"

He finally looked up at me. "Kids."

"Ah. You don't want them."

"I'm not a huge baby person. Older kids, teenagers, I can hang with. But you obviously have to raise children for a decade before they morph into those, and I don't think I can, or want to, do that. The accident solidified it for me.

"I told her from the beginning, but she would always blow it off and say something like, 'Well, we will see about it in the future'. She finally realized I wasn't going to change my mind two and a half years into our relationship, and I think she tried to talk herself out of having kids for my sake. But she deserved children if she wanted them, so I called things off. I had no problem being the fall guy if it meant she could have the life she wanted."

I could see the muscles in his face tense and his jaw clench after his confession, but when his eyes met mine, his features softened. Throwing back the whiskey, Landon set the empty glass on the counter before standing and making his way over to me. When I took his outstretched hand, he led us to the couch in front of the fireplace. Falling onto the cushions, he patted the spot next to him. I tipsily obliged.

"Are you feeling a tiny bit better?" he asked.

I sat with my legs curled underneath me, my elbow resting on the top of the couch, and my head in my hand. "Honestly, yes. Between the shower, the food, the wine, and you, I am feeling much better. Better than I thought I could feel at this point."

He smiled. "What time are you supposed to be at the courthouse?"

"Ten-thirty."

"I don't start work until ten, so I'll cook us breakfast before we leave."

The room around us was spinning ever-so-slightly, but Landon remained steady.

"You're really gorgeous, do you know that?" The alcohol made me brave and loopy. "And you're such a good person. It blows my mind that you're single."

Shaking his head, he stared at me. "I'm not single. I'm with you."

My cheeks flushed pink. "Which I don't understand," I started, and he shot me a look that was somewhere between frustration and exhaustion. "But I'm trying to," I finished, and he relaxed.

"That's all I'm asking. I just want you to try to see yourself the way I see you."

"And how is that, exactly?" I teased, praying the wine vastly improved my flirting abilities.

"Smart," he said, inching closer to me. "Beautiful. Funny. An amazing mom. An incredible human being." At this point, our knees were touching, and my skin felt like it was smoldering beneath his pajama bottoms.

"Hot as hell in my clothes," he added, his voice low.

In one movement, he pulled me onto his lap, and my legs immediately spread apart on either side of his toned lower body. Running his fingers up and down my sides, he gave a slow, content sigh. "I wish you were here on better terms because I've been imagining this night for a very long time."

I leaned forward, pressing my chest against his, and whispered in his ear. "Thanks to you, I have momentarily forgotten how terrible this week has been, and would love to make it somewhat redeemable by being with you." As I pulled away, I felt him harden underneath me.

Grabbing a fistful of my hair, Landon's lips met mine. Unlike in the restaurant parking lot, this kiss was calm, unhurried. His hands combed through my tresses and slowly trailed down my back, tracing the curve of my spine. Without realizing until it was too late, I let out a low moan. His touch felt so damn good.

Determined not to break our kiss, he carefully lifted up the bottom of my shirt and slipped his hands under, resting them on my hips. He tried to pull me closer, but the space between us had closed long ago.

The whiskey on his breath tasted sweet, and every time I inhaled, the scent of his soap and cologne filled my lungs. Being this close to him was intoxicating. My worries had temporarily abandoned me, my depression was momentarily absent, and warmth radiated throughout my entire body. What I wouldn't give to feel this way for the rest of my life.

Still lip-locked, I leaned back, feeling for the hem of his shirt. Mimicking his ease, I drew it upward, gradually revealing his suspectedly impressive abs and chest. He quickly pulled his arms away from me, slipping them out of the sleeves before returning his hands to my body. I slid it up to his chin, pausing our kiss so I could finally remove the fabric that separated my torso from his. He was nearly gasping in anticipation after the shirt passed over his face, and I tossed it onto the floor behind us.

"My turn?" he asked, and I nodded.

Moving his face next to mine, I could feel his breath against my cheek and the low, steady vibration of an appreciative hum in my ear as his fingers grazed my skin. Inch by inch, he bunched the material in his hands as he made his way upward. When he reached my shoulders, I took the shirt from Landon's grasp and yanked it over my head, throwing it to the floor in the same vicinity of his abandoned shirt. Between the heat from his stare and the warmth from the fireplace behind me, I was burning up.

"God, you're beautiful," he sighed. "Jaw-droppingly, mind-blowingly stunning."

I leaned into him again, breaking his gaze out of desperation to feel more of him against me. As we kissed, I tucked my hands behind his back, gliding them down toward his pants. Finding his belt, I encircled his waist and moved my hips away to gain access to the buckle. Landon threw his head back and groaned before moving one hand off my back and onto his pants.

"Sam," he breathed. "There is nothing I want more right now than to make love to you."

The hesitation in his voice made me freeze.

"But I want you to be in a clear state of mind before we do this. I don't want you to regret anything, nor do I want you to feel pressured into having sex with me because of…everything."

I did not see that coming. Pulling back even more, I discovered even *he* was starting to spin. Crap, I was drunk. "I realize now that I am very inebriated, so I'm not going to argue with you. If it's any consolation, though, I will still want to have sex with you when I'm sober. This is not a drunken-fueled desire, I promise."

He gave me a sad smile. "I hope not. I just don't want there to be any regrets on your end. I'm sorry I got carried away. I see you and," he paused, sighing. "It's a struggle to control myself. I hope you aren't mad."

Ungracefully, I slid off his lap and onto the couch next to him. Why was everything moving so quickly? Closing my eyes, I replied, "I can't be mad at you for being a gentleman. I'm a little surprised, but also feel incredibly respected." Opening one eye, I watched as he ran his fingers absentmindedly up and down the inside of my leg.

"The room is spinning," I whispered, and he smiled again. I shut my eye, gaining relief from the shifting walls around me.

When I came to again, I recognized Landon's room from my brief walkthrough. After settling in beside me, I curled up against him, relishing in an unfamiliar feeling. For the first time in a long time, my head wasn't filled with thoughts and anxiety. Instead, it contained blissful nothingness.

Taking advantage of my silent mind and tired body, I allowed myself to drift off to sleep, with Landon's arm draped heavily around my body, almost as if he were protecting me from what was to come.

CHAPTER THIRTEEN

The smell of breakfast roused me from my slumber, my stomach grumbling with hunger. At some point during the night, I had taken two ibuprofen from the bottle on the nightstand next to me, which I assumed Landon had strategically placed there before we passed out. I tentatively stretched, waiting for the body aches that followed a night of drinking to remind me that I was too old to partake in that, but nothing happened. Wiggling my limbs, I was shocked to realize I felt okay, albeit tired. Pulling the covers away from my body, I saw I was still shirtless. Did I dare?

Feeling clear-headed and somehow maintaining some of the braveness I had last night while drunk, I decided that yes, I *did* dare. Pausing to mouthwash and finger-comb my hair in Landon's bathroom, I made my way out to the kitchen wearing only a bra and his pajama bottoms. To my delight, he was also still shirtless, frying up eggs and bacon over the stove. Two slices of bread were sitting patiently in the toaster, waiting to be burnt to perfection. His hair was disheveled, and a pair of pajama bottoms clung to his hips.

Coming up behind him, I placed my hands on both of his biceps and leaned into him.

"I don't think it's safe for you to cook bacon shirtless," I whispered.

He moved his head to kiss me. "It's definitely not.

161

I've already had a few grease casualties. But it's worth it now." He slid us away from the stove before wrapping his arms around me and gently pushing his tongue into my mouth. The warmth from last night instantly returned, and my legs felt wobbly.

After a few seconds, the bacon began to angrily pop and sizzle on the skillet. Landon sighed and gave me a final kiss before refocusing his attention on the food. "Did you sleep okay?"

Sitting on my barstool, I nodded. "The liquids and the drugs you left on the nightstand? Both were a very good call. I'm feeling much better than I should, thanks to you." I watched him while he cooked, admiring his toned back and shoulders.

As he offloaded some bacon onto a nearby plate, he half turned to look at me. "Did you and Charles date long before you got pregnant with Raegan?"

His question made me second-guess my decision to stay shirtless, as discussing my history with Charles wasn't exactly…romantic. "A grand total of two months, I believe? And I'm not sure you could even call it dating. Casually sleeping with is probably more accurate. Of course, I wasn't on birth control, and Charles, being the fantastic guy he is, assured me he would pull out every time. Surprise, surprise," I said, wrapping my arms around myself as if there was a sudden chill.

Landon faced the stove again. "And then his family basically forced you to get married?"

"Yes, so our pregnancy out of wedlock wouldn't tarnish the family's pristine reputation." I rolled my eyes. "They paid for an apartment off campus so we could live together as a 'family' while Charles finished his degree. No one ever gave me the option of continuing my education, because after all, it was *my* fault I got pregnant."

He sighed and shook his head. "And Harrison?"

I leaned back, gathering my hair into a ponytail. "Harrison was the product of a drunken night, not unlike the occasion Raegan was conceived, but that time, I was on birth control. Even though Raegan was only two when I got pregnant with Harrison, I knew my relationship with Charles wasn't going to last. I didn't want to risk having another kid with him. But only abstinence is one hundred percent effective, and one missed period later…" I trailed off.

He grabbed two plates from the cabinet and served up breakfast. Joining me at the island, he cocked his head, a fork dangling loosely from his grip. "Would you have stayed with him if it wasn't for the cheating?"

I stared at the plate of food in front of me, wondering when the last time my breakfast consisted of more than a cup of coffee and a protein bar or pastry. "No, but I couldn't tell you when I was going to leave him if it weren't for the picture I received in an anonymous email. Like I said, I knew from the beginning we were doomed. You can't change a person. Charles was, and still is, a philanderer, and his mother always bails him out of difficult situations. I never wanted to marry him, but I was young and they pressured us. I would have been fine raising Raegan on my own without being legally tied to Charles. Even after we were married, I was always a single parent, and I had a feeling that's how things would stay.

"I hoped he would come around the first few years after the kids were born. But he didn't. He ignored them just as much then as he did up until a few days ago, and

I would bet everything that he's not spending time with them now. I can guarantee he strictly relies on Raegan and the nurse he hired to care for Harrison and treats Raegan like she doesn't exist.

"And it took me so long to understand this, to fully comprehend he didn't care about his own children. When the realization did hit me all those years later, I was too exhausted to fight. Between raising Raegan and Harrison and then later, working, I didn't have the energy to even contemplate divorce, much less file the paperwork. Once they got older and things started to mostly settle down, though, that's when I started really thinking about it. Then, lo and behold, I was emailed a picture of Charles shagging his secretary, and that was it. My suspicions were confirmed. And he was gone. He doesn't know about the picture, but he didn't argue with me when I accused him of cheating."

Absentmindedly, Landon moved his eggs around. "It's mind-boggling how men can just check out of relationships. I'm not saying it happens all of the time, obviously, but I frequently hear of men deserting their families because they were just...done. Burnt out, couldn't take the pressure, whatever their excuse was. And regardless of their reasoning, it's always selfish. Do husbands think their wives never experience burnouts? Day in and day out, raising kids, working, trying to maintain a household? And yet, it's rare that a mom just up and leaves her family; it's most often the father. And society has somehow made it seem acceptable. 'Oh, he wasn't feeling appreciated.' Or, 'Oh, he was tired of supporting his family'."

Now gripping the fork so tightly that his knuckles were white, he began jutting the prongs angrily into his eggs. "Mothers hardly ever feel appreciated. Wives hardly ever feel appreciated. I think it's safe to say women usually suffer more than men when it comes to mental health-related issues, and yet, when women ask for help, they're weak and are scoffed at. 'They aren't trying hard enough'. 'They're overthinking things'. Our world has set men up to succeed regardless of their behaviors and attitudes, and women are destined to fail, no matter how hard they try not to."

He finally released the fork, its clattering onto the plate echoing throughout the kitchen. "I'm going to step off my soap-box now. Bottom line, I'm sorry you had to go through all of this. And even though it took a while, I'm glad you were finally able to separate yourself from him. You never deserved the life he and his stupid family forced you to live."

I tilted my head and blinked a few times to ensure the person sitting next to me was real and not a figment of my imagination. Landon was the type of man I never thought could exist in my world after nearly resigning myself to a terrible marriage. Now here I was on the road to divorce, and here *he* was, cooking me breakfast shirtless and expressing his frustration regarding the unreasonable expectations and standards society placed on women.

Talk about an incredible turn of events.

Bringing his barstool as close to mine as possible, he kissed me again. "I'm also glad you feel okay after last night. I was unsure of how things would go down this morning with the amount of alcohol you had. No judgement—I'm honestly impressed."

"Yeah, well, if I hadn't drunk that much, last night could have gone differently," I pointed out. "Even though I'm not hungover, I still have regrets."

His eyes lingered on mine, and I saw they were filled with the same fervor from hours earlier. Noticing the clock on the wall behind him, I deduced we had a couple of hours before we had to leave. Grabbing the fork and loading it with eggs, I began shoveling the food into my mouth.

"In a hurry?" he asked, his eyes widening.

I pointed to the time. "You have to go to work in a few hours, I have to be at the courthouse soon after that, and if we are going to finish what we started last night, we need to get moving."

He stopped mid-chew. "Seriously?"

"I mean, I would say we could do it now, but the food is helping absorb the small amount of alcohol left in me. Besides, I'll probably perform better with food. It's on my label."

He began eating at a pace that rivaled lightspeed. "I wasn't sure you would still want to," he said, his voice muffled by a mouthful of bacon. "Again, don't feel pressured. Hopefully we will get many more opportunities, and by the grace of God, under better circumstances."

Clearing my plate, I stood up and placed it in the sink on my way to the pantry. Grabbing another water bottle, I returned to his side, but this time, I faced outward with my elbows resting on the island. "We can't *not* finish what we started last night; circumstances momentarily be damned. And like I said, the alcohol didn't make me want to be with you more than I already do when I'm sober. It's impossible. Nothing could make me want to have sex with you more," I said, but then eyed his pants. "Cancel that. Those on the floor with our shirts would drastically increase my desire to sleep with you."

Landon dropped the piece of bacon he was holding and stood up so fast the barstool tipped over. Lifting me off the ground, he carried me into his room within a matter of strides and placed me on the bed. "You were done, right?" he nearly growled.

I fell back against the duvet. "Very much so." Our lips met as he hovered over me, his long, muscular body dwarfing mine. Moving his kiss from my lips to my shoulders before pausing at the tops of my breasts, I slowly raked my nails down his back, causing him to arch against me. Every inch of him was hard, and I could feel my own desire increasing.

Lowering himself onto his elbows, he reached around to unclasp my bra. "Is it okay if I touch you here?" he asked, staring at my breasts. "I know people have triggers, and I don't want to—"

I shook my head, cutting him off. "It's fine. Everywhere you want to touch me is fine. In fact, *please* touch me everywhere."

He smiled and nodded before unhooking my bra and pulling it forward. After my arms slipped out, he tossed it onto the floor with sheer abandon. Caressing my right breast, he took my nipple in his mouth and began gently sucking. My body curved to meet his, a groan escaping my lips. After a minute, he switched to my left breast, deliberately taking his time while I writhed under him.

My hands wandered from his back to his glutes, and I cupped them slightly, pulling his hardness closer. I wasn't against foreplay—hell, it was a much-needed thing—but because I hadn't had sex in ages, it wasn't taking much to turn me on.

"I need you naked, now," I commanded, and Landon pulled away from me, his eyebrows raised.

"Are you not enjoying this?"

My chest was heaving; my breathing was erratic. "I'm enjoying it too much, that's the problem. I want you inside of me before I finish." Without hesitation, he rolled off of me to free himself of his pants, and it took everything in me not to gasp. It was officially safe to say that every inch of Landon was utterly astounding, and the temporary shock of seeing him, *all* of him, made me pause long enough for him to move between my legs.

"If I do this," he began, reaching to hook his fingers over the waistband of my bottoms, "slowly…" He tugged lightly, making them gradually slide down my hips as he moved backwards. "Will you…" I squirmed in anticipation. This man was killing me.

"Landon," I said, my voice stern. "For the love of God, get these damn pants off and stop torturing me. Or I will get you back for it later."

A slow grin crossed his face before he finally discarded the pajamas onto the carpet. After standing back to gaze at me, he got onto his hands and knees and inched his way up my body, stopping and kissing my skin every so often. When our faces were parallel, he slid his hand under my head and pulled me close, exploring my mouth with his own. With his erection throbbing against my thigh, I reached down and stroked it while he kissed me, causing him to emit a guttural moan.

I placed my other hand against his chest, my fingers tracing his abs. "I don't know if I've mentioned this before, but you are so unbelievably attractive," I said between kisses.

He chuckled. "I pale in comparison to you."

Pushing him back against the bed, we shifted so I was on top. "Condoms are in there," he breathed, his eyes darting toward the end table. I moved off of him to access the top drawer and grab the box. Tearing the packet open, I slipped a condom on his incredibly impressive shaft before straddling him and tossing the box and wrapper in the direction of the nightstand.

His blue irises bore into mine as I slowly lifted my hips and slid him inside of me. Resting my forehead against his, I ran my fingers through his hair and kissed him while leisurely moving up and down. He began to shift underneath me, attempting to quicken my speed, but his efforts were in vain. Purposefully maintaining my unhurried pace, my lips trailed off his so I could whisper in his ear. "I told you I would get you back for tormenting me."

He groaned. "This is evil."

After a few minutes, I realized I was torturing us both and quickened my motions to match his desired rhythm. He reached up to caress my breasts, and the overwhelming arousal that swept through my body made me painfully aware of the fact that I wasn't going to last much longer.

"Landon." I tried to say his name with a sense of urgency, but instead, it came out as more of a sigh. Moving a hand from my breast to my back, he ducked slightly, his mouth now where his fingertips had been seconds earlier.

"Landon," I said again, my voice somehow stronger. Between the sensation of him throbbing inside of me and the tug of his lips on my breasts, I knew I was hurtling toward a mind-blowing orgasm. Understanding my tone, he sped up; his hips thrusted faster and harder against mine. Shifting my hands from his biceps to his headboard, I sensed our euphoria was about to peak.

"Sam," he gasped, bringing my face down to his and kissing me as he relentlessly drove himself inside me. That was it. I felt myself grow tighter around him before I spiraled, and as I came, Landon stilled under me and groaned against my lips, his own release rendering him immobile.

Once our bodies relaxed, I placed my hands on his chest and grinned. "That was definitely worth the wait."

He stared up at me, his face content. "What I would give to stay like this forever."

Laying against him, Landon ran his fingers through my hair as I listened to his heartbeat. The heat from his body and the steady sound of his heart were making me drowsy, and after a few minutes, I begrudgingly lifted myself off of him. He moaned in protest, but turned to face me as I curled up next to him, sliding an arm under my pillow. "Thank you for the best night and morning of my life."

"I think you just mean morning, since all we did last night was drink and pass out. Well, all *I* did was drink and pass out."

He shook his head. "I mean night and morning. Just sleeping next to you, being close to you…" he trailed off. "Since the night of the accident, I have nightmares every so often. But feeling you next to me—I slept amazingly well. Even though you were snoring a little bit. It was still magical." He winked.

I scoffed. "I was not snoring."

Pulling me against him, our lips met once more. "You were. Just a tiny bit, though. If I had been asleep, I wouldn't have noticed. But I was awake, staring at you like a stalker, because I can't get over how lucky I am to have you in my life."

I studied his face, trying to memorize every line and feature in that moment. "The feeling is mutual. You pulled me out of my comfort zone, stood up for me and my children, and made me feel like a normal human being. You picked me up, literally, when I was at my worst. I don't know what I did in a past life to deserve you, but it must have been epic."

He smiled. "It's probably all of the things you've done in *this* life. Don't sell yourself short, Sam. You're amazing. And I will do all those things one hundred times over if it means keeping you in mine."

We laid in bed for a few minutes, basking in the post-sex glow and dopamine until he let out a long sigh. Sitting up, he slowly removed his arm out from under my head before making his way to the bathroom. I awoke a few minutes later to him kissing my forehead.

"Let's go, Sleeping Beauty. I have to get you back to your place so you can get ready for court."

When we pulled up to my house, he insisted on walking with me to the front steps. "You really didn't need to get out of the car," I said, unlocking my front door. When I turned to face him, he grinned and pulled me in for a kiss.

"I wanted to make sure you got into your house safely. Plus, I can do this without having to lean over a center console. It's a win-win."

I slid my hands into his back pockets and drew him close. "I would have to agree." We kissed again—this time longer—and I could feel my stress momentarily lessening. Eventually, I brought my hand up to his face. "Thank you for everything," I whispered, and he rested his head against mine.

A few seconds passed before he reluctantly moved away from me and stepped off the porch. As he walked to his car, he called back to me. "Please let me know how court goes."

I watched him drive away before I stepped into my house and closed the door behind me. Leaning against it, I shook my head. I wanted to spend more time thinking about Landon and how we spent our morning, but the reality of the rest of the day was hitting hard now that he was gone.

The *ex parte* was only a small battle in the overall war between Charles and me, and once the kids were back in my care, I needed to work with Jules to ensure that asshole could never disrupt our lives again. After that, I could spend every available second engrossed in thoughts about Landon, but until then, I needed to focus. My children's wellbeing depended on me, and I couldn't let Raegan and Harrison down again. I had to fight as if our lives depended on it, because they did.

CHAPTER FOURTEEN

Like a lost puppy, I trailed behind Jules as we walked to our assigned courtroom. "Charles isn't going to be here?"

Abruptly turning to face me, Jules narrowed her eyes and pursed her lips. Even though she was my attorney, her lawyer persona scared the daylights out of me. Place her in a courtroom, and like flipping a switch, she transformed from a happy, friendly person into a blood-seeking shark. Her reputation of being both feared and respected in the divorce attorney industry was why I hired her, despite her incredibly steep retainer. "His attorney knows we are filing an *ex parte* application for a custody order, but neither of them needs to be present. You are the one filing—you are the only one who needs to plead her case in court. And you need to be prepared for the judge to know and admire Charles, since everyone in this damn city is in love with that man." She paused to roll her eyes.

"You need to be honest, but you also have to keep your emotions at bay. You must be factual and explain why Charles isn't fit to have custody of the children at this time. The judge needs to understand that Charles is using your children as pawns in this divorce and he does not have their best interests at heart."

I gulped. We definitely should have rehearsed this more than the two times in front of the courthouse only a few minutes earlier.

A bailiff opened the door and motioned for us to enter. "This meeting will be held in chambers," she informed us, and we followed her through the courtroom and into a room off to the right of the judge's bench. A man with receding gray hair, glasses, and a black robe sat behind a desk, and he barely acknowledged us as we approached him. Finally, he glanced up at Jules and me, then returned his gaze to a stack of papers in his hand. "An *ex parte* application against the mayor, huh?" Jules and I wordlessly stared at him.

"Why do you think he is unfit to care for his children?" the judge asked.

Jules nodded at me, and I took in shaky breath. "Your Honor, Charles does not have the skills or training to care for our children, especially Harrison, my fourteen-year-old son. He has cerebral palsy and has been under my care, as well as under the supervision of a thoroughly vetted, trusted caregiver since birth. Charles hasn't—"

The judge held up his hand, halting me. "The mayor lived in your home with you until a few months ago, correct? So why do you think he doesn't have the skills or training?"

I nodded. "That is correct, sir, but just because Charles resided with Harrison doesn't mean he knows how to care for him."

The judge raised his eyebrows before leaning back in his chair. After folding his arms across his chest, he released a long sigh. "Mrs. Hawley, as I'm sure you're aware, I, along with nearly everyone else in this city, have known the Hawleys for decades. I'm having a hard time believing Charles would purposefully neglect or not care for his children while they are with him. He's had them for what, two days? I'm sure there is a learning curve when it comes to caring for a child such as Harrison, and because you don't have concrete proof that Charles isn't meeting his children's needs, I feel inclined not to remove them from his home."

My cheeks grew hot as fury surged through my veins. I'd lost this *ex parte* application before it had even started, simply because of who I was married to and how much everyone in this godforsaken community worshipped him and his family.

Jules cleared her throat. "Your Honor, if Mr. Hawley had any intention of caring for his children following his exit from his shared home with Ms. Hawley, he would have had everything Harrison needs ready to go *prior* to taking them. He did not, Your Honor. He took my client's items, instead. This proves he never planned on caring for his children following his separation. Until now, that is, but I'm not going to interject my thoughts about Charles and his timing."

Jules' logic made the judge furrow his brow. Rubbing his forefingers together, he gently rocked back and forth in his chair, the squeaky sound of the protesting seat hinges filling the otherwise uncomfortable silence. Eventually, he shook his head. "I'm sorry, Mrs. Hawley. I believe Charles can care for his children. I'm going to deny this *ex parte* application for a custody order without prejudice. I will, however, schedule a status conference for next Monday regarding the divorce proceedings and a noticed motion for the following week."

Jules reached out and clenched her hand around my wrist. "Let's go, Samantha."

She swiftly ushered me out of the judge's chambers

and courtroom at breakneck speed, knowing all too well what was about to happen. Dragging me down the courthouse steps and off to the right of the grounds, she located a park bench next to the municipal building and beelined for it. After forcing me into the seat, she knelt in front of me. "Breathe, Sam. You need to breathe."

I stared at the ground in an attempt to stave off the nausea and dizziness that was threatening to overtake me. I registered voices of those passing by, but they all sounded distant, almost foreign. Everything, including my line of vision, was starting to narrow.

"Sam." Jules snapped her fingers, breaking my vacant stare. "BREATHE."

Gasping for air upon her command, the world came rushing back to me; the surrounding noises roaring in my ears like trumpets. Filling my lungs once more, the full reality of his denial hit me like a freight train. I wasn't getting my kids back. They weren't coming home today. They weren't coming home for who knew how long. Harrison was at risk; Raegan was sinking into depression. I lost my kids *again*.

"Now you're taking too many breaths," Jules pointed out. "This was always a possibility, Sam. The next step is to get everything in order and try again on Monday. Charles' attorney hasn't even sent us his discovery, leading me to believe they haven't completed it, and it's been months since you've filed for divorce. I don't care if Charles and the judge on Monday have matching tattoos—Charles has to give us his discovery. It's the law. If he doesn't, he can be held in contempt."

"What if something terrible happens to Harrison?" I asked, my voice hollow. "What about Raegan? She hasn't gone to school since she was shot. She's doing home study at Charles' insistence, which means she's missing her friends and therapy. I haven't heard from her in days; I'm sure Lydia took her phone." Burying my face in my hands, I allowed my tears to fall freely through my fingers and onto the cement below. "What happens if I show up at Lydia's house and ask if I can see the kids? Just for a few minutes to make sure they're okay. Or demand that Raegan and Harrison come home with me? Could I get in trouble?"

Jules sighed. "Lydia and Charles would pull a power move, no doubt. They'd probably threaten you with trespassing, claim harassment, or some other bullshit. You and I are aware that Charles having the kids is a disaster on so many levels, but like the judge said, Charles has only had the children for a few days. As awful as it is, we need to give him at least a week to prove he is incompetent. If you try to see or take the kids back now, especially after the *ex parte* was denied…you won't look good in court."

Groaning, I shook my head. "I'm such an idiot. I never should have let it get this far."

"Sure, we should have followed up with the divorce and drafted a custody plan sooner, but I also understand where you were coming from. If Charles wasn't trying to take the kids after he moved out, which I know was your main fear when filing for divorce, why rock the boat? But now here we are, fighting the worst-case scenario.

"I know this isn't what you wanted or needed to hear. It's absolutely asinine that you can't have your children right now. Charles isn't equipped to handle himself, much less his children. The entire situation is just…bullshit. It's all bullshit." She stood up to join me on the bench and gently took my hand. "I'm not going to lie, though. If we get another judge who favors Charles, our future court hearings are going to be battles. And seeing how many people in this city know the Hawleys, I think it's safe to assume we are going to need to be prepared for a major fight to finalize this divorce and get your children back."

I should have waited until Harrison was eighteen years old to file for divorce. I should have sucked it up like Lydia and endured a loveless, terrible marriage for the benefit of my children. "What happens if I don't get my kids back?" I whispered. I could feel bile creep up my throat as the words crossed my lips, burning every inch of my esophagus.

Jules shook her head, her curls bouncing. "It won't happen. The worst-case scenario is they split custody fifty-fifty. Raegan is of legal age in a few months—they will listen to her testimony, and we will get a few more people on our side. If they still ignore the evidence..." she paused. "We will see what happens if we get there. For now, go home. Tomorrow, we start planning."

****

Somewhere in the middle of my mental breakdown in the courthouse parking lot, I managed to call Landon with the sole purpose of relaying what had happened with the *ex parte*. Twenty minutes later, he appeared next to my car, softly knocking on the window.

Gently urging me out of the vehicle, he slid into the driver's seat and motioned for me to sit on his lap. Collapsing against him, he rested his head atop mine and began rubbing my back in slow, methodical circles.

"I hate today. I hate the judge, I hate Charles, I hate this stupid city, I hate myself for putting my children in

178

this position," I sobbed.

He said nothing, his breathing remaining slow and steady and his touch constant against my skin. Whether it was his presence, the calming techniques he was inadvertently using, or both, I managed to pacify my frantic brain much faster with him here. After a few minutes, I wiped my eyes and sat up.

He studied me, his shoulders lowered and the brightness in his eyes vacant. "What can help you right now? Rage cleaning? Although I'm fairly certain your entire house is spotless at this point. A walk, maybe? Drinking? If we start at two after my last appointment, I'll be sober long before I have to go to work tomorrow morning."

A small laugh escaped me. "I don't think I can drink that much two days in a row, though it sounds very tempting. I should not have taken five days off from work. At least the hospital keeps me busy. Apart from my meeting with Jules tomorrow, I have nothing to do but sit and hate myself for the poor choices I made. Clearing my schedule was a huge oversight."

"We can get the hell out of this place and go to dinner. Atlanta? It's a little far, but there's obviously a ton of restaurants to choose from. Whatever you want to do, I'm down," he said, putting his hand in mine.

"I would love to burn this entire city to the ground," I said.

He nodded. "Let's kidnap the kids and make it happen."

Leaning back against his chest, I sighed and closed my eyes. What would be a legal equivalent to lighting the city on fire? Then it hit me. It was catty and ballsy, but I was immediately in love with the idea. "We go to dinner." I straightened, staring at Landon with a tentative smile.

He tilted his head. "When you shot up that fast, I thought you were going to suggest something illicit. I got lowkey excited."

"Here's the plot twist, though. We go to dinner *in Madison*."

His eyes widened. "Oh, damn. Are you sure that's what you want to do with everything going on?"

I was talking fast, my excitement overcoming any and all logic. "Everyone already hates me and thinks Charles can do no wrong. I'm done hiding and living my life quietly. If he wants to make me out to be the bad person, I'm going to live it up, and the entire population of this community can kiss my ass while I'm doing just that."

A smile broke out across his face and his eyes sparkled. "It's brilliant. I would love to flaunt you around the city on my arm, and if we can stick it to Charles and all his minions at the same time, it's a win for both of us."

When I opened my front door to him four hours later, he stared at me for five seconds without blinking. "I'm sorry," he said, taking me by the waist and leading us into the house. Pressing me up against the nearby wall, his hands were all over me, his tongue finding mine. "I don't think we're going to make it to dinner if you're going to wear this dress. I don't want to leave the house," he breathed.

Deciding to go all out for tonight, I stopped by a boutique on the way home from court and found a navy-colored dress that was probably meant for girls half my age. It fell about three inches above the knee and had a high halter neckline, a fitted bodice, a flowy skirt, and sheer lace straps on the back. I also bought strappy black heels that tied above my ankles and a cute lace cardigan to complete the outfit. My hair was down and loosely curled, and I had applied enough makeup so the wrinkles and dark circles under my eyes were a thing of the past. Even I had to admit I was impressed with my appearance, and that rarely happened.

"I could say the same about you." I smiled as I grabbed his tie and pulled him against me. He was wearing the same dress shoes he wore on our first date, but tonight, he was sporting a light blue dress shirt, a gray dinner jacket, and a pair of gray fitted dress pants. I knew we had dinner plans, but the overwhelming desire to get naked and ditch that reservation was mutual.

Placing his hands on my thighs, he lifted me up and I instinctively wrapped my legs around his waist while snaking my arms around his neck. Our kiss never breaking, he carried me to the couch and sank onto the cushions. I could feel his hardness growing under me, and my breathing hitched in my throat. Lacing his fingers through my hair, a moan escaped his lips before he suddenly froze and dropped his hands at his sides. "I can't mess up your hair." He broke away from me. "I'm sorry I got carried away."

I stared at him, panting. "I don't want to go to dinner anymore. I want to finish what we've started. Then we can revisit the topic of a public meal."

Landon shook his head. "We can't. We have to go to dinner now, because once I'm done with you, your hair and makeup," he gestured, "won't look presentable."

Jesus, take the wheel.

Slowly moving my legs out from behind him, I slid off his lap. "I know you're concerned about how I feel regarding dinner tonight, but how are *you* feeling about this? You have a lot at stake, too."

He put both hands on his knees, exhaling slowly. "I have no problem with the people of this city knowing I'm crazy about a magnificent woman. Raegan isn't under my care, so they can't say anything about me crossing any boundaries. I mean, they can, but it will be a lie. And anything else they want to say, let them. I only care about you and the wellbeing of your kids."

"When you say stuff like that, it makes me want to accept the challenge of you making me completely unpresentable," I warned, putting my hand on the inside of his thigh.

Placing his hand over mine, he slowly moved it toward the middle of his leg. "I already need a minute to recover from our greeting. You touch me *there*, and going out will be off the table for the entire night."

"Don't threaten me with a good time." I winked as I stood up.

He remained seated for a few minutes, pinching the bridge of his nose and his eyes tightly closed. Finally, he stood, and I eyed the zipper area of his pants. It was no longer tight against him.

"Ready?" I asked gleefully, and he shook his head.

"I swear, Sam," he said, as we headed to his car, "you drive me crazy in the best possible way."

We decided to seal our fate at The Eatery for its notability and amazing food, but the open floor plan that allowed guests to see other patrons didn't hurt, either. As we walked toward the restaurant, hands intertwined, I noticed a line wrapped around the building, which seemed excessive for a Wednesday night. "What's happening here?" I glanced around at the crowd.

Landon shrugged. "There may or may not be a school fundraiser happening in one of the event spaces." Everyone in Madison supported the local schools— especially the two high schools. Friday night lights was everything to this community.

I paused, still far enough away from the restaurant that we were out of everyone's line of sight. Did I really want to do this? I had been angry earlier—angry at Charles, angry at the judge, angry at the entire community—and I still was. But was I ready to face the inevitable inundation of harsher stares and louder whispers from here on out? Everyone would think *I* was the cheater, regardless of what I knew and the evidence I had to prove it.

On the flip side, a majority of the community had disliked me from day one. I was an outsider who "trapped one of their own," a woman who never joined their cliques, and a mother who worked fulltime. I would almost bet my life I could have sex with Landon in the middle of the restaurant and no one would hate me more than they already did.

"We can leave," he said, sensing my hesitation, but I shook my head firmly.

"No. We are going to have a great dinner, enjoy each other's company, return the stares of everyone glaring at us, and then go home to finish what we started."

Sure enough, small, audible gasps could be heard as we walked by the crowds of people waiting in line, and I couldn't help but smile as Landon and I made our way to a table against the main dining room wall. He pulled out my chair and waited for me to sit before taking the seat next to me and rubbing my thigh. I could feel dozens of people staring at us, their glares like daggers. The clinking of silverware against bowls and plates could not mask the amount of whispering happening in that moment.

Completely unfazed, Landon picked up the menu and casually glanced at it. Following his lead, I also put the leather-bound booklet in front of my face, but left it low enough for me to see the room. I stared at the menu for a few seconds before covertly shifting my eyes to the tables in front of me, mildly shocked by the number of individuals blatantly staring at us. No one made any attempt to hide their looks of disdain and disbelief; their mouths were all hanging open and their eyes were narrowed. The audacity of them judging me made my anger from earlier resurface. Shifting my menu, I moved a hand to Landon's leg.

His irises darkened slightly. "If that hand moves any closer in one direction..." he trailed off.

"Really? Even here?" I asked, amazed.

He held up his menu to hide his words from the rest of the room. "You turn me on when you simply *glance* at me. When you touch me, it's a struggle to maintain my composure. I'm not lying when I say you drive me crazy. I feel like a teenager again. Actually," he stopped. "I never even felt like this when I was a teenager. It's just what *you* do to me." Leaning over, he kissed me softly, and someone behind us uttered a sigh of disgust.

A server, who appeared to be about Raegan's age, materialized in front of us, and even she couldn't hide her shock. "Dr. Ford?" she asked, her jaw dropping. Looking from him to me, her mouth fell open even further. "Mrs. Hawley?"

I gave her the sweetest smile I could muster. "Soon to be Miss. Can we get two glasses of water, please? And a bottle of wine?" I directed the last question at Landon, who simply nodded. I turned back to the server. "And a bottle of your best merlot, please."

She stared at us for a beat before turning around and heading toward the kitchen.

He raised an eyebrow. "I know you feel like this is the first time you've taken control of your life and shown people your true colors, but this fierce woman sitting before me," he looked me up and down, "is the Sam I've always seen. I'm glad you're not picking and choosing who you show it to anymore, because everyone deserves to know the real you. It's magical and frightening, all at the same time."

I pressed my lips together and smiled. "I've been screwed over ever since I got here, so it's about damn time. Retribution, baby."

Dinner arrived promptly after we ordered, and as we ate, the background noise in the restaurant all but disappeared. Landon and I were lost in great conversation, and the food was divine. When the bill arrived, he went to take it, but I grabbed it out of the server's hand. "I said I was getting the next dinner, and this is the next dinner." He held up his hands in surrender, and moments later we were walking out of the restaurant, our arms wrapped around each other's waists and his jacket around my shoulders.

Just as we were about to step down into the parking lot, I felt someone tug at my purse. Turning around, I saw Mrs. Peters, the bookstore owner, and her husband waiting for valet to bring their car around.

"Well, I declare—" she started, but I cut her off.

"Mrs. Peters!" My falsetto was so high, I was sure neighboring dogs were howling. "What a pleasant surprise! How was your dinner?"

She sneered. "It was a bold move, having dinner with one of our own after just filing for divorce from another one of our beloved neighbors. The mayor, of all people." Her eyes narrowed.

I disengaged my arm from Landon's frame so I could fully face her. "Bless your heart, Mrs. Peters, for being so involved in my business. I just figured after almost eighteen years of living here, people should really get to know the woman they've hated solely based on assumptions and rumors. Give them something to really talk about. Because you know what assuming does."

When we were safely inside his car, Landon looked over at me. "I knew you were a badass the second I met you, but seeing you in action telling someone off…we need to get home."

As the city rushed past the car's windows, I couldn't help but grin. I had officially done it—I had shown everyone that I was stepping out of Charles' shadow and image, and in doing so, I was leaving my timid, meek persona behind. If the people of Madison wanted someone to hate, fine. But I was going to ensure they hated the real me; the person who wasn't going to take their crap anymore. The gloves were off, and I was ready to fight.

CHAPTER FIFTEEN

Removing my phone before tossing my purse onto the entryway table, I spun around to face Landon. He immediately wrapped his arms around me and brought his face to mine. "Where were we?" he asked.

Leaning against the wall in the same spot we found ourselves hours before, I put my foot just above the baseboard to steady myself. The alcohol we had consumed at dinner was making me feel really, *really* good and I could no longer trust my sense of balance.

His hands resuming their place in my hair, Landon traced my jawbone with his lips. "You are so damn gorgeous in this dress," he murmured, creating a trail of kisses from the space behind my ear down to my bare shoulder. Feeling his lips against my skin, my heart began beating erratically, intensifying my headrush. My hands slid down his waist and settled low on his hips, encouraging me to pull him close. Moving his hand out from behind my head and onto the wall behind me, he kissed me. Hard. "That entire dinner, though," he breathed, "I spent fantasizing about getting you out of it. Full disclosure."

I smiled as his lips brushed against mine. "Imagine how I feel. Every shirt you wear fits as if it were tailored to your body. The way they cling to your arms and shoulders—I never thought I could be jealous of clothes." Raking my hands down his abs, I stopped at the top of his slacks. Unbuckling his belt and discarding it on the floor, I started to undo his pants, but he gathered me in his arms and started up the hallway before I could finish.

"Bedroom," he commanded. "The things I want to do to you would be difficult to accomplish against a wall." We barely made it to the edge of my bed before he started undressing me. With my legs hanging off the side of his lap, Landon undid the small button on the halter neckline. When it draped freely against my back, he then moved to the zipper, gently separating the material. I pulled the top half of the dress down around my shoulders and was about to remove my arms from the fabric when he stopped me.

"You're doing my job." Scooping me up, he stood and laid me across the bed. Letting out a contented sigh, he gradually made his way over to me on his hands and knees. "It should be known that I love this dress even more now that I know you don't wear a bra with it." Tugging the top portion of the dress downward until it reached my stomach, he moved his mouth slowly from the base of my neck to the space between my breasts, shifting his weight onto his elbows.

With a sudden sense of urgency, Landon bunched the material in his fists and moved off the bed, removing the rest of my dress in one fluid motion.

As he stood, he began unbuttoning his shirt, his eyes filled with hunger while he admired me on the bed wearing nothing but a flimsy thong and strappy heels. Just as he started to remove his pants, I motioned for him to join me on the bed. Once we were parallel, I hooked a leg over his side to straddle him.

"Now *you're* doing *my* job."

His growing erection made it challenging to remove his pants, but once they were off, I tossed them onto the floor and laid next to him. "Tell me I'm not dreaming," he whispered, his eyes boring into mine.

"If you are, I'm right there with you."

He drew his left hand up my thigh and slowly moved it between my legs. Feeling my wetness, he groaned. "These are now coming off," he said, his hands temporarily leaving me to rid himself of his boxers. "And these," Landon added, removing my underwear and heels. Planking over me, his elbows began to relax, bringing his body closer to mine. When our skin touched, he paused. "I have a condom in my wallet," he said, starting to leave the bed, but I stopped him.

"My tubes were tied after Harrison, and I haven't been with anyone before you. If you aren't worried and you trust me, you don't have to put one on. I will in no way be offended if you want to, though."

In one movement, he was back on his elbows with his legs between mine, hovering at my entrance. "I've never trusted anyone more." He started to ease into me, and I grabbed his thighs, pulling him close, desperate to feel him inside me again.

We moaned in unison, and he began moving at a slow, steady pace once my body adjusted to his. Closing my eyes, I allowed myself to get lost in the moment, willing myself not to come undone with every thrust. He placed a hand under my head and lifted my face to his. "I love you, Sam."

My eyes shot open. "Really?" I asked, instantly realizing my reaction was borderline mood killing.

Undeterred, Landon continued to move in and out of me, his eye contact unwavering. "Since our first dinner together. You agreed to go out with me, despite so many potential obstacles, and you stayed after I told you about the accident."

"Well, you have me beat then, but only by a few hours. I knew I loved you when you offered to go to jail for me."

This caused him to pause. "Going to jail for giving those parents a piece of my mind about their lack of gun safety is one of the less serious offenses I would do on your behalf. It's taken every ounce of self-control not to go after your asshole ex. Anyone who hurts you or your children infuriates me beyond all belief."

Putting my hand on his chest, I stared up at him. "And this is Exhibit A as to why I love you more than you'll ever know." Shifting under him, the anger that temporarily clouded his eyes gave way to uninhibited desire once more. As our lips connected, he began to speed up, and I could feel the slow, pleasure-filled burn start to build inside me. My fingers wrapped around his arms, my nails digging into his skin.

"I'm not going to last much longer," I nearly gasped.

His tempo increased. "You drive me wild, Sam," he whispered.

Starting to tighten around him, I could hear myself moan. "Landon."

He kissed me. "Come for me, Sam." My orgasm came crashing down around me, and seconds later, I could feel Landon's own release.

A little while later, Landon's voice interrupted the silence that had nearly lulled me to sleep. "Sam?"

I turned to him, nuzzling my face against his chest. "Mm-hmm?"

"I mean it—I love you. It wasn't just a spur-of-the-moment thing." He kissed the top of my head.

Listening to his heartbeat, I smiled. "I know. I meant every word, too."

****

Dozens of text notifications popped up on my phone's lock screen as I shut off my alarm the following morning.

Raegan—*You went out with Dr. Ford to The Eatery?*—

I would bet money her phone was going off all night long.

Me—*Yes. I take it you know the girl who was our server?*—

Raegan—*Yes, but she wasn't even the first person I heard it from. Lydia is furious. Definitely called you a few rude names last night. Their phones have been ringing for hours. Good job, Mom.*—

Her message was followed by a winking emoji.

Exiting out of her text, I went to the next message.

Drea—*Peach. How did it go?*—

Drea—*I'm dying over here.*—

Drea—*I need details, please. I'm assuming you spent the night with Landon, and that's why you aren't answering me. That's the only excuse I will allow.*—

Drea—*How was dinner?*—

Drea—*Did everyone stare at you?*—

Drea—*Did Landon Ford murder you and bury your phone with your body?*—

Drea—*Oh my gosh. PEACH.*—

Drea—*ARE YOU STILL HAVING SEX WITH HIM?!?!?!?!?!*—

Drea—*You are. That's why you're not answering me. Oh my gosh.*—

Drea—*You better call me in the morning, girl. I need detaillllllssssssssss.*—

Drea—*I'm serious. Call me.*—

Drea—*I can't believe you had sex. Finally. Good for you, girl.*—

Drea—*But really, call me.*—

Slowly waking up, Landon moved his hand from around my waist to my shoulder. Propping himself up on an elbow, he kissed my skin before peering over my arm. "What time is your meeting with Jules?"

"Eight-thirty. I need to get moving."

He traced my spine with his finger. "Moving…like we did last night?" I rolled over to see a mischievous grin plastered across his face. "I'm just saying, I could really get used to going to bed with you and waking up beside you."

Giving him a quick peck on the lips before getting out of bed, I grabbed a bra and underwear from the dresser on my way to the bathroom. "And how about showering with me?"

Landon appeared in the bathroom doorway seconds later, in all his naked glory. An hour later, he was driving back to his house, and I was heading to Jules' office in Atlanta.

"Georgia is a fault and no-fault state," she said the second I walked into her office and closed the door. She was facing away from me, staring at a whiteboard. The space was divided into two sections: *Divorce* and *Custody*. "Originally, you were going to claim irreconcilable differences, or no-fault. Is that still how you want to proceed?"

I bit my lip. When I first filed, I wanted the process to be as simple and hassle-free as possible. But now that

Charles was messing with me and the kids, I wanted the real reason for the end of our marriage to be known. "No," I finally said.

Jules spun around. "Are we going the adultery route?"

Sitting down at her desk, I nodded. "I'm tired of saving face. If people want to know the real reason why my marriage ended, I'll tell them; whether they choose to believe it or not is their problem."

Jules couldn't hide her smirk. "I fully support your choice, but just know, it means more work for us. Do you still have the picture?"

"I have it printed and saved in multiple locations. No one could find or destroy them all, but I don't think Charles even knows proof of him cheating exists."

"And you don't know who sent it?"

I shrugged and shook my head. "I didn't care to investigate at the time."

Jules turned to her whiteboard and wrote, *photographic evidence* under *Divorce*. "And alimony?"

My leg began to bounce. "Hear me out on this. What if we ask for full physical and legal custody in exchange for Charles forgoing alimony?"

Jules stared at me. "Are you sure you want that?"

"He hasn't helped financially in any way since we separated, and I'm doing fine. I don't need his money. I want my children, and I want him out of my life for good. He's so greedy and money-hungry, I'm fairly certain he would forgo his parental rights in exchange for me not pursing alimony."

"I don't know." She drew in a long breath. "I think you should go for full custody *and* alimony, but let's see how everything plays out. And when it comes to custody,

Carissa Hyde

he hadn't seen or contacted the kids since you kicked him out until Sunday's incident? Six months of radio silence proves him suddenly expressing interest in the kids is a ploy, but because everyone in this city is in that man's back pocket, we will need to have an army behind us. And as much as I hate to push it, we will most likely have to have Raegan testify to really drive the matter home."

I despised the thought of having my kids pick sides and fight against their other parent in court, but Raegan already hated her dad, and Harrison didn't have the ability to testify. My leg jittered faster as my anxiety intensified. This was all such a nightmare.

Folding her hands across her chest, Jules sighed. "Speaking of Raegan, how is she holding up?"

I put my head down on her desk, my leg movement temporarily ceasing. "Charles hired a tutor since her injury, so she's missing her friends and therapy at school. I spoke with her Monday and she texted me this morning, but I have a feeling Lydia is restricting her phone usage."

Jules wrote *prevention of therapy* on the side under *Custody* as I straightened.

"How many other people do we need to testify against Charles? I'm thinking we can get Harrison's primary care doctor, because she knows Charles has rarely shown up for Harrison's appointments over the years. Hospital staff, too. If McKenna is willing and able, we can bring her in. She can testify Charles hasn't been around within the last six months. And even before that, if we're being honest." I raised an eyebrow.

Jules nodded. "Perfect. Send me her information and I'll set up a time to talk with her before the end of next week."

"Anything else?" I asked.

194

Jules rested both hands on her desk and leaned forward. "Monday is just a status conference, so there shouldn't be too much back and forth. We've done everything expected of us, but Charles hasn't. Whether he's pals with the judge or not, he's already in trouble for not handing over what he needs to. The judge will probably give him a few days to give us what we need, since the noticed motion is the following week."

"And the noticed motion will be the hearing for the divorce?" I asked.

She nodded. "Possibly the first of many. I am going to ask if you can have the kids starting next Monday, since that will mark one week since you've seen them. I'm praying the judge will think it's a fair custody swap, but then again, no one sees this man for the monster he truly is."

After texting Jules with McKenna's contact information and the picture of Charles having sex with his secretary, we parted ways and I found myself leaning against the exterior wall of her office building. Lighting my first cigarette in weeks, I inhaled slowly, reveling in the nicotine. I could not wait for all this insanity to be over.

****

I thought it would be difficult returning to work after having five days off, but the chaos that greeted me at six the following morning forced me to hit the ground running. Landon had stayed the night *and* insisted on making me coffee before I left, so I was feeling good for a multitude of reasons. But as always, my warm coffee became chilled after hours of neglect due to rounds and fetching items for patients.

Midway through my shift, I collapsed behind the

nurses' station with the goal of updating patient files. As I stared at the computer, though, I could feel fatigue creep in and my desire to work drastically decrease. Maybe sitting down had been a mistake.

Just as my fingers were hovering over the keyboard preparing to strike, I heard the double doors leading to the geriatric floor open. Before I had a chance to look up, Drea was leaning over the counter, her face in front of the computer monitor. "Ding, dong."

I couldn't help but smile as I stared at her, my head tilted sideways. "Hey, Drea."

She sauntered around the station and plopped into a chair next to me. Throwing her feet up on the desk, she stared at the side of my head as she opened a bag of chips and dug in.

Determined not to be distracted, I updated patient files until I could no longer handle the sound of her chewing and her stare drilling holes into the side of my scalp. Dropping my hands, I widened my eyes and gave her a fake, toothy smile. "Can I help you?"

"I'm just going to wait until you're done with whatever it is you're doing so you can tell me about your new, dare I say it, *boyfriend*."

I shook my head. "My job. I'm doing my job. And you're going to be waiting a long time, because I'm very behind. Not having been here for the last few days is really messing with my motivation to work now that I've sat down. I'd rather be at home, in bed."

"With Landon," Drea finished, and I smacked her arm. "I'm not wrong, though," she pointed out.

I shrugged. "No, you aren't."

Drea let out a long, high-pitched squeal as she crinkled the chip bag in her clenched fists, causing fried potato particles to scatter onto the floor. "I can't believe this!"

"It's a good thing a majority of my patients are deaf, because you would have just killed what little cochlear hairs they had left with that damn screech."

"Peach, you're *glowing*. I mean, you still look like crap because your ex is an ass and your kids are gone, but there's a slight glow under the dark circles and apparent exhaustion! You have a manfriend! Who stuck up for you and Raegan in front of Charles! I got chills when you told me that story. Tell it again. I love it." She clasped her hands together like a child begging for a cookie, the poor chip bag now decimated from excitement.

I chuckled. "Thank you for being happy for me. If I momentarily forget that Charles all but stole my kids from me and is making the divorce process ten times harder than it needs to be, I'm pretty happy, too."

She put her feet down and moved closer to me. "What's going on with all that? You said you have a status conference Monday?"

I nodded. "We've filed our stuff and he hasn't filed his, so I'm hoping they hold him in contempt and I get the kids back. The two situations aren't related at all, but if Charles can't fill out simple paperwork and provide necessary documents to move the divorce forward, he shouldn't be allowed to have the kids. I'm praying the judge sides with me, but he didn't for the *ex parte*, so I'm not feeling super confident."

"That judge better realize he's going to end up under your care sooner than later, since he's old as dirt and you're the charge nurse on the geriatrics floor at the only hospital in Madison," Drea cackled.

I had only entered one more patient file into the system after Drea left before someone sat in the same chair she abandoned. Moving only my eyes, I saw Linda and two other nurses standing behind her.

"Landon Ford, huh?" Linda asked, and the two other nurses smiled.

I was never going to get the patients' information entered into their charts. "Landon Ford." I nodded, my heart skipping a beat when I said his name.

"Everyone's talking about it," Linda said, wiggling her eyebrows.

I pursed my lips. "I don't doubt it. There's not much else to do in this city but gossip."

Ignoring my comment, the brunette nurse to the left of Linda spoke up. "Are you dating him?"

"Yep, I am." I kept typing, hoping I was sending the message that I didn't want to discuss my personal life with random coworkers.

"Is it serious?" she questioned.

Shutting my eyes to grant myself a second of peace, I inhaled slowly and turned to them. Before I could open my mouth, Linda stood. "Sorry, Sam. I know you're trying to work. But the mayor's estranged wife dating the high school psychologist? It's like a local soap opera. We'll hound you later, though." She turned and gestured for the other two women to follow her.

Shaking my head, I called after them, "Yeah, but it's not a soap opera, it's my life. And it would be wonderful if everyone could stop being so damn nosy about my business."

All three of them laughed. "Sorry, Sam, but if that's what you wanted, you are in the wrong place," the brunette said as they disappeared down the hall.

Like that thought hadn't occurred to me every day since I moved here.

When I got home that evening, I barely registered Landon's car parked on the street as I traipsed from the driveway to the front porch. Turning the key, I opened the door to a delectable smell wafting toward me from the kitchen. Dropping my purse next to my shoes, I walked into the living room to see him wearing an apron and cooking something at the stove.

Hearing me enter, he looked over his shoulder and smiled. "Hey, beautiful."

"What is all of this? And how did you get in? Not that I mind in the slightest," I added, doing a slow spin and realizing he had already set the table and lit a candle. On the kitchen island was a bouquet of fresh flowers in a vase.

He stared at me as if I were speaking an unknown language. "I'm making dinner. And I know where the hidden key is now, thanks to Raegan's intel."

I shook my head, laughing. "But why?"

He narrowed his eyes slightly and formed a straight line with his lips. "Because you're my girlfriend and I wanted to make you a meal?"

My chin jutted out as my eyebrows raised. When was the last time someone made me food in my own home? *And I was his girlfriend?*

His face mirrored mine. "Please, Lord in Heaven, tell me someone has cooked for you before I came around."

I sat down at the kitchen table, my legs splayed in my typical un-lady-like fashion around the spindles. "Uh…" I wracked my brain, but I truly didn't think anyone had made me dinner after I moved out of my parents' house.

"Charles never cooked?" he asked.

"Does that surprise you?" I countered, and he cocked his head.

"Initially, yes, but you're right. I shouldn't have expected him to. Guys like him do the waiting, not the waiting on."

Pointing at him, I said, "Exactly."

Returning his attention to the stove, he relayed the evening's menu. "I'm making shrimp linguini with a white sauce and cheesy broccoli, because you need to eat vegetables, but no one ever said they had to be in their natural, disgusting form. My thought—add cheese to everything that tastes gross, and viola. Suddenly delicious."

Coming up next to him, I slid my arms around his waist and stood on my tiptoes to put my head on his shoulder. "Thank you for dinner. Truly. After the day I had, I was going to heat a microwave meal and call it a night."

He nodded toward the hallway. "Why don't you shower, relax a little, and I'll bring you dinner in bed?"

I groaned as I released him and leaned against the nearby counter, my hand over my heart. "You're spoiling me."

He put down the wooden spoon he was holding and stepped in front of me. Pulling us together, his lips met mine. "Someone has to."

I returned the kiss, my hands finding their way into his back pants' pockets. "I'm so glad that someone is you."

Once I got out of the shower and crawled under the duvet, Landon brought us dinner and wine in bed. Sitting next to me, he took his wine glass off the nightstand beside him and raised it.

"To an amazing woman. May she continue to put up with me breaking into her house and cooking her dinner."

I raised my glass. "To a delirious man who thinks *his girlfriend*," I said in a singsong voice, "will ever prevent him from breaking into her house for any reason, but especially to make her dinner."

"Cheers," he grinned, clinking his glass against mine before leaning in to kiss me.

"Cheers," I whispered.

CHAPTER SIXTEEN

I stared at myself in the mirror. My makeup was applied, my hair was blow-dried and pinned back, and my pantsuit was ironed and ready to go, draped across my bed. Landon was beside me, straightening his tie and fussing with his already-perfect hair. When he was satisfied with his appearance, he came up next to me, and we both looked at ourselves in the mirror, expressions serious. Rubbing my arms, he continued to look at my reflection.

"You've got this," he said confidently. "You've met with Jules and you know what's going to be discussed—there shouldn't be any surprises. And if the judge has an ounce of humanity, just a smidgin of integrity, you should get Raegan and Harrison back today for at least a week."

I bit the inside of my cheek, resisting the urge to smoke this early in the morning. Today was definitely a day I could go through an entire pack of cigarettes, but I knew I shouldn't. Instead, I fidgeted with my watch strap. "Charles is friends with everyone in this damn city, though," I whispered. "What if everything I've done isn't enough? What if they just keep letting him slide?"

Landon shook his head. "If they ignore the law, you go above that judge. Jules said she could do it. It's a hassle, yes, and it will probably prolong the entire divorce process, but it can be done. You two will do whatever it takes to make sure those kids are safe, and if that means going outside of Madison for future court hearings, then so be it. Let's just hope it doesn't resort to that. I have faith in Jules, and more importantly, I have faith in you."

Breaking eye contact with him in the mirror, I turned to face him. "I can do this."

He nodded. "If there is anyone in the world who would fight until death for their children, it's you. Jules will be right beside you the entire time, and we know how she is in court."

I leaned in and kissed him, getting a small taste of mint-infused mouthwash. "I've got this." After putting on the pantsuit, Landon and I gathered our stuff and exited the house.

"Call me at any point, alright? If you need someone to bail you out of jail, or if you just need to vent, my phone is on loud and I am prepared to duck out for a few minutes, if necessary." He kissed me before opening my car door and waiting for me to get in.

Once I was inside, he went to his own car and climbed in. We headed down my street in the same direction, but when we came to the main drag, Landon turned left toward the school, while I continued straight. After pulling into the courthouse parking lot, I lit a cigarette and took a few quick drags before opening the car door and stamping it out on the cement.

Jules met me on the steps wearing three-inch heels, a blazer, a pencil skirt, and a look that could kill. For a moment, I almost pitied Charles and his lawyer, because Jules gave off the vibe that she was ready to fight someone until they either died or ran away screaming. Her hatred of Charles had been steadily growing since we first discussed my case, and it wasn't just because of how he treated me and my children. She could tell he was a spoiled little rich kid in a man's body, and she had made it her mission to bring him down.

Locating our assigned courtroom, we sat on an uncomfortable wooden bench, waiting for the status conference to begin. Charles was nowhere in sight, and our hearing was supposed to start in twenty minutes. Hands in my lap, I began flexing my fingers as I bit the inside of my lip. "Can we pray he doesn't show up?" I asked.

She snorted. "We can pray, but we also know he's not going to let you off that easy. I'm sure even if he is late, the judge will forgive him because he's Charles-freaking-Hawley."

Jules was no stranger to small Southern communities, as she was born and raised in a North Carolina town that had a population of less than three thousand people, but even she was shocked to learn just how bad the nepotism with Charles was in this city. When I moved here, I wasn't sure if everyone saw how awful he was and just accepted it, or if they didn't say anything because he was one of their own, or if they were simply blind to his blazingly apparent flaws. Whatever the reason, it was baffling to see so many people support such a jerk for years.

Four minutes before our hearing was due to start, Charles waltzed in with his lawyer, dressed in his most expensive suit and loafers. Time had not been kind to him, and his once boyishly good looks and Southern charm had given way to a beer belly and early signs of balding. I wasn't sure why he let himself go, seeing as how he had all the time in the world to hit the gym, but perhaps now that he was worth millions, Charles' money meant more to him than his appearance.

Staring at him as he approached us, it was hard to recall how and why I ever liked him in the first place. I do remember that he was charismatic, and I, like many others, was wooed by his handsome face and what I thought was a confident personality. I was too naïve and young to realize his charm was fake, his good looks wouldn't age well, and his disposition was that of a narcissistic asshole.

Charles' lawyer offered Jules a weary stare before sitting next to Charles on the wooden bench opposite ours. "I can't believe you're traipsing around this city, *my city*, with the high school psychologist," Charles muttered loudly.

Jules whipped her head around to stare at me. Her eyes were blazing but narrowed, communicating that I should not respond to Charles' comment. I knew as much, but it was difficult not to engage with him when every word out of his mouth infuriated me beyond all belief.

At ten a.m. sharp, the courtroom door swung open, revealing a bailiff, who ushered us into the courtroom like sheep. "Petitioner over there," she called, looking back at me and Jules as she pointed to the right side of the courtroom. "Respondent over there," she said, gesturing to the left side of the room while turning to nod at Charles and his attorney. Walking down the middle of the divided seating area, she pushed her way through the swinging door and stood outside of the judge's entrance.

The bailiff waited for us to be seated before clearing her throat. "Judge Orwell, the judge who ordered this status conference, is out sick today. Judge Thurman will preside over this proceeding from here on out."

She started toward her station, but Charles' attorney stopped her. "We can't have a different judge. Judge Orwell knows our case. We have to reschedule for a date he's available."

Jules shook her head. "Absolutely not. I'm ready to get this ball rolling. I would like this status conference to take place today, as scheduled."

The bailiff gave a solitary nod toward Jules. "There will be no rescheduling of the status conference. Judge Thurman is perfectly competent to preside over your case." Her eyes wandered over to Charles, who released an exasperated sigh.

Thoughts flooded my mind as Charles and his attorney exchanged hushed whispers. Maybe Charles didn't have the same relationship with Judge Thurman as he did with Judge Orwell, and that's why his attorney wanted to reschedule. Perhaps this new judge wasn't as far up Charles' ass as the first one. *Fingers crossed.*

When Judge Thurman appeared, everyone in the courtroom rose and sat down again when instructed to do so. Shuffling papers around, he readjusted his glasses several times before peering over his bench.

"Charles Hawley," he said, lowering his spectacles to the bridge of his nose. "I haven't seen you since you were a teenager. How are you doing? How is the family?"

Charles grinned, and I suppressed a groan. My theory was just blown out of the water. "My mother is doing great, Your Honor. Still misses my father dearly, though, I'm afraid. He was the love of her life."

The judge moved his eyes from Charles to me. "And this woman, apparently," he said, "is not the love of *your* life, or we wouldn't be here right now."

Understatement of the year, buddy.

"According to her, Your Honor, no. She is not. Though I thought she was. We have two beautiful children together, but she kicked me out of our house without any warning and filed for divorce."

Judge Thurman was still staring at me, and I side-eyed Jules. *I wasn't supposed to respond to any of this, was I?*

As if she could read my mind, Jules gave me a small, nearly unnoticeable head shake.

"May I ask why you are seeking divorce from Mr. Hawley, Ms. Hawley?" the judge asked.

Jules stepped in. "You can see Ms. Hawley's reasoning for a divorce in the paperwork, Your Honor."

More papers were shuffled before Judge Thurman addressed the room. "Adultery?" He narrowed his eyes at Charles. "And you were served with these papers…nearly four months ago?"

Charles' lawyer nodded. "We were served with papers stating irreconcilable differences four months ago, yes. The adultery claim was added last week, which is a blatant lie. There's absolutely no proof my client was unfaithful to Ms. Hawley at any point during their marriage."

And here I was thinking everyone had to tell the truth in court, but I guess no one was under oath, as of yet.

"And the discovery process?" Judge Thurman inquired.

Charles gave his attorney an unreadable look. Shaking his head, the lawyer cleared his throat. "Your Honor, we have not finished the discovery process. My client was honestly hoping to reconcile with his wife prior to last week. But Ms. Hawley made it known to him that she did not reciprocate my client's feelings nor desire to save their marriage."

The judge raised an eyebrow. "Because filing for divorce wasn't a big enough hint?" he asked, and I had to duck my face to keep my smile hidden. Judge Thurman was redeeming himself.

Charles' attorney sighed. "What can I say, Your Honor. My client is a hopeless romantic."

Jules was the one who audibly snorted then, causing Judge Thurman to shoot her a warning glance. Pursing her lips, she regained a serious expression.

"Mr. Hawley," the judge began. "The law states you have a certain number of days to complete the discovery process. That time has long since passed, added adultery claim or not, and I can hold you in contempt of court."

Please, for the love of God, do it. Hold him in contempt. Finally hold the man accountable for something.

"However, seeing as how you are a Madison native and mayor of this fine community, I am giving you until Wednesday to complete AND send the discovery items to Ms. Hawley's attorney. Is that clear?"

Dammit.

"Yes, Your Honor," Charles and his attorney said simultaneously.

Judge Thurman glanced at Jules. "I know Judge Orwell set the noticed motion for next Monday—does a week give you enough time to gather everything you need?"

Jules nodded confidently. "Yes, absolutely, Your Honor."

He grunted, satisfied with her answer. "Then it's decided. Next Monday is the first scheduled hearing. Any other questions?"

"No, Your Honor—" Charles' attorney started, but Jules cut him off.

"Actually, Your Honor, we were hoping to determine when Ms. Hawley can see her children again."

The judge moved his head to the side and squinted. "What do you mean, *when* she can see her children again? Was there an order I missed about Ms. Hawley *not* being allowed to see her children?"

Charles' attorney noticeably stiffened.

"No, Your Honor, but Mr. Hawley took Harrison and Raegan without any prior warning two Sundays ago, and after our *ex parte* application for a custody order was denied last Wednesday, my client has yet to see her children."

With both eyebrows raised, Judge Thurman shifted in his seat. "Mr. Hawley, when were you planning on returning your children to Ms. Hawley?"

I stared at Charles, who simply looked at his attorney. "We were unclear how long the children were going to stay with Mr. Hawley," his lawyer began, but the judge waived him off.

"Until we get custody sorted, the children will spend seven consecutive days with each parent."

Jules spoke up. "Does this mean my client can pick her children up after we are dismissed?"

Judge Thurman nodded. "Yes, and she will be expected to return the children to Mr. Hawley's residence by noon next Monday, unless they will be accompanying you to court."

Banging the gavel to signal adjournment, I waited

for Charles and his attorney to clear the room before I hugged Jules. "Thank you," I said, fighting back tears at the thought of seeing Raegan and Harrison after what had been the longest week of my life. "Truly."

She rubbed my back. "It's the least I can do. Let's get your kids back."

Twenty minutes later, I was standing next to my van in the bricked circular driveway that led to Lydia's mansion on the outskirts of Madison. Her home embodied old Southern wealth, with its towering white columns supporting a giant front porch, a box hedge garden off to the side of the house, and nearly 14,000 square feet of living space. I had only been inside once—the day we told Lydia and Charles' father I was pregnant, because after dropping that bombshell, I was never welcomed back into their home. I do vaguely remember the interior being more lavish and ostentatious than the outside, however, and that said a lot. A grand oil painting of Charles and his parents hanging over the mantel in the main sitting room flanked by large taxidermized deer heads was not a memory I would soon forget.

I hung back as Jules made her way to the front door. She didn't want Lydia getting in my face, and I wasn't going to argue with her. As long as I got my kids back, I didn't care who went to the door to inform Lydia of the custody change. Although I would hire a serial killer if I had a choice.

From my vantage point, I could see clear to the front door, and when Lydia opened it, it was apparent Charles hadn't told her what happened in court that morning. She ran her eyes over the document that explained the temporary custody agreement before disappearing into the house. To my complete and utter surprise, there was no yelling, no arguing. Jules glanced back at me. *How odd.* I thought for sure Lydia was going to fight us.

Minutes later, Raegan appeared, limping slightly, and when her glance met mine, tears started streaking down both of our faces. Lydia steered Harrison to the front door, the duffel bag I had given her filled with his necessities hooked over one of the wheelchair handles. Once they crossed the threshold, Jules took over, and Lydia shut the door firmly behind them.

With Lydia safely inside, I nearly ran to meet Raegan, who dropped her backpack and threw her arms around me the second I reached her. "Rae of Sunshine," I whispered into her hair, squeezing her for dear life. "I missed you so damn much."

"I missed you, too, Mom," she said, her voice muffled against my shirt.

Hearing Harrison and Jules come up behind her, she moved aside. After embracing Harrison, I crouched down in front of his wheelchair and grasped his hands. "I missed you, too, Handsome Harry. More than you'll ever know. What do you say we go home and momentarily forget this ever happened?"

Harrison grinned and moaned happily. Raegan looked from him to me. "He didn't smile once the entire time we were here."

Still standing behind Harrison, Jules shook her head but remained silent.

I rubbed his knee. "I'm so sorry you weren't happy, baby. But for the next seven days, you're all mine, again, and we are going to make them the best seven days yet, you hear?" He smiled again as his legs jerked— something that only happened when he was overjoyed.

Wiping away tears, I stood and embraced Jules once

more. "Thank you for getting my kids back," I sniffed.

As we parted, she clasped my shoulders. "Just remember, this is only the beginning. Call me after Wednesday and we will schedule a time to meet up later this week."

Once I loaded Harrison into the van and we were all safely locked inside the vehicle, I drove us home, my right hand clutching Raegan's hand the entire time. After settling in, I called McKenna, and her initial scream of happiness turned into hysterical sobs. Finally, she managed to relay that she would be by within the hour, despite me insisting she stay put.

She burst through the front door thirty minutes later and enveloped each of us in a minute-long bear hug. "I've never missed you guys more in my life. Seven days without seeing y'all was brutal." She looked at me. "I can't even imagine how you must have felt."

I started to gather ingredients for Harrison's favorite lunch smoothie, but McKenna nudged me aside. "I got it. Go change, update everyone you need to," she urged, so I did just that. Sitting on my bed, I sent a quick text to Landon.

Me—*I got them back. Temporarily, but I'll take what I can get at this point.*—

His response was immediate.

Landon—*Oh my gosh, Sam. That is amazing. Do you want me to stop by after work? Or do you want some alone time with them, just the three of you?*—

Before I could overthink it, I replied.

Me—*You're a part of our lives, now. It's the four of us. I can't wait to see you tonight. I love you.*—

As I walked into the living room after throwing on a pair of sweatpants and a hoodie, my phone buzzed.

Landon—*I'll be there with pizza and celebratory balloons. I love you, Sam. See you in a few hours.*—

He appeared in the entryway of my house three hours later with a giant bouquet of balloons in one hand and three pizza boxes in the other. "The party is here," he said, grinning. Standing on my tiptoes to give him a kiss, he dropped the balloons and wrapped his arm around my waist. "You did it," he whispered, his face against mine. "You got Harrison and Raegan back."

"The judge is making us swap custody every week until things are sorted out, but for the next seven days, my babies are all mine." He kissed me again, and when we pulled away from each other, we noticed Raegan and McKenna staring at us from the living room. Raegan seemed mildly amused as well as slightly disgusted, while McKenna's eyes welled again.

Walking over to McKenna, Landon stuck out his hand. "You must be McKenna. Sam has told me so much about you. Thank you for all that you do for Sam, Harrison, and Raegan. I learned very quickly you're an invaluable part of this family."

McKenna's face softened even more; her tears were now dangerously close to falling. "Geez, Sam. Way to put me on a pedestal."

He then walked over to Harrison and knelt down in front of his wheelchair. "Hey, Harrison. I'm Landon, your mom's…" He looked back at me for assistance, but I just shrugged. "I'm a very good friend of your mom."

Raegan folded her arms. "Emphasis on the *very*."

I swatted her arm as McKenna snorted. "Raegan Marie."

She feigned innocence. "What?"

Ignoring us, he continued. "I've heard so much

about you, and I'm really excited to finally meet you. Is it cool if we have dinner together?"

We all watched as Harrison studied him. Finally, he gave Landon a cautious smile. "Alright then," he nodded. "I'm stoked I get to spend some time with you. Maybe this upcoming week we can do something fun together. I heard you like action movies, and there's a new one I've been wanting to see."

Harrison gave him a bigger smile upon hearing the word "movie," and I grinned. Landon remembered the way to my kid's heart. As we gathered around the table, I prepped and started Harrison's G-tube before sitting between him and Landon. Conversation and laughter filled the room, and as I stared down at my plate, I held back tears as an overwhelming sense of gratitude washed over me. These people were all that mattered. They were my everything. And for the first time in a long time, I felt truly happy.

Knowing this was the calm before the storm, I soaked in every moment of the evening. After McKenna left and the kids were in bed, Landon and I sat on the couch, a pair of wine glasses on the ottoman in front of us. "I was talking with Raegan earlier while you were putting Harrison to bed," he said, resting his head on my shoulder.

"Oh yeah? About what?"

"Her stay with Charles. She said it was awful and that she despises Lydia. Her exact words were, 'Lydia is a garbage human being'."

I snorted. "She should have met Charles' father before he died. He was equally as charming."

"But she did say she understands why Charles is the way he is, because Lydia is so terrible. Raegan said she kind of feels bad for him, now that she's had a small glimpse into his life, but also still hates him, because he chose to follow in his parents' footsteps. I thought her psychological insight was impressive and told her she could give me a run for my money."

"Ah, the student becomes the master," I nodded, feeling proud.

"You know what she said next?" he asked. I could hear him smile. "She said, 'I think I'm going to stick to cosmetology, but thanks. It's nice to know I might have something to fall back on'." He chuckled to himself as I shook my head and grinned. "She was so nonchalant about it, as if it is something everyone can do." He gave a low whistle. "She's going places, Sam."

I laughed softly. "If Raegan is known for something, it's her tenacity and stubbornness. I can't imagine where she gets it from."

"I'm pleading the fifth on that one. How did the status conference actually go?" he asked, sitting up. "I didn't want to ask earlier in front of the kids."

Leaning forward, I grabbed my wine and took a sip.

"Stressful?" he volunteered, watching me. "I am getting a subtle whiff of cigarette."

"Sorry," I muttered, trying to scoot away from him, but he put his hand on my knee, halting my movement.

"I didn't say that because it bothered me. I just know you only smoke when you're stressed."

I stared into the glass, trying to translate my feelings into words. "We have a different judge now, and while I was hoping he would be more in my favor, he also seems biased toward Charles. The noticed motion is still set for next week, and I have an awful feeling this whole thing is going to span weeks, maybe even months."

Landon moved his hand off of my knee and began rubbing my back. Feeling his skin against mine, I closed my eyes and felt the tension my body had held on to all day finally lessen.

"I'm sorry," he said softly. "Can I do anything to help?"

I shook my head before facing him. "You already help by just being here. I appreciate you more than you'll ever know."

He kissed my forehead as I drew myself into him. "We just have to survive the next few months. Then hopefully we can all move on without Charles interfering."

CHAPTER SEVENTEEN

"I'm sorry." Landon's voice rang out in the silence, startling me awake. I was facing away from him, but I tentatively planned on turning over if it happened again. Inadvertently holding my breath, I waited, blood pounding in my ears.

"I'm so sorry. I tried to stop, but it was too late." His entire body began to tremble as slow, mournful cries emanated from his lips.

Freeing myself from the blankets and spinning around, I could see that his eyes were squeezed shut and an indescribable pain was etched across his face; his lips were taut, his breathing ragged. My heart stopped as I watched him battle his inner demons.

"Landon," I said quietly, placing my hand on his shoulder and gently shaking him. He didn't react—his crying was more violent than my attempts to wake him. "Landon," I said louder. "Landon, wake up. It's a nightmare."

Tears were now falling from his tightly-closed eyes, temporarily staining the pillowcase below him. I couldn't bear to see him like this. "Landon, please. LANDON."

He jolted awake, his eyes flying open and his body stilling. His gaze moved around the room before it landed on me.

"It was…" he started. "It felt…"

I laid parallel to him, my face level with his. "I know. I'm sure it felt real, but tonight, it was a nightmare."

Breathing slowly, our eye contact remained steady as he reoriented himself; the trails of tears across his cheeks were illuminated by the glow of the bathroom nightlight. Desperate to rid him of his torment, I brought my hand to the space just above his beard and wiped the traces of anguish from his skin. "I'm so sorry you're still haunted by those memories."

He said nothing as he took everything in. Finally, he gave a long, slow sigh. "I didn't mean to wake you. I'm sorry."

I studied him, my hand still on his cheek. "You don't ever have to apologize for this. It's not something you can control."

Resting his hand atop mine, he closed his eyes. "This is the first nightmare I've had since I met you," he whispered.

I gave him a slight smile. "I must be losing my magic."

He shook his head. "It's not that. I can guarantee it's because I've been stressed lately, more so than normal. With everything going on...I just feel helpless."

I slowly pulled my body away from his. "What do you mean?"

His eyes opened to reveal darkened irises where there were normally crystal blue pools. "Everything going on with the trial, and Charles, and the kids...I've watched you suffer, and I feel useless. I can't solve your problems, even though I want to. I so badly want Charles to just disappear and leave you and the kids alone. I..." He raked his fingers through his hair as he pulled himself into a sitting position. "I just want you to be happy." His voice waivered. "And you can't be happy until all of this is over and it goes in your favor. Nothing I do or say can make this situation better, and I hate it."

It was my turn to sit up, but instead of joining him against the headboard, I moved even further from him, sitting cross-legged down at his knees. He watched me, his eyes dazed with confusion and sleep. "Why are you so far away?"

My jaw opened as I shook my head, trying to organize my thoughts. "I need to look at you straight on when we have this conversation, and I need you to see me." Taking a deep breath, I looked away while I mentally waded through all the issues I wanted to discuss. After a beat, my eyes returned to him. "I feel awful—I had no idea you were feeling this way. I realize now how selfish I've been, and I'm sorry. I've asked a lot from you and haven't checked in once to see how you are doing during all of this."

He looked down. "No. You've asked nothing from me, and that's partly why I'm feeling this way. I *want* to help. I wish there was a way I could make this better for you and Raegan and Harrison, but what can I do?" He sighed. "You've spent so much of your life fighting in some way. You've advocated for Harrison since he was born, you've overcome so much to become a nurse, and now you're fighting for your children because Charles is an asshole. It's been incredibly difficult sitting here, watching you fight yet again, when I'm right here. I'm more than willing to aid in your battle, but I can't, and it's frustrating beyond all measure. And I know you're strong and independent and you don't really *need* my help, but sometimes I catch myself wondering why I'm even here if I can't contribute in some way."

I held up my hand. "I know everything seems worse when you're mentally struggling, but Landon, there's no way you can look at me and not see just how much you've helped me. If you weren't in my life…" I looked around. "I honestly don't know where I would be. In jail, for taking out Charles? In a mental hospital for losing my mind after he took Raegan and Harrison? I would definitely be closer to a lung cancer diagnosis, because the amount of smoking I would be doing would be absolutely shocking."

When my eyes landed on him again, he was still looking down. "I need you to understand, while you may feel useless and helpless, I see you as the complete opposite. You literally picked me up off my floor when I was at my worst. You've supported me throughout all of this; you've been here for me ever since that moment in your car on our first date when you pulled over and listened to me vent. Am I strong and independent? One could say that, sure, but it's because the life I chose made me this way, and that's not necessarily something I'm going to go brag about. And do I need you?" I shrugged. "Maybe not. But I *want* you."

He slowly raised his head, and I ducked mine to ensure he was looking at me. "You simply existing in my life has changed me, and the fact that you decided to take a chance on me, and love me, and make me feel like I'm worthy…" I paused, momentarily at a loss for words. "You being in my corner since day one has brought back a version of me I thought I would never see again. That Sam, she was buried under years of depression and regret and reluctant submission to ensure peace was kept at home. Then you came in, showed me how a healthy relationship should be, and here I am, in the process of divorcing my piece of crap husband and nearly getting into fights with old ladies in restaurant parking lots."

A slow grin spread across his face.

"I know you say you feel like you can't do anything to make my situation better, but Landon," I whispered, my eyes blurring with tears, "you've been the only thing making this entire nightmare livable."

Leaning toward me, he wrapped his arms around my waist and pulled me onto his lap. My hands returned to his face, gently brushing his beard with my fingers. "Please believe me. Besides my kids, you've been my only other source of joy during all of this. You mean the world to me."

"I could hire a hitman for Charles," he said into my hair.

I let out a small laugh. "I mean, that would definitely make my life easier. But truly, please don't let these feelings of helplessness cloud reality—you've done everything possible to help me, and I appreciate it more than you'll ever know. You can't fight my battles, but having you here gives me the motivation to completely demolish Charles in court and leave my old, pitiful self and marriage behind."

As I huddled against his chest, his arms still enveloping me, I could feel him slowly begin to relax. "I'm sorry," he whispered, exhaustion making his words slow and heavy. "I think I'm used to being needed, and it's an odd feeling being with someone who can handle her crap better than I probably ever could. Your independence is a little intimidating, at times."

I bit my lip. "Being wanted, though, is far superior to being needed. If I needed you, I might feel stuck with you, and vice versa. Because I want and choose you, I'm actively keeping you in my life—you bring something to the table that I like. Well, you bring a lot of things to the table that I like. And my love for you isn't out of obligation, it's out of desire."

He nuzzled his forehead against mine. "Samantha Hawley, everyone: Independent, intelligent, and gorgeous."

Grinning, I kissed him softly. "Has any of this made you feel better?"

He yawned and slid us back under the sheets. "Yes. I'm sorry we had to talk about it now. I should have brought it up sooner. It just felt so trivial bringing up my feelings of inadequacy while you're dealing with this whole mess."

"Your feelings are just as important as everything else going on. If staving off your nightmares means discussing things at," I glanced at my alarm clock behind me, "five in the morning, it's worth it. *You're* worth it, Landon."

"I love you, Sam," he mumbled, sleep already overtaking him. "Thank you for wanting me."

"I love you. And always."

****

Between working and having the kids back home, the rest of the week flew by. I cancelled Raegan's home study Charles had established, and by Wednesday, she was back in school and seeing Dr. Ridley. The difference it made having her amongst her friends and regularly seeing her therapist was amazing, but not at all surprising.

I saw so much of myself in Raegan as she got older, and this was one of those instances. Years of me shutting myself in with the kids when they were little made me nearly socially inept for a very long time, and I struggled for years to overcome my fear of social situations. Being isolated could break a person down within a matter of hours, and while Raegan wasn't an overly social teenager, those few days she had been cooped up in Lydia's home had negatively affected her. By Wednesday evening, though, she was more talkative and voluntarily shared how her day was at the dinner table every night after. She was also exceling at physical therapy, which I drove her to twice during the week. Her limp was still noticeable, but she was getting stronger with every session.

Like Raegan, Harrison had also been out of sorts the first few days he was back. Because he had never been away from me for more than a few hours, I was terrified he wouldn't recover from the days he spent with Charles. I wasn't quite sure how he perceived his time with his father, and I feared I broke his trust.

On Wednesday when I got home from work, he was refusing to eat the smoothie McKenna had made him, and I could tell she was nearing her wit's end. Lifting him out of his wheelchair and carrying him to the couch, I put him on my lap and held him. He didn't need to be verbal to tell us he was struggling—it was glaringly apparent by his actions and demeanor.

We sat there for nearly half an hour, me cradling him and explaining the entire situation. I told him it was hopefully temporary, and after a few weeks, he may be back with me and McKenna full time. Eventually, he started to squirm, so I returned him to his chair, and when McKenna tried the smoothie one last time, he reluctantly swallowed it. On Thursday, McKenna was happy to report that he was far less combative and more willing to do things, and by Friday, he was seemingly settling into his old routine.

Because the kids were with me, Landon stayed at my place every night, taking it upon himself to cook us breakfast and dinner every day. He even memorized a few of Harrison's favorite smoothies and watched while I fed Harrison through his G-tube. Our homelife wasn't the easiest to adjust to, but he was making strides at fitting in. When the following Monday rolled around, Raegan and I were sitting at the table, eating the French toast and scrambled eggs he had served us the moment we walked into the kitchen.

"Is this what normal partners do?" she whispered, eyeing him. He was happily whistling to himself while frying up another batch of French toast, completely unaware of our stares.

I shrugged. "I've heard rumors, but your dad was the only man I've ever lived with. However, now that I've experienced it for a short while, I would highly recommend getting with someone who treats you like you're an equal."

She grinned as she tore away a corner from her toast. "I'm glad he's here. You've been really happy lately, despite all this crap with Dad. I didn't realize just how long it had been since I'd seen you smile until he showed up."

I nudged her. "What are you talking about? I smile all the time."

Nudging me back, she shook her head. "Not the way you smile when he's around."

Turning away from the stove, Landon caught my eye and winked at me. Biting the inside of my cheek, I leaned against Raegan. "I hope we have even more reasons to smile after all this crap is over."

"The hearing this morning—what is it for?"

I stood, my plate all but licked clean. "Everything. It's the beginning of the entire divorce process." Leaving Raegan and Landon in the kitchen, I walked up the hallway to check in on McKenna and Harrison before heading to my bedroom. I had laid a pair of black dress pants, a white ruffled top, and a black cardigan on the bed before breakfast, and a pair of black heels sat in the doorway. Falling onto the bed, I deliberately got dressed at a pace that rivaled a sloth. I was in no rush to see my kids off for the next week, and I was especially not in a hurry to head to the courthouse.

After spending fifteen minutes putting my clothes on and another twenty minutes doing my hair and makeup, I couldn't stall any longer. Reluctantly, I made my way to the kitchen to find Raegan and Landon cleaning up and McKenna and Harrison at the table. McKenna was feeding him his smoothie, but he paused to give me a grin. I tried to return the gesture, but smiling felt dishonest. He was about to get shipped back to Lydia's, and there was nothing I could do about it.

Facing McKenna, I said, "I'm going to take the car to drop Raegan off at school and then head to the courthouse. Would you mind bringing Harrison to Lydia's in the van sometime before noon? And because I can almost guarantee Charles hasn't purchased it yet, would you be able to put his seizure monitor in the duffel by the front door? That bag has to go to Lydia's too—it has everything Harrison needs for the week."

She nodded, refusing to meet my eyes.

Hunching down in front of Harrison's wheelchair, I

rubbed his knees. "I love you, Handsome Harry." I tried to keep my voice strong. "I'll see you next week, okay? I love you so much, and I'm sorry this is happening. I'm trying my best to resolve it as quickly as possible." A single tear slid down my cheek, but I quickly wiped it away. I didn't want to upset him.

Landon met me by the front door, my purse and keys in his hand. With her backpack slung over her shoulder, Raegan walked past us, giving Landon a high-five before opening the door and squeezing between it and the doorframe to wait for me in the car.

"I'll finish cleaning up here before heading out," he said, clasping my hand. I tried to look at him but failed; instead, I stared down at the floor. I knew if my eyes met his I would start crying, and I had spent a lot of wasted time on my makeup. "Hey," he whispered. "You've got this. He would be an idiot to fight you now that he's seen the proof." We had to submit the picture of Charles cheating into evidence before today's hearing, meaning Charles and his attorney were aware of the photograph I'd had in my possession for months.

"But he *is* an idiot. That's the problem," I muttered. "I swear I could have a video of him cheating on me and he would try to deny it. He's scum."

He nodded. "That, he is, but I've seen you tackle some pretty harsh scum on the bottom of your shower, and if you attack him with half the power you used with that sponge, he doesn't stand a chance."

Despite the overwhelming sadness I felt in every inch of my body, I let out a quiet laugh. "Thank you."

He dropped my hand and gently pulled me against him. "Call me when you can."

Climbing into the car with Raegan, I glanced over at

her in the passenger seat before turning over the engine. I drove slowly to the school, not realizing I was barely keeping up with the flow of traffic until someone honked. When we pulled into the parking lot, Raegan was looking at me. "Do you want me to come with you?"

I shook my head. "I'm fine, but thanks for offering. I'm just…dreading it. Dreading everything about this. I hate that I won't see you after school. I hate that your brother is there without proper help. The whole thing is just," I paused, not wanting to unload my issues on her. "It's just not ideal."

Raegan sighed. "And to add to the stress, I realized I should be hearing back from colleges within the next couple of weeks. You know I didn't apply to any colleges in Georgia, but now the thought of leaving you and Harrison makes me regret not applying to something closer."

I leaned over to embrace her. "No matter what, Rae, your brother and I will be okay. If your dad is going to fight for custody, Harry and I will stay here until he turns eighteen. Is it what I want for us? Not at all. But I promise you, the day after Harrison's birthday, we will join you wherever you are. Right now, at this time in your life, you need to do what you want to do. You deserve to get out, live on your own in a place where you want to be. We've all been trapped here for far too long—it's due time one of us escapes."

She pulled away from me. "As much grief as I give you, it was really hard being away from you while we were at Dad's last week, and it was only for seven days. If you aren't within a reasonable driving distance when I move away for college…" she trailed off as she stared out the window. "I don't know. I'm sure I'll be fine, but maybe I should apply to a college closer to here, just in case."

I firmly shook my head. "Absolutely not, Rae. You will be fine on your own. There's an adjustment period, of course, but your fear shouldn't overtake your aspirations. If you get accepted to your dream college, you will go. I won't let you stay here because of us. And besides," I added, "no matter where you end up, if I'm not with you, I will always be a phone call away."

She was still staring out the window, watching her peers walk up the steps to school. "Regardless of what happens, we will be okay. Right? We've adjusted to life so far, and whatever changes the divorce brings, we will adjust to those, too. We've dealt with hard things before, and we can do it again."

I couldn't help but laugh. "I'm sorry, when did you start sounding like a full-fledged adult?"

Raegan shrugged as she turned to me. "I'm eighteen in a few months. I have to practice."

Patting her thigh, I smiled. "I'm in denial about your upcoming legal status, so, on that note, get going to school. Please call me whenever Lydia isn't around this week. I feel so much better hearing your voice and having updates on Harrison. I definitely sleep better knowing you are both doing alright." Holding back the tears that didn't fall earlier when I was saying goodbye to Harrison, I managed to utter, "I love you, Rae of Sunshine. I'm so happy you're my kid."

Raegan gave me a half-smile. "Love you, Mom. See you next week."

I watched her disappear into the main school building before I drove to the courthouse. Similar to last week, Jules and I sat outside our assigned room twenty minutes prior to our scheduled hearing time. After a few seconds of small talk, silence fell between us, and my legs began to jiggle nervously.

Please let today be as uneventful as possible, I silently prayed to anyone who was listening. *Please let the judge be fair and not enamored with Charles like everyone else in this city.* I hadn't been to church in ages, but today, I was desperate.

The sound of a single person's footsteps on the marble courthouse floor made me snap out of my Hail Mary and raise my head. McKenna, dressed in a flowy top, dress slacks, and ballet flats slowly approached us. Launching myself into a standing position, I started toward her. "Is it Harrison? Is something wrong?"

Jules grabbed my hand before I could get to McKenna. "Sit down, Sam. Harrison is fine, right?"

McKenna stopped a few feet away from me and nodded. "He's fine," she said, but her ever-present clear, confident voice was gone. Instead, her cadence was soft and wavering. As she looked at both of us, she began wringing her hands, further proving she was nervous.

I turned to Jules, confused. "What is going on?"

My attorney shot me an unreadable look. "She's here for the trial, Sam. She's going to be a vital part of today's hearing."

CHAPTER EIGHTEEN

A vital part of today's hearing? What the hell did that mean? And why did I not know about any of it?

McKenna sat down on the other side of Jules. "Sorry I'm late."

Jules patted her knee. "You're right on time. Thank you for coming."

Something weird was going on, and I hated the fact that I had absolutely no clue as to why McKenna was here. Just as I was about to implore further, Charles and his attorney strolled up. Unlike last time, Charles kept his snide remarks to himself and refused to make eye contact with any of us.

Once we were in the courtroom, Charles, his attorney, Jules, and I sat on our respective sides, and McKenna took a seat behind me. Judge Thurman stared down at us. "Mr. Hawley, I know we covered this briefly last week, but you understand Ms. Hawley is claiming adultery? I know the original filing stated irreconcilable differences."

Charles nodded, his face stoic.

"Ms. Hawley, you have proof of this adultery?"

Jules spoke on my behalf. "Yes, Your Honor."

"Everyone has seen and approved the list of witnesses?" This time, both attorneys verbally agreed, and I looked around to ensure no one else had snuck in. It was still just McKenna behind us, but having her as a witness in my divorce hearing didn't make any sense. I was beyond confused.

"Okay. Ms. Hawley, please proceed." The judge settled back into his chair, his hands folded in his lap.

Jules grabbed the clicker from the table in front of us and aimed it at the projector behind Judge Thurman's head. The blank white screen that hung on the wall opposite the jury box flickered to life, presenting the picture of Charles fornicating with his secretary. "There's the proof, Your Honor," she said, shrugging.

Charles' attorney didn't miss a beat. "Your Honor, obviously we are going to need verification this picture wasn't doctored or altered in any way."

Jules nodded. "Your Honor, I would like to call our first and only witness for the day, Miss McKenna Ruiz."

She rose from the seat behind us and began slowly making her way up to the witness stand. Raising her right hand and swearing to tell the truth, she eventually sat down and stared at Jules, who quickly glanced at me before nodding at her.

"Miss Ruiz, you are the one who took this photograph, correct?"

My jaw dropped. *McKenna took the picture?*

She purposely kept her eyes on Jules. "Yes."

"And why, may I ask, did you feel inclined to take this photo?"

And why would she be so secretive about it? Why couldn't she have just told me?

McKenna swallowed hard. "I went to Mr. Hawley's office to discuss something when I stumbled across him…being unfaithful to Ms. Hawley."

"And this photograph has not been altered in any way, shape, or form, Miss Ruiz?" Jules questioned.

McKenna vehemently shook her head. "No, ma'am."

Another glance from Jules in my direction. "Miss Ruiz, why were you meeting with Mr. Hawley?"

I was still so hung up on the fact McKenna had taken the picture and not told me that I hadn't even processed why she was actually there and able to take the photo. McKenna finally looked at me, her eyes beginning to well. "Mr. Hawley," she started, but a small sob escaped her.

An alarm went off in my brain, my stomach roiling as an indefinable weight constricted my chest. *Please tell me she wasn't about to say what I feared she was going to say.*

After regaining some composure, McKenna opened her mouth once more. "Mr. Hawley was harassing me, and I went to ask him to stop."

The second she uttered those words, my blood turned to ice. No.

Judge Thurman subtly leaned forward in his chair, his eyes fixated on McKenna.

"Harassing you how?" Jules pushed.

Bile started creeping up my throat.

"When he still resided with Ms. Hawley and was home while Ms. Hawley was out, he would say things to me. Inappropriate things. They started small; like, he would say I looked pretty or asked if my pants were new. But then, he started 'accidentally'," she air quoted, "brushing up against me."

My esophagus was burning now. I wouldn't throw up, I chanted to myself. Don't throw up. But I was overwhelmed. Guilt, disgust, and rage filled my head and heart, and the room was starting to spin. *Charles assaulted McKenna.* This was something I never saw coming, and I felt ashamed, embarrassed even. I had let McKenna down. How did I not see any of this? How did I not sense it?

"I would be standing at the kitchen island, making food for his son, Harrison, and his hand would brush across my lower back. Then it would move lower. When I would call him out, he would apologize, pass it off as an accident. But it happened too often to be an accident each time."

Don't throw up.

"What caused you to confront him?" Jules asked.

Somehow managing to turn my head toward Charles, I saw he was caressing his forehead while gazing at the floor. His poker face was gone, and to me, that was his sign of admission. My stomach lurched.

"He began texting me from a burner phone. Asking me to meet him at a hotel room. He even left me a voicemail once. It was clear he'd been drinking. He said he'd liked me from the moment he saw me and that he could ensure I was well taken care of if I started a relationship with him."

I couldn't sit through this any longer. Standing, my legs felt like gelatin as I staggered toward the main aisle.

"Ms. Hawley? Where are you going? You can't just up and leave during a hearing," the judge boomed, but I couldn't speak. If I did, all that would come out would be breakfast.

Instead, I continued to half run, half stumble out of the courtroom. I heard Jules ask for a ten-minute recess before the door slammed closed behind me. Eyes darting, I couldn't find any glaringly apparent signs for the bathroom, so I carried myself through the courthouse entrance, down the steps, and halfway around the side of the building. Placing one hand on the brick exterior of the courthouse to steady myself, I leaned over a row of hedges and threw up.

The breakfast Landon had spent so much time preparing was out of my system within seconds. My eyes swam as my temples throbbed. McKenna was sexually assaulted. By my ex. Charles harassed the woman who cared for our son. Not just once—multiple times. Dozens of times, even.

I threw up again and again, until nothing was left but a bitter taste in my mouth. Whether it was solely from the vomit or in addition to this morning's revelation, I didn't know. Footsteps approached me, but I couldn't look up.

"Sam," Jules said, rubbing my back. I held up my hand, silently begging her not to continue. She'd withheld this information from me on purpose.

"Sam," she said again, this time ignoring my plea for silence. "I didn't tell you because I knew how you would react; I know how much McKenna means to you. I couldn't tell you and risk you doing or saying something to Charles before the hearing. Plus, I only found out about all of this on Friday." She stopped, and we finally made eye contact.

"I called her to my office to see what she could tell me about Charles never being around and never helping with Harrison. She fell apart within minutes. I hate to exploit her like this, but this community needs to see Charles for the disgusting, adulterating man he is. I'm sorry we caught you off guard, but I feel like I didn't have any other choice."

She was right. Had I known this sooner, I would

have lost my mind. McKenna was like a daughter to me. How dare he lay a hand on her in any way, shape, or form. "Charles cheating on me didn't affect me nearly as much as this does," I breathed, fighting off any and all urges to throw up again. "How did I miss this? How did I let this continue for years? And why didn't she tell me?"

Jules' shoulders dropped. "She didn't want to upset you. She said you've dealt with so much stuff already, she didn't want to add to it. It goes without saying that McKenna cares deeply about you and the kids, Sam. I honestly don't know if she would have ever told anyone had I not called her in."

"I feel terrible," I whispered. "I feel like I should have protected her."

Jules shook her head. "How were you to know? We do need to get back in there, though and I beg you, please, please don't say anything to Charles. Pretend he's not there, if it's easier. We have to make him suffer in a way that's legal."

I managed to straighten and smooth out my clothes. "I don't know if I can be in the same room as him. How can someone be so disgusting and terrible?"

She shrugged. "But once we're done, hopefully everyone else will see him that way, too."

"Are you better now, Ms. Hawley?" Judge Thurman asked as Jules and I entered the room again.

I nodded shakily and headed back to my seat. McKenna was still on the stand, her face splotchy and tear-stained, her eyes filled with regret and softened with sorrow. Knowing I would break down in front of everyone if I looked at her long enough, I quickly averted my eyes.

"Continuing where we left off, Miss Ruiz," Jules said, once again taking her place below the witness stand.

The judge interrupted her. "Do you have this voicemail, Miss Ruiz?" he asked, causing McKenna to shoot a worried glance at Jules.

Jules nodded at her.

"Yes, I do."

Judge Thurman peered over the tops of his glasses at her. "Can you play it, please? I am interested in hearing it."

I shuddered away the urge to gag. I didn't know if I could bear to hear it.

Jules gave McKenna another approving stare before she withdrew her phone from her purse and set it on the witness stand. Seconds later, Charles' voice rang throughout the courtroom.

"McKenna, it's me." He was slurring. "Listen, you keep rejecting me, and it's honestly hurting my feelings. No one has rejected me before. Well, Sam has, but that's why I'm looking elsewhere. I never should have married her. I should have denied getting her pregnant and let her fend for herself. My life would have been so much better without all of this bullshit."

I clenched my fists, silently seething. *The feeling was mutual, asshole. You could thank your family for pressuring me into 'all of this bullshit'.*

"Anyway," Charles' voice continued. "I don't understand why you don't like me. I'm rich. Don't all women love money?"

Glancing at Charles, it was apparent the voicemail hadn't been submitted for evidence. His face was buried in his hands, and his lawyer's dumbfounded appearance was almost comical, had it been any other occasion. Shoulders slumped, face drooping—the poor attorney was the picture of defeat. At least he was getting paid well to represent a client who was a garbage human being.

"Just call me, okay? I can't stop thinking about you."

The phone went silent, as well as the entire courtroom. Judge Thurman stared at the floor in front of him, his eyes unblinking. He remained motionless for what felt like minutes, causing McKenna to stare uncertainly at Jules. She shrugged, also at a loss of how to proceed. Finally, the judge brought his pointer fingers to his temples and rubbed them.

"Can I continue, Your Honor?" Jules asked, her chipper voice echoing in the otherwise soundless room.

He simply nodded, still massaging his face.

"You started working for the Hawleys as a caregiver for their son when he was around nine years old, correct?" Jules faced McKenna.

She nodded. "That's correct."

"You were eighteen years old?"

"That's right."

"When did Mr. Hawley start making advances toward you?" Jules asked.

"About a month after I started."

Five years. This poor woman had endured five years of harassment, and it started when she was only a few months older than Raegan was now.

"And you never said anything to Ms. Hawley?" Jules asked.

She shook her head. "No."

"Why?"

"Ms. Hawley has been through so much as it is, and I knew she would lose her mind if she found out. She sees me as part of the family, and had she known her husband was inappropriate with me…it would have killed her."

I would have killed Charles long before I offed myself in this situation.

"I was also afraid if Mr. Hawley found out I told someone, he would somehow force me to quit, that he would tarnish my reputation. I'm finishing my teaching credential, and as the mayor of Madison, I was concerned he would pull strings so I couldn't get a job in the county."

"But you're coming forward with everything now," Jules said.

She nodded. "I can't stand back anymore and watch Ms. Hawley take flak for her choices regarding Charles. He's done nothing but cheat on her and ignore his children for years, and it's time people know that."

Charles' attorney stood. "Objection, Your Honor."

The judge stared at Charles' lawyer. "We don't have a jury, Counselor. Sit down."

Jules spun around on the points of her heels to face Charles and his attorney.

"Your witness."

****

Charles' attorney forwent questioning McKenna, and they pleaded no contest to the adultery accusation. She quietly stepped down from the witness stand and resumed her position in the second row of benches directly behind Jules and me.

Judge Thurman glanced at the clock on the wall directly to his right and sighed. "Well, Mr. Hawley. I, for one, can say I didn't expect any of this. I'm calling it for today. We will continue this hearing next Monday. Alimony and custody will be at the forefront of discussion." Right before banging his gavel, he shot a weary glance at Charles. "Also, Mr. Hawley, might I suggest the next time you claim a woman is the love of your life, don't cheat on her."

Charles and his attorney swiftly exited the courthouse, with Jules, McKenna, and I trailing slowly behind. The entire walk to the parking lot, I thought about what I could say to McKenna. What I should say. But I had nothing. There was nothing that could convey the amount of regret I had—the amount of shame I felt. When we all reached the parking lot, I turned to her.

"McKenna," I managed to say before she stepped toward me. Instinctively, I pulled her small frame against mine. She melted into me, her body shaking and her arms pulled up against her chest.

"I am so, so sorry," I whispered. "I wish you had told me. I would have kicked him out five years ago. Never would I have questioned you. I trust you with my kids—I will take your word above anyone else's every damn day of the week."

Jules rubbed my arm before nodding at me. "I'll see you on Wednesday at my office to discuss the custody information."

McKenna pulled away from me a few minutes later, wiping her eyes with the cuff of her sweater.

"Do you want to get out of here? Do you need alone time? Do you never want to see me and the kids again?" I asked, and she jerked her head up.

"Nothing would ever make me *not* want to see you, Harrison, and Raegan," she said. "I thought I'd made that abundantly clear by now."

Touché. "I don't know what to do say or do, Kenny. I feel like a lifetime of apologies will never begin to make up for the amount of damage Charles did to you. I wouldn't blame you if you didn't want to see us again. The terrible memories you must face every time you walk through our front door…" I trailed off, my nausea returning.

McKenna shook her head. "Those memories are nothing compared to how elated I feel when I get to hang out with Harrison. Or when Raegan and I talk for hours on the couch. Or when I see you and we can talk about adult things. My parents are hours away, Sam, you know that. You're *my* family, too. I would never just up and leave you."

"Do you want a drink, then?"

She smiled. "Goodness, yes. That sounds amazing."

When she and I walked into the nearest bar five minutes later, the server couldn't even manage a "hello" before I ordered two glasses of wine and a basket of biscuits.

"Do you think Charles is going to fight you for full custody?" she asked as we climbed into the nearest booth.

The wine appeared in front of us, and I took a sip before responding. "I'm not sure. I thought he was going to fight the adultery thing until the judge asked you to play the voicemail. The fact he conceded that quickly gives me some hope, but I truly don't know. I don't have physical evidence he's a terrible father. Just the word of many, many people."

I wasn't sure if her vulnerability in court inspired me to share something personal or it was my guilty conscience, but after taking another swig of wine, I folded my hands on the table and looked at her. "I mean, in all honesty, I didn't start out as the world's greatest parent, but at least I eventually stepped up. "

She rolled her eyes. "I call bullshit."

Giving a small laugh, I shook my head. "When Raegan was a newborn, I was no better than Charles or any other parent who neglects their kids. I was young and overwhelmed. I didn't know how to raise a child, but I was too scared to get an abortion and adoption wasn't something I really considered. The first few months of Raegan's life, I just stared at her. She would cry, and I would change, feed, and burp her, almost robotically. But sometimes that wouldn't help. She would cry, and cry, and cry, and eventually, because I was home alone with her so often, I would put her on the floor with the television on and lock myself in the bathroom.

"I spent so much time in there, hands over my ears, trying to block out the sound of a kid I didn't know how to care for. Finally, I called my parents, and they managed to make it out here. My mom could hear in my voice how much I was struggling. When she arrived, she quickly realized I was raising Raegan on my own. Charles was never around, even then."

McKenna cocked her head. "What changed?"

"My mom pulled me aside about a week into staying with us and gave me a heart-to-heart. Told me I was waiting for someone else to step in and care for Raegan, when there would never be anyone else. I chose to have her, so it was my responsibility to saddle up and take care of her. Raegan was the one suffering, and it wasn't her fault. She didn't ask to be there."

"Damn," she muttered.

I pursed my lips. "Yep. It was a come-to-Jesus moment, and that was what I needed. I walked back into the house, took Raegan from my dad, and didn't let her go for nearly a year after that." I laughed. "With Harrison, I was slightly older, but no matter how old you are and how many kids you have, nothing prepares you for a child who has special needs. That was an entirely different adjustment, but we did it. However, after Harrison was born, it was difficult to split my time evenly between him and Raegan. It still is, and because she's older and more independent, she doesn't always get the attention she deserves. I just hope one day she doesn't hate me because of it." The biscuits had arrived at some point during my confession, and I offered one to McKenna before grabbing my own.

She examined the circular quick bread, her head still tilted to one side. "As someone who doesn't live in the same house as you and the kids but knows you all pretty darn well, I'll tell you this: neither of your children hate you, Sam. I don't think they ever could. Harrison was so overjoyed to be back at your house this last week once he realized he wasn't unexpectedly leaving. I know you know, but he was in such a funk when he got back from Lydia's. I'd never seen him so downtrodden before. Even during his hospital stays, he's happier than he was after spending time with Charles. But when he knows he's with you, he's elated. He knows you're his safe place.

"And Raegan," she continued. "She's going through a lot right now, but she's just as strong as you are. Maybe even stronger, which is wild to think about. Two intimidating women in one family," she winked.

"You are the second person to call me that within a

matter of days, and I find that odd. I never really saw myself that way until I decided to take a stand against Charles," I admitted.

She shook her head. "You've always been fierce. Maybe a little quieter about it, but come on. All the stuff you do for your kids? And all the stuff you've accomplished in life? You are a phenomenal mother, nurse, friend, and partner, judging by how Landon always stares at you. He's the human version of the heart-eyes emoji whenever you're around."

I could feel my cheeks flush. "I think he's deranged for wanting to be with me, but at the same time, I'm done questioning it. Now I'm just sitting back and enjoying the fact that he wants to stick around. He's an amazing guy."

She smiled. "And you're an amazing woman. Dream team, right there."

After we finished our wine and biscuits, we headed back to the courthouse. Both exiting my car, I walked around the vehicle to stand beside her. "Have you considered pressing charges against Charles?"

"I don't think there's much of a point," she said, shaking her head. "You know this city. What will he get? A slap on the wrist? It's not worth dredging everything up yet again. Although, because of all of this, I think Kevin and I are going to move out of Madison once I graduate. That way I don't have to worry about seeing him ever again."

I put my head in my hands. "Again, I am so sorry about all of this. I'm sorry about Charles, and I'm sorry you had to unearth all those feelings again because of my divorce. Please, let me know if I can do anything. I'm really, terribly sorry."

She stepped close to hug me. "You can annihilate Charles' ass in court. Divorce him, get one hundred percent physical and legal custody of the kids, and leave this place in your dust. That's what you can do for me. Make yourself blissfully happy while he suffers."

"From your lips to God's ears."

Hearing me pull into the driveway, Landon opened the front door and met me on the front steps. He was wearing his signature school psychologist outfit, and had it been any other day, I would have jumped at the chance to do potentially psychologically damaging things to him in the bedroom. But after the shitshow that had been today, I couldn't fathom doing anything but putting on pajamas and going to bed. I was mentally and emotionally exhausted.

Walking up the steps, I placed a hand on his chest. "You'll never believe what went down today in court."

CHAPTER NINETEEN

Landon's jaw didn't close for almost an entire minute after I finished relaying the day's events, a dazed look plastered across his face. We hadn't made it past the foyer before I explained what had happened.

"He…he assaulted McKenna. For years. And she didn't say anything." His eyes were pinballing back and forth as he tried to digest what I had told him.

I nodded. "Instead, she came back here, every day, and cared for Harrison, because she loves him that much."

"Just when I think I know everything about Charles and believe he can't be any more of an asshole, he takes Raegan and Harrison. *Then* we learn he's assaulted McKenna. I just…"

I dropped my purse on the entryway table and kicked off my heels. "I know. It was shocking. I never suspected any of it. And what I don't understand is how could someone assault anyone, but *especially* an eighteen-year-old girl who is caring for their son? How awful can a person be?"

He ran his fingers through his hair as he stared at the floor, shaking his head. "Now more than ever, I hope you get full custody of the kids and never have to deal with that man ever again. Is she going to press charges? Because she really should."

"I asked her the same thing, but she said there isn't

any point. And as sad and infuriating as that is, she's right. After witnessing the bias toward Charles firsthand, I can't imagine McKenna having too much luck. She did say she was going to move out of Madison, though, once she graduates. My heart breaks for her. I feel like I should have been there for her somehow."

"You didn't know. It's not like you were aware of what was going on and ignored it. You had no idea."

I brought my hands up to my jaw and massaged it. Between fighting the near constant nausea and forcing myself not to verbally and physically attack Charles in court, it had been clenched for hours. "I still feel so guilty."

Finally looking past Landon, I noticed the blazing fireplace and a blanket topped with two plates and cutlery where the ottoman once sat. It had now been pushed off to the side, making way for the indoor picnic Landon had apparently planned. "Did I miss a special occasion?" I gawked, eyeing the romantic setup.

He stared at me, momentarily confused, until he turned around. "Ah, I forgot about all of that for a second. You didn't miss any special occasion—you have to stop thinking that me making you a nice meal warrants something to celebrate."

I tore my eyes away from the fireplace and stepped in front of Landon. "Sorry, I'm not used to thoughtful gestures like this. But it's a wonderful thing to have to adjust to."

Wrapping his arms around my waist, he kissed me softly, at first, but it quickly escalated. Just as I was about to reach for his shirt, he pulled away. "We need to eat dinner first. It's salmon, and cold fish is not ideal."

The thought of dinner *and* getting Landon naked

after had me almost salivating. "How did I manage to land a man like you in this city, of all places? And after being in a terrible relationship for so long? How lucky am I?"

Grinning, he kissed me again. "I'm the lucky one. Now come on, dinner awaits." Taking me by the hand, he led me over to the blanket. A restaurant-level looking plate presented glazed salmon and broccoli rice. The broccoli rice, of course, was covered in cheese. I pointed to it. "Because if you're going to eat vegetables—"

"They have to be covered in cheese," he finished, smiling. I sat down as Landon went to fetch a bottle of wine from the counter. Joining me on the blanket with a cabernet and two wine glasses, he pulled a multitool from his pocket and uncorked the wine. I raised an eyebrow.

"You carry a multitool in your work pants?"

He shrugged. "You never know when you'll need it. This is the South, babe. A multitool is the least dangerous thing people carry here."

With the wine brimming in both glasses, we carefully toasted before taking a sip. I was bringing my fork speared with salmon and scooped with rice to my lips when Raegan's ringtone sounded on my cell. Instantly dropping the cutlery, I jumped up and raced to get my phone from the entryway. "Is everything okay?" I asked, fear gripping my voice.

"Mom!" she screamed. "I just got the email! From USC's business school! I GOT IN!"

Moving the phone away from my ear, I put her on speaker. "Say it again, Rae, Landon's here and you're on speaker now." The weight of her announcement slowly seeped into my brain as she screamed her news again at an ungodly volume. In my mind, she was jumping up and down somewhere in Lydia's house, her hands balled into fists of pure joy and triumph. I was immediately saddened by the fact I wasn't with her to celebrate the news in person, but I also felt relieved she couldn't see me in this moment. After the unimaginably emotional day in court, her news stirred up more feelings I didn't want to deal with—I didn't have the energy. I fell into the nearest kitchen chair, scrambling to pull myself together and gather my thoughts. Tears began rolling down my cheeks, and I frantically wiped them away.

"I'm so proud of you, baby," I managed. "I knew you could do it."

"I can't believe it, Mom. USC is my first choice. I got accepted to my FIRST CHOICE COLLEGE. Like, is this real life?"

Part of me almost wished today had been a nightmare. Trying to speak in a neutral tone and failing, my voice cracked as I said, "I can totally believe it. I didn't doubt you for a second." I paused, using what little energy I had left to make a joke. "Well, the time you missed five English assignments, I was a little worried. There was definitely a hint of doubt."

Raegan laughed, and the falsetto cracked through the line.

"Thank you for calling me and letting me know, Rae. Go call your friends. Maybe your dad will let you go out and celebrate tonight." Letting my phone clatter onto the table, I buried my face in my hands as Landon walked up and knelt in front of me. Placing his hands on both my thighs, he glanced up at me. "Well, this is a great way to end an already very emotional day, isn't it?" he asked, offering me a half-smile.

I sniffed. "I'm so, so happy for her. She's always wanted to go to college on the west coast. And like she said, USC is her dream. But it's *USC*. How in the hell am I going to afford it? And what if I don't get full custody of Harrison? Raegan turns eighteen in July—she can leave Georgia and never look back. If Charles fights for custody of Harrison, I'm stuck here for another three and a half years. And that is awful for so many reasons. I never imagined living across the country from either of my kids." I was sobbing, now; the day's feelings were finally spilling out of me.

What would life even look like with me and Harrison still in Georgia, and Raegan in California? The fact that I hadn't emotionally prepared for something like this to happen seemed negligent on my part. I knew Raegan was going to be accepted to most of her university choices, so why hadn't I figured out how to handle it sooner? And today, of all days. The universe couldn't have dealt me one life-changing event or piece of news a day—spread it out a little?

"It's a lot to take in, but especially after today's shitstorm," he agreed. "And I know it's hard, but try not to think worst-case scenario right now. I mean, today was mostly successful, though also heartbreaking. McKenna's confession may force some people to realize that Charles is an adulterer in addition to being a pervert who harasses barely legal women, *and* you're one step closer to being divorced. Let's play best case scenario." Taking my hand, he led me back to the blanket in front of the fire. "What's the *best* outcome of all of this?"

Staring up at the ceiling as I wiped under my eyes, I sniffed and leaned against the ottoman. "Best case scenario, I get full custody of Harrison. Raegan applies for and receives scholarships and student loans. We move to Southern California. Harrison and Raegan can meet their grandparents. Well, Raegan has technically met my mom and dad, but she was two months old. She doesn't remember them."

His features softened. "This all sounds amazing."

I turned so that my eyes met his. "And you would come with us."

He smiled. "That would be best case scenario for me, too."

"Would you want to move with us? Could you?" I asked.

Landon joined me in resting against the ottoman, his hand finding its way into mine. "You and I both know how I feel about being back here. I would move in a heartbeat. With my parents gone, nothing is keeping me here except you. If you move, and you want me to come with you, I'm coming with you."

Leaning my head on his shoulder, we both gazed at the flames dancing inside the brick-encased fireplace, the light casting shadows on the surrounding walls. "Have you been to California?" I asked.

"Oddly enough, I haven't. There was a psychology conference in Los Angeles I signed up for a few years ago, but then the pandemic hit, and the event turned virtual. I've heard good things, mostly. Some people say it's snootier the closer you get to Los Angeles, but Los Angeles folk have nothing on Southern women," he grinned.

I bobbed my head in agreement. "There are definitely ugly people in Southern California as a whole, but there aren't as many small cities to feel trapped in, so it evens out. If there are gossipy people in the community you move to, it's fairly easy to avoid them if you live in a bigger city. Where I'm from, it is the best of both worlds. If you want to see people you know, you shop at certain local stores, and if you want to avoid those familiar faces, you drive ten minutes away and shop for your groceries in peace amongst strangers. Here, there's not really any means of escape unless you want to spend an arm and a leg for gas and travel on the highway for a bit," I said.

Landon caressed my hand with his thumb. "I applied to so many colleges in bigger cities, including a few in Southern California, with the intention of leaving small-town living behind forever. But when I was accepted to Wesleyan in Connecticut, I traded my dream of living in a big city for attending my dream university. To make matters worse, the college requires all undergraduate students live on campus, which is basically like living in a micro city. And I thought Madison was bad." He chuckled. "During my master's program, though, I lived a few miles off campus, but it was still a small community. When I went to Harvard for my doctorate— that was my happy medium. Cambridge isn't a huge city by any means, but in comparison to Middletown and here, it felt massive.

"I always hoped my parents would follow me when I told them I planned on staying in New England, but like so many people here, they only knew life in a small community. The idea of moving to any other place, much less a larger city, was scary to them. And I understand that. They were third-generation Madison natives. Cutting roots that run that deep would be a struggle," he admitted. "But for me, I never felt attached to this place like they did. Even when I was young, I fantasized about living elsewhere. I watched too many movies that romanticized popular cities, and I was itching to get out and explore other places. The accident was my final sign to get out when I could."

I rubbed his arm with my free hand. "I'm sorry you had to come back."

Shrugging, he shook his head. "It was a rough first couple of weeks, but I'm glad I got to be there for my parents when they needed me. And ultimately, of course, coming back here led me to you. I consider moving home worth it." He kissed my forehead before resuming staring into the fire.

I closed my eyes, allowing myself to get caught up in the idea of moving to California and getting the hell out of this place, returning home, and seeing my parents. The thought of them seeing Raegan and Harrison would be a dream come true for them *and* me.

Relocating to Southern California also meant Harrison could experience the beach, the nearly unlimited amount of sunshine, and the picturesque mountains bordering almost every city. It was hard not to get as giddy as Raegan, visualizing all the possibilities for Landon, me, Raegan, and Harrison starting over in my home state. But it also made the possibility of it not happening that much harder to bear.

Opening my eyes, I sighed. "Best case scenario seems far-fetched, though."

He rubbed my leg. "Maybe it is, maybe it isn't. But for now, let's celebrate today's small victories and acknowledge the fact that McKenna is a strong, brave, badass woman who has suffered through years of bullshit and is still here for your family. You couldn't have found someone better to care for your son. Also, your daughter being accepted into USC is pretty freaking awesome. You should be proud of Raegan and your parenting skills."

Grabbing our glasses from the ottoman, we clinked them together. "Cheers," we said simultaneously before throwing back the wine. We ate dinner in silence, simply enjoying each other's company and processing the day's events. When we finished, he took the dishes and started the dishwasher, further proving he truly was one of a kind.

Returning to the blanket, he stood over me, hand outstretched. With my palm in his, Landon hoisted me off the floor and pulled me close. Offering me another grin, he started to aimlessly dance us around the room.

"We don't have music," I laughed as he spun me around in slow circles.

Pulling out his phone, he chose a song I couldn't see before slipping it back into his pocket. "Yours," by Russell Dickerson filled the room.

"There's that country music I always knew you listened to." I winked.

Grinning, he replied, "You can take the man out of the South, but you can't take the South out of the man. Plus, this song perfectly sums up my feelings for you."

I laid my head against his chest as we moved quietly throughout the living room, listening to the lyrics.

"Sam," he said softly. "Even if you end up facing the worst-case scenario, we can suffer living in Georgia together for another few years, no problem."

"I know," I smiled, moving my face close to his.

Our lips met, and we kissed until long after the song was over. Eventually, we danced our way back to the blanket, where he took me in his arms and laid me on the floor. I stared into his eyes as he hovered over me.

"Thank you," I said, wrapping my arms around his neck and bringing him close to me. When his face was next to mine, I started kissing the space where his collar ended and his bare skin began.

"For what?" he asked, groaning as I moved up to his ear.

Pulling back slightly, I stared at him. "So many things. Like being patient with me and sticking around. I know the last few months haven't been easy. There were plenty of opportunities when you could have left and never given me another thought. But you didn't. You stayed."

He moved off me and onto the blanket. "Once I met you, I knew I could never leave you. You are what I never knew I was missing in my life, Sam. You have all of me, always, no matter what." Propping his head up with his hand, his eyes moved up and down my body. "On a completely unrelated note," he grinned, "I'm not sure I'll ever get over just how beautiful you are."

Rolling onto my side, I began unbuttoning his shirt. "And I'm not sure I'll ever get over the fact that you think it's okay to walk around the house with a shirt on when the kids aren't here."

He smiled. "Would it lead to this every time?" he asked, quickly ridding himself of his pants once I yanked his shirt open.

"Probably, most definitely, yes," I panted. As he removed my clothes, I tried to remain calm and collected, but it was a struggle. Knowing what was about to happen caused my breathing to sound almost frantic and my heartbeat to race. I wanted him all over me—his skin against mine, immediately.

After our clothes were tossed onto the couch, he gently spread my legs apart with his shoulders. When his lips touched my skin, an uncontrollable groan escaped me. His tongue swirled around me, his arms forcing my legs wider. Running my fingers through his hair, my body writhed uncontrollably as his face moved against me.

"Landon," I breathed, dragging my elbows up to my sides. Watching him go down on me immediately backfired, as my arousal rapidly increased. Falling back onto the blanket, I bunched the fabric in my hands and moaned. "I think you should be inside me. *Now*."

Pulling away, he glanced up at me, his eyes darkened with lust. "You come this way, and then we can do things however you want." Dropping his head and placing his tongue on me once more, I gasped as his mouth created even more heat against my skin. Without warning, my back arched and my orgasm swept over me, causing me to cry out his name as I came undone.

When my body stilled, he planked over me, smiling. "You know what two sounds I love most in the entire world?"

Still trying to catch my breath, I shook my head.

"The final dismissal bell on Friday and you calling out my name. Both do different things to me, but I will never get tired of either." He gave me a devilish grin, and I couldn't help but laugh.

"It's weird to refer to school when we are having sex, but to continue down this path for a second—just imagine if I was in your office, on top of you, calling out your name as the final bell rang," I taunted.

"Oh, God," he said, momentarily closing his eyes. "Don't make me finish without you."

I put my hands on his chest, gently forcing him off me. Rotating onto his back, his eyes were wide with surprise until I climbed on top of him. "I saw that face. Did you really think I was going to leave you high and dry?" I asked coyly.

He smiled. "I hoped not, but even if you did, I still got what I wanted."

Without warning, I sank down on top of him, my body adjusting to him within seconds. I had every intention of taking my time as I slowly flexed my hips, but Landon wasn't having it.

Pushing himself deeper inside me, he drew my body close and tightly wrapped one arm around my waist. The room spun, and I was on my back before I could even register what had happened. It was his turn to stare down at me, his eyes sparkling in the last bit of firelight.

"If you think I'm going to last long after going down on you, you are so very wrong," he said, bringing his lips to mine and pushing his tongue inside my mouth. Dizzy with anticipation and pleasure, I felt him start to move. His pace was urgent, his motions intense.

"God, Sam," his breathing heavy, "what you do to me…" he trailed off as he thrusted faster.

I could feel another orgasm starting to build. Closing my eyes, I wanted this moment to last forever, but in reality, I knew both of us weren't going to last another minute.

"Sam," he said, starting to slow down ever so slightly.

"Come for me," I whispered, kissing him. Gripping his biceps, I could feel myself tighten around him. Moaning, he stilled as he came, causing me to follow suit seconds later.

Curling up next to me, he and I lay shrouded in darkness, as the fire had exhausted its last flame minutes earlier. "You really have no regrets about asking me out all those weeks ago?" I asked.

Spent, Landon lifted his head a mere inch off the blanket to stare at me. "Do you?"

"Absolutely not."

His head lowered again. "I have never been more certain about anything in my entire life. The day I saw you, I knew that was it."

"And all the drama that has unfolded along the way?"

Landon shifted from his back to his side and draped an arm over my midsection. "It just makes our story that much more exciting and epic."

CHAPTER TWENTY

Judge Thurman peered out into the courtroom from his seat on the bench. It was a week later, and this time, it wasn't just McKenna, Jules, and me on my side of the room. Behind us was an entire team of people who were ready and willing to testify that Charles had never been around for our children, and one of them was Raegan. To the left of us sat Charles and his attorney, the benches completely empty behind them. I was mildly surprised Lydia hadn't shown up, but the fewer people to contend with, the better.

I knew I should have felt confident, ready to challenge Charles with the support of nearly a dozen people, but I still felt uneasy. Judge Thurman could easily take pity on Charles and grant him what he felt was fair, despite what the other witnesses and I would say.

"Custody, child support, and spousal support are on the agenda today, and with the amount of witnesses Ms. Hawley brought, today is going to be a very long day," the judge said. He moved his eyes between Charles and me before sighing. "Well, Ms. Hawley, since you seem to have brought the calvary with you, why don't you go first. We will start with custody—please tell us what you desire in terms of legal and physical custody."

I nodded, taking a deep breath before standing. "I'm asking for full physical and legal custody of Harrison and

Raegan."

Charles immediately stood, but his attorney placed his hand on Charles' arm. Reluctantly, he slid back into his seat but not before shooting me a nasty glare.

"And why do you want full physical and legal custody of Harrison and Raegan?" Judge Thurman asked.

Forcing myself to address the judge and not Charles, I said, "Because I've been there for my children from day one, and I know for certain Charles cannot say the same. Or at least, he can't prove it."

The judge nodded at Charles. "And what do you want, Mr. Hawley?"

I lowered myself into my chair as Charles stood. The anger radiating from him was unmistakable—his cheeks were flushed, and his hands were shaking. His somewhat irrational rage caused me to feel both annoyed and nervous. He was angry, with little or no proof to counter my accusation, and I had an army. But at the end of the day, the judge would make the final verdict.

"I wanted to be reasonable and ask for fifty-fifty."

"For physical and legal?" Judge Thurman clarified, and Charles nodded.

"Do you honestly think you and Ms. Hawley can amicably agree on all things legal regarding Harrison and Raegan?"

Charles all but threw up his hands in frustration. "I was willing to try, Your Honor, but now with her asking for full legal and physical, I may ask for the same."

The judge shook his head. "Mr. Hawley, you just said you were asking for fifty-fifty. Are you changing your mind? Do you now want full legal and physical custody?"

Charles looked at his attorney, who in turn, stared down at the desk in front of him. Taking his silence as an objection, Charles inhaled slowly and exhaled forcefully before answering. "I want fifty-fifty."

The judge shook his head once before turning to me again. "Ms. Hawley, who do you have with you today to aid in your fight for full custody?"

Turning, I stared at the faces of the men and women behind me, a lump forming in my throat. The fact that this many people were willing to take time off from work to help me was astonishing. I swallowed hard before beginning. "The group you see behind me consists of a handful of Harrison's doctors and nurses who care for him now or have in the past. There's Miss Ruiz, whom you met last week. She has been Harrison's caregiver for five years. There's also Grace Parker, my former neighbor and daughter Raegan's former babysitter, and lastly, Raegan."

Judge Thurman could not hide his surprise when I mentioned Raegan. Both eyebrows raised, he lowered his glasses. "Raegan, how old are you?" he asked.

Raegan stood. She was wearing a pair of my dress slacks, a black tank top, and a navy cardigan. I'd told her she could dress semi-casual, but she had rolled her eyes in response. "If I want him to take me seriously, Mom, I have to look professional. Otherwise, I'll just seem like a dumb teenager." I hadn't argued with her.

"I'm seventeen, Your Honor." Her voice rang clear, and I was momentarily jealous of her confidence. Had I been as brave as Raegan when I was her age, I probably would have had a different life.

"When do you turn eighteen?" he asked.

"In three months, Your Honor."

The judge pushed his glasses up the bridge of his nose. "And you're here in support of your mom?"

Raegan nodded. "Yes, Your Honor."

"Where is Harrison?" Judge Thurman asked, and I answered before Raegan could.

"He's at home with my friend, Andrea Mitchell, who is a registered nurse. She cares for him on the rare occasion when Miss Ruiz and I cannot."

Judge Thurman nodded, his lower lip jutting out. "I'll be interested to hear what you have to say, Raegan. Ms. Hawley," his eyes met mine. "Who is taking the stand first?"

Harrison and Raegan's pediatrician, Dr. Katherine Reed, was sworn in before taking a seat on the witness stand. Jules walked to the area in front of Judge Thurman, standing only a few feet away from Dr. Reed.

"Dr. Reed," Jules began, "how long have you known the Hawleys?"

"Since Raegan was a toddler," she replied.

"And you see Harrison often?" Jules asked.

Dr. Reed nodded. "Harrison's diagnosis of cerebral palsy requires routine checkups. We attempt to monitor everything—his vitals, bloodwork, etc., to ensure he's receiving the best possible care." She was calm and collected, as if testifying in court was a frequent pastime, but I knew for a fact that this was her debut court hearing. When Jules had asked her if she would testify, she disclosed that she'd never been a part of anything like this before, but she would gladly take the stand if it meant Harrison could stay in my care.

Watching her and Jules, I knew they had rehearsed their conversation, which, I assumed made the whole process easier for Dr. Reed. But for the rest of us, it was unfolding like a stereotypical courtroom drama TV show. We all knew Jules' questions were leading to something; we just didn't know what.

"How many times, estimated, of course, has Ms. Hawley attended Harrison's appointments?" Jules asked.

My stomach clenched. There it was—the first shot, and Dr. Reed's answer was going to start the war of custody. Everyone in the courtroom stilled, waiting for her response.

"Every time, ma'am. I can't remember a single instance that Ms. Hawley did not accompany Harrison."

Jules nodded. "And how many times has Mr. Hawley attended Harrison's appointments?" Second shot.

Dr. Reed paused, thinking about Jules' question. "I believe he came to a few of Harrison's appointments back when he was a baby. It wasn't a lot, but I can't tell you a number."

Turning slightly, Jules rubbed her hands together. The clicking of her high heels against the tile was the only thing filling the silence before she spoke again. "So, it's been a while since Mr. Hawley has gone to one of Harrison's routine care appointments."

Dr. Reed moved her head in affirmation, causing Jules to glance at Charles' attorney. "Your witness," she said, returning to her seat beside me.

Charles' attorney stood up, straightened his tie, and took the same place on the floor where Jules had been. "Dr. Reed, thank you for joining us," he started. "Now, I know you said Mr. Hawley hasn't gone to any of Harrison's appointments since he was a baby. Why do you think that is?"

Dr. Reed shook her head and shrugged, but I could

tell she was trying to buy herself some time to think about how to properly answer the question. Cross-examination wasn't something that could be rehearsed, and I knew his goal was to fluster Dr. Reed so she would say something he could use against us. As a doctor, I knew she worked well under pressure, but I prayed she could maintain her focus while being pummeled with persistent questions in court.

"I'm not sure, sir," she finally answered.

Charles' attorney paced the floor in front of the witness stand and judge's bench. "Do you think it's because Mr. Hawley doesn't care? Or do you think it is because of his work schedule?"

Another shrug from Dr. Reed. "Again, I'm not sure why Mr. Hawley rarely attended, or attends, Harrison's appointments. I grew so accustomed to seeing only Ms. Hawley that I never questioned it."

"I just want to make it known that Mr. Hawley never went out of his way to miss Harrison's appointments. He manages his own accounting business, as we all know, and he is the mayor of this beautiful city. Granted, none of that takes precedence over his son, but some things can't be missed for routine appointments."

Now would be a great time for our next witness. I looked to Jules, who subtly nodded before returning her gaze to Dr. Reed and Charles' attorney.

"Again, sir, I never questioned it. I'm just stating facts—Ms. Hawley has been to all of Harrison's appointments, while Mr. Hawley hasn't been to one in a very long time," Dr. Reed concluded.

Charles' attorney nodded. "Thank you, Dr. Reed. We are done, Your Honor."

Jules rose. "Our next witness is Dr. Melody Taylor.

She is one of the ER doctors at Morgan Medical Center."

The redheaded doctor stood, papers in hand, and affirmed everything she was about to state would be the truth before sitting behind the witness stand.

Jules stared up at her. "Dr. Taylor, how many times has Harrison been in your care?"

Dr. Taylor stared at the podium before answering. "Just confirming with my notes, ma'am, but Harrison has been seen by me in the ER eighty-six times. More often when he was younger, but he's been in the ER once this year already."

"And how many times has Ms. Hawley accompanied Harrison in the ER?" Jules asked.

Dr. Taylor didn't need to inspect her notes before answering. "Every time, ma'am."

Jules nodded. "And Mr. Hawley?"

Dr. Taylor scanned the papers in front of her. "Two times, ma'am."

The judge raised an overgrown eyebrow while Jules started to walk the floor. "Two times in the last fourteen years, is that correct, Dr. Taylor?"

She nodded, staring down at Jules. "It was the first two times Harrison was admitted to the hospital."

"And did you ever ask why Mr. Hawley wasn't present during these emergency visits?" Jules questioned.

Dr. Taylor nodded. "Actually, yes, in the beginning. Caring for a child with special needs can be very overwhelming, and when Harrison was younger, I could see Ms. Hawley was stressed, as are all parents of special needs children, on some level. I thought having Mr. Hawley there would help ease her anxiety, but she would always tell me he never answered her calls."

"And did you ever try to call Mr. Hawley yourself?" Jules asked. I cocked my head as I watched Jules slowly walk back and forth below the judge's bench and witness stand. *Why would an ER doctor take it upon herself to reach out to the other parent if they were absent during a visit?*

Dr. Taylor shot me an apologetic gaze before looking to Jules. "Yes, actually. I called him on three separate occasions. Having worked in Madison for two decades, I know the Hawley name—they are a highly regarded family in this community. When Ms. Hawley told me he wasn't taking her calls, I felt that it couldn't be true. I thought maybe she was purposely trying to withhold information from him."

My jaw dropped. I never got the impression Dr. Taylor didn't like or believe me when we first met. Because I was not only her coworker, but also a frequent emergency room visitor, I was fairly confident she and I were on good terms now—but apparently at one point, she thought I would lie about Charles. What type of person and mother did she think I was?

"I wanted to see if she was telling the truth," Dr. Taylor continued. "The first time I called was during Harrison's third trip to the ER. He did answer the phone, but told me he was unable to step away from work at the moment and that he would be there as soon as possible. Again, as the mayor and a business owner, I understood that he was an incredibly busy person, so I didn't think anything negative about his response."

"But did he ever show up?" Jules asked, and Dr. Taylor shook her head.

"No, ma'am, he did not. And that struck me as odd, seeing as how his infant son, who has special needs, was in the hospital. Having a non-disabled infant in the hospital is terrifying, but when a child who has special needs is in the hospital, depending on their disability, of course, some things can go south very quickly. I thought Mr. Hawley would want to be there in the event something unexpected happened, for both his son and his wife's sakes."

"When was the next time you called him?" Jules asked.

Dr. Taylor shuffled through some pages on the witness stand. "During Harrison's eighth trip to the ER and on his twelfth visit. I got the same story. After that, I stopped trying. I would see Ms. Hawley out in the hall on her phone, trying to reach him for at least the first few hours after Harrison was admitted. I heard her leave him voicemails time and time again. I knew then it wasn't her lack of trying or purposely trying to exclude Mr. Hawley. Mr. Hawley just couldn't be bothered by his son's health issues."

Whether or not she thought I was a liar at some point, she just redeemed herself with that comment.

"Your witness." Jules nodded at Charles' attorney, who stood.

"Dr. Taylor," Charles' lawyer said, approaching the stand, "you said Harrison was a patient of yours eighty-six times in the last fourteen years. Is that correct?"

Dr. Taylor nodded. "Yes, sir."

"And how often do both parents show up at their child's bedside when their child is admitted that many times?" Charles' attorney asked.

Dr. Taylor shook her head. "I can't definitively answer that, sir. I don't keep track of other patients, just my own, and I don't see a lot of children like Harrison."

Charles' attorney kept going. "Ms. Hawley was unemployed for many of those visits, correct? She didn't become a nurse until Harrison was older."

Dr. Taylor shrugged. "Sir, it's not my job to keep track of my patients' parents' employment history. I am solely responsible for my patients."

The lawyer sighed. "The point I'm trying to make, ma'am, is that Ms. Hawley would have been the most logical person to stay with Harrison at the hospital a majority of the time, since she was unemployed."

Dr. Taylor stared Charles' attorney straight in the eye. "If that's true, then what is Mr. Hawley's excuse now that both he and Ms. Hawley are employed? If anything, Mr. Hawley runs his own business and can make his own hours. He can adjust his schedule according to his children's needs. Ms. Hawley is at the mercy of the hospital scheduler, and yet she manages to make it every time."

Charles' lawyer shook his head, knowing very well Dr. Taylor just put him in his place. "No further questions, Your Honor."

Next to take the stand was Grace Parker, my former neighbor and Raegan's former babysitter. I hadn't seen her in years, as she and her husband moved away right before Raegan turned ten years old. I had passed along the only number I had for her to Jules, and apparently, she had been successful in reaching Grace, because now she sat behind the witness stand, her arms folded across her chest. A few additional wrinkles and a hunched frame made me realize just how much she had aged since I last saw her, but I doubted her mind had deteriorated along with her youth.

"Hi, Mrs. Parker," Jules greeted her. "It's nice to

finally see you in person, after our initial few meetings over video call."

Grace nodded at Jules; her face was emotionless, and her body was rigid. She had been one of the original homeowners in my neighborhood and was known for being a grump, which I'd discovered the hard way when Raegan was little. Grace had wandered over to my front yard, where Raegan sat playing in the grass wearing nothing but underwear.

"You know, we have chiggers here," she'd drawled, giving me a disapproving stare.

It had been hotter than blue blazes that afternoon, and Raegan had screamed at me for thirty minutes to go outside before I gave in. She had sweat through her clothes within minutes, so I stripped her of her outfit and plopped her down in the shade with a coloring book while I watched from the front steps, exhausted from hours of morning sickness due to being newly pregnant with Harrison.

"What in the hell are chiggers?" I'd asked, earning me an even more belligerent glare. We hadn't spent a whole lot of time outside during the summer months since we moved because of the humidity, so I had no idea what she was referring to. And I sure as heck didn't grow up with those things in Southern California.

"You out-of-staters move to the South and have no idea what goes on around here," she'd tsked, walking over to Raegan and plucking her up off the grass. Surprised by her brazenness, Raegan and I both stared at her, our eyes wide. Being a stereotypical toddler, Raegan instantly went for Grace's glasses, ripping them off her face while manically giggling. From our very brief interaction, I thought Grace would be furious, but instead, she smiled and let Raegan wave her glasses around in the air like they were sparklers on the Fourth of July.

"They're nasty little suckers that will make you itch until you bleed," she finally answered. "I would highly suggest putting clothes on the child if she's going to be in the grass."

I nodded slowly. "Okay. Thanks for the head's up."

Gently taking back her glasses, Grace set Raegan in my lap and walked back into her house.

"When did you first meet the Hawleys?"

Jules' questioning made me snap out of my walk down memory lane.

Grace sighed, as if being here was a huge imposition. "I knew Lydia and Charles—the first Charles, that is—that their son and his wife had moved in next door after he finished college. I was aware that the wife stayed at home with their young daughter. I didn't speak to any of them, though, until about two and a half years after they moved in. I saw that woman," she nodded at me, giving me the same contentious look she had given me all those years ago, "put her daughter in the grass almost completely naked one day in the middle of summer. I felt I needed to go over there and tell her about chiggers, because I knew she wasn't from around here."

Jules couldn't help but smile. "How did you wind up being Raegan's babysitter?"

Grace looked at me and I could see her surly expression lessen ever so slightly.

"Ms. Hawley came pounding on my door in the middle of the night about a year after our first interaction. She was crying, saying something along the lines of her infant son was being rushed to the hospital because he had a seizure, and she had no idea where her husband was." Now the disapproving stare shifted to Charles. "She begged me to come to her house and watch over Raegan while she went to the hospital to be with Harrison. After raising four kids of my own, I wasn't interested in watching someone else's, but since Raegan was asleep and Samantha needed help, I agreed.

"Samantha ended up coming home a few hours later because she still couldn't get ahold of Charles—the second one, that is—and she didn't want to put me out longer than she already had."

The cantankerous attitude faded as Grace's story continued. "I saw how exhausted Samantha was. I learned it wasn't Harrison's first time in the hospital, nor was it the first time she couldn't get ahold of Charles in the middle of the night. She told me she normally took Raegan with her to the hospital when needed, but that night, Raegan hadn't been feeling well and Samantha was afraid to wake her. I ended up staying that whole day so Samantha could sleep and visit Harrison. I learned very quickly Raegan was a vivacious little thing, but cute as a button. Watching her didn't turn out to be that big of a nuisance."

"How often did you interact with Charles?" Jules asked.

Grace was shaking her head before Jules even finished speaking. "Never. Never once did I interact with him, and I rarely saw him the entire time we lived next door. I moved right before Raegan turned ten, so I was around for quite a while. His never being there wasn't shocking to me, though. He is a carbon copy of his father."

I brought my tongue to my top lip, trying to mask my smile. If Grace was still the same person she was when I knew her, she was going to elaborate.

"A lot of people in this city were smitten with Charles Sr., but I knew the truth. He was a cheating, lying politician who—"

Nope. The woman hadn't changed one bit, and I loved her for it. Audible whispers came from behind me, and Judge Thurman banged his gavel. "That's quite enough, Mrs. Parker. Thank you."

She shrugged, completely unfazed.

Jules resumed her place next to me, obviously content with how things went down.

Charles' attorney looked at Charles before standing. "We have no further questions, your Honor."

Grace harrumphed as she stood to leave the witness stand. As she passed through the half-doors leading back to the benches, she shook her head at Charles' lawyer. "I drive all the way here from Nebraska, and you don't even question me? You *must* know your case is doomed."

Judge Thurman banged his gavel again as nearly everyone on my side of the room erupted in nervous snickers. "Mrs. Parker, if you're going to disrupt the hearing again, I'm going to have to ask you to leave."

Grace kept walking, raising her hand in the air and waving off the judge. "No need. I'm driving back home. There are a multitude of reasons why I left this place, and I ain't sticking around long enough to remember all of them." With that, she pushed open the courtroom door and was gone.

CHAPTER TWENTY-ONE

Judge Thurman called for a fifteen-minute recess after Grace's dramatic exit. Everyone stood and shuffled out of the stuffy courtroom, no one daring to utter a word until they reached the hallway. Charles and his attorney went one way, and Jules, Raegan, McKenna, Harrison's care team, and I went the other. A few people used the restrooms, but most of us huddled around, too nervous to stray far from the area.

"It's going really well, right?" Raegan asked Jules, who simply shrugged.

"If this was any other case, I would say yes, it's going freaking amazing. But because your dad has so much clout in this city, I can't honestly tell you how it's progressing. Even if I think it's going in our favor, that judge could turn around and give your dad whatever he wants solely because he grew up with the Hawleys."

Raegan's chin jutted out and she forcefully expelled air, momentarily scattering her bangs before they fell neatly back into place. "I don't understand why he thinks he has a shot. He's never been there for us, and he's an idiot for trying to dispute the counterarguments of all these people who actually have."

I shook my head. "Again, Rae, the judge has the final say. It may not matter what type of evidence or testimonies we bring to the table. But I know he will listen to you, seeing that you are your father's child.

Everyone else here," I gestured to the crowd around us, "they are helping us build the case. You are the one who is going to have to bring it home. That is, if you still want to. In no way do I want you to feel like you have to be here. It's my battle, after all."

She picked at a cuticle before staring at me. "It's not just your battle, though. He made it mine too, when he had the audacity to think he could care for Harrison and me. If I have to spend one more week with that man and his awful mother, I'm going to lose my mind. I will also bill him for my much-needed future therapy."

Pulling her in for a hug, I whispered, "I'm so sorry you have to do this. I hate that we put you in this position."

Raegan moved away from me slowly. "It's not your fault, Mom. You've always been there for us, and I'm fairly certain you would have stuck it out with Dad had he not slept with who knows how many people, just to keep Harrison and me 'safe'," she said. "But safe doesn't always mean better. Your leaving him is the best thing that has happened to all of us for so many reasons."

Jules peered at the clock. "It's time." Everyone in the group nodded at each other before we all solemnly returned to our seats in the courtroom.

"Who's up next?" Judge Thurman asked, and Jules looked back at the seats behind us.

"Your Honor, I would like to call Zachary Chase, a nurse at Morgan Medical Center."

In the span of an hour, Jules went through all the nurses who routinely cared for Harrison; all gave similar testimonies to Dr. Taylor and Dr. Reed. If Charles showed up to any of Harrison's appointments, it was early on, and they hadn't seen him in years at his son's bedside while under their care.

With minimal to no cross examination by Charles' attorney, we swiftly made our way to McKenna. "Miss Ruiz," Jules motioned for McKenna to take the stand once again.

I grimaced. I hated seeing her up there just as much as I dreaded the idea of Raegan sitting behind the stand, but even more so now because of what McKenna had gone through last week. The poor woman had to spend yet another day in court with the man who assaulted her, thanks to me and my terrible choice for a husband.

Judge Thurman nodded at McKenna after she was sworn in. Once she was seated behind the witness stand, Jules stood in front of her, ready with her list of questions. "Miss Ruiz, you're Harrison's caregiver while Ms. Hawley is away from the home, correct?"

McKenna nodded. "I care for him while she is at work, if she has a doctor's appointment, things like that."

"And you cared for Harrison while Mr. Hawley still resided with Ms. Hawley?"

"Yes, ma'am. Mr. Hawley only moved out a few months ago."

Best few months of McKenna's life, I bet. That asshole, Charles.

"Did you ever watch Harrison while Mr. Hawley was home?" Jules asked. "I know a few of us already know the answer to this based on last week's interview, but I would like to further ensure *everyone* is aware of Mr. Hawley's involvement with his children."

Or lack thereof.

McKenna paused, inhaling slowly before responding. "Yes, ma'am. There were many times I was there when Mr. Hawley would return home from work or elsewhere. The first time he returned to the house while I was working, I texted Ms. Hawley to see if I needed to stay until she got home. She acknowledged that it was an odd situation—me sticking around when Harrison's father was home—but she asked me if I could continue watching Harrison until she came home, even on the random days Mr. Hawley returned before her." She shot me a remorseful glance, but she had nothing to be sorry about. It was the truth. I never trusted Charles alone with the kids because he was so incompetent and uninterested in their lives.

"Was Mr. Hawley ever home the entire duration of your staying with Harrison at any point over the last five years?" Jules asked.

Without missing a beat, McKenna nodded again. "Yes. Again, I initially found it weird, but after working with the Hawleys for a few months, I realized why I was needed when Mr. Hawley was 'home'," she quoted.

"Can you clarify, Miss Ruiz?" Jules questioned.

"If Ms. Hawley hadn't told me Mr. Hawley was home on various occasions, or if I hadn't briefly seen him in the common areas, I might not have known he was present while I was with Harrison. There were many occasions I never saw him, or if I did, it was only for a short time." She momentarily shut her eyes. Of course, he only stuck around long enough to assault her before disappearing. "I'm assuming he locked himself away in his study each time he was home, but I never investigated."

Jules shook her head slightly. "So, you're telling me you were asked to care for Harrison while Ms. Hawley was away, even though Mr. Hawley was home?"

"Yes, ma'am," McKenna answered.

"This happened multiple times?" Jules asked.

"Yes, ma'am. Not incredibly often, but quite a few times, yes."

"Did you ever ask Ms. Hawley why you were needed if Mr. Hawley was home?" Jules asked.

McKenna nodded. "Ms. Hawley said Mr. Hawley was uninvolved in his children's lives, but kind of like Dr. Taylor, I thought she was being dramatic, at first. Then, as I spent more and more time with Harrison and the Hawleys, I realized she was right. Even when Mr. Hawley would come home from work, never once did he say anything to his children. Raegan and Harrison would be there on the couch, or doing homework at the dinner table, and he would walk past them as if they didn't exist. Never once did I hear him ask how their days were. He never offered to help Raegan with her assignments. He would walk in, drop his stuff in the kitchen, and head down the hallway." Finally, McKenna glanced over at Charles, causing me to do the same.

He was staring straight ahead, not registering either of our gazes.

"To recap, Mr. Hawley never paid attention to his children and was incapable of caring for them while Ms. Hawley was away," Jules said.

Charles' attorney stood up with a huff. "Objection, Your Honor. That is hearsay."

Judge Thurman shook his head. "Again, there is no jury present, Council. You have no one but me to sway, and I wouldn't worry about that one comment."

The lawyer sank into the chair, his eyes lowered in defeat.

McKenna stared at Jules, who nodded in her direction. "Thank you, Miss Ruiz, for once again taking the stand, especially after your testimony last week. Your witness, Council," she gestured toward Charles' attorney.

"No further questions, Your Honor," the lawyer muttered. I felt that if he questioned McKenna about anything, it would somehow circle back to her claims of Charles assaulting her, and he didn't want to bring that up again. Maybe he was smarter than he looked, although he *had* agreed to take Charles' case.

Judge Thurman glanced at the clock on the wall. "We have time for one more witness."

Jules turned, staring into the sea of people behind me. "Your Honor, we are calling Raegan Hawley, Ms. and Mr. Hawley's daughter, to the stand."

Charles watched Raegan as she slowly made her way to the front of the courtroom. Just as Jules was about to open her mouth, the judge raised his hand to stop her.

"Raegan, before we begin, I have to ask, do you want to be here today? Are you okay with testifying in court, seeing as how these are your parents?" He gestured to both Charles and me.

Not even batting an eye, Raegan nodded. "Yes, Your Honor. In fact, it was my idea. My mom didn't want me to be here."

Judge Thurman looked at me. "And why is that?"

"Because she didn't want me to feel like I was in the middle of their problems."

"And you don't feel that way?" he asked, his voice raising an octave.

Raegan shook her head. "No, Your Honor. I was never in the middle of their problems. I've always been on one side." She stared directly at me, her face unreadable.

I wouldn't cry. Instead, I studied the table in front of me and folded my hands in my lap. Slowly cracking my knuckles, I listened as Jules began.

"Raegan, do you remember your father, Mr. Hawley, being present when you were growing up?" Jules asked.

Well, we were just jumping straight into this, weren't we?

Raegan glowered at Charles. "No, ma'am."

"Did he ever attend any of your extracurricular activities? School events?"

Unlike her stance with the rest of the witnesses, Jules abandoned pacing below the witness stand while Raegan was up there. Instead, she leaned against the small wall that separated the witness stand and the judge's bench, her hands placed on either side of her. She seemed cool and collected, and I knew it was because she didn't want to heighten Raegan's already-present nerves.

Raegan cocked her head. "Yes and no. If he knew a lot of community members would be present, he would attend. Almost always he would appear at school functions and my little league games. When I was younger, I thought it was because he was proud of me and wanted to see me participate in these activities. But as I got older, I realized it was for show."

Jules rapped her fingers lightly on the wall. "Why do you say that?"

"Because when there weren't a lot of people in attendance, he wouldn't show up. I had private singing lessons for a bit, and only the parents of the kids belonging to the studio were allowed to attend the showcase at the end of the year. My dad never came to those recitals. There weren't enough people there for him to impress."

Never once had Raegan said any of this to me, and it made my heart hurt. I tried so hard to make up for the fact Charles was rarely there during games and performances. I would bring flowers, cheer loudly, clap long after everyone else had stopped. But my efforts were clearly in vain. Raegan had been young, but she wasn't fooled. I rubbed my face with my hands, forcing myself to take slow, steady breaths. There was nothing I could do about any of it now anyway, but the guilt was still there. I had a feeling it always would be.

Jules exhaled slowly. "Did your mother ever talk about your father in a negative way around you and Harrison?"

Raegan couldn't help but glance in my direction, and it was my turn to give her a poker face. "Not that I can ever remember, ma'am. Even to this day, my mom has a hard time speaking badly about my father in front of me and Harrison. And Lord knows she has plenty of ammunition."

"When was the last time you were in your father's care?" Jules asked, breezing past Raegan's last comment.

"A week ago, when the court ordered my brother and me to spend every other week with him. This past Monday through this morning was my father's scheduled week to ignore—I mean, 'spend time with us'."

I raised my hand to my mouth and coughed quietly to stifle a snort. God help anyone who chose to cross Raegan during her lifetime.

"And before this temporary custody agreement started, when was the last time you saw your father?"

"Excluding the brief second he was yelling at my mother while I was in the hospital, over half a year ago when my mom was kicking him out of the house."

Jules shifted her weight. "Did he ever try to contact you after he moved out?"

Raegan shook her head. "No, ma'am. Never texted, never called."

"And how is it spending time with him during his custody week?"

Sighing, Raegan leaned back in her chair and crossed her arms. "It is just like how my life was before he moved out. And after he moved out, honestly."

"Can you clarify what you mean?" Jules asked.

"He ignores me and Harrison, even when he is home. Lydia, his mother, is around, but really, she just hovers over me to make sure I won't communicate with my mom while she pays an incompetent nurse to care for Harrison. I mainly spend the week at my dad's ensuring my brother is fed and clean, since it was very clear early on that the nurse has no idea what she's doing."

Raegan had said as much to me, but every time she tried to get photographic or video proof that the nurse wasn't properly trained or able to care for Harrison, Lydia would be close by, watching Raegan. There were even a few instances when Lydia took Raegan's phone, preventing her from using it for days at a time. Apparently, Lydia learned from Charles' mistake and would not allow any solid proof to surface regarding her and her son's ineptitudes.

"Are you saying your father, Mr. Hawley, doesn't tend to Harrison himself while he is home?" Jules asked, causing Raegan to emit a burst of laughter before quickly throwing both hands over her mouth.

"Sorry, Your Honor," she mumbled, and the judge simply waived his hand. "No, ma'am. He didn't care for Harrison the first fourteen years of his life—why start now? He hired someone for around-the-clock care, but if I had to guess, this nurse has never cared for a person with cerebral palsy. Instead, I take care of Harrison. My father is not equipped to take care of my brother, and Harrison is not safe in his home."

"How is Harrison unsafe, Raegan?"

She held up her fingers and started ticking things off as she went. "He doesn't have the correct equipment for Harrison, and if he does, he doesn't know how to use it. Harrison requires a special bed, which my father doesn't have, and he needs his smoothies to be prepared in a specific way so he doesn't choke. My father doesn't know how to use the G-tube, and the nurse isn't confident in her own ability to use it, either. He finally ordered the seizure monitor for Harrison's bed, but who knows if it's hooked up. I spend every night in Harrison's room while we are there, just in case he has a seizure and needs help."

"Is your father aware of what he needs to do to properly care for Harrison?" Jules asked.

"The thing is, ma'am, if my father had paid any attention to us at all when he lived in our home, he *would* know. He wouldn't need to be told by anyone what is required to provide a safe home for his own son. But he has no clue.

"That first week my father had custody, I would bet my life that my mother told Lydia and the caregiver at least what the bare minimum is that needs to be done to make sure that Harrison is safe at Lydia's home. After my father all but kidnapped Harrison at the park, if I may add. He never asked permission from my mother to take Harrison; he hijacked Harrison from McKenna while they were outside of our home and my mother was with me at the hospital. But, I digress. My father wasn't prepared to care for Harrison these last couple of weeks, and unless they hired a competent nurse and took classes on caring for children with cerebral palsy, they *still* aren't prepared to care for Harrison this next week."

Jules pushed off the wall and stood a few feet away from the witness stand.

"Raegan, in your opinion, after spending fourteen years with your brother and knowing what he needs to ensure he is happy and healthy, can your father, Mr. Hawley, take care of Harrison? And another equally important question—can he take care of you?"

Raegan eyed Charles. "I'm not worried about me, ma'am. I'm almost eighteen years old—I can take care of myself. But when I am at my father's house with Harrison, I am constantly worried about Harrison's safety and wellbeing. I believe, as well as probably every medical professional in this room, that my father is not equipped to care for my brother at all. Harrison is not safe under my father's care."

"But you feel he is safe at your mother's, Ms. Hawley's, home?" Jules asked.

Raegan nodded vigorously. "Absolutely. My mother has been there for Harrison since the day he was born. And when she isn't able to be with him, she has extensively vetted caregivers who are beyond medically qualified to provide Harrison with exceptional care."

Jules turned away from Raegan and the judge, tapping her fists atop one another. "Two final questions, Raegan. Do you want your parents to have split custody?

Or would you rather one parent have one hundred percent custody of both you and your brother?" She turned to face the front of the courtroom again.

Raegan slammed her hand down on the podium, causing us all to jump. "Absolutely not, I do not want my parents to have split custody. My brother and I deserve to reside in the one place that is safe with the one parent who keeps it that way. We not only want, but deserve, to be with my mom one hundred percent of the time."

Jules smiled as she faced Charles' lawyer. "Your turn, Council. Thank you, Raegan," she called over her shoulder.

Charles' attorney rose and walked to the same area Jules stood seconds earlier. My lungs started to burn, and I realized I hadn't taken a breath since Jules finished questioning Raegan. Shooting her a quick glance, I inhaled slowly before closing my eyes.

Charles' lawyer was going to give Raegan hell, and because she was young and emotionally-driven, I had a feeling it would be easy to twist her words and make Raegan so confused that she would begin to question things. Sending up a prayer to anyone who would listen, I pleaded for Raegan's resiliency and tenacity to shine through while her father's attorney questioned her. The Hawleys had worn me down within a matter of months when I moved here. I didn't want their attorney, in a last-ditch attempt to make Charles seem like a good guy, to do the same to our daughter within a matter of minutes.

As if she could sense my fear, Jules reached for my hand and gave it a small, quick squeeze. I took another breath and waited for the inquisition to begin.

CHAPTER TWENTY-TWO

"Hi, Raegan." Charles' attorney decided to lead with a greeting that, maybe in his mind, made him seem trustworthy and approachable, but Raegan only glared at him, her arms folded and her back firmly pressed against the chair.

Realizing she wasn't going to answer him, Charles' lawyer cleared his throat and continued. "When you were little, were you aware of what your father did for a living?"

Raegan continued to stare at him. "I guess not. Does any little kid completely understand their parents' jobs?"

Undeterred by her attitude, the attorney pushed on. "Of course not. But this means you didn't understand why your father, Mr. Hawley, could show up to some of your games and recitals, but not all of them."

Raegan raised an eyebrow. "That's not a question, sir." The 'sir' had been full of snark, and I worried the judge would comment on her attitude. *Calm down, Rae.*

"You're right. I apologize. Do you agree that you were too young to understand why your father didn't come to every one of your events?"

Raegan slowly nodded. "Yes. But then I got older. My way of thinking and seeing things changed, but his behaviors did not."

Charles' lawyer nodded. "Your father is a busy man, Raegan. He runs his own accounting firm and is the mayor of Madison. I'm sure he would love to spend every waking moment with you and your brother, but unfortunately, he has to work."

I could see redness creep from Raegan's neck onto her cheeks. "He can make his own schedule since he has his own company. And does he *really* have to work? His trust fund will more than hold him over for the rest of his life. The only thing he's spending money on is himself; he hasn't helped my mom pay for any of our stuff since he moved out."

The judge's eyebrows shot up in surprise, but he stayed silent.

"How do you know he doesn't help your mother, Ms. Hawley, pay for things related to you and Harrison?" the attorney asked.

That was a great question, and I, too, wanted to know the answer. Never had I brought that up in front of Raegan. At least not knowingly.

"I overheard her telling Dr. Ford one day."

"And who is Dr. Ford?" Charles' attorney asked.

Shit. I *knew* they were going to somehow drag Landon into this, and Raegan unknowingly walked into their trap.

"Dr. Ford is the man my mother started seeing a few months ago." She was talking slowly, now, her spitfire attitude finally subsiding. She recognized she was entering dangerous territory regarding Landon, and now she had to truly think before she spoke.

Charles' lawyer nodded. "And was she seeing Dr. Ford prior to her kicking your father out of the house?"

My hands clutched the arms of the chair. Of course, they would go there. Jules moved her hand onto my leg, which I noticed then had started bouncing up and down.

Ceasing the movement, I exhaled slowly.

"No. Up until a few months ago, my mother rarely left the house to do anything other than work or take Harrison to appointments. Maybe this is a statement McKenna—Miss Ruiz," Raegan clarified, "can confirm, but my mother hasn't asked McKenna to stay outside of work hours and for the occasional random appointment in a very long time, maybe even ever."

Judge Thurman eyed McKenna. "Is this true?"

McKenna stood long enough to answer. "Yes, Your Honor."

Charles' attorney kept going. "But of course, your mother could have found another sitter. Or perhaps, invited Dr. Ford to your place of residence."

Raegan snorted. "I would have noticed if someone other than McKenna watched my brother while I was home. And I'm home a lot, by the way. I don't have a car. More proof my father doesn't help us pay for anything. Plus, do you really think my mother was dumb enough to invite another man into our home while my father still lived there? We had a doorbell camera and security cameras pointed at every door and window in our house before my father left, thanks to his paranoia. Everyone, including my father, would have known if another man was sneaking around our home."

I hadn't even remembered the cameras until she mentioned them. After kicking Charles out, I removed them all and threw the heap of security systems in the trash. A ceremonial burning was seriously considered by all of us, but setting electronic devices on fire was a hazard.

Charles' lawyer gaped at Charles, making it clear Charles had also forgotten about the cameras. "Did your mother start dating Landon Ford while you were his patient?"

I stared at Jules. Were they seriously trying to get Landon in trouble? Were they stooping that low? Jules didn't meet my eyes. Instead, she kept her hand on my knee.

"No, that would be a conflict of interest, along with a bunch of other issues. I had been seeing Dr. Ridley for a bit before Dr. Ford went out with my mom. Why are you so focused on Dr. Ford and my mom's relationship, anyway? She isn't the cheater. My dad is. My mom tried for so long to keep our family together, even though everyone with a pulse knew it was falling apart years ago, including me. I noticed things growing up; things my friends' parents did that mine didn't do, like show affection for one another. Most of my friends' fathers were around, too. Mine never was—business owner and mayor or not."

I was starting to feel like Charles' lawyer wasn't going to succeed at breaking Raegan until he asked his next question.

"Can you say your mother is there for you, Raegan?"

I felt like someone had punched me in the stomach. She and I both knew I hadn't been there for her as much as I should have. More than Charles, granted, but definitely not as much as I needed to.

"She's been there for me more than your client has," Raegan shot back, her attempt at deflection painfully apparent.

Charles' attorney shook his head. "That's not what I asked, Raegan. Is your mother there for you when you need her?"

Slowly, Raegan's arms dropped into her lap, and her deathly glare softened as her gaze fell to the floor. She was starting to break down, and I couldn't blame her. "My mom is there for me as much as she can be, between working and being a single parent with two kids."

"Do you often feel like you fall through the cracks under your mom's supervision?" the lawyer asked.

"Again, my mom does her best. I don't understand how this is relevant," Raegan said.

Charles' attorney approached the witness stand slowly. "A few weeks ago, your mom let you attend a party."

Jules' hand clenched my knee. *No.* They couldn't do this. They couldn't use that against me. Could they?

"And?" Raegan asked, but she also sensed where this was going, causing her tough façade to lessen even more as panic began to creep in.

"Your mom allowed you to go to a party where you were shot, Raegan. You could have been killed. All the while, your mom was on a date with Landon Ford forty-five minutes away."

I struggled to regulate my breathing. Every time I inhaled, I took short, silent gasps, but somehow forgot to exhale. In turn, the stagnant air caused my lungs to slowly balloon inside my chest, and the lack of oxygen made the room feel like it was shrinking around me.

I already blamed myself for Raegan's accident, and having it used against me in a custody battle made me hate myself even more. A completely new and powerful wave of guilt washed over me, catching me off guard. What would happen if the judge also blamed me for the incident and granted Charles full custody? Would rewarding Raegan for completing her assignments be what caused me to lose custody of my children? I should have never allowed her to leave. I should have told Landon no and stayed home. I should have—

"Stop," Jules said, her voice barely audible. "Don't do this. Don't let them get to you. They know this is their only shot at custody. They are trying to get you to succumb to their one and only argument. Don't do it. Don't let Charles screw you over yet again. Breathe, Samantha."

I knew she was right, but mom-guilt never listened to logic. It listened to the heart and outside forces; the pressure of the world always increased the ever-present shame every mother inevitably felt dozens of times throughout her children's lifetimes. If I hadn't allowed Raegan to go to the party, she wouldn't have gotten shot. I could have prevented it, plain and simple.

"Do you think if my dad had been home, he wouldn't have allowed me to go to that party?" Raegan's response caused my head to jerk up. Her arms were folded across her chest once more, her glowering eyes misted over with unshed tears. "Again, even when my dad lived with us, he didn't care about us. He wouldn't have known I wanted to go to a party. He wouldn't have tried to stop me. My mom was trying to be nice. The kids' parents were home. She let me go to the party knowing adults were present. It wasn't a frat party at some random college."

"And how are your grades?" Charles' attorney asked, not missing a beat.

Raegan shrugged. "Great."

"But they weren't a few months ago, correct? They started to slip?"

Raegan leaned forward, resting her crossed arms on

the witness stand. "Sir, I'm not sure how this is relevant to my mother, but yes, they did slip for a minute in one class. Want to know why?"

Charles' attorney stared up at Raegan, waiting for her response. I think he was hoping it would help his case, but he should have known better. Even though she faltered for a brief second, she hadn't broken under the lawyer's pressure, and she was now closing in for the kill.

"My English teacher assigned us an essay. She wanted to know what this city symbolized to each student. Knowing I couldn't give the response she wanted, I started to slack off and not turn in subsequent assignments. But the second my mom found out, she made me write the essay, as well as complete the rest of my missing work. Can I enlighten everyone as to what my response was to my teacher's essay prompt, sir?" Raegan asked, but she didn't give Charles' attorney a chance to respond.

"My thesis stated that this community symbolizes brokenness. My father, the man everyone knows and loves in Madison, shattered our home. He destroyed my mom's heart and trust. He shattered my dreams of having a father who cared about me and my little brother. This city," she gestured around her with her hand, "symbolizes the devastation my mom, Harrison, and I have felt for a very long time. Madison not only represents, but supports, my father's terrible, neglectful behavior, in my opinion. And you know what, sir?" she asked, nearly yelling at this point. "I got an A on that essay, and I now have an A in the class, bringing my GPA to a 4.0."

****

Raegan's testimony caused Judge Thurman to demand another fifteen-minute recess before dashing into his chambers like the courtroom was on fire. Raegan shakily stepped down from the witness stand and walked into my outstretched arms as Charles and his attorney left the room.

"Holy crap, girl," Jules muttered. "I didn't see a lot of that coming, but you handled it like a freaking champ. You ever think about becoming a lawyer?"

The moment my arms wrapped around Raegan's body, she collapsed against me. "I'm so tired, Mom," she said, her head against my chest.

"I know, baby," I said. "I'm sorry you had to do that. But Jules is right. That was absolutely amazing."

"I almost let them get to me," she whispered.

"Me, too, baby girl. It's hard not to let them rattle you. But you stayed strong. I'm so proud of you, Rae of Sunshine."

Removing my arms from around her shoulders, I cupped her chin and stared into her eyes as she pulled away from me. "I don't know if I have said this since this entire circus started, but thank you, honey. I hope I never made you feel like you had to support me or go against your father in any way, but I truly appreciate you standing by me and helping your brother and me throughout this entire disaster. I don't know what I would do without you."

She leaned into me again. "The look on your face when the lawyer brought up the party…I saw you go pale and start to panic. That's what made me snap out of my own spiraling—seeing you realize Harrison and I could be taken away from you. I can't let it happen, Mom. I won't."

I hugged her until Jules tilted her head toward the judge's chambers, bringing to our attention that the door had opened and Judge Thurman was making his way back to his bench. Reluctantly, I let go of Raegan, and she sat next to McKenna, who immediately reached for her hand.

Charles and his attorney made their way back to their side of the courtroom a few moments later, and after everyone was seated, the judge cleared his throat. "I'm afraid to ask, but are there any closing statements from Mr. and Ms. Hawley before we move on?"

Charles and his lawyer shook their heads, but Jules nodded at me. Standing up, I started talking before I could psych myself out. "Your Honor, there is nothing more important to me than my children. They are the first people I think about when I wake up every morning, and the last people I think about before I close my eyes each night. They are my entire world, and no matter what decision is made here today, I just want them to be happy and safe. That's all I want for them now and for the rest of their lives. Please help ensure my children are cared for and loved, because it's what I've spent the last seventeen and fourteen years fighting for."

The judge nodded as I resumed my place beside Jules. "Good job," she murmured from the side of her mouth. "Short but sweet."

"Now, when it comes to financial matters, I'm expecting Mr. Hawley to pay spousal and child support, seeing as how he makes more money than Ms. Hawley. The amount will be determined outside of court. Are there any oppositions to this?" Judge Thurman asked.

Jules stood. "Your Honor, because my client is seeking full physical and legal custody, she will not be asking for child *or* spousal support *if* she is awarded complete custody."

The judge peered over the bench. "She is legally entitled to receive spousal and child support, despite the custody ruling."

Jules nodded. "She is aware of this, but she is afraid if she asks for money in addition to full legal and physical custody, Mr. Hawley will put up a fight. My client doesn't care about money—she cares about her children."

Judge Thurman's eyebrows raised far above his glasses. "And if she isn't awarded full custody?"

Jules answered, "Then we are seeking a fair amount of spousal and child support from Mr. Hawley, seeing that he has more than enough to support himself, Ms. Hawley, and his children."

Charles and his attorney had their heads down, discussing something in hushed tones.

"Mr. Hawley, your thoughts on all of this?" the judge asked, and Charles' attorney stood.

"We would like to hear the custody ruling, Your Honor, before saying anything regarding financial support."

Judge Thurman removed his glasses and rubbed the bridge of his nose. Everyone in the courtroom watched him, collectively holding their breaths. "Mr. Hawley," he finally began. "This trial has certainly been an eye-opening experience for me. Knowing your father, not all of it was shocking, but today's revelations have been…disconcerting. If what your daughter says is true, and I *am* inclined to believe her, I've been duped by you. In fact, most of Madison has. And seeing that you're a politician who comes from a long line of politicians, maybe that's on me. I believed you were a great partner and father.

"But your infidelity proves my first belief wrong, and your daughter's statement, as well as the rest of the statements," he gestured out to the room in front of him, "shows that my second belief is also wildly inaccurate. And while I want to believe you care about your children, I can't help but think you did all of this to level the playing field with Ms. Hawley. A possible retaliation for her seeking divorce."

"Your Honor—" Charles started, but the judge held up his hand, halting Charles.

"Would you find it acceptable if Ms. Hawley had full physical and legal custody of Raegan and Harrison and you kept the amount of money you would owe in spousal and child support each month?" he asked.

Charles glanced at his attorney, who openly shrugged. That poor man was done.

He then studied me before moving his eyes to Raegan. "Would I be able to visit them, Your Honor, if I wanted? Maybe for a lunch or dinner or something every once in a while?"

The judge turned to face me. "Ms. Hawley?"

If I got the kids, it would only be fair, but I doubted he would actually request time with them. "Yes, Your Honor, I would find that acceptable. But complete transparency, Raegan has applied to multiple universities throughout the country. Depending on the custody ruling, my wish is to follow her with Harrison to ensure Raegan has support wherever she attends college."

Judge Thurman stared back at Charles, waiting for a response. Eventually, Charles nodded. "Okay."

"Then it's settled. Mr. Hawley, you will be divorced

from Ms. Hawley once the final paperwork is submitted and approved, and Ms. Hawley will receive full physical and legal custody of Harrison Hawley and Raegan Hawley once those papers are signed and approved. Ms. Hawley will not be receiving any financial support, spousal or child, in spite of my belief that she's having a lapse in judgement. After all these weeks, this final session is adjourned, and I hope I do not see the two of you back here for a very long time. Or ever."

With that, the judge banged his gavel, stood up, and left the courtroom. Jules shook hands with Charles' attorney, and before I could say anything to Charles, he stormed out, his attorney shadowing him. As the door closed behind them, the entire room erupted in cheers and applause. Raegan and McKenna were hugging each other and crying, while Harrison's doctors and nurses were shaking hands and embracing one another.

"You did it, mama," Jules smiled. Even her eyes were glistening.

Making the first move, I pulled her in for a hug. "I couldn't have done it without you, Jules. You're amazing. I will be indebted to you for the rest of my life, in more ways than one," I laughed.

Jules grinned as she stepped back. "I have a reasonable payment plan, but for now, let's not worry about that."

McKenna wrapped an arm around Raegan's waist, and Raegan did the same to mine as we made our way out of the room, through the hallway, and down the courthouse steps. We were flanked by Harrison's team of doctors, and based on the amount of people I had around me, I felt like a celebrity who had just stood trial.

Accepting congratulatory remarks from the medical

team behind us, I wasn't paying attention as we reached the sidewalk separating the courthouse from the parking lot. Raegan clearing her throat and poking my side caused me to look at her before noticing him in the background. Standing in the parking lot was Landon, his hands in his pockets and his eyes wide with uncertainty.

"Did you…?" he asked.

Dropping her arm from my waist, Raegan and McKenna slowed their pace, giving me room to approach Landon. "We won. I got full physical and legal custody," I said, the reality and relief of the trial's results fully hitting me. Tears ran down my cheeks as he closed the gap between us and threw his arms around me.

"You did it," he said, his voice cracking. "You freaking DID IT."

"We all did it," I admitted, briefly turning to admire the crowd behind me. "Every single person testified and did an amazing job. If it hadn't been for all of them, I might not have gotten the outcome I wanted."

Landon grinned. "They all testified to the truth, and any judge would be an idiot to ignore that." Wiping away my tears, he tilted my face up to his. "I'm so damn proud of you, Sam. This whole thing is over—the nightmares have passed. Your kids are back for good."

I stared into his eyes. "Thank you for holding me during the bad dreams."

Bringing his lips millimeters away from mine, he whispered, "Always."

My lips met his, and he wrapped his arms tighter around me. Behind us, McKenna started clapping, and Raegan gave a loud whoop.

"I feel like I'm in some cheesy rom-com movie," I laughed as we parted.

"Small city, big conflict, satisfying ending, I would have to agree." Landon smiled.

After I hugged and thanked everyone profusely, Harrison's team disbanded and left McKenna, Raegan, Landon, and me standing in the parking lot.

"Does this mean we can go home to Harrison and forget this mess ever happened?" Raegan asked.

A huge grin spread across my face. "Yes. That's exactly what this means. It also means we can properly celebrate you getting into USC, if that's where you're choosing to go."

"Hell yeah, it is. I can't wait for California. Is it ready for all of us?" Raegan wiggled her eyebrows.

Landon spoke up. "I'll stop by the store on the way home. Pick up some party items and food. I'll see everyone back at the house in forty minutes?" He and I kissed once more before we got into our cars.

Stepping inside my house minutes later, I couldn't help but cry again upon seeing Drea and Harrison. My kids were now safe and would no longer be exposed to the toxic environment their father and grandmother created. *I* would no longer be exposed to Charles and Lydia's bullshit.

Leaning against the front door, I inhaled slowly. Best case scenario was actually happening after years of thinking it never could, and honestly, it was about damn time.

CHAPTER TWENTY-THREE

My cell phone vibrated against the pen in my scrubs pants' pocket, amplifying the already noticeable buzzing sound. Giving my patient an apologetic smile, I finished helping her into bed before snatching the pen away from my mobile and moving it to my shirt pocket. The vibrating eventually ceased, only to start up again seconds later.

I let out an annoyed sigh. If it was an emergency back home, McKenna knew to call me at work before attempting to call my mobile, and I knew Raegan and Landon were at school. Eliminating those three people meant no one important was calling me, but their persistence was aggravating. When it buzzed a third time, I rolled my eyes and fished it out of my scrubs.

It was an unknown number.

"Hello?" I didn't even try to hide the annoyance in my voice as I walked into the hallway.

"Samantha, it's Lydia."

Was this a joke? I was mentally prepping for a car warranty salesman to be on the other line, not my ex-mother-in-law.

"Are you there?"

I cleared my throat. "Yes. How can I help you?"

"I would like to meet for lunch, but I don't want anyone to see us, so we must drive out of Madison. Are you at work right now?"

What in the hell? Lunch? She asked so casually, like it was something we had done every weekend for years. "Yes, I'm at work. But to be honest, I'm confused as to why you want to have lunch with me, since you have wanted nothing to do with me for the last, oh, eighteen years?" Was I being a bitch? Maybe. But *she* was always a bitch, so I felt I had the right.

"I don't want to talk about anything over the phone. It must be done in person. Do you work tomorrow?"

I stared up at the ceiling. This woman and her constant need for drama. "No, I don't work tomorrow. Let me see if I can get McKenna to—" I started, but Lydia interrupted me.

"Great. I will send a car to pick you up at eleven a.m. sharp." She hung up before I could argue.

As if she could sense trouble, Drea came up beside me, her signature bag of chips in one hand, a half-eaten chip in the other. When she saw my face, she shoved the partial piece back into the bag and stared at me. "What's happening? Why do you have that face?"

Shaking my head, I said, "You'll never guess who just called me."

She narrowed her eyes. "Charles."

I stuck my bottom lip out and nodded. "Excellent guess, but not quite."

"Someone I wouldn't suspect…" she trailed off, lost in thought. Then, her eyes lit up. "Lydia!"

"BINGO," I said, pointing at her. "Freaking Lydia. I picked up on her third attempt, but I should have kept sending her to voicemail."

"What did she want?" she asked, her brown eyes wide with both shock and intrigue.

"She wants to meet me for lunch to discuss things

Carissa Hyde

she cannot talk about over the phone. Oh, and she doesn't want us to be seen together, so she is having a car pick me up and drive me to who knows where."

Drea tilted her head. "Is this some kind of murder plan?"

I shrugged. "Honestly, because it's Lydia, I wouldn't put it past her."

"Okay, well, be sure to drop a pin and share it with me and Landon when you get to wherever you're going, just in case we need to tell the police your last known location."

When I got home later that night, Landon was just as shocked as Drea. "What could she possibly want to discuss with you after you divorced her son and outed him as a cheater nearly two months ago?"

"I have no idea, but I'm not looking forward to this meal at all."

The next morning, Lydia called again. "Wear something nice," was all she said before hanging up. A town car arrived in front of the house at eleven, and McKenna shot me a worried glance as I headed out the door. "Please be safe!" she called.

A man wearing a suit and newsboy cap opened the rear passenger door for me before climbing into the driver's seat and taking off. "Are you allowed to tell me where we are going?" I asked him, and he simply shook his head in response.

Fantastic.

After driving for nearly an hour, we pulled up to a fancy restaurant I would drive past on the way into Atlanta. Climbing out of the car and glancing up and down the street, I sighed for the umpteenth time that morning. Why in the hell did we need to go all the way to the outskirts of Atlanta for lunch? What could this woman possibly want to tell me?

I attempted to keep my annoyance at bay as the driver led me into the restaurant and to the back corner of the building. Just when I thought we were going to head into the restaurant kitchen, there was Lydia at a table that looked like it had been purposely moved to that location to appease her. She was wearing a pantsuit and hat, and I couldn't decide if the hat was an accessory for her outfit or if she was using it as an aid in her attempt at being unrecognizable.

"Lydia," I said coolly as I slid into the seat opposite her. She glanced up at me before her eyes darted around the restaurant.

"I'll call you when I'm done, Paul," she said, and the driver disappeared. Pulling the menu to her face, she studied it with the intensity of there being a quiz when the waiter appeared.

Not even caring about the food options, I stared at her, hoping she would tear her eyes away from the menu for five seconds to address why we were here. Instead, she continued to act like I hadn't even shown up, so I lowered the top of her menu, forcing her to look at me. "Lydia, why am I here?"

Shaking her head sternly, she pointed at the food list. "Find something to eat. When the waiter comes to our table, I want to order every course so they won't disturb us again."

I used every ounce of self-control not to throttle her and instead, gripped the menu with one hand and angrily turned the pages with the other. When the waiter appeared, I ordered the first three things I thought sounded appetizing. Once he took our menus, delivered our drinks, and vanished into the kitchen, Lydia finally made eye contact. "I think what you did—divorcing Charles, I mean—was really ballsy."

She brought me here to *chastise* me. I should have suspected as much.

Leaning forward, she folded her hands on the tabletop. "When Charles first told me he had gotten a girl pregnant at college, the only thing I could think about was how the exact same thing happened to me with Charles' father. Unlike you, I had made it three semesters into college before getting pregnant with Charles, but the end result was still the same. I dropped out of college to care for him, while his father finished his degree."

She wasn't yelling at me, yet. I was confused.

"The second that test read positive, I knew my life was over," Lydia continued. "My parents stopped talking to me. Charles' father's parents hated me. They made me get a paternity test after Charles was born."

None of this surprised me, but it did give me some insight as to why Lydia was the way she was.

"I didn't want my son to live the same type of life— having to think about a child and a wife while still in college. It puts a lot of stress on a person. But Charles is so much like his father. Stubborn, determined, and honestly, cruel."

This was the first time I had ever heard Lydia speak negatively about Charles, and my eyes widened into saucers the size of the table.

Registering my shock, she nodded. "I know, I know. It's hard to admit when your child is wrong or acting unacceptably, but it's true. Charles the second is just like Charles the first. Determined to sleep with every woman who pays him any mind while climbing the social ladder with ease.

"He was going to leave you, you know. When he told us you were pregnant, he was going to split. He didn't want the responsibility. But I told him he had to do the right thing and be a good person. Especially because of who we are and where we are from. If word got out that Charles had gotten a woman pregnant and abandoned her and the baby, it would hurt our entire family's reputation. The apartment during college and the house you're in now—it was all a bribe to ensure he kept our name clean and his actions reputable."

I sighed. "I know all of this, Lydia. I lived it up until a few months ago. I don't really want to sit here and—"

She put up a hand, not letting me deter her speech. "But just like his father, Charles couldn't uphold a sparkling, clean reputation forever. I, just like you, I'm sure, suspect he cheated on you long before you found out, but I had no right calling him out when I hadn't called out my own husband during our forty-five years of marriage. Charles' father was never faithful to me, but his family did exactly what we did for you and Charles. Bribed him with money. No Hawley can turn down money."

Wasn't that the truth.

"Even though Charles turned out just like his father, I tried to raise him differently. I would fight with his father for hours, trying to make him see the way he and I were raised wasn't right. But it wasn't any good. Charles' father was abusive, and I felt trapped."

I tensed, straining to hide my shock. Charles had never once mentioned his father's violence towards him or his mother. "Did he ever hit Charles? Or hit you in front of Charles?" I interrupted, my voice low—partially out of shock, and partially out of discreetness.

Lydia gave me a sad smile and shook her head. "You know better, Sam. The Hawley men only do forbidden things behind closed doors. They never flaunt it. Their reputation means everything to them.

"If I talked back, I was hiding bruises all over my body for weeks. For my own safety, I stopped attempting to change Charles' father's mindset on parenting. Instead, I just watched as the nightmare of my son turning into my husband and my father-in-law unfolded before me. I vowed to stand by Charles' father and ultimately Charles, for better or worse. And I hated it. I hated myself for it. But most of all, I hated Charles' father. I despised him for putting us in that position."

A loud clatter from the kitchen doors behind us nearly made me jump out of my chair. My focus had been so intense on Lydia and her story that I had lost all sense of my surroundings. Never could I have imagined having this conversation with her—especially now, after everything we had been through.

She glanced around the room. "You and I are alike in the sense that we both know what it feels like to be in a loveless marriage. I know you wouldn't have married Charles if his father, and subsequently I, hadn't forced you. But you went along with it, just as I did, and you suffered, along with Raegan and Harrison.

"I hope Charles didn't physically abuse you, but I can only imagine what he may have said and done over the years to emotionally and mentally hurt you. Make *you* feel like you were sinking with your failed marriage, just the way I felt for decades. But this is where you and I are different." She hesitated, clasping her hands together and slowly rocking them back and forth.

"I remember sitting in the driveway one afternoon, delaying going inside like I always did, but on that day, a particular song came on the radio. It was popular country song from the 2000s about poisoning, killing, and stuffing an abusive husband's body in a trunk, the victim and her best friend driving around with it while the women lived their best lives. Bought some land, sold jam…something like that." Lydia began fiddling with the utensils wrapped tightly in a blindingly-white napkin.

I knew exactly which song she was referring to, and it was still one of the best revenge songs to this day, in my humble opinion.

"Doctors blamed Charles' father's passing a few years later on liver disease due to his excessive drinking, and no one questioned it. Lying was easy for me at that point, as I had spent our entire marriage feigning happiness and putting on a show for the good people of Madison."

I was trying hard to maintain a straight face, but it was a struggle. *Did she…?*

"When I cried at his funeral, those were tears of liberation. And maybe a bit of sadness, too, because at one point, I really did love Charles' father." She sighed, dropping the utensils. "But those feelings were felt very early in our relationship, and I could barely recall what being in love with him was like at the end. What truly depressed me was the fact that Charles wasn't living at home anymore to experience a life without his father looming over him. His father had already damaged Charles. My son would never know a life of happiness and true love within the walls of our home."

Lydia stared at me; her gaze was unwavering. "Like I said before, I know my son isn't a good person. I know he mistreated you and the children and never even gave your relationship a chance, just like his father didn't give ours a chance. But Charles is my son. Regardless of his wrongdoings, I love him. He's my baby, and I always try to support him. However, watching him try to care for Raegan and Harrison when they were at my house...I quickly realized just how absent he had been in their lives. He couldn't properly raise them, and when he told me he was going to fight for custody, I tried to change his mind. I told him he shouldn't mess with his children like Charles' father had messed with him—especially because of Harrison and his needs."

I couldn't believe it. Lydia just acknowledged that Charles was an unfit father. It took them basically kidnapping my kids for her to see it, but she admitted it. I blinked, reveling in her statement. The fact that she had finally recognized all of her family's flaws was possibly more shocking than her almost-confession of killing Charles' father; though not by much.

"But he was hellbent on it. Probably because he was angry that you were actually leaving him. What you said at the hospital that one day was, I think, accurate. I'm fairly certain he thought you would be like me and just suck it up and stay in a terrible marriage for the sake of saving face. But again, he doesn't know what happened to his father." I swear she winked at me then, but she moved too fast for me to be certain.

"When you stepped inside our home all those years ago, I had a feeling you weren't going to put up with Charles' nonsense. I never got to know you because I thought you would up and leave long before you actually did, and to be perfectly honest, I was jealous of you. You are driven and you go after what you want. I never had the courage to return to college and finish what I had started. Instead, I gave up my dreams and dedicated myself to ensuring Charles' father's dreams became a reality. I masked my misery with needless spending and by holding large, extravagant social gatherings whenever possible.

"But you—even though it took some time—you got your degree. You raised Raegan and Harrison alone and managed to get a job; make your own money. You're a strong person, Sam. And after spending time with Raegan and Harrison over those last few weeks of your marriage to Charles, I realized thankfully, they are strong, too. I was glad Charles conceded in the end; although I'm sure it might have had more to do with the fact that you said you would forego all financial support if you were awarded custody."

At some point during the latter portion of our conversation, all three courses of our lunch had arrived at the table, and Lydia slid a plate in front of her.

"Anyway, to wrap this all up, I commend you for sticking to your guns and actually divorcing Charles. I know that entire process wasn't easy, but you didn't back down. I wish," she said, slowly removing the fork out of the napkin, "I wish I had been as brave as you. I wish I had gone back to school so I didn't have to rely on Charles' father for support. Had I gotten my degree, I could have divorced him and left with Charles; I could have given him a better life. Instead, I was a coward, and we all paid dearly for my mistakes." She examined the cutlery before stabbing it into her salad. Now privy to cryptic information about her late husband's passing, I was grateful we were meeting in a public setting with food cooked by professionals. I didn't want to risk anything at this point.

Glancing down, I couldn't fathom eating the soup, salad, or the grilled chicken breast that lay ornately on the plate after Lydia dropped her bombshells. Instead, I peered at her as she ate. Mouth closed and head nodding after her teeth sank into the first bite of food, she was absorbed in her lunch, giving me free reign to observe her.

She and I had never spent more than a few minutes together since our initial meeting when I was in college, so my opportunity to study her never really presented itself. As I sat across the table from her, I finally had the chance to truly see the woman who had been a stranger to me for all those years.

She had the same prominent nose as Charles, but her green eyes were softer than his. Wrinkles were starting to appear around her eyes and mouth, despite her many Botox sessions and likely plastic surgeries. Her hair was blonde, but it was apparent she dyed it, as it had the coarseness and texture of naturally graying locks.

Before Charles and I separated, she had been a large, threatening presence in my mind, but being here with her now, I saw her for what she truly was—a small, beaten-down, exhausted woman who succumbed to living her life for her husband and the public eye. Time and age were starting to deteriorate her body, causing her spine to hunch and her fingers to knot with arthritis, further dwarfing her stature.

When she finished eating, she glanced up at me. "You haven't touched your food. Is there something wrong with it?"

My stomach grumbled in protest at the thought of eating. "This has all been a lot to take in—I'm not that hungry."

She shrugged and waved at the waiter, who arrived seconds later with the bill. I started to go for my purse, but she shook her head. Wordlessly, we walked out of the restaurant and onto the curb. Less than a minute later, two black town cars pulled up in front of us. Lydia nodded at the first driver, and I recognized the second driver as the man who drove me to lunch.

Turning to me, she said, "I'm sorry everything turned out the way it did, Sam. But I'm happy you can now live a life you want instead of the one you felt forced to accept." She dug around in her purse for a second before producing two envelopes—one labeled for each of my children.

"Raegan's envelope has a bank statement and debit card in it for an account I opened for her. I heard she got into USC, and since Charles isn't paying spousal or child support, it is going to be difficult for her and for you to afford her education. This should pay for all four years of her degree, plus a car, because a vehicle is necessary in Southern California, I hear.

"Harrison's envelope has information regarding his account and a debit card, as well. I know you receive money from the state and such, but in the event something happens to you and Harrison needs long-term care, hopefully this can help."

My hands were down at my sides, and when she realized I wasn't going to reach out to take the envelopes, she grasped my hand and forced them into my palm. I glanced down at the crisp white stationary before staring at her. "Lydia, I can't. We can't. This is too much; we can't accept this," I stammered.

She stared at me. "Samantha, I know you are capable of providing for your children but let me help ease the pressure a little bit. Please don't reject it. You and I both know you want what's best for Raegan and Harrison, and this money will help them."

I glanced around. Had I stepped into another dimension where Lydia suddenly became an actual human being? "Lydia, I—"

"You're welcome, Samantha," she said softly before disappearing into her town car.

On our return to Madison, I stared out the window, my mind processing the afternoon's events as small Georgia towns and cities disappeared behind us. As much as I hated to admit it, Lydia had been...nice. She had unsuspected murderous tendencies and hid behind a bitchy persona a majority of her life, but today, speaking with her had been almost pleasant, and definitely eye-opening.

I thanked the driver as he pulled away from the curb half an hour later, and I turned to stare at what was my first, and last, house in Madison. A "for sale" sign had arrived yesterday, and while I couldn't ignore the sadness of seeing my home for sale, I couldn't let it overshadow the overwhelming amount of joy and relief I felt. Within a few weeks, Landon, Harrison, and I would be following Raegan to Southern California; a pipe dream that was becoming our reality. By this time next month, we would be in a new city, in a new state, and starting new lives—together.

CHAPTER TWENTY-FOUR

"So, it's really happening, huh?" Landon surveyed the empty house while wiping a bead of sweat from his brow. It was the middle of June, and even though it was early in the morning, the humidity was intense and unforgiving.

A lump formed in my throat as I nodded. "I sure as hell hope so. We just spent the last two days loading up that damn moving truck. If you and I are having second thoughts, it's too late to voice them now."

Grinning, he stepped forward and kissed me. "I have no second thoughts."

I slowly turned, staring at the house that had been filled with so many memories from the day I first moved in. Not all of them were good, but a lot of them were, and while I had wanted nothing more than to leave this hellhole for years, now that the time was finally upon us, I found myself overcome with emotion.

"Hey," Landon said, placing his hand on the small of my back. "It's okay to be sad. Even though this home wasn't always filled with happiness, it was the house where your children were born and raised. Raegan took her first steps in this house. You and Harrison learned how to navigate cerebral palsy within these walls. And as much pain as this city brought you, it also brought you some joy. None of that can, or should, be forgotten."

A single tear rolled down my cheek as I turned to

face him. "I hated being here for so long, I thought I would drive one hundred miles per hour out of this place, maniacally laughing like some movie villain the entire time. In a cruel turn of events, I'm crying and nostalgic."

We both looked around, then, and I noticed I had missed some of the confetti from Raegan's graduation party a few weeks ago during my final cleaning. She had moved to California a few days after the ceremony, claiming she needed time to get used to the area and state. She and I both knew that was a lie—she just didn't want to help Landon and me pack up the entire house.

Instead, McKenna had stepped in, and now she was standing outside, saying farewell to Harrison. While part of me wanted to be there for both of them during the process, I knew my heart would break into a million pieces witnessing her telling Harrison goodbye. He was going to be heartbroken for quite some time once he realized McKenna wasn't going to be around anymore. We had a few caregivers lined up and ready to meet once we made it to California, but no one would ever replace McKenna.

Drea threw a going away party at the hospital on my last day of work three days ago, which was bittersweet. I was finally leaving the city and people who detested me just as much I disliked them, but I was also leaving the few good friends and a job I had grown to love. I had an interview scheduled at a local hospital as an ER nurse a few days after the move, which I was nervous but excited about.

So many things were changing, and I knew if I paid my anxiety any mind, I wouldn't be able to leave the house, much less move across the country. Instead, I tried to focus only on the positives, which was a difficult thing to do after preparing for the worst for so many years.

Landon had flown to California a week before Raegan's graduation, and had gotten word the day of the ceremony that he would be the new high school psychologist for a school in the San Fernando Valley. Harrison, Landon, and I decided to move to the suburbs just outside of San Fernando so the commute would be minimal for Landon and the drive for Raegan manageable whenever she felt inclined to visit.

After I insisted on doing one more walkthrough of the house, Landon and I walked out onto the front porch and locked the door behind us for the last time. McKenna was standing in the driveway next to Harrison, and when we made eye contact, she immediately turned away from him, her body shaking with emotion.

"I'll get Harrison into the van while you say goodbye to McKenna," Landon whispered, stepping past me and heading toward Harrison. He gave McKenna a brief but kind hug before taking off with Harrison.

Descending the steps, I took in a deep breath, willing myself not to cry. The second I saw McKenna's face, though, I was done for. Pulling her close, we both started sobbing.

"Kenny," I managed, and she cried even harder. "I don't know how I will ever be able to thank you for everything you have done for Harrison, Raegan, and me these past five years. After everything you went through with Charles, you still found the strength and courage to return to our home, day after day, to care for Harrison. You made me feel comfortable about returning to work. You gave me the peace of mind I needed to leave Harrison with someone other than me. You restored my faith in humanity by being the kindest, most compassionate, most dedicated person I've ever met.

"You are a superhero, McKenna. You have a heart of gold and the soul of an angel. I will never forget you and everything you have done for my family. If you and Kevin ever consider moving to California, please know you will always have a place with us. You're family, sweet girl. I hope you know that."

Pulling away from me, she could only manage to nod. Wiping a few tears from her cheeks, I embraced her again before starting toward the van. Landon was standing next to it, the driver door open. "Are you ready?"

Looking up at McKenna, who was still crying in the front yard, I moved my eyes to Harrison and gave him a confident smile before turning to Landon. "Yes. Let's do it. Let's get the hell out of here and never look back."

And that's exactly what we did. As Harrison and I drove away in the van, Landon behind us in the moving truck, we watched as Madison slowly vanished in our rearview mirrors. Once we crossed the state line, I couldn't help but choke up again. Eighteen years ago, I came to Georgia with Charles, completely unaware of what I was getting into and how my life would unfold. Nearly two decades later, I was leaving with two children, an incredible partner, and hopes for a future I never thought would be possible.

The drive to California took us a week. Not only was it difficult for Harrison to sit in the car for more than a few hours at a time, but we also wanted to see the sights as we drove through the country. I couldn't imagine ever doing something like this again, so taking our time felt like the logical thing to do. When we reached the house we were renting in California, Landon parked the moving truck in front of the driveway and traded places with me in the van. After readjusting the seat and mirrors, we were off yet again.

"Raegan is still meeting us, right?" he asked, his eyes sparkling.

The nerves that had disappeared once we were a safe distance from Georgia resurfaced suddenly, and my leg started bouncing up and down in the passenger seat. I had waited for this moment for years, but now that it was here, I was inexplicably nervous. I couldn't believe it was finally happening.

When we pulled up in front of the condo, I saw my old car and Raegan leaning against it. Even though she had only been out of Georgia for a few weeks, she looked like a different person. When I had talked to her on the phone, she'd sounded happier, and now seeing her, I noted the happiness wasn't just in her voice—it was radiating from her entire body. We hugged for a few seconds before helping Harrison out of the van, and the four of us stood on the curb, staring at the condo in front of us.

Raegan inhaled slowly. "You ready for this, Mom? No one is going to have a heart attack, right? I don't know first aid or CPR."

Landon grinned. "Well, your mom's a nurse, and I've had training if she also passes out. But hopefully it doesn't amount to that."

All eyes were on me as I continued studying the building. This was almost twenty years in the making. The one thing I dreamed about, but never thought would be possible after I married Charles and our lives unfolded across the country. But here we were, after all that time had passed. Would they even recognize me?

My forceful exhale through closed lips caused my cheeks to puff. Shifting my weight, I gathered my bearings and finally nodded. "Let's go."

Landon steered Harrison up the cement walkway as Raegan and I took the lead. When we reached the front porch, Landon cleared his throat.

"Do you want me to hang back? I don't want to interrupt this moment."

I turned and cocked my head. "You belong here just as much as the rest of us do. We are a family. Besides, if you don't meet them now, you're going to meet them later." I squinted at him. "Are you nervous?"

He shoved his hands in his pockets. "Of course, I am. This is a huge deal. I know how much this means to you and how important they are to you. What if they hate me?"

Stepping back and leaning around Harrison, I gave him a quick kiss. "They won't hate you. And even if they do, I promise they won't hate you more than they hated Charles."

Raegan snorted and Landon laughed. "Fair point. I'll be right here next to Harry, then." He put his arm around Harrison, who grinned.

Resuming my place next to Raegan, she glanced at me. "Ready?"

I nodded. She glanced back at Landon, who also agreed. After taking a deep breath, Raegan rang the doorbell, and a minute later, a gray-haired woman who had Raegan's eyes opened the door. My vision immediately blurred behind tears. Seeing her face after all these years was bittersweet. It was difficult to see how old she had gotten while I was away, but it was nothing short of a miracle that she was still with us.

Glancing from me to Raegan, then from Landon to Harrison, I could see the confusion in her eyes before a moment of clarity hit her.

"Oh my gosh." She brought a wrinkled, shaky hand up to her mouth as small sobs escaped her. "This can't be real; this can't be happening. You can't be here. I—" she faltered. "Martin!" she called behind her, and a tall, also graying man appeared beside her seconds later.

"What the—*Sammy*, is that you?" he asked, and before I could answer, his arms were around me, pulling me close as if no time had passed. Breathing in his scent of sawdust and Dove soap, more tears fell in rapid succession. God, I had missed this. I had missed them so much.

When he released me, I wiped away my smudged makeup and gestured behind me.

"Mom, Dad, I want you to meet Landon, my partner, and your grandchildren, Raegan and Harrison."

****

"You're acting really strange, Rae. Are you sure everything is alright?"

It was the third Saturday of the month, marking our recuring mother-daughter date—something we had initiated when Raegan started at USC last year. She was constantly busy with school and working at the on-campus library, and I learned early on if we didn't schedule things in advance, I wouldn't see her for months.

A flowing olive-colored dress hung loosely on her frame, and a pair of strappy sandals were balanced on the center console. A few months into college, she had stopped dyeing her hair, and her now natural brown locks hung down in waves around her shoulders. Normally we didn't do anything too fancy on our dates, just lunch and maybe a movie. But today, Raegan wanted to go to a new brunch spot and a show at the local playhouse.

This meant I had to dress up too, and after much debate, I picked a peach-colored wrap dress and wedges. Landon was away at a psychology conference this weekend, so I couldn't get his opinion on my attire, but I did send a picture to Drea.

Me—Does this outfit look okay? Miss you.—

Drea—You look stunning, Peach. Miss you bunches. Can't wait to visit in a few weeks.—

Harrison was at home with Melissa, the caregiver we hired a few weeks after settling in. She wasn't McKenna, but she was a close second, and Harrison quickly adapted to her, now offering her the same smile he gave McKenna every time she walked through our front door.

Raegan glanced over at me. "I'm not being weird. I've just never been here before. A couple of girls from school recommended this place, but I've never been to Pasadena, and you know how I am with navigating. If we talk, we may end up in Canada."

I shrugged, but I still didn't entirely believe her. She was even uncharacteristically quiet when she came to pick me up, but I didn't want to make something out of nothing and ruin the day. Half an hour later, we pulled off the freeway and onto a main street before turning down a small side road. Reading her phone, Raegan whispered the address to herself before returning her eyes to the road. After passing a few small shops, we pulled into a small carpark.

"The restaurant is down a little bit, but this is the

closest place to park," she announced.

Sure enough, a few blocks later we came upon a rustic-looking eatery. Raegan held the door open for me, allowing me to walk past her into the building. There were a handful of small, bistro-like tables inside the room opposite what appeared to be the kitchen and take-away counter. Staring straight out from the front entrance, there was a glass door leading to a garden with outdoor seating options.

"Outside?" The maître d' appeared out of nowhere, holding menus.

Raegan nodded, and we followed the woman as she led us to an unexpectedly gorgeous alfresco dining area.

There were dozens more bistro tables scattered throughout the mostly shaded area, with flowers and hedges sprinkled throughout. The most impressive part of the garden, though, was the giant oak tree in the middle of the grassy yard. Someone had built a deck around the trunk, and a white railing encircled the deck and tree.

"Wow," I said, after the maître d' sat us at the table closest to the tree. "I was not expecting something like this. This place is beautiful. And oddly…vacant." Doing a double take, I realized no one was inside the restaurant when we entered, and no one was occupying any of the tables outside. *Was this place really terrible, or just unknown?*

Raegan was studying the menu and barely acknowledged me when I spoke.

"Rae, babe. Seriously. What's going on? Is something happening at school? Are you struggling with a class? Do you need extra help?"

Before she could answer, I felt a hand on my

shoulder. Shifting in my chair, I saw a grinning Landon, donned in black dress pants and a white button-down shirt. My heart flip-flopped when my eyes met his.

Glancing over at Raegan, he nodded. "Nothing is going on at school. She's just a terrible liar." He laughed. Raegan all but threw down the menu.

"I am. I'm a terrible liar. I knew if we started talking on the way down here, I would blow it." Her signature smile returned to her face, having been absent since she picked me up.

Moving my eyes from Raegan back to Landon, I squinted. "I thought you were at the conference this weekend?" Giving Raegan a quick wink, she stood up and he took her place at the table. I watched her walk inside the restaurant before turning my attention to Landon. "What is going on?"

Landon smiled. "I was at the conference all day yesterday and this morning, but I left early to come here."

I cocked my head. "Why? Are you okay?"

A server appeared with two glasses and proceeded to pour us red wine.

"Today is the anniversary of us moving to California," Landon said, raising his glass once the server disappeared. "One year ago today, we got the hell out of Madison and haven't looked back since. And not to brag, but we are doing pretty darn well here, if I do say so myself."

Hesitantly, I lifted my glass and clinked it against his. After we both took a sip, I returned the glass to the table and folded my arms over my chest. "You left the conference to celebrate our one-year moving anniversary?"

Landon smiled, leaning back in his chair. "You know, if someone had told me twenty-five years ago that I would get into a horrible car accident at sixteen years old, I would have been shocked. If someone then came back and told me nearly a decade after the car accident that I would be a therapist, working with children who have experienced similar or worse trauma, I would have told them they were crazy." He moved his hands from his lap to the tabletop, sliding both arms across the space to grasp mine.

"But if someone had told me that when I was thirty-eight years old, I would meet the woman of my dreams and her two amazing children who would restore a sense of normalcy and peace in my life, I would have openly laughed and had them committed."

Birds chirped happily from the oak tree above us as my mind tried to process everything.

Wait. Was he…? Was this…?

Rubbing a thumb over my left hand, Landon gave a satisfied sigh. "Yet here we are, and all of those things happened," he said softly, staring down at our hands. "Unfortunately, regarding the accident, but fortunately, in terms of everything else." He paused. "When I met you, Sam, I knew my heart was no longer my own. I know you thought I was certifiable, but I couldn't stay away—as we both know." His lips formed a smile, but he still wasn't making eye contact with me. "You had your reservations, rightfully so, but you still agreed to give me a chance, and because of that, you have made me the happiest man alive.

"Your children," he glanced over his shoulder toward the building, "are shining examples of how amazing and how dedicated you are as a parent. Your ability to lessen my anxiety and stress just by being in your presence is some kind of witchcraft that I will never understand, but will forever be grateful for, and it proves just what an amazing partner you are."

He stared at me then, his head tilted and his eyes glinting in the sunlight. "I love you so much, Sam. Thank you for giving us a chance all those months ago. Thank you for including me in your life and inviting me on this adventure with you in California. Thank you for loving me, even when it's difficult. Thank you for being there for me on the nights my nightmares get the best of me. Thank you for the most amazing year and a half of my life." His blue irises bore into mine, confirming what was happening. It took me long enough, but I understood.

Pulling away from me, he reached into his front pants' pocket as he slowly slid out of his chair and onto one knee.

"Samantha Hawley," he started, and I quickly glanced at the building behind him. Raegan was standing in the doorway, flanked by Harrison and Melissa, with one hand over her mouth, the other wrapped around her midsection. When the light shone through the tree just right, I could see tears glinting in the sun on her cheeks.

Moving my eyes back to Landon, he smiled up at me. "Will you marry me?"

"Oh my gosh, Landon," I said, my heart thudding in my chest. I stared at him, the ring, and then back at Harrison, Raegan, and Melissa. My hands rose to either side of my face. "How did Melissa and Harrison get here?"

He laughed. "We planned this months ago. Granted, the psychology conference changing its dates last minute nearly ruined it, but I just decided to skip out early and carry on with the plan. Melissa and Harrison followed you and Raegan here."

"I can't believe this." I shook my head. "And I can't believe Raegan was able to lie about it for months. She must have been dying."

"She really was," he admitted, smiling. "She would call me every few days or so and confess that she almost told you, or almost accidentally mentioned it as the day drew closer. I mean, it's a good thing she struggles with lying, but she almost outed me multiple times."

Finally refocusing on Landon and the ring, my eyes widened even further. "Is this—" I began, pointing at it.

"It's your mom's. Your dad gave it to me after she passed away. I wanted to propose before your dad left us, too, but you were right. He couldn't live without your mom. I couldn't pull everything together in a week. I decided to wait until summer—on the anniversary of our move to California."

Now I was the one crying. "My dad knew?"

"I asked for his permission within a month of moving out here. He said he had to get to know me a little better before he let his little girl go off and marry another guy he didn't know, since it ended so badly the first time."

"That sounds exactly like something my dad would say." I tried to laugh, but it came out as a sob.

"He finally told me I could marry you right after your mom passed and gave me her ring. He knew how much it would mean to you."

Moving a hand from my cheek to my mouth, I shook my head slowly. "I can't believe you pulled this all off. Everything…everything is perfect."

He smiled. "I had to ask Raegan and Harrison's

permission to marry you, too. Raegan made me promise I would include her and Harrison in the proposal. This is what we came up with. I rented out the restaurant, ditched the conference, and here we are. But you still haven't answered my question." He shifted nervously as the server started to cross the lawn, holding a bottle of champagne. Stopping a few feet behind Landon, she held it up.

"Is it a yes?" she asked us, and Landon stared up at me expectantly.

Grinning, I bent over and kissed him. "Of course, it's a yes. It will always be yes."

A word about the author…

Carissa Hyde fell in love with writing at a young age when she realized using the alphabet to create stories was more enjoyable than using it to solve math problems. She lives in Southern California with her husband, their three children, and their beloved family dog. Georgia Peach is her debut novel. You can connect with Carissa on Twitter @HydeandC and on her website at carissahyde.com.

Thank you for purchasing
this publication of The Wild Rose Press, Inc.

For questions or more information
contact us at
info@thewildrosepress.com.

The Wild Rose Press, Inc.
www.thewildrosepress.com